SANDSTORM

STORM

Alan L. Lee

FORGE® A TOM DOHERTY ASSOCIATES BOOK | NEW YORK

SANDSTORM

Copyright © 2013 by Alan L. Lee

Design by Mary A. Wirth

A Forge Book
Published by Tom Doherty Associates, LLC
175 Fifth Avenue
New York, NY 10010

www.tor-forge.com

Forge® is a registered trademark of Tom Doherty Associates, LLC.

ISBN 978-0-7653-3494-7 (hardcover)
ISBN 978-1-4668-1960-3 (e-book)

Forge books may be purchased for educational, business, or promotional use. For information on bulk purchases, please contact Macmillan Corporate and Premium Sales Department at 1-800-221-7945 extension 5442 or write specialmarkets@macmillan.com.

First Edition: June 2013

Printed in the United States of America

0   9   8   7   6   5   4   3   2   1

To my brothers, John and Ronald . . .

and

in loving memory of my parents.
"Thank you" somehow seems lacking.

It gives me comfort to know you still
watch over me from above.

ACKNOWLEDGMENTS

To my Executive Editor Bob Gleason at Forge, thank you for your enthusiasm and seeing the potential. Your gentle guidance has meant a lot. I do enjoy our chats about all things nuclear.

The Forge team has been nothing short of amazing. Thanks to Tom Doherty for the opportunity to get my story out there. It's a privilege to be published under your imprint. I still pinch myself from time to time.

Thank you, Kelly Quinn. I'm not sure of everything an editorial assistant does, but you wear a number of hats well. You held my hand throughout this entire process, making everything fall into place smoothly. Go Bruins!

M. Longbrake, you're the English teacher I wish I'd had. As copy editors go, you're a shining star. Your suggestions and edits were dead-on. I owe you lunch!

Art Director Seth Lerner, it was as if you were in my head. Thanks for creating a totally amazing book jacket. It will forever be a fixture in my man cave.

Mary A. Wirth, even though I'd looked at and read the book numerous times, your text design really made it come alive for me.

To Kate Folkers, getting *Sandstorm* to where it is today is a testament to your unyielding belief. We were down to the eleventh hour, but this being your last deal as a literary agent was the best stay of execution I could have ever hoped for.

To Sharlene Martin of Martin Literary Management, your vision inspires dreams of big things to come.

Vince Flynn and Brad Meltzer are true inspirations who offered friendship, insight, and support. Thank you both for being exemplary people.

In Jeff Zaslow, mankind lost a brilliant storyteller. Your wit, poise, talent, and nurturing manner are sorely missed. Thank you for your encouragement.

To the men and women who serve, whether on the front lines or in the shadows, no amount of gratitude is enough.

Thanks to anyone who took the time to answer any dumb question I might have posed. I guarantee I'll have many more.

To my sons, Spencer and Drake, I am blessed to have two wonderful examples of what love truly means.

Finally, to my wife, Sean. Thanks for holding down the fort while I was locked away in the man cave writing. Your support and patience were unwavering. This journey has meant so much because you've been by my side.

SANDSTORM

CHAPTER 1

Erica Janway reflected on her past because she had no future.

Forty-eight years of living, most of them good. A decent childhood. No serious health issues other than a brief fondness for alcohol. The usual amount of bad dates before the right one showed up. She was proud to have served her country with honor, no matter what some of the assholes at the CIA thought. She'd get a black star chiseled into the white face of Vermont marble on the Wall of Honor at Langley. Her husband, Paul, was the rock of her foundation and the main reason the drinking stopped. There was plenty more to reflect upon, but she was out of time.

The ominous figure clad in a dripping wetsuit stood motionless a few feet away in her Annapolis, Maryland, kitchen. She knew his presence was of her own doing. She hadn't been able to keep her nose out of things. When they'd reassigned her from station chief in Moscow back to Langley, she'd been able to deal with the indignity only for so long before it had really pissed her off. Working from a desk, she'd searched daily for trouble, and once she'd stumbled upon it, resisting the temptation to dig further had been impossible. She'd wanted to take her suspicions up the ladder to her superiors but had lacked concrete proof. Plus, she could ill-afford another blemish on her record.

As a puddle formed on the tile, Erica figured he'd been watching her for a long time from the inlet off the Chesapeake Bay, the water's edge just a chip shot away. She'd been on the deck for most of the evening and hadn't heard or seen anything unusual.

Erica stared at the 9 mm pistol pointed at her chest. "If it's money you want, I only have about sixty dollars in the house." She was trying to buy time. She knew he wasn't here for money. Common criminals didn't walk around with silenced weapons. She coyly eased toward the knife holder on the counter.

The intruder, of course, recognized what she was trying to do. He almost wanted to give her a fighting chance. While watching from the water, he'd discovered there was something playfully amusing about her. She hardly came across as the cold-hearted threat she was portrayed to be. But he'd never been given a reason not to trust his handler's orders.

He focused his weapon squarely on Erica's heart as she stood next to the knife holder. She didn't bother to make the attempt, knowing it was futile. She prepared herself as best she could. There was nothing to say that would alter her predicament. The thought that she would not die in vain gave her a degree of comfort. She'd prepared a package to be sent in the event that something happened to her. They would have no way of knowing that.

She decided not to scream. There really was no point. The house was hidden away behind ample foliage down a path. One of the attractions about the property had been its privacy.

Erica closed her eyes, thinking of Paul. She heard the muffled *thump* as a bullet left the chamber and tore through her heart.

———————

On his way out, Janway's executioner paused to look at several notes she had scribbled on a notepad while sitting on the deck. As he read, he observed that some were pertinent to why he was here. In the lower right-hand corner, framed by subconscious doodling, were two letters firmly repeated a couple of times. They meant nothing to him, but as he tore the pages away, he decided he'd make sure "NM" was run through every database of Janway's life. At this point, there could be no loose ends.

CHAPTER 2

Maneuvering her way through the throng of people choking the Spanish Steps should have awakened her to the fact that she'd been aimlessly walking the streets of Rome for quite some time. She'd passed countless cafés, bars, and clubs, the nightlife openly beckoning. Nora Mossa was oblivious to it all.

She recalled seeing on television—maybe on the National Geographic channel or during Shark Week—that several species of shark had to keep moving or they'd die. She could relate. *Obligate ram ventilators.* That was the term. They had to swim forward in order to force oxygen-containing water through their mouths and over their gills. The shit you remembered at the weirdest times, she thought.

Like a great white, she wanted to rip something apart. Not necessarily to feed, but to get rid of the rising aggression overtaking her system.

She'd been waiting on a phone call that had never come, and now, the deadline had passed. Nora fought back the urge to vomit. Not getting that call meant that in all likelihood, her friend and mentor, Erica Janway, was dead.

Not caring about the risks, she took as many shortcuts as possible back to her Piazza Navona neighborhood. Three blocks past the Pantheon, she was at her apartment building. Instead of taking the elevator, Nora climbed the steps of the thirteenth-century building to the second floor. She leaned against the thick wooden door of her apartment after shutting it, taking a long, deep breath. She took a moment to focus on what she had to do next. Erica and the CIA had trained her not to panic. Procedure would help clear her mind. She was on her way to the bedroom when the faint smell of lavender and sandalwood tickled her nostrils.

She ducked just in time.

The move thwarted the man's attempt to wrap a beefy arm around her neck, leaving him nothing to grasp but air. His momentum forced him to take an extra step, leaving him slightly off balance. Nora pivoted to his left side and put all her weight behind a punch that nearly doubled him over. He cringed but countered with a sweeping right hand. Again, she managed to avoid the effort. She took advantage of an opening to deliver a pair of sharp strikes just below the rib cage. She then took a step and knocked him forcefully backward with a kick to his midsection. He crashed into a table, nearly falling because he only tried to brace himself with one hand. Nora understood why when she located the knife in his right hand. Judging from how he tried to attack her from behind, she was sure it was sharp enough to slice her throat open in a single pass.

The next move was easy to anticipate but difficult to defend in the relatively close quarters of her living room. Nora backpedaled, her arms searching behind her while she kept the rapidly advancing man in front of her. He was within arm's length when she grabbed a dining room chair. As his right hand zigzagged forward, searching for flesh, she brought the chair around, punishing his arm, dislodging the knife in the process. His quickness and recovery caught her by surprise. His left hand shot out and wrapped around her neck like a python, squeezing tighter and tighter. He lifted her up and shoved her against the wall. It was nearly impossible to get air into her lungs. Nora couldn't loosen his grip, but she clenched her left hand and swung down onto the bridge of his nose as if trying to chop a tree trunk. She felt cartilage break as he quickly released his grip, trying to regain his equilibrium through watery eyes. Nora kneed him in the crotch and then used her knuckles to deal a blow that shifted his larynx. He staggered to the ground, clutching his throat. Nora went to retrieve the knife, knowing she had to hurry. Fighting through the pain, he attempted to pull out a gun, but the attached silencer's bulk wouldn't easily clear his jacket. Nora picked up the knife and, without thinking much about aim, let it fly. A hurried shot sailed a few inches past her head. The knife, however, found a target. All five inches of the blade sliced through the man's left eye into brain matter. His body went limp after a few erratic jerks.

He was professional enough to not carry identification, but he had made the mistake of wearing cologne, which had given his presence away. It made her wonder if he had been out on the town when called away to go do a job. The body lying on the floor confirmed one thing for sure. She had to hurry. What if he wasn't alone? And even if he was, he would be expected to report: when he didn't, someone else would definitely come to see why.

She scurried from room to room in the apartment, making on-the-spot decisions about what was essential. The options were narrowed by what could conveniently fit in the small piece of luggage sprawled open on top of the bed. Several times she stepped over the dead man's body as if it were an apartment amenity. Washer. Dryer. Corpse.

"Take the black dress!"

"No time!"

"There's plenty of time. Take the black dress!"

"No time!"

"Take the black—"

"Damn it. Shut up!" The irritated utterance startled her, especially since the words surfaced from deep inside her head, which at the moment was running a marathon of emotions. Nora stood perfectly still until her nerves settled.

Given the circumstances, she shouldn't have allowed herself to even entertain the frivolous thought of packing the black dress. Just taking a moment to consider it was stupid and a gross misuse of valuable time. Granted, it was a Versace that accentuated her figure in head-turning fashion. At over twelve hundred dollars, it was the single most expensive article of clothing she'd ever purchased. Still, it wasn't worth dying over. From here on out, every move required extreme thought and caution.

Nora Mossa had to disappear.

Nora Mossa had to become someone else.

She had two fake identity kits supplied by the CIA. She'd pack them but had no intention of using either. There was a third, kept totally off the books. Hiding behind a fictitious identity wouldn't guarantee safety, but it would buy time. And she needed time to figure this whole mess out and decide whom she could trust. Someone would have to be responsible for bringing her back in.

Erica Janway was missing, maybe for two days by now. A package had been waiting for Nora when she returned late from a date last night. It was addressed to Vivian Ward. Seeing the name had nearly made her heart skip a beat. "Vivian Ward" was Julia Roberts's prostitute character in Nora's favorite chick flick, *Pretty Woman*. It was also her code name designating extreme danger. She had immediately ripped the package open, revealing a series of notes and a letter addressed to her from Erica. She focused on every word. Erica was not a person prone to paranoia. She instructed Nora that if everything was okay, she'd phone her by noon Eastern Time the next day to alleviate her fears. Nora barely slept that night as she contemplated what it all meant. She wanted desperately to hear her friend's voice. She hoped that this was just a precaution the two of them would laugh about one day while getting caught up. She had nervously stayed in her apartment, keeping a close eye on the comings and goings on the street below. By early evening, she couldn't bear to stare at the clock any longer, so she went for a walk. No return call had come in the time allotted. In that scenario, Erica had been specific in her instructions.

Run.

Run.

Quickly!

The sound of her suitcase shutting echoed throughout the bedroom. She had been stationed in Rome for just over a year and was beginning to like the sound and feel of calling it home. Sadly, that was about to end. Satisfied that nothing essential was being left behind, she headed for the door and exited. With the key about to lock away a part of her life, she paused for reflection. She stomped her feet and hurriedly went back into the apartment. When she emerged in the hallway, slung over her arm was the black Versace dress. There were some things a woman just couldn't do without.

CHAPTER 3

The jet's turbulence jolted Nora awake from what was a deep, fatigue-induced sleep. Her journey from Rome had begun with good intentions and meticulous preparation. She had spent an entire day at a hotel on the outskirts of the city, perfecting her look. She was no longer a blonde with hair that fell below the shoulders. Her hair was now brunette and short, fuller at the top and cropped neatly around the ears, sloping in toward her neckline. The eyes were also different. Gone were the light green opals, replaced by vibrant blue contact lenses. Her passport matched her newly acquired French accent as well. Nora wasn't ready to embrace where circumstances were taking her, but there was little choice. Her life was inexplicably in danger. Her friend was missing and likely dead. But why? What had Erica uncovered? Some of the answers would come from the package Erica had sent. That information would have to be sorted out, and Nora knew she couldn't go at this alone. She needed help, and that meant turning to someone capable of handling the situation—but more importantly, someone she could trust. That list was regrettably very short. If she had followed protocol after the attempt on her life, an emergency number should have been dialed immediately. Arrangements would have been made to bring her in safely. But Erica worked for the CIA as well, and there had to be a reason why she hadn't alerted her superiors. Nora prayed the person she had to contact would help. They hadn't been on speaking terms for years. An association and romance had both ended badly, and each had vowed not to see or speak to the other again. Now, she felt that same man was the only person capable of helping her. How could she convince him to help when, years ago, in a similar situation, she had doubted him? This was a man who used trust and faith as huge measuring sticks. He didn't suffer fools gladly. He was capable of being kind and gentle in one setting and highly lethal in the next. She once loved him dearly. If he wouldn't help, she felt her days might be numbered.

She was traveling under the name Nathalie Tauziat, French national, born in the seaport city of Calais. She was unmarried, an only child, making a good living as a corporate headhunter, a job that often required lots of travel as the stamps on her passport indicated. Given the stress of her job, it made perfect sense to pamper herself with a vacation. Plus, the name also belonged to a former professional tennis player. If questioned, the name would pass casual inspection, drawing perhaps a polite smile from a knowing customs agent who might have remembered a moment at Roland Garros Stadium. The age and physique of this Nathalie Tauziat would end any speculation on the spot.

The flight was roughly on schedule: the landing gear touched down at Charles de Gaulle airport two hours and ten minutes after takeoff. Nora had over six hours to burn before she had to return to the airport for a flight to JFK in New York. She decided to get lost in the mix, so after storing her bag in an airport storage locker, she opted to take the suburban express train into Paris. She took the train all the way to the Cluny–La Sorbonne station. She looked particularly comfortable as she exited the station with only her purse in tow. She'd changed clothes during the flight, and the effect allowed her to blend in well with the hundreds of young women who walked around the Sorbonne University campus. She sat on a bench, pulling out a paperback novel she'd purchased before boarding her flight. From time to time she scanned the surroundings from behind dark sunglasses, relieved to discover there was nothing out of the ordinary.

––––––––––

On the flight to New York, Nora's mind refused to shut down. She landed and found a hotel near the airport. Unable to sleep much, she studied Erica's notes once more. It was all just a collection of names, dates, and financial documents that appeared to be a complex set of monetary transfers between foreign banks. Two words circled in the notes with a question mark stood out in the middle of one page—*Nuclear capability?* Following it was a list that read like a who's who of National Security nightmares: *The Middle East? Iran, Pakistan, Syria, North Korea? China? CIA???* The names of individuals didn't register with her. Two were Arabic. Others were Asian, German, Russian, and American.

Early the next morning, she boarded her flight at the last moment. Nora was sure her body was going to make her pay for all this travel, but it couldn't be helped. Perhaps there would be a moment to rest where she was now headed.

It was both comforting and nerve-racking to hear the pilot announce that the plane was making its final descent for landing. There were a number of possible outcomes ahead. The absolute worst of all, she couldn't bring herself to think about. It would take all her powers of persuasion to elicit help from the person she was going to see.

As the plane skidded down the runway, the flight attendant announced gleefully, "Ladies and gentlemen, welcome to the Caribbean and the beautiful island of St. Thomas. The temperature is a delightful eighty-six degrees."

CHAPTER 4

There were times Dmitri Nevsky was convinced he was born in the wrong era. He should have been at Stalingrad in the winter of 1943, the temperature minus thirty degrees Celsius, Germany's Sixth Army finally defeated. Deaths in the tens of thousands, a human·toll for sure, but pride restored after bleeding the German army dry, a pivotal turn of World War II. He missed the Cold War as well, working not for the KGB but for its replacement, the Federal Security Service of the Russian Federation, or FSB. It was a career, but not as meaningful as it could have been.

The challenges had become predictable. Skilled practitioners like him found themselves working for countries that often cut their balls off at the first sign of real trouble, preferring instead to seek a diplomatic alternative. It eventually made him sick, and he couldn't stomach the weakness anymore. When the time came, he was welcomed by those who didn't give a damn about the rules. They helped to make him financially stable, his family wanting for nothing within reason.

Nevsky's thoughts on this dark, dreary day were extremely focused. A drum solo of rain pelted his umbrella, some of it splattering off to wet his full-length triple-XL black trench coat. He kept his other hand concealed inside one of the coat's deep pockets, comforted by the handle of a semiautomatic pistol. As he took in the frenzied activity before him, he was glad everything was progressing smoothly. Through his years as a member of the FSB's elite covert division, he had become a man who placed stock in preparation. Paying attention to details went a long way toward staying alive. He was living testament to that. There had been close calls in the Middle East, and a particularly harrowing moment in Bucharest where a bullet narrowly missed a major artery. Everything about this operation had been played out in his mind countless times. Trouble was, this was only the beginning.

Located approximately sixty miles from Moscow in the city of Obninsk, the Institute for Physics & Power Engineering did very little to draw attention to itself. The building's exterior, much like the darkened sky, did not portray friendliness. There had been a time when the institute's work and research were vital to the nation's survival and interests. But those were brighter, more prosperous days. In the wake of the Soviet Union's collapse, the institute and the workers who stayed were forced to adjust to a changing marketplace. The center still possessed valuable commodities high in demand, but those buyers were outside Russia's borders. The ability to modify inventory to fill specific orders greatly changed the institute's mission statement.

The loading dock was located in the rear of the expansive, two-story structure that over the years had taken on a faded Pepto-Bismol color. The rear of the property was enclosed with perimeter fencing, an electronic gate providing the only entryway. Nevsky's group of men seemed oblivious to the weather as they labored on the loading dock, darting back and forth from the building to the two oversized trucks. Each trip from inside was like a carbon copy of the others. Every crate carried was the same size and weight.

The purchase order was bogus. The material packed inside the rectangular boxes being loaded wasn't copper or other precious metals, as the purchase order stipulated. Nevsky didn't give a damn about the inaccuracy as he watched his men move about with precision. He was thankful not to hear a sound from the Bluetooth device attached to his ear. His guards stationed on the roads two miles out in each direction had nothing to report. His orders were simple. Babysit the shipment by whatever means necessary. The journey wouldn't conclude until the cargo was housed briefly at a trading company in Gomel and then finally handed off at a destination not even he was privy to yet. He was told the job might require more than just delivery. That worried him the least of all. His men were well trained and, perhaps most importantly, loyal.

It was a rush order, which he detested, since details of his route had been arranged and taken care of by others. Because he was being paid a significant amount of money, he would go along—careful, however, not to place faith in anything or anyone.

The plump, red-cheeked manager, who greeted him upon arrival, stepped onto the loading dock from the building. He avoided the rain as if he were allergic, waving for Nevsky to come inside. Nevsky left his post from in back of the trucks.

The manager had a nervous way about him, his eyes darting from side to side, scanning the area. "Five more crates and we're done," he said, slightly out of breath. "Then, you and your men can go."

Nevsky nodded. "Fine." He looked beyond the manager to the final load being picked up. "My count is as it should be."

"Good," the manager said, as uncomfortable as a kid who needed to relieve himself.

Nevsky started to turn and then pretended to be deep in thought, as if he were trying to jog his memory.

"Oh," he said, almost as an afterthought. "I, of course, have something for you." He waved at his men in the back of the truck. An oversized duffle bag was ushered to him. The manager's balancing act eased when he saw it. "I believe the agreement is half now and the balance delivered when we make our next destination," Nevsky said, watching the gleam in the man's eye. "A representative will bring you the rest." In truth, he hadn't forgotten at all. It was just that he hadn't had any fun all day.

The manager followed the bag as if witnessing a baby's first steps. "Yes, that is the agreement."

Nevsky turned his attention to the last crate being loaded, and his men quickly closed and locked the doors on the back of the trucks. Two other trucks had previously followed the same procedure. He addressed the plump manager one last time. "Then, we are finished here." The trucks were already pulling away when Nevsky stepped off the dock and into a waiting Range Rover. The driver waited for instructions.

Nevsky motioned forward with his arm. "Everything is fine so far."

With that, the vehicle pulled away as the manager hurriedly slid the loading dock doors shut.

"Yes, everything is okay," Nevsky repeated in his mind.

And yet, as he glanced beyond the rain-streaked windshield, he found little comfort in the statement.

CHAPTER 5

Every now and then he'd open his eyes, and except for cloud formation, the same powder blue sky stared back at him. On the horizon, the deep water of the Atlantic Ocean was a perfect navy blue, preceded by a hue of green, which grew increasingly lighter until one could see the glistening row of white ripples closer to shore. It was another in a long stretch of beautiful days in paradise.

Alex Koves felt the sun warm his body, his eyes shielded from the bright glow behind a pair of sunglasses. An unconscious move brushed free some of the excess water lodged in his black mane of hair, the remnants of several jaunts into the refreshing water. His six-foot-two-inch frame stretched out comfortably on the oversized beach towel. The sand beneath him was warm and molded to the contour of his body like a Temper Foam mattress. Drifting in and out of sleep, he lost sense of time and that was just fine with him.

It required more work to maintain, but his body was still chiseled from the days spent as a world-class athlete. With the Sunday afternoon poundings of football behind him, his body felt the best it had in years. As an added blessing, the headaches were gone as well.

Stereo speakers scattered about delivered soothing sounds of jazz from a boastful music collection. It was a musical taste handed down from his father who played it constantly in the household as he grew up. Many hours were spent listening and being educated on the various musicians and their style. Charlie Parker, Coltrane,

Monk were like relatives. When his father took him as a preteen to see Dave Brubeck in concert, there was no turning back.

The volume was set low so it complemented rather than drowned out the audio provided by the ocean's waves and the swaying leaves of palm trees. The setting did wonders for maintaining his equilibrium. This was as tranquil as life could get. The private stretch of beach served as the backdrop for the two-story house his family had purchased as a vacation haven when he was a young boy. Back then it allowed them to escape the cold, harsh Chicago winters whenever they wanted. Years later, after convincing his parents to sell the property to him, he put the house through a major renovation. It was now an architectural showplace of three bedrooms, a tech-rich media room, gourmet kitchen, and wraparound deck suitable for serious entertaining.

Nature provided a safeguard with tall trees and brush that lined the sloping, curved entrance road, preventing the casual observer from discovering the riches that lay beyond. With over a hundred feet of private beachfront, it was total tranquility.

The long month was finally winding down, but like every year, it would exit with a bang. Decorators and caterers were due to arrive shortly to begin preparations for his annual Carnival party tomorrow night. St. Thomas was a totally different place around Carnival time. From early April 'til the first weekend in May, it was as if the entire island took a deep breath from months of tourist overuse and indulgence. And while Carnival meant roughly a month's worth of added abuse, it was pleasurable energy being exerted: during this respite, the focus shifted back to Virgin Islanders—their pleasures and desires came first. If outsiders didn't understand the attitude, the atmosphere, or the slight delay in service, that was too bad. The island was in a constant state of celebration. Roberts Stadium held a battle of the bands, a costume competition, and calypso singers, while Emancipation Garden hosted the gluttonous culinary delight of the Cultural Fair. The waterfront provided cramped access to the spirited, socially driven nights of food and drink at Carnival Village.

After a late night of indulging in all that Carnival Village had to offer and still suffering the aftereffects of the four a.m.

bump-and-grind of J'ouvert Morning, relaxing on the beach was exactly what the doctor had ordered. By now the children's parade would be wrapping up in town. Many of the parents of the kids participating in the parade had been right alongside him at Carnival Village and J'ouvert Morning. By late afternoon, they'd go home and have a good nap, then awake to put the finishing touches on any floats or costumes for the adult's parade. That activity would be followed up with another night of revelry at Carnival Village. Hell, Carnival only came once a year. Live it up. There was always Sunday to recuperate.

The wind, surf, and soft music concealed the footsteps, which would have been hard to hear anyway since they were made in sand. Alex felt the sun's disappearance but paid it no mind, figuring the clouds had once again cut in between. His peaceful existence remained undisturbed until a voice interrupted the calm.

"Hello, Alex."

He should have been startled, but the tone wasn't alarming—it sounded almost apologetic, in fact. He squinted through his sunglasses, trying to identify the person behind the voice. He couldn't make out who it was, but the mystery offered promise, the voice extremely puzzling.

"Hello," he responded, inching up on his elbows. "Do we know each . . . ?"

"It's been a while," the woman said, anticipating the question. "A lot of distance between us."

His mind was racing. There was something about her voice. "Well, damn, if this isn't intriguing."

He took off his sunglasses as he began to stand up. On the way, he couldn't help but glance at the woman's body, nearly bumping against it. She was toned, but not overly muscular. Long, shapely legs led to a trim waist and firm breasts. His gaze finally rested on the woman's face.

"You still don't recognize me?" she said, sensing his apprehension. "All things considered, I suppose that's a very good thing."

He stood back for a moment, not wanting to believe what his mind was telling him as he cut through the layers of disguise.

Damn!

The hair was shorter and brunette, not blond. The eyes he remembered were not the blue hue that stared at him now. The eyebrows were thicker and darker as well.

"Nora," he managed to say quietly, painting by numbers until the canvas took total shape. "Nora Mossa."

"Guilty," she said with raised hands.

He put his sunglasses back on and dropped down onto the oversized beach towel. "Thanks for stopping by," he exhaled. "You look great. Enjoy your vacation or whatever it is you're doing. Now, if you don't mind, you're blocking the sun."

She ran her hand through her hair, not yet comfortable with its shortened length—a petty concern, given her present situation. She knelt beside him, sandals dangling in her hand. She bit her upper lip while trying to find the words. Nora glanced at the ocean for a moment. From Rome, to Paris, to New York, to this tropical paradise, she had thought countless times of what to say. She knew playing on the emotion of their being former lovers wouldn't be persuasive. Revisiting the past surely wouldn't rouse any sympathy from him. She'd tried every way possible in her mind to make this moment less painful and more likely to promote understanding. The bottom line was, she needed his help. He was the only one she could trust and depend upon, even though, when he had needed those things from her years ago, she had failed him miserably. She was fully aware that she had some nerve being here, and maybe that was where to start. Maybe he would respect that. If not respect it, perhaps he would at least understand the desperation that had driven her to seek him out.

"Alex—" She reached out to touch his shoulder but stopped short. She gathered herself. "I won't say I'm sorry. I conveyed that several times years ago. That's ground already covered. I do wish I were here on vacation, and heaven knows I would not have sought you out if I were."

"Nora, whatever it is"—she could see a raised eyebrow above the rim of his glasses—"I don't give a damn. So traveling all this way, you've totally wasted your time."

Part of her wanted to strangle him. Another part totally understood his reaction. "Damn it, Alex!" She tried not to significantly raise her voice. "Do you have any idea how hard this is for me? I would never attempt to reenter your life if at all possible. Not after the way we left things. You made your feelings toward me painfully clear. I'm only here because I have nowhere else to turn."

Alex used his elbows as support again. "I'm sorry to hear that. Sounds like you've got yourself in what you *perceive* to be a bad way. But your life and your world is one I don't live in anymore."

"Alex, my life is in danger. I—" He cut her off with a raised hand.

"Save it. Really." He shook his head. "I mean, whatever it is, what the hell do you think I can do? As I said, that's your paranoia. Your world. Look around you. This is me now. It's quiet. It's peaceful."

She knew she was fighting for her life, so everything was fair game. "Does that mean you've totally forgotten? I don't really see how that's possible."

"Forgotten!" Alex exploded. He took a moment to calm himself. "No, I haven't forgotten. Let's see if the names ring a bell with you. Cowl. Accord. Fitness. Why don't you go ask them for help? Oh, that's right, you can't. Because they're dead. I could go on. And that's precisely the point: no, I haven't forgotten. I just don't want to remember it all every day anymore."

"It's because you haven't forgotten that I'm here. I need the old Alex. My life depends on the old Alex."

"Well, I've got some bad news for you. That Alex doesn't exist anymore."

She ran her hand over her face before continuing. "Believe me, if there was another way, another avenue—" Her head sunk into her hands. "I would have explored it. We've been through a lot together, and I'm praying that deep down inside, you can understand that enough to help me."

Crap! She didn't want to cry. She could feel the moisture forming in her eyes and tried to hide it by turning her head and wiping her face. "Look, I have my life savings. Nearly a hundred thousand dollars. It's yours."

He studied her through his sunglasses. He recalled the time when their lives had been entwined. She was a strong, competent, tough woman who could more than take care of herself. Though her facial features had changed a little, this was hardly, at the moment, that same Nora Mossa. He noticed her hands were trembling.

"Alex . . ."

He let his name trail out to the ocean, only to hear it come back.

"Alex, please," she begged, realizing all her dignity was lost.

He fixated on the sky. "Nora, like I said. You've wasted your time. The answer is no. It's not my place anymore. Now, if you don't mind, I'm trying to ease out of a hangover."

There was nothing left for her to say. She knew of no other way to persuade him. For the first time, she fully grasped how deeply she had failed him. After all these years, he had not eased an inch on how he felt about her. The way he left it was the way it remained. Dismissal. Total and permanent. As Nora got to her feet, the tears that ran down her cheeks weren't out of self-pity but of compassion. The clock couldn't be turned back. There apparently was no way to fix this.

"Thanks for your time, Alex. I'm sorry to have bothered you. I guess this really is good-bye." She got no response. "If you change your mind," she mumbled, "I'll be at Frenchman's Reef until Sunday afternoon. Room 410."

She exited just as quietly as she had entered.

CHAPTER 6

The smell of fresh coffee in the early morning hours always provided the illusion that all was right with the world. Unfortunately, that euphoric state hardly ever lasted beyond a full cup.

Sitting behind his desk, George Champion, the director of the National Clandestine Service, stole a few minutes of government time to indulge in the aroma of a freshly brewed pot of French roast beans. The coffee itself would certainly end the fantasy. After all, how many times in his life had he truly enjoyed a perfect cup? Still, the odds of that were damn far better than those of solving the mountain of problems that greeted him today, none of which had any easy solution.

He pulled out a file he knew all too well. Erica Janway. If the gender had been different, he'd be looking over the file of a bona fide high-ranking member of the CIA. A person he very well could have been answering to. What had gone wrong for Janway before her death? Since she'd filed a discrimination lawsuit, no one at the agency dared to even look at her the wrong way. It had been a bad situation. The office of general counsel had insisted she be assigned to desk duty at Langley until the matter was fully investigated. Was her lawsuit merely the result of being disgracefully reassigned from her post as station chief in Moscow? That administrative move alone pretty much placed a ceiling on her career. The allegations that led to her removal were serious, but never fully proven. Just the word of two male agents who claimed that Janway sexually harassed them and that when her alleged advances were turned down, she failed to give them top-level assignments. There were also the reports of excessive drinking. To her credit, she had admitted that perhaps, due to the pressures of the job, she took a drink or two more than she should have, but she had insisted that it never clouded her judgment. When her husband had suggested she had a slight problem, she did get help. So why would a woman so obviously up-front and competent jeopardize her career with a stupid decision to chase some mid-level subordinates? Sure, men had done it for years, but Janway knew what the stakes were. She was smarter than that.

Champion had worked with her on one occasion. While he was station chief in Berlin, they ran a joint operation together. It was a large-scale undertaking, and her professionalism and problem-solving skills were impressive. This one red flag on her record, though, proved to be a major downfall. The fact that one of the accusations came from the son of a prominent US senator—a senator who also served on the subcommittee charged with overseeing the nation's intelligence agencies—was a deadly thorn in her career.

Janway was reassigned to an important post at Langley, but essentially, it was desk duty. She withstood the injustice (as she perceived it) for almost a year before filing the lawsuit. If her career wasn't over before, it certainly was then. Now, she was dead.

Add to that, the latest headache provided by the station chief in Rome. Nora Mossa, who Janway mentored, was AWOL. Her apartment had been searched and secured when she failed to make a scheduled check-in. Field assets like her were known to go off grid at times, but she wasn't on an assignment, and after several hours, an alert was sent out. Factor in the Janway connection, and Mossa's disappearance became even more concerning. The agent was now actively being searched for all over the world. A heads-up was even sent out to other governmental agencies. The organizational chart of the CIA was much like any other major conglomerate, which meant Champion, near the top, rarely met or even knew a majority of those on the lower rungs of the ladder. Mossa was an exception. He knew her name. She'd been part of that joint operation with Janway. She was one of Janway's most prized assets. Mossa's file indicated a result-oriented field agent who didn't mind getting her hands dirty. She was also well trained, able to assume new identities and disappear with ease. That's all he needed at the moment, an experienced field agent who, when she didn't want to be found, likely couldn't. It would take a lot of resources, but she *had* to be located. Until evidence was presented to the contrary, he was going with the assumption that she hadn't met the same fate as Janway.

Outside his partially opened door, Champion could hear that his administrative assistant, Mrs. Prescot, had arrived. She was a carryover from the office's previous occupant and the one before that. Loyal and efficient, she'd likely be in that outer office until she chose otherwise. He could tell she was making a fresh pot of coffee before settling in her chair. Shortly after, there were voices, and then came a polite knock at his door. Mrs. Prescot poked her head in.

"Good morning, Mr. Champion."

"Same to you, Mrs. Prescot."

"Mr. Peters is here to see you."

"Show him in, please."

She opened the door fully, motioning Karl Peters into the office. Smartly dressed in a dark suit, the Hofstra alum carried a small brown paper bag, slightly moistened at the corners.

"Can I get you anything, Mr. Peters?" Mrs. Prescot asked in a nurturing way. "We have coffee, tea, water, soda."

He sheepishly held up his brown paper bag, careful to put a hand under the bottom. "No thanks," he said. "I stopped for a latte on the way."

"Very well then." Mrs. Prescot was closing the door when she paused. "By the way, Mr. Champion . . ."

"Yes?"

"Your coffee is getting much better, but . . ."

"But it would be better if I wait for you to make it."

Mrs. Prescot smiled and closed the door behind her.

Champion still had a warm look on his face when he addressed Peters. "Latte! What the hell?"

Peters removed his beverage from the soiled bag. Licking his fingers, he said, "What can I say? Acquired taste. Double chocolate mocha, to be exact."

Champion just nodded. "To each his own." He raised his coffee mug and took a drink.

Peters slurped his still-hot latte, the sound of which produced a pained look from Champion. Peters looked up innocently. "Sorry, sir." He cleared his throat before beginning. "On Janway's computer at the house were files that pertained to nuclear capability for Pakistan, North Korea, China, and Iran. Essentially, just background stuff on who has what, and in the case of Iran, how far they are from getting nukes and by what means they might acquire the materials needed."

Champion swiveled in his chair and peeked beyond his office windows at the workforce beginning to filter in. He gave the discovery a moment of thought. Janway was assigned to WINPAC (Weapons, Intelligence, Nonproliferation & Arms Control Center), so it was certainly within her scope to have such information. Peters seized the opportunity to sneak in another sip of his latte, concentrating on drinking more quietly. "Forensics went over the place twice and came up with nothing. Neighbors along the street didn't hear or see anything out of the ordinary, and it's generally quiet down there. She did have some e-mail correspondence with Nora Mossa that dates back a few months. Trivial stuff, basically, and nothing recent. Still, it's being analyzed to make sure nothing is coded. On the Mossa front, it's been three days. No communication. No sightings. However, some sort of altercation took place in her apartment. Furniture was broken, and it looks like she packed in a hurry. Traces of blood were found on the floor, but the DNA wasn't hers. There's no husband. No serious boyfriend. She hasn't made contact with her mother in Oregon."

Champion seemed uncomfortable when he told Peters, "Of course, we're not sure she wasn't taken either." He didn't wait for a vague supposition. "We need to find her and quickly. If she's running, it sounds like she has a reason. It bothers me that she hasn't made an attempt to be brought in. Intensify the search. Let the other agencies know this is now a priority for us."

Peters knew when he was being dismissed. Rising, he said, "I'll see to it, sir." He was half out the door when Champion called out.

"Did you talk to the husband yet?"

Peters shook his head. "I tried briefly. He's pretty torn up and not exactly in a cooperative frame of mind, especially considering who's asking."

"He's a big-time lawyer who can generate headlines we don't need. Give him a few days to reflect and try again."

"I'll give it a shot," Peters said, regretting the choice of words.

CHAPTER 7

At sixty miles an hour, the screeching tires indicated the current rate of speed was ill suited for the tight roadway. Sharp turns were maneuvered with varying degrees of pressure on responsive brakes. The vintage Porsche convertible jolted forcibly forward upon entering a straight section of road and then proved its craftsmanship when precise handling was called for.

The difficulties of making it from one section of St. Thomas to another required an elevated level of patience and skill, since there was mazelike traffic feeding into Carnival Village. Several horns along the way cursed at Alex as he finally made it past the logjams and then beyond Havensight Mall, where the cruise ships docked. It would be smooth sailing from here; up into the mountains for a short stretch along Frenchman's Bay Road, down again and then rising once more, where an impressive view of Charlotte Amalie's waterfront revealed itself.

The brisk, refreshing wind tossed his hair about and helped soothe his distressed nerves. The car's stereo system was cranked nearly all the way up, the last fifteen minutes devoted to Sting. Even though Alex sang along, there was no canceling out the thoughts uppermost in his mind. For years he had been able to stow away fragments of his life. Images, thoughts, and emotions, all neatly tucked away, lying dormant. Now, all the healing and comfort of a new life had been ripped apart; shattered in one unexpected brush with the past. No matter how hard he tried to dismiss the intrusion, the damage was done. Yesterday on the beach marked the first time in four years he had uttered the code names of those who'd been betrayed. Men and women who had placed their trust in his hands, a miscalculation that cost them their lives. There were detractors who had questioned whether the bright Alexander David Koves had been thrust into a lofty position too soon. When he claimed a trusted government source was a traitor, responsible for the deaths of his assets, he had few supporters left. What hurt the most, though, was the absence of backing from the woman he loved, Nora Mossa. He could handle the weight and pressure from his superiors but not the skepticism from one he held close to his heart. So he returned to Langley, walked into CIA headquarters a government employee, and an hour later, was escorted out, no longer on the US government's payroll. It was the only thing he had quit on in his life.

Unable to fully enjoy his annual Carnival party, he made a stealthy getaway from the packed crowd, promising to return shortly in a better mood. He realized only one solution would ease his mind.

He greeted the guard on duty at the entrance to Frenchman's Reef Hotel with sympathy, understanding the man's lack of enthusiasm: the guard was missing the last night of Carnival Village. The two recognized each other, having played pickup basketball together at Griffith Park. He waved Alex through. Familiarity often made life a lot easier on St. Thomas. Alex parked and bypassed the hotel lobby, heading for a side elevator. A few minutes later, he found himself hesitating before knocking on the door. His arms felt the weight of his decision and resisted. Was this what he really wanted? Did he miss the action that much? He got off the rock enough to exorcise the boredom, but an element of excitement was missing. In the final analysis, there was the pain he knew would never escape him if Nora got killed after pleading for his help. Her death would haunt him ten times more than the souls that already did.

He took a leap of faith and willed his right arm to knock. Through the peephole, he could see the light inside eclipsed by movement. When it was determined he was friend, not foe, the door opened.

"Let's go. You're making me miss my party," he said.

Nora stood slightly stunned. "Does this mean—"

"It means tonight you're going to a party," Alex cut in. "We'll address that other thing tomorrow." Nora was still motionless.

"Well, let's go."

Back at his house, the party was lively. The deck was full of bodies and the overflow was positioned on the beach. Some were dancing to the music, but the conversations and laughter spoke volumes to the level of entertainment. The abundance of food and drink were set out on a lengthy buffet table, caterers making sure there was never a shortage of anything.

The house brought back memories for Nora. They had been a couple when she was last here. She had nearly forgotten about Alex's past as a professional football player. He never talked about it much, and the only visible tribute to those days was an oil painting of him when he was an Oakland Raider. It hung in the family room above the fireplace, his fierceness when fully engaged as a strong safety perfectly rendered. When she read sports stories about him, it was said he delivered hits with all the force of a runaway train.

Alex made introductions when necessary and told Nora to make herself at home. The party consisted of people who all seemed to enjoy each other's company and stories. It was the first time in days that Nora felt secure enough to let her guard down. She drank, ate, and danced like it was a weekend back in college at the University of Oregon. Every now and then she would observe Alex moving about, being the perfect host. She was grateful beyond words that she had been right about the kind of man he was.

CHAPTER 8

Alex had thought Nora was completely out of his life for good. He'd made that intention clear years ago—ironically, in this very city.

As the Lincoln Town Car sedan rolled along the Arlington Memorial Bridge, it dawned on Alex that he hadn't been in the nation's capital since shortly after the day he'd walked away from the CIA.

The sun was retreating on the Virginia side of the Potomac, slowly making way for the moon to work its photogenic shift under a virtually cloudless sky. Joggers with varying degrees of athleticism made their way across the bridge, sweating in the humid air.

There were few architecturally designed wonders that could rival the view provided by the Lincoln Memorial and the Washington Monument when they were lined up. Crossing the bridge, Alex momentarily witnessed the postcard. The Town Car glided up 23rd Street and then turned onto K Street, heading east. Downtown Washington was still experiencing some residual after-work traffic, mere child's play compared to the actual rush-hour madness. The sedan stopped in front of the Mayflower Hotel. Alex dutifully tipped his driver but waved off the hotel bellhop, handling the single suitcase himself. He checked in and a moment later was relieved to discover not much had changed in the expansive luxury suite. He stretched out on the outer-room sofa and once again studied the notes and materials Nora had given him. He'd already gone over them several times and was no closer to an answer. Feeling he needed a set of expert eyes, he'd made copies and forwarded them to a knowledgeable party prior to departing St. Thomas. That person was one of the main reasons he was back in Washington. Alex hooked up his laptop, logged on, and sent two e-mails. Each contained his room number and the same short message. "I've arrived. Come now."

Since Nora was also staying at the hotel, she was the first to show up. She didn't come empty-handed. Alex accepted the quart of rum and liter of Coke as she entered. Despite a sheepish smile, she looked depressed. She was a woman used to being in control, and the past few days had totally thrown her for a loop. Every morning since she had hastily left her apartment, Nora had checked the Internet offerings of several Rome newspapers. There were no headlines about a dead man being found in a missing woman's apartment. By now, the decomposing stench of a dead body would've forced neighbors to inquire. No headline and no scandal could mean only one thing. The body had to have been removed. Doing so would require resources and more than one person.

Thirty minutes after Nora's arrival, the second e-mail recipient was at the door with a briefcase in hand. Before stepping in, the taller man on the other side of the door looked down at Alex in silence. It had been nearly two years since they'd seen each other. After a few seconds, Duncan Anderson said, "One black man reporting for duty."

"Get your ass in here," Alex responded, embracing the larger man as they chuckled.

Duncan's deep voice resonated throughout the suite as he and Alex engaged in banter that brought about boyish laughter. Their chatter stopped when Duncan encountered the statuesque brunette who now stood slightly before him.

He was truly taken aback. "As I live and breathe . . . Nora Mossa." The two immediately embraced. She concentrated on fighting back tears, but one managed to slip through.

"It's so good to see you, Duncan," she offered, wiping away that trace of emotion. "He didn't tell me."

Duncan looked quizzically at Alex, who gave no explanation. "I had no idea this involved you, either."

Nora laughed slightly. "Well, considering the new look, and

how long it's been, I don't know if it's such a good thing you recognized me so quickly." She gestured toward Alex. "It took other people a little longer."

Alex let the remark slide. He was hoping Duncan's presence would be a calming influence. Seeing another familiar face might give Nora's psyche, badly bruised by events real or imagined, a big boost.

"All right, enough of the homecoming," Alex said. "Let's get to it." They sat at a large table, and Alex beckoned Duncan to begin. The big man sized up Nora one more time before proceeding. Even though it'd been years, he could sense this wasn't the same confident woman. Not once could he recall ever seeing her shed a tear. She was as tough and capable as they come. Or had been.

Nora recognized the look. She'd seen it for the first time when she was eleven. As she stood by her mother's side, a graying doctor looked down at her trusting, yet frightened face, and then to her mother, who nodded it was okay. That nice doctor with a wonderful bedside manner went on to deliver news that shattered a perfectly happy family's life. Her father wasn't expected to survive his massive heart attack. That same gaze was now in a friend's eyes.

Duncan's oversized hand withdrew a stack of papers from his leather briefcase and laid them in a neat pile in front of him.

"Erica Janway was murdered at her home in Annapolis," he began. Nora's eyes glazed over but no tears fell down her cheeks this time.

"How?" she asked calmly.

Duncan understood that she and Janway were close. He felt compelled not to coddle her in any way.

"Single shot through the heart."

Nora stored the image in her mind. She prayed she'd get close enough to those responsible. Someone was going to answer for her friend's death. "Please continue," she advised.

Duncan sifted through the stack of papers, pulling out a section. He handed copies to Nora and Alex. "I've been trying to figure out exactly what the hell Janway was up to. The package she sent you may be a bunch of disjointed notes, but within them is some eye-catching stuff. The names, they're key as well. Some I recognize as dealers on the black market. I've got feelers out, trying to get some background. I feel certain we can take the mystery out of one name. 'Champion.' Given the arena we're operating in, I'd say that's your current boss, Nora, and"—he locked eyes with Alex—"your old boss, mi amigo: George Champion. In case you haven't been keeping up, he's now director of the National Clandestine Service. The other names, unless something rattles my memory, are a complete and utter mystery to me. Just names on a page at the moment."

Alex stood to go make a drink. "In that case, let's discuss tomorrow."

Nora was the only one surprised by the subject. "Tomorrow?"

"Yeah." Alex made rum and Cokes for himself and Duncan, having been waved off by Nora. "Before we go any further, we're going to discover if your concerns have merit or whether we can just drop you off at Langley. So, we have to prep."

Nora felt part of this was payback. She had failed to believe in him years before, and it proved costly for them. "Would you mind telling me what you have in mind?"

Alex smiled. "Not at all. It'll essentially be your ass on the line."

CHAPTER 9

Seven heavily armed men were a bit much for what was supposed to be a simple business transaction. Perhaps they were being cautious or feeling nervous. The briefcase Dmitri Nevsky carried did, after all, contain a large sum of money. More money than any of the seven men had ever seen in their lives.

Nevsky immediately sized up two of the seven, since they were the ones to greet him and his two-man entourage at the warehouse door of the TTI trading company. The two men had the smell of cheap alcohol and outdated cologne. Their clothes were nothing fancy, worn more than once a week, Nevsky surmised. Instead of the finer things in life, their money was spent on the tools that no doubt garnered them respect in the circles in which they traveled. Both men proudly flashed their guns as if they were holding onto their private parts. One carried a Heckler & Koch automatic. To a less-seasoned man, it would make a statement. Nevsky merely made note of it, as he did of the other man's Uzi. He had little doubt the weapons had been fired at human flesh just to make a stupid point.

Once inside the warehouse, two additional armed guards met Nevsky and his men. They joined the parade that eventually led them to an open, dimly lit storage area. Rays of sun managed to sneak through the dusty, grimy side of overhead windows. Three other men were congregated behind a long, battered table. They stood up from their chairs, postures filled with bravado. From the diversion of eyes, Nevsky knew whom he'd be talking to behind the table. He was also the best dressed of the seven, wearing a rich silk shirt hanging over imported jeans. The only part of the shirt tucked into his jeans revealed a polished automatic pistol.

The guard with the Uzi walked over to Silk Shirt and whispered in his ear. He then returned to his position on Nevsky's flank, along with Heckler & Koch.

Silk Shirt raised an arm, motioning behind Nevsky. "So where are your trucks of merchandise?"

"Close by," Nevsky coolly answered.

"So you represent our friend from Sverdlovsk?"

It had been a long journey. Rain-soaked days and nights, bumpy roads, less than stellar sleeping arrangements, risks around every corner, and now this. Nevsky glanced around the mostly empty storage area.

"You expecting someone else?"

Silk Shirt accepted the observation with a smile. "No. In fact, we cleared the place out just for you."

"Good. Then you're ready to house the trucks."

"I'd like to and will," Silk Shirt said, bowing his head before raising it triumphantly. "That is, as soon as we finish our negotiation." His hand inched slightly closer to his gun.

Nevsky noted the position of the armed men and then his own. He let out a sigh. "I'm not aware that any part of the arrangement is open-ended. I was told this was a done deal."

"It's a long way from Sverdlovsk to Gomel. Things change. Inflation kicks in. Have you not seen that the economy is in the crapper? We have unexpected overhead. As the Americans say," he searched for the words, "life is a bitch."

Nevsky laughed softly. "I've heard that one." Everyone produced a smirk. The storage area's ambiance became more noticeable as things got quieter. There was a dull hum of air conditioners. From an unseen office, a radio could be heard. The storage area smelled of dampness and stale cigarettes. Nevsky was aware that the seven men began to shift their stance.

He directly addressed Silk Shirt. "So, how exactly have things changed?"

"In addition to what you have in the suitcase . . . our accountants and financial advisors calculated that we need an additional five million rubles."

"Whew," Nevsky whistled. "That's quite a change." He gave his men a hand signal that went unnoticed by the seven. He then made a move to the inside of his jacket.

"Well—" A millisecond or two behind where they should have been, hammers were shifted into place and the seven men all had their weapons carefully trained on Nevsky and his crew. A surprised look surfaced on Nevsky's face before he slowly withdrew his hand from a breast pocket. In it was a cell phone. "I'm not the one who can authorize five million rubles. A call has to be made."

With gun in hand, Silk Shirt motioned Nevsky to continue. "Go ahead. We are in no hurry here." He looked affirmatively to his men as if to say, I told you so. They all relaxed a little.

Nevsky had an anxious look as he waited for the call to be answered. After several rings, someone did. "It's Dmitri. We have a slight problem. An additional-five-million-rubles problem." After listening, he removed the phone from his mouth for a second. "You are Petrov?" he asked Silk Shirt, who nodded in turn. Nevsky returned to his conversation. "Yes, Petrov." He continued to listen, filling in a mumbled response as he did.

Nevsky tried to reassure Petrov, producing a pained smile to indicate this wasn't going to last much longer. "Yes . . . Yes . . . I understand. Not to worry." At last he ended the call and returned the phone to his breast pocket.

Nevsky placed the briefcase on the table as he took in his counterpart. At the moment, he was full of contempt but was careful not to display it. This poor, stupid fool, he thought. A low-life thug who was attempting to make a name for himself by muscling his way into the big leagues. The man ran a small operation of organized crime wannabes, and the money in the suitcase wasn't enough? Hell, it would have made their year and then some.

"Well, Petrov. What can I say? You are right. Things change," Nevsky said. The words comforted the seven but more importantly, got them to ease up even further. "My employer wants this transaction completed in the worst way, so he has instructed me to take care of the matter."

With the money already being spent in his mind, Petrov chuckled. "Good. Glad we can do business." He gave his men a look of triumph and conviction.

His mood changed quickly. In a span of seconds, the speed with which his mind couldn't fully comprehend, Petrov realized he wouldn't be spending that money after all. A bullet from Nevsky's automatic burned a hole through his throat, shattering vocal cords and splattering blood on his expensive silk shirt. Petrov's shocked system sent his hands to his throat to check if this was really happening. Then, he fell backward, landing on the cold floor.

The man holding the Heckler & Koch, behind to the left, was equally caught off guard as two bullets fired by one of Nevsky's men ripped open his midsection. Nevsky's other companion neutralized the guard carrying the Uzi by knocking him to the ground with a sideways kick. At the same time, he placed two bullets to the head of the other man on his right, who was frozen in amazement.

Having used just one well-placed bullet on Petrov, Nevsky was able to address the other two men behind the table, whose reactions were lagging. Again, he was efficient and accurate. Each man stumbled to his death with a bullet to the head.

The remaining man on the left dropped his gun in surrender just as one of Nevsky's men was about to pull the trigger. The man holding the Uzi was on the ground, waiting for the shot that would end his life, but instead his weapon was knocked away. Petrov's surrendering guard was directed to get behind the table. He was joined by the remaining survivor, who favored his left side after the kick to his kidney. The air smelled of burnt flesh, and the hum of the air conditioners could no longer be heard due to the gurgling noises from Petrov, who lay squirming on the floor.

"Now, do we still have any negotiation problems?" Nevsky asked the survivors. Both men enthusiastically indicated they did not. "Then this," Nevsky grabbed the briefcase and walked around the table, "will soon belong to you. We'll be back within the hour with the trucks."

Nevsky hovered above Petrov, who now only held one blood-soaked hand over his throat. The other lay by his side, no longer responding to commands. The man's eyes were watery, devoid of all the sureness they once held. Nevsky bent down.

"Petrov, you are partly right. Life is a bitch. But to finalize the statement for you, Americans sometimes complete the expression by saying, *Life is a bitch . . . and then you die.*" Nevsky fired a lethal shot to the head. He and his men began their exit.

"An hour, comrades," he said forcefully. He then stopped to address the stunned pair.

"Congratulations on your promotions."

CHAPTER 10

Alex returned a flirtatious smile as he held the door open, allowing an attractive blonde and her less impressive friend to exit. He knew, at times, he could be quite shallow.

The morning edition of the *Washington Post* pinned beneath his arm, he entered the Starbucks on Dupont Circle at precisely eight a.m. While in line, he perused the front page of the *Post*, which offered updates on the usual spattering of hot spots. The war on terror waged on, gas prices were edging up again, and the District was in for another warm day.

He ordered a medium coffee, doctored it up with cream and a couple of sugar packets. At least three other people were waiting for a seat in the crowded coffeehouse when he made his way to a window seat occupied by a slender woman wearing a black and white two-piece dress. If she saw him coming, she made no indication of it, and yet, as he approached, she gathered her coffee and purse and got up to leave.

"Finished?" Alex asked innocently.

"All yours," she responded, brushing by him with barely a look.

"Thank you."

Alex plopped his frame into the seat, took a momentary glance at the hustle and bustle on the street, and then returned to his paper. He pulled out his cell phone and laid it on the table. Dressed in a gray polo shirt and black pleated microfiber pants, Alex was not only comfortable, he also blended into the landscape without drawing any attention. He opened the sports section and headed for the box scores to find the breakdown of the Cubs game. It was early in the season, but seeing them only three games out of first place was encouraging. Thinking about Chicago reminded him he was due to make all the necessary family calls. He hadn't talked to his parents for two weeks, and his California-sunshine sister had now left a phone message and two e-mails. Her last message started out with, "Where in the freaking world are you?"

Alex turned a page of the newspaper and in doing so, slid over a napkin that had been lying on the table ever since he sat down. Written on it inside a circle was a simple plus sign. Anyone else would have interpreted it as simple doodling, but to him, it meant all area surveillance cameras were under control and everything else necessary to pull off his plan was in place and ready to go.

Satisfied, he took one more look around. Grabbing his phone, he sent a text message to several people. It read, *Send Bambi into the forest.*

Five minutes later, a taxi pulled up in front of the coffeehouse and Nora emerged. It was startling for Alex to see her this way because with the aid of a blond wig, she now looked like the Nora he remembered. She entered the establishment and got in line, glancing at Alex only as a reference point. She used her debit card to pay for her order. It bore not the alias she was using to travel halfway around the world, but rather her real name. With order in hand, she looked for a seat. A man dressed in construction gear and a Redskins hat dotted with paint drippings motioned her his way. When she arrived at his stool along the countertop, he was happy to get a closer look. He offered his seat, saying it was time to get to work.

Alex covertly followed her movement. He could tell, even from his vantage point, that her eyes were devoid of contact lenses, revealing a set of green eyes that had once captivated him. The long-haired wig was virtually undetectable as being a fake. Alex wanted more than anything for this charade to end. The next ten or fifteen minutes would provide the answer. He didn't want to think about what his future would bring should he be wrong about this situation. He wanted to walk away clean, send Nora on her way, and perhaps fly to Chicago to see his parents and take in a Cubs game. After that he'd entertain flying out west to surprise his sister. That sounded like a plan, much better than the one hastily put in place now. He drew some comfort in knowing that quality people were involved and that therefore there was little, except for the unexpected, that could go wrong.

CHAPTER 11

Even though the bland navy blue sedan had no distinguishing markings, any native Washingtonian could guess with a high degree of accuracy that it either belonged to the feds, District police, or one of the local TV news stations. It essentially was a case of hiding in plain sight.

Karl Peters was in the back seat, his mind racing. He didn't usually get to utilize the services of a driver, and he hadn't really said much of anything to the man, but then he realized they were heading west on New York Avenue. To save time and aggravation during the morning rush, his driver was avoiding the backlog of the Beltway. This route would take them along K Street Northwest, a straight shot to the Whitehurst Freeway that accessed the George Washington Parkway and its gradual climb to Langley.

"Luis, no rush," Peters said. "In fact, let's take the scenic route."

Having grown up in the District and being an avid bike rider, Luis had been a human navigation center long before technology caught up. He acknowledged Peters's request by switching lanes through heavy traffic just in time to make a left-hand turn onto North Capitol Street Northeast. Like Peters, he was single, and every now and then, a private perk on company time was a welcome thing. It was shortly after eight in the morning on what promised to be another spring gem in the nation's capital. The various Metro stops would be emptying the District's vast female workforce (Union Station was a gold mine) and Congress was in session, all of which guaranteed a beauty pageant.

With the heavy traffic load, they had no choice but to coast around the House and Senate buildings. Peters was impressed with his driver's innate knowledge. "Something tells me you've done this before."

"Yes, sir," was the response as a shapely brunette in a floral dress crossed in front of them at a stop sign. "I certainly have."

Rolling into the heart of the District along Massachusetts Avenue, Peters took note of the time. Sadly, this distraction would have to come to an end. There was much work to be done. Once at Langley, he'd spend a large chunk of time getting briefed by legal before having to return to the District for a late-morning sit-down with Janway's husband at his firm. They had debated sending a legal representative with him, but decided that doing so would send the wrong message. In the final analysis, Champion felt Peters's down-to-earth disposition would make the sympathy he expressed believable and possibly get Paul Janway to relax somewhat. If legal teams got involved and motions started flying back and forth, everyone would lose.

The sight of a Starbucks ahead reminded Peters that he had yet to get his morning latte. He knew that by now Champion would be on at least his third cup of coffee, so he'd brownnose it and get his boss some quality ground beans. The man did love his coffee.

"Drop me off at the Starbucks on the next block," Peters requested. There was absolutely no place to park, so Luis stopped the vehicle in traffic and was more than willing to double park for as long as it took, no matter how many angry looks or horns he had to endure. Peters told him the dedication was unnecessary. Grabbing the door handle, he said, "Shouldn't take too long, so just drive around the block. No need to piss people off. Do you want anything, Luis?"

It was the second time this morning Luis was impressed with his passenger. This had been only the third time in over a year he'd chauffeured Mr. Peters around. Luis was flattered that the man had cared enough to remember his name, let alone be considerate enough to ask if he was thirsty or hungry.

"No thanks, sir. But I appreciate you asking. I'll just circle a couple of times and pick you back up in a minute."

Exciting the vehicle, Peters followed procedure and buttoned his sport coat, in order to conceal the holstered weapon he would probably never have to fire. He entered the noisy, packed coffeehouse. It was always amusing to him how a company like this had found the formula of appealing to people's laziness and desires in one successful swoop. Too busy to make coffee at home? Or too lazy? Whatever the answer, it added up to profit.

There were so many people engaged in their own distractions that Peters, trying to pay attention to the line moving, totally missed the stunning blonde passing by him on her way out. He did manage to casually catch a glimpse of her from behind as she opened the door. His attention got diverted to his cell phone. The customized beeps indicated it was an urgent message. Grabbing his phone, he stepped out of line and speed-dialed Langley. The line was answered on the first ring.

"This is Peters, I just got notified to call."

His eyes widened as he was relayed information. He headed toward the exit.

"Where?" he shouted into the phone, pressing it firmly against his ear, trying to hear over all the noise. The answer stopped him dead in his tracks. He immediately looked up and began searching faces in the coffeehouse.

"Are you sure?" he asked. "Shit, I'm there! I'm standing right in the place. I'll get back to you." He ended the call, pocketed the phone, and in the process unbuttoned his jacket. Looking over the crowd, he didn't see what he hoped to find. He reached into his jacket pocket and pulled out a photograph and then bumped his way past grumbling patrons to the front of the line.

The cashier said, "Excuse me sir, but there's a line," and motioned for the customer behind Peters to step forward. Peters quickly flashed his identification and holstered weapon before holding up the photo of Nora.

"Have you seen this woman? She might have just been here. Paid with a debit card."

The freckle-faced girl was now a little nervous as her coworkers began to take notice. "No, I haven't, but . . ." She looked behind her. "Steve. Steve!" She motioned frantically. "Get over here!"

A slightly older man came sauntering over, wondering what

the urgency was. She pointed to the man from the CIA. Steve took a look at Peters's credentials and immediately straightened up. Peters hurriedly tried again. "Have you seen this woman? She paid with a debit card just a few minutes ago."

The worker produced a look of admiration. "Yeah, I served her." He glanced beyond Peters into the seating area. "She was just here, took a seat. But I don't see her now." Peters didn't bother saying thank you as he rushed for the exit.

With all the noise in the coffee shop, few people noticed the momentary change in its pattern, and yet Alex registered the slight commotion unfolding at the cashier's counter. Though he couldn't hear everything, he did hear *Seen this woman?* when a man held up something in his hand. Alex went into a state of disbelief. This couldn't be happening this fast. From his window seat he could see that Nora had a slight head start as she strolled down the street. Still, she was clueless as to what was now taking place. Alex had to deal with the situation fast. What concerned him most was not knowing if the man had backup waiting outside. Alex calmly rose from his seat and managed to maneuver himself a few steps behind the man as he hurriedly pushed through the exit door. Alex's appearance on the street so soon—without having sent anyone a text with instructions—was a warning to others in place that something was wrong.

The bright sun greeted Peters as he frantically looked up and down the street and across it, examining every woman moving. He stopped when he saw the woman who had momentarily caught his attention in the coffee shop as she was leaving. He began walking at a faster pace toward her as she sauntered down the street. His mind was in rapid mode, analyzing. Long blond hair. Physically fit. Just left the coffeehouse. Had to be. But it didn't make sense. No matter, that would get sorted out later. He was now just a few yards behind. Close enough to be heard.

"Nora," he shouted. "Nora Mossa."

The woman didn't stop. She didn't speed up or slow down either. She seemed oblivious to his calls. He could be wrong.

"Nora Mossa. Stop!"

This time the woman came to a halt. Peters reacted by slowing down to almost a crawl. He inched his hand closer to his holstered weapon as he approached.

"Nora Mossa," he said, under control. "Turn around . . . very slowly."

She did not move, keeping her back to him instead. He was now five feet away, and his hand firmly gripped his weapon, ready to draw if necessary. At that instant, Peters's peripheral vision caught a figure reflected in a storefront window. It was a man. That much he could tell, and that the man was directly behind him. Gun now out of its holster, Peters tried to turn, but the blow that descended at the base of his neck was lightning fast and well placed. It made the nerve endings in his body go haywire. A swift kick was delivered to the back of his already buckling right knee. The gun dislodged from Peters's hand before he hit the pavement. He could see his weapon being kicked away by the same foot that had brought him down. That foot then reversed itself and came crashing into his face, sending him into near unconsciousness. Peters didn't give in totally to the dizziness that enveloped him, but he couldn't move a muscle in his body. He did manage to hear his assailant yell at the woman.

"Get going."

Peters wanted to look up and assess the situation, but he couldn't. He merely saw the man's shoes walk out of view, and then he blacked out.

Alex paused until Nora got into a waiting car that spun off down Connecticut Avenue, then he returned to the man lying on the ground. Knowing he had to work fast and hoping no one in the growing curious crowd had the presence of mind to use a camera or mobile phone to capture the moment, he kneeled and checked the fallen man's pockets. He found a photograph of Nora, taken recently, and replaced it. He then quickly inspected the man's wallet. Satisfied, Alex got up and darted across the street.

"Idiot," Luis said under his breath as he hit the brakes to avoid hitting the man in a gray shirt and dark slacks that ran right out in front of his vehicle. He watched the asshole duck into the morning crowd before disappearing down into the Dupont Circle Metro Station. Luis continued on his way, and not seeing Peters waiting outside the coffeehouse, he slowly maneuvered the sedan around the corner. He paused to take a look inside to see if Peters was on his way out, but was then drawn to an area up the street that seemed to captivate the interest of a number of people. The sedan continued its lazy progress. Luis strained his neck to see what was going on. Through a couple of legs he managed to see the figure of a man lying on the ground. And then he caught a slight glimpse of the man's clothing. Luis slammed the brakes again and was out almost before the car was shifted into park. He was not polite as he pushed people aside. "Damn," he muttered to himself. He checked to make sure Peters was still breathing. Relief set in when the man began moving.

"Sir, we need to get you out of here. You need medical attention."

Luis, although small in stature, was in excellent shape from his bike riding, so picking up Peters and putting him over his shoulder was not that difficult a task. "Anybody see what happened here?" he asked the parting crowd.

A man wearing a short-sleeved flannel shirt that screamed *tourist* spoke as Luis made his way to the car. "Some guy hit him from behind and knocked him to the ground. Robbed him too, I think."

Luis nodded as he gingerly deposited Peters in the back seat and was then caught off guard as the Good Samaritan stood behind him holding a gun.

"He dropped this too."

Luis slowly stepped to the man's side and gathered the weapon delicately from his hand.

"I'm on vacation from Louisiana."

Luis nodded. "Sure you are." Seconds later, tires screeching, the sedan headed for the nearest hospital, which Luis determined was the George Washington University facility.

As soon as Luis's tire-induced echo dissipated, another car came flying up the street, horn blaring and lights flashing as it barely dodged pedestrians and cars. It made a stop that jolted its occupants forward. Doors flew open and two men rushed into the Starbucks. Onlookers on the street weren't sure how to react as everything was happening so fast. Shortly after the two men entered the coffee shop, another car appeared; it, too, carried a set of men, whose movements mirrored the first.

Parked across the street the entire time, a white van inconspicuously pulled out of its parking space and joined the morning traffic. Duncan smiled behind the wheel, satisfied he had taken good pictures of the license plate numbers of the two vehicles that hurriedly arrived. The smile, though, hid what he and Alex had feared the most. Nora Mossa indeed had a serious problem.

CHAPTER **12**

He wore an Armani jacket that covered a jacquard sweater tucked neatly into pleated trousers. Expensive, cushioned sneakers made his feet feel special as he moved easily through the growing mob of people, each step well placed on the historic pavement. His casual manner indicated familiarity with the surroundings. To him, the City of Lights never looked better than it did at the onset of dusk. He had traveled the world and seen countries and cities at their best and worst. He always felt Paris was the most beautiful.

A slight gust of wind filtered in from the Seine, making its way through most of the narrow streets of the Île Saint-Louis neighborhood. Every now and then, the breeze tousled strands of his jet-black straight hair back and forth along his forehead. He loved Paris, but on occasion, he missed his homeland. He tried not to think of it often, and the only reason it entered his mind this time was because of the man he was to meet shortly. He didn't need to reference a calendar or diary. It had been fifteen years since he last set foot in Israel. The reason for his exile was simple. It was not a safe place for him.

At age nineteen, having never forgotten a face, especially *those* faces, he'd exacted his revenge. His actions set in motion what eventually became an occupation and the reason why he had to stay away.

They had been violent men who most assuredly were going to make more families grieve. Their attacks against Jews were so frequent, they had forgotten most of their victims. He was far removed from that young man now. Sometimes not even old photographs could restore the memories of innocence and optimism.

His world had been shattered in an instant on a bright sunny day in his hometown of Netanya. He had run for blocks, as he was apt to do at ten years old, in order to catch up with his father as he got off work from yet another day of protecting Israelis from the worst. Despite the daily dangers he faced wearing a military uniform, his father always preached there was good in the world. Not all Palestinians were murderous monsters. The good ones, in fact, often lived in fear of those who were set on never giving peace a chance—by which he meant the militant groups Hamas and Hezbollah, about whom he had nothing good to say. To him, they were savages worthy of oppression.

With sweat starting to soak his clothing, he had nearly caught up with his father when he gleefully called out. As his father turned with a smile upon hearing his son's voice, two men encroached upon the decorated soldier from behind. A large hand covered his mouth, yanking his head backward in the process. The young boy slowed down, recognizing danger. When he saw the huge blade appear, he ran as fast as he could. His father tried to resist, but the other man helped to restrain him. In seconds, a wave of crimson dotted the wall of the building his body fell against. The two men were smiling when the boy came in low, swinging his fists with all his power. His father was on the ground, making the most awful sounds. The boy's blows were fierce for one so young, and even as the man hit him hard in an attempt to drive him off, the boy didn't pause. Finally, the boy had no choice but to end his onslaught because the pain of the knife inserted into his back was too much for him to withstand. He fell forward next to his father, unable to do anything as his father's life drifted away.

For nine years, he lived with that day. If he had run faster, would it have made a difference? Had he been stronger, could he have helped his father subdue the bastards who had attacked him from behind, like cowards? Over time, he had dreamed about what he'd do if he ever caught up with the pair. He'd learned the assailants were skilled killers for Hamas, well financed and protected. Eventually, however, he'd realized his thoughts of revenge were mere dreams. He didn't possess the stomach to kill. In having to take care of his mother, he'd developed a gentler side. He'd tried so hard to make her laugh. It was obvious he had become her life. In response, rather than go abroad for college, he decided to stay close to home. The hate had eventually escaped him. Or so he thought—until the day he saw them through the window of a restaurant.

They were *laughing*. To conceal his glare, he pretended to look at the menu. He remembered they'd also been smiling after they'd taken his father's life. Since he'd only been ten when fate brought them all together, they would not know him now, but their faces were ingrained in his mind. A life filled with brutality and constant anxiety had taken its toll on them, but there was no mistaking who they were.

His hands started to shake, and he was unsure of what to do. His mother was shopping at a boutique down the street. He wanted to run and tell her that the men who destroyed their happiness were eating breakfast. But in the time it would take, they might disappear once again. Besides, what could she do? How would he prove to the authorities these were the men responsible for a decade-old murder?

Instead, he made a decision that would change his life. He entered the restaurant and made his way to the kitchen area in the back. He encountered a waiter and asked if the manager was on duty. The waiter raised an eyebrow and mockingly laughed, referencing the time. Thinking on the spot, he informed the waiter he was a new hire reporting for work. Since the restaurant was filling up, any help was welcome. He was given an apron, a pat on the back, a menu to learn quickly, and then orders to get busy.

The killers were cleaning up the last portions of their meal. From his vantage point, he could tell they were low on orange juice, and there were coffee cups on the table. He grabbed a waiter heading back into the kitchen, asked where the coffee and juice was, and rushed to get both. Sweat beads formed in mass on his forehead, and the hairs on his neck stood on end. He approached the two men, praying for his knees not to buckle.

"More?" he managed to get out of his throat, holding up the

pot of coffee and carafe of orange juice. It took every bit of concentration he possessed to keep his hands from shaking. The one he had tackled nine years ago and tried to beat with his then-tiny fists turned and said yes to coffee. The one who took his father's life and stabbed him in the back waved him off. His eyes were lifeless and menacing. He was not an attractive man by any standard. His face bore the scars of many altercations.

At that moment, the young man knew if he went through with his developing plan, Dead Eyes would have to be taken care of first. He sensed the man was the more dangerous of the two. Later, he would wonder how he arrived at that conclusion so readily, surprised it came to him with such clarity. As he started to leave the table, the man with scars called out to him. He turned around slowly, fearing he'd been identified, a knife waiting for him.

"Yes, sir?" he said, making eye contact.

"Bring the check," the man said gruffly before returning his attention to his companion. The young man nodded and headed for the kitchen. Once behind the safety of the doors, he found a large sink and threw up. Rubbing cold water over his face and neck, he continued to bend over the sink until he started to gather himself. He looked around the kitchen and discovered what he was looking for. He sauntered over and took the most impressive knife off the rack, carefully concealing it in the back of his pants at the waist. His next move was to the waiter's station, where the customer checks were kept. He picked up one with a particularly large tab and made his way back to the table.

"Here you are, sir," he said, placing the bill in front of the man with the blank stare and scarred skin. There was no going back now. He then went to the other side of the table and started to stack the dirty plates.

"This is the wrong bill," the man said disgustedly.

"Excuse me, sir?"

"This is not our bill." He held it up as evidence.

The new hire came around to the man's side, positioning himself at an angle slightly behind him. To gain leverage and a firm stance, he rested his left hand on the table. The man laid the bill out and explained that they didn't order that much food. The young man listened and pretended to examine the bill. While doing so, he slowly reached for the back of his pants. The move was shielded from the man sitting across the table by the mass of his partner. And besides, both were concentrating on the bill.

"My apologies, sir. In fact, I don't think you have to worry about paying, at least not for this," he said. Before the man could look up to ask what he meant, he moved swiftly, cupping the man's chin with his left hand, forcing it back strongly. He was no longer that weak little boy with tiny hands. His right hand came into view and the long, sharp butcher's knife in it ripped a deep straight line through the man's neck. The blood splattered across the table, partially blinding his friend. That was an added benefit for the young man as he made the short steps to be within arm's length. With all his might, he drove the knife directly into the second man's heart, jerking it while it was inside to achieve maximum damage. When he withdrew the knife, he returned his attention to the first man. He had heard that sound before. Nine years ago, in fact—the last desperate gasps of air escaping a life. The rest of the restaurant's patrons started to realize what was happening, and the place filled with screams and customers rushing to exit. The young man reached into his pocket and laid a photo on the table.

He made sure Dead Eyes was focusing.

"Remember him?"

The man, of course, couldn't speak as he fixated on the image of the soldier wearing an Israeli army uniform.

"You killed my father nine years ago and then stabbed me when I tried to help him," the young man whispered in his ear. The man remembered now. Stabbing a boy had only occurred once in his life, and until now, he had thought little of it. In a strange way, he admired his attacker, even as a final thrust was plunged into his back.

Weeks after the incident, even though authorities had no clue as to the assailant's identity, his mother was deathly afraid for his well-being. He had killed two high-ranking Hamas members, and although the Israelis wouldn't press very hard to find him, the militant group was paying good money for information. They had to avenge this act. His mom, meanwhile, reached out to an old friend of her husband's. She knew that in doing so, it would more than likely mean severing contact with her son, but she knew of no other way. Word of the young man had spread throughout the ranks of those who would be impressed by such deeds. One of those people was a friend of his father's who'd ascended to more meaningful work within the walls of Israel's secretive Mossad intelligence group. At the urging of his mother, he decided to listen to his father's friend. What the man offered seemed to make sense, and it was appealing. Intense training ensued. The young man proved to be smarter than the majority of recruits, physically gifted, and above all, seemingly oblivious to danger. He turned out to be a natural for Mossad's Metsada division, which was responsible for the agency's special operations assignments. His mother would have never believed her fun-loving son, the one who spent years making her laugh, had turned into one of the most skilled and feared operatives Mossad had ever produced. He proved to be a propaganda success story as well, because the Arabs had given him near-legendary status, fearing him immensely. To make matters worse for those who sought to harm Israel, there was no accurate description for the man Arabs called "The Devil."

His real name was Nathan Yadin. He had killed many since that day in the restaurant. He often struggled spiritually with the violent nature required to get the job the done. And yet, even though he truly didn't like killing, he was not one to hesitate when the time came. Through his training and situational adaptability, he now possessed a diverse and lethal skill set. Because of his reputation and expertise, it was necessary for him to live outside his homeland. With a price on his head, there were those who hunted him on a continual basis, as if this were the Old West. They might as well have been chasing shadows.

He guarded his identity so closely that not even his handler knew of his true residence. Each requested meeting was arranged by e-mail, and the location was always his choice someplace in the world. No discussion. On this particular encounter, he realized he was taking a gamble. Not with the man he was due to meet, but by the location he'd chosen for the face-to-face. He actually lived on

Île Saint-Louis. The last half hour had been spent walking around, getting a feel for the crowd. It seemed normal enough for an early evening. He'd decided to take the meeting here because he was tired, and once it was over, all he wanted to do was have a short walk in order to collapse in his bed. The last two weeks had been especially taxing, and there had been virtually no time to relax while in Washington, DC. His only pleasure had been polishing off a bushel of crabs one night at a Bethesda, Maryland restaurant.

Yadin really couldn't complain too harshly, though, about his work. He was well compensated for his troubles by the Israeli government, and in addition, opportunities sometimes arose for him to make money off the books. There was once a Hamas official who pleaded with the Devil for his life, offering millions in a foreign bank account to spare his pitiful soul. Yadin accepted the offer but rejected the terms of the contract. He eventually collected the money, knowing that not doing so would ultimately result in its funding the deaths of countless others. Thus, he could more than afford the pricy lifestyle of the upscale Paris neighborhood. His command of the language was flawless and his love of the culture immense.

Yadin continued on his path, pleased it would permit a guilty pleasure stop. There was already a line forming outside Berthillon ice cream parlor, a Paris institution. Rather than wait outside, he made his way through to the tea room in the back and found a seat. Shortly after, he returned to the street with ice cream cone in hand, appreciating the little things that made life enjoyable.

Unfortunately, it was time to double back a couple of blocks to take his meeting. Along the way, he checked for all the faces cataloged in his memory from having just traveled this way. He once again encountered those that were supposed to be there and was satisfied that others had moved on. Just ahead was a face he knew very well. Over the years, he had watched it progress from youthful vigor to its current state, which was approaching retirement. Time had proven it to be a face worthy of his trust. But not even this face knew he lived just a few blocks away. It was better for both of them that way. If the old man were ever kidnapped, he wouldn't be able to resist intense torture, and if he knew where

Yadin lived, he'd be forced to give up his location. The two men exchanged a heart-felt hug. As a youngster, Yadin remembered the numerous occasions that Yosef Ezra had been a visitor in the family's home, a dear friend of his father's. It was Ezra his beloved mother had reached out to in a plea to protect him.

"You look tired, Nathan," Ezra said, a well-placed hand gently nudging him forward as they began to stroll.

Yadin didn't try to hide his discomfort. "Washington was draining."

"But successful," Ezra confirmed. "The woman was resourceful, a credible threat to our success. You did well."

Ezra knew the words would comfort his former protégé. He had become a perfectionist, a man who took pride in getting results. This was not the same playful, joyous child he'd first encountered in the Yadin household, the apple of his father's eye. Instead, the events that shaped his life had produced a calculating, meticulous, distrusting and all-too-deadly man. The perfect weapon for Mossad. At first, Ezra had his doubts. A near-fatal stab wound had forced Nathan to miss his father's funeral. That alone would crush the spirit of any youngster who'd worshipped his father, let alone watched him die. When Ezra met him again years later at the request of his mother, Nathan had grown into quite the young man, possessing qualities that reminded Ezra of his father. But he was no longer fun-loving, that much was evident from the very beginning. He was distant and seemingly unconcerned about the danger he was in for killing two prominent Hamas members. Ezra had sat with him until the wee hours of the morning. There was something special about the young man. Ezra had presented him with three options. He could flee the country and start over elsewhere in the world. Or, like his father, he could join the Israeli defense forces and opt for a career there. His college studies had already given him exempt status from mandatory service in the military, but surely, it was much too dangerous to return to collegiate life. Nathan had accepted the third option. That was when it had been revealed to him that Ezra served as a high-ranking official for Mossad. No guarantees were given, but based on their lengthy conversation, Ezra had told Nathan he thought a rewarding career was there for the taking. In the long run, both had come to understand that the right choice was made.

"The next and most important phase is progressing on time," Ezra said now. "The shipment is in transit. Your studies are up to date?"

Yadin chuckled. "Do you really want to hear a lecture on how enriched uranium can form the core of a nuclear bomb?"

Ezra returned a smile. "Perhaps some other time." He came to rest at a spot that offered an excellent view of the Seine and the brilliant lights of Paris across it. "As we draw closer, my concern is that we have never asked you to do anything of this magnitude. There are so many variables. Any one of which could fail."

"I trust you've done your homework as well, Yosef. The world is filled with danger, and the potential of this particular threat can no longer be ignored or accepted. While we strive for peace, we cannot let our guard down against the wolves howling at the gates."

"As you know, there will only be a shell of support available to you. Everything must fall into place."

"You're the master planner."

"Even I am capable of overlooking something. We've launched this effort on so many fronts. There is support from the West, but not fully."

"Have faith, Yosef. You've dedicated years of planning to this operation. And was it not you who taught me to always expect the unexpected?"

CHAPTER **13**

Alex was knocking back drinks like it was happy hour, but there was definitely nothing to celebrate. He had thought he'd be on his way to Chicago to see his parents, having said a final good-bye to Nora, dismissing her paranoia in the process. Instead, her mind was probably in a fog, as his was. She was crossing the Atlantic by plane headed for London after boarding at Philadelphia International Airport, once again traveling under the guise of Nathalie Tauziat. What she didn't know yet had Alex and Duncan slightly on edge as they lounged in the sitting area of his Mayflower Hotel suite.

Alex took another swig of his rum and Coke. He was trying to get a grip. "Okay, okay," he said impulsively to his friend Duncan sitting next him. "The guy from the CIA had to be a freaking coincidence. He made a phone call after he was in Starbucks and then started asking questions."

"I'll give you that. But"—Duncan sat up on the sofa to gather papers from the coffee table in front of him—"the Department of Defense and the FBI! Who knows who the hell showed up after I booked. She's on a serious watch list."

"Yeah, it's fucked up, all right. I'm not sure what the hell I can do here. I've been out of the loop for too long. This isn't my thing anymore. I should have stuck with my initial impulse and not gotten involved."

"That *was* an option, mi amigo," Duncan said, tapping Alex's chest with a couple of fingers. "That ol' heart of yours, though, wouldn't let you do it."

"Yeah, yeah, I hear you."

Duncan could tell his friend was at a crossroads. He wanted to walk away, but he had given his word, and now Nora was depending on him. That she was a former lover only made it tougher.

"Look, for what it's worth, you looked pretty damn efficient out there today," Duncan said, raising his drink in a toast.

Alex exhaled as he fell back into the sofa's cushion. "Physically I can get the job done, but this requires a whole lot more than muscle."

"You've still got some connections out there. You pulled today off. Like it or not, you got involved. Getting Nora on a plane for London to do a job, you're already thinking ahead. She's a strong woman, but right now, she's alone and the world is getting smaller. Janway was killed for a reason, and judging by today's circus, some people are very nervous about her association with Nora. So, from where my drunken ass is sittin', you don't have much of a choice."

"Is that right? Well, I suggest you pack a bag as well, because you're in it now too."

Duncan chuckled. "Wouldn't have it any other way. Where are we going?"

"You said you recognized a name in Janway's little packet of misinformation?"

"Yeah. A big player on the black market. This guy could get you ice water in hell."

"To hell it is, then."

CHAPTER 14

It was obvious the director of the National Clandestine Service was not a happy camper. George Champion was known to be calm under fire, so his present demeanor warranted treading lightly. Little had been said so far during this hastily scheduled early morning meeting.

The four other people seated at the lengthy, polished table were anticipating the fall of the proverbial axe, even though none of them felt responsible for the matter at hand—none, except for the man with the bandaged face, for whom the others unconsciously made plenty of room.

Karl Peters used every ounce of concentration he could muster to remain focused. The stitches just below his hairline tightly sealed a nasty gash that was extremely uncomfortable. The bandage under his black and blue right eye made it challenging to focus. Every move of his neck painfully reminded him of his carelessness. He was holding off on taking the prescribed painkillers because he wanted to remain as lucid as possible.

Champion lifted his head from the folders in front of him, briefly diverting his eyes to Peters. The man was like a devoted dog with little bite. Peters didn't have much field training; his present state was evidence of that. He should've still been under observation in the hospital with the concussion he suffered, but he refused to accept the doctor's recommendation, promising instead to take it easy.

Seeing Peters's condition only served to raise Champion's blood pressure. He was pissed someone had given his operative a swift, calculated beat down. That wasn't all he was steamed about, though. The rapid response by several government departments to a Nora Mossa sighting was puzzling. Such cooperation usually didn't manifest itself so readily.

Every person seated at the table had a folder in front of him or her, and all were given ample time to familiarize themselves with its contents. Champion interrupted the silence with a bit of sincerity. "Karl, are you sure you're feeling up to being here? Your presence, though helpful, is not totally necessary." Champion knew the answer before Peters waved him off.

Careful to keep his head still, Peters replied, "Thanks for your concern, sir, but I'll be just fine."

Studying the contents of the folder had kept Champion at the office until nine o'clock last night, much to his wife's frustration. He surveyed the group, and then began speaking as calmly as he could.

"We know Erica Janway and Nora Mossa had a working relationship that developed into a friendship. We also know that Mossa, for some reason, is on the run and hasn't communicated that she wants to be brought in." Champion's eyes scanned the room once more. "Judging by the events of yesterday, we can say with certainty that she's not out there alone."

A bespectacled Adrian Jennings, who didn't feel comfortable in the suit he had scrambled to find in the back of his closet when news of this meeting awoke him, felt Champion's attention land on him. "That's right, sir," he said, reaching for his notes. "Ordinarily, there would be surveillance video from a number of sources in the Dupont Circle area, but all the cameras in the vicinity of that Starbucks were circumvented for thirty minutes. Static interference on every one. It's highly unlikely that was a coincidence." Jennings shook his head. "This looks like a very professional jamming job, and going through Miss Mossa's background, that kind of expertise is not there. We've been monitoring all transportation outlets, but that takes time. For the last twenty-four hours we've been concentrating on those in the US."

Champion extended his appreciation. "Thank you, Mr. Jennings. Mr. Bonderman, how is she getting around?"

Jason Bonderman was thankful to realize that his time, like Adrian's, would be short, and he just wanted to get it over with. Being in closed-door meetings with the upper-floor types was not his forte. "She undoubtedly has access to good fake documents. It's the only way I see that she's getting around. If she uses any of the agency-supplied aliases and documents, red flags will go up immediately, but I don't anticipate that happening. She's too skilled to make a mistake like that, unless it's intentional, which I believe yesterday was. The debit card she used is her personal one. Her credit cards have not been used, though the accounts are still active. Find the name she's traveling under, and we can establish a pattern and pin her down. Of course, there's the chance she could change identities at any moment. We can freeze her debit and credit cards, but I suggest we keep them open should she use them again."

Champion pondered his options and realized at the moment, they were few and far between. "Keep with it. I need all eyes on this. Mr. Bonderman, Mr. Jennings, again, thank you. You can get back at it now."

Once Bonderman and Jennings exited, only Peters and a woman dressed in a smart business suit remained. Sara Garland didn't visit Langley often. Being around suits and management was, for her, the epitome of boredom. After a couple of trips, the mystique of the compound sort of lost its luster. There was no comparison to being out in the real world, in the thick of things.

The sun hadn't been up for long, and already Champion could feel the initial onslaught of fatigue. A busy workday would force the symptoms to subside. "Sara, profile this for me. If you're Nora Mossa, how are you moving about?"

Though Sara held him in the highest regard, she didn't feel the slightest need to impress Champion. Before she had worked with him, she had heard through the grapevine that he respected ability. She had been pleased to discover the grapevine had been right, and he had subsequently become a mentor to her career. The folder in front of her contained a great deal more information than the packets distributed to Jennings and Bonderman. Before she could respond, Champion interrupted, his eyes pacing back and forth between Garland and Peters. "I'm sorry, it just occurred to me you two don't know each other. Sara Garland, Karl Peters." An obligatory nod followed the introductions.

"Karl, I asked Sara to do background work on Mossa once she went AWOL in Rome. She's pretty much up to speed. And Karl, if you're up to it, you two might be working this together."

Sara cast Champion a quick, curious glance that he noticed but dismissed. Peters looked at Sara, sizing her up. "I'm up to it, sir."

"Good. Sara, please continue."

She swallowed quietly and focused on her notes. "Nora Mossa is well trained. Excellent in self-defense, high marks with weaponry, intellectually sound." Sara flipped a page, searching for the most relevant material. "She speaks several languages: Italian, French, Spanish, Russian, and at last report was working on Arabic. She has kills to her credit, so she's not a stranger to getting her hands dirty. If she wants to hide, the world is her playground. As Mr. Jennings mentioned, because of her covert status, I'm sure she has several identities that we don't know about. There is no lover or boyfriend of consequence, but she does date. She hasn't contacted any of those individuals so far, nor has she called her mother."

At the end of the table, Peters took notes more to keep his mind off the pain than anything else. So far, he knew most of what Ms. Garland was saying and would lay odds Champion knew it as well. He was aware of Mossa's skills: they were the reason he'd drawn his weapon and kept his distance. For him, the gun was the equalizer. What he hadn't counted upon was her having backup. Though he didn't know who Sara Garland was, he surmised she might not have made that same mistake. He figured Champion knew that as well, which was probably why she had been working this case unbeknownst to Peters.

"I assume all active assets she's worked with in the past have been notified and that they should report immediately if contacted?" Sara asked of Champion.

He confirmed her assumption, which prompted a response. "Then we have to do some detailed background work, which is going to be time-consuming for sure. I'll need clearance for that." Sara turned her attention to the beat-up Peters on her left. "As for yesterday, it was no mistake on her part. I believe it was a fact-finding exercise. With the surveillance cameras manipulated, the coffee shop was a perfect vantage from which to see what's coming your way. A woman with a multitude of skills who's on the run, all of a sudden stupidly uses a debit card under her real name? And"—Sara raised an eyebrow, "a woman who trusted someone else to watch her back."

"What's her next move? Where would you go?" Champion got up to walk around, trying to jump-start his system. Was it really only six-forty-five?

"Once alerted to the circus that ensued," Sara said, "I would get my ass out of Dodge, so to speak. Knowing I had that many prying eyes on me—and knowing the watchers have a ton of resources readily available—I'd get out of the country before a containment plan could be put together. The quickest available flights departing anywhere would suffice. And one other thing," Sara added as she closed her file.

"I wouldn't trust anyone at this point. Least of all, the CIA."

CHAPTER 15

Some useful elements of his past were slowly returning.

On this particular night they were serving Alex well. Conducting surveillance under these circumstances was a bitch, and yet, his target was well in sight and unaware he was being tailed. Duncan was half a block ahead of the subject while Alex kept pace a short distance from behind, careful not to bump into pedestrian traffic going in the opposite direction or onlookers who stopped in their tracks to survey their varied options.

The streets were dimly lit by the red neon glow that stretched from building to building. Amsterdam stood out on the world map because it had succeeded in maintaining a sense of age-old beauty, while also addressing the wants and desires of the human condition. Its acceptance of most soft drugs, especially marijuana, was an eye-opener for those who visited from much stricter locales. Couple that with legalized prostitution, gaudily on display in the infamous Red Light District, and it was easy to see why Amsterdam was a destination for those who wanted to experience what their own countries would never come to understand. For all its vices, Amsterdam had little crime except for nuisance pickpockets and low-level dealers of hard drugs.

Alex and Duncan had eyes on their subject the moment he exited the fashionable Hotel InterContinental Amstel. He promptly called for a taxi and was let out a block from the Red Light District. Alex was being extra cautious because there was a chance that another set of eyes was on the subject or that he had veiled security watching. If the latter were the case, they would be very skilled. Even though Nora told him the man was traveling alone, Alex checked anyway to make sure no one was watching his flank.

The man's name was Neville Schofield, a card-carrying member of Britain's elite security service, MI6. He was also someone Alex once considered a friend. The years had been kind to Neville. His curly red hair still possessed volume and was perfectly suited for the animated face it topped. Alex used to poke fun at him over his resemblance to the lead singer of Simply Red. There were a few wrinkles on his face, but other than that, he appeared to be the Neville of old. The next fifteen minutes were spent watching him delight in the process of shopping for his next sexual escapade. He finally made a choice and was ushered into the working woman's office, the curtains steadfastly closed after an arrangement was agreed upon. There was nothing for Alex and Duncan to do now but wait. Making the down time interesting was a small wager on just how long they'd be waiting. While Duncan kept watch, Alex ducked in a bar to grab a couple of beers to go.

"You ever?" Duncan asked, motioning toward the sexual smorgasbord.

Alex shook his head. "Not as long as I can get it for free."

"Yeah, I don't get the fascination either. Granted, the whole experienced thing I understand, but just thinking about all the guys before you . . ." Duncan's face constricted as if something sour passed his lips. "Plus, no emotional attachment at all. I mean, when you're with a woman, even if it's a one night stand, in some respect she's there because she digs you."

"Never knew you were such a romantic." Alex finished off his beer. "Also, you owe me fifty bucks."

Duncan looked up to see Neville emerging from the apartment. "Damn," he muttered as he reached in his pocket and handed over his debt.

Neville grabbed another taxi back to the hotel. Instead of heading for his room, he made a detour to the lobby bar. He chose a table overlooking the Amstel River, flagged down a waitress, and ordered. After his drink arrived, Neville managed two sips before he was interrupted. Duncan blocked him in by occupying the outside chair, and Alex followed by taking a seat directly across from Neville. His momentary unease was replaced with a toothy smile.

"Talk about a sight for sore eyes."

Alex nodded. "Still like big tits, I see. Now, what's Mrs. Schofield going to say about that?"

The smile disappeared from Neville's face for just an instant. "You bastard! You've been following me?" he said, shaking his head. "To answer your queries: yes, I still have an affinity for large breasts, and there is no Mrs. Schofield anymore. We divorced two years ago."

"Sorry to hear about that," Alex offered sincerely.

"Don't be. As you so aptly put it, she did have ample reasons to leave me." Neville turned his attention to Duncan, whose smirk was as unnerving as his size. "And who might Bigfoot be?"

"Sorry, didn't mean to startle you," Alex proclaimed. "Neville Schofield, meet Duncan Anderson." They shook hands, and Neville was taken aback by the size of Duncan's hand.

"Nice guy to have around," Neville observed.

"As friends go, he's pretty damn good."

Neville made a reference to not drinking alone, and the alert waitress, sensing a sizeable tip might be in her future, was quick to take new orders. The bar was beginning to fill up, and for that, Alex was grateful. More noise meant the trio's conversation could carry on without much concern for privacy.

"Now, back to this *following me* business," Neville said with a raised eyebrow.

"I've had someone on you for two days."

Neville traced his memory. A man of his position was supposed to notice such things. He was embarrassed that he hadn't. "I do have business hours. A lot less intrigue involved with a making an appointment."

"Don't let it bother you too much. She's very good."

Neville was at least thankful for that. "Still, it's tricky business here, Alex. It's been years since we last tossed a few back, and if memory serves me right, you're no longer . . ."

"Correct," Alex confirmed. He could tell Neville needed to

hear more before this impromptu get-together could proceed in the direction Alex needed it to go. "And this has to be off the books for you."

"How far off?"

"A matter of time more than anything," Alex answered as he produced a sheet of paper. "I need a couple of days, a week at most. If you're asked after that, feel free to give it up."

"I've always known you to be an honorable man in a dishonorable profession. Doesn't sound too compromising, as long as it doesn't jeopardize queen and country."

Alex chuckled, "Yours, I'm not worried about."

Neville directed his focus upon the single sheet of paper Alex pushed across the table to him.

Duncan provided some background on what he was looking at. "I believe these are names of arms dealers. A couple I recognize, strictly small-time stuff. Guns, ammunition, that gray area you government types allow to fly under official scrutiny so that you can keep friends in dark places. There's three on here I don't know, and that's where we're hoping you can help out."

"So if I can, you want me to identify their level of commitment to world order?"

Alex waited until the waitress finished placing drinks on the table. "Here's the bonus question. Any of those three names capable of procuring nuclear elements?"

It was part of Neville's job at MI6 to know the world's movers and shakers, especially those who tried to operate covertly. They did so for only two reasons: profit or ideology.

Neville studied the names and then looked up. "Anything here I should know about? Something possibly crossing my radar?"

"To early to tell, but I highly doubt it," said Alex. "As I mentioned, I'm not concerned with the tea and crumpet set. I'm looking for Moby Dick."

Neville returned to the list. "All right, Captain Ahab, I can make this a little easier for you. Ostermann is no longer with us. Not much fanfare on his demise; he drowned in Greece. Official report said he had too much to drink. Now, reportedly, he did like his alcohol, so it was a darn good cover story if other factors were involved, which may be the case. I'll get to that in a minute. Rafiq Nawaz Khan . . . Pakistani. Well educated—US, in fact. He's helped a number of countries increase their regional bargaining power. At first, though, it was to accelerate programs. Now it's more directed at maintenance. The shift, I believe, can be explained by pressure from Israel. The thinking being, if I know precisely what you're equipping someone with, there's less concern, because I can adequately monitor that. Besides, the maintenance business promises a steady paycheck, and you're alive to cash it."

Duncan shook his head with an understanding look. "That was the name I knew. So much for my usefulness."

"It's a complex business with constantly moving boundaries," Neville assured him. "This brings us to the third name on the list. Tobias Baum . . . German. The A-list guy of high-level black market stuff. Of course, officially his wealth comes from the shipping industry and well-placed investments. Klaus Ostermann was an associate of his. As I mentioned, Ostermann is dead. Some saw his *accidental* death as a message to Baum."

"A message from the Israelis?"

Neville shot Alex a wink and pointed a finger. "Ah, you may be out of the game, but how it's played hasn't left you. The Israelis went out of their way to let it be known they weren't involved with Ostermann's timely demise. I say *timely* because Mossad was putting pressure on Baum to cease his dealings with certain Middle East countries, namely Iran. Israel gets a little testy when someone is trying to facilitate a WMD program for a country whose leader has publicly said they should be wiped off the face of the earth."

"I take it Baum is a bit headstrong."

"There's that. Plus, countries keep throwing millions upon millions in his face to take calculated risks on their behalf."

"So you think this Ostermann thing didn't exactly put the fear of God in him?"

Neville waved his hand, dismissing the supposition. "A guy like Baum would take all the necessary precautions, create the illusion that the message—if it was a message—was received loud and clear. But Baum, with all his assets and connections, would also think no one could pry that deeply into his affairs and come up with anything concrete. You see, the other theory about Oster-mann—" Neville paused to down his drink. "—is that Baum got rid of him because he felt the Israelis *did* get to him."

"Fair enough. I know the type," Alex responded.

It was getting very noisy in the bar so Duncan leaned in close to be heard. "So, there's only one question that remains." Neville was puzzled.

Alex smiled. "Where can I find Tobias Baum?"

Anticipating a night of engaging stories and plenty of alcohol, Neville proved his worth. "My friend, I can do you one better than that."

CHAPTER 16

It was not the way Alex liked to work, but he had to remind himself he'd done more with much less. And the stakes during those instances were far greater than they appeared to be now. Not letting his psyche get too far ahead of itself, he also acknowledged those were days gone by. He was putting himself at risk for the woman that sat across from him. What the hell was he doing here? The impulse to get up and walk away simmered just below the surface. For now, he held it in check. Besides, leaving would put him on equal footing with her, and though her desertion was very much in the past, making that distinction was mostly what kept him seated.

Nora had followed Neville Schofield from London to Amsterdam, but Alex was adamant about keeping her out of sight. If questioned, he wanted his friend to have total deniability on whether he'd seen or heard of her.

Thanks to information supplied by Neville, Nora and Alex now sat outdoors at a Brussels restaurant along the Rue des Bouchers. They were just an attractive couple enjoying a leisurely mid-day meal. Five tables away were Tobias Baum and a bodyguard. The reddish, brick-paved street was for pedestrian travel only, and the myriad restaurant choices lining both sides attracted a constant stream of foot traffic. They provided ample cover for Alex and Nora. Apron-clad waiters selling their various establishments to passersby provided further distraction. Across the narrow street inside another restaurant, Duncan kept watch through a window seat. His vantage point allowed him greater visibility of the entire street, and he labored through the process of trying to check out every person who crossed his sight line. It was Duncan who'd alerted Alex that in all likelihood, Baum was about to have company, and true to Duncan's observational skills, two men had walked up and joined the German.

So far, Alex had to hand it to Baum. Certainly wealthy way beyond his life expectancy, Baum either understood innately or had come to learn that not drawing too much attention to one's self in his line of work eliminated a lot of trouble. Others, more paranoid or bent on displaying their self-importance, would surround themselves with a small, attention-grabbing entourage. Alex, Nora, and Duncan had concluded that Baum's regular detail consisted only of two men. One pretty much stayed within reaction distance, serving as both protector and companion. Alex took detailed notes in his mind about the man. How he moved, on which side did he carry his firearm, were there any physical ailments he was trying to cover, like a bad knee? Did his muscular frame reduce his quickness, thus making him more apt to use a weapon than his hands or feet? The other bodyguard either trailed a safe distance behind or took a position ahead of the pair to make sure the horizon was clear of hidden danger. There had been no incidents that might have offered the opportunity to judge their readiness or skill level, but given Baum's wealth and penchant for the finer things in life, it was likely that the bodyguards were among the best in the business. Alex knew that in Afghanistan and Iraq, there was a serious market for men of such expertise. In order to protect its fragile but valued interests, the US often recommended the services of ex-military specialists as personal bodyguards. The clients sometimes balked at the specialists' hefty fee, but they soon acquiesced when the realities of survival took over. Though the bodyguards were outsiders, they were at least men that could be trusted. Their political and religious beliefs aside, they worshipped the proper execution of their job and the almighty dollar. Those bodyguards sat with Baum at the table, preparing to eat lunch. A smart man would go one step further and make the task of protecting him more than just about the money. From all appearances, Baum didn't treat them like pieces of furniture. The personal touch could go a long way toward extending how far his protectors were willing to stick their necks out.

The fourth occupant at the table was a new face, and though Alex couldn't hear the conversation, he concluded it was a business meeting of some sort. Judging from the seemingly relaxed nature of everyone, and from Baum's moments of short laughter, it must be familiar business.

Nora sat with most of her back angled to Baum's table. She also donned fashionable dark sunglasses that covered a large portion of her face. Her hair was tied back and mostly tucked beneath a hat bearing the logo "FFF": France's national soccer team. There wasn't much conversation taking place at the table. Duncan felt compelled to speak through his Bluetooth device.

"Hey you two, you're supposed to be a romantic couple enjoying each other's company on a beautiful day in which love is in the air," Duncan offered, finding it impossible to contain a smirk. "Come on, chat it up. Hold hands."

Nora took the ribbing to heart, forming a guilty smile. Alex, assured that Duncan was watching, ran his hand along the side of his face as if wiping something away, retracting four fingers, leaving only the middle digit to scratch away.

"Nice," Duncan replied. "Such class."

Alex returned his attention to the menu. He had no idea whether Baum planned on staying for any length of time. So far, his table had only ordered drinks, but they all did look at menus.

The plan was simple enough. If Baum left, Duncan would exit his location and maintain surveillance at a safe distance, giving Alex and Nora time to pay for their food, finished or not, in a seemingly relaxed manner. They would then catch up with Duncan and broaden the tail. Discovering if Baum kept any semblance of a regular schedule would be vital to whatever action they might have to take later. Was there a good place to neutralize or separate the bodyguards, should it be necessary? Other than sleeping, did Baum ever require personal time? Was there a lover? If so, perhaps her place would be an ideal location to make a move on him. Alex did at least know any lover would be a woman, even though less than thirty-six hours ago, he'd never heard of Tobias Baum. It was the kind of detail anyone could acquire, given a little diligence, but Alex had not needed that diligence: Neville had been courteous enough to send Alex an e-mail that contained a condensed, somewhat sanitized bio of Baum. Neville had sensed Alex's hourglass had a rather wide opening, so he had decided to provide a little headache relief. And whether the bio was sanitized or not, Alex knew how to read between the lines and connect the dots.

It was apparent Baum was a major supplier. A vast majority of merchandise was steady and legitimate through his shipping business, while other transactions were off the books. The former kept him in good standing with authorities, the latter kept him on the lips of governments around the world who either sought to improve their territorial position or maintain influence afar covertly. Alex would bet good money the US had, from one time or another, used Baum's services, and judging from Neville's immediate knowledge, Britain probably had as well. The death of Baum's associate, as Neville hinted, was probably a strong message sent by Israel. The question was, would a guy like Baum back down, or would he use the threat to up his payday from potential buyers? The selling point would be, "I'm taking a huge risk for you. I can deliver, despite your enemies' pressure and watchful eyes. How badly do you one day want to be able to stand up for yourself?" That kind of comfort and risk-taking was expensive.

Baum's lunch engagement lasted long enough for everyone to finish their modest orders. Sticking to the plan, when one of Baum's bodyguards departed, Duncan did too, retrieving the nondescript rental car. He stayed hidden around the corner until Baum's Mercedes had arrived to pick him up. It was only a matter of minutes before Baum, the remaining bodyguard, and Baum's lunch guest walked to the waiting vehicle. Shortly after the three were whisked away, Duncan came into view, keeping a safe distance behind.

Alex and Nora remained seated for at least another five minutes before settling the bill. There could be an extra set of eyes checking to see if anyone was interested in Baum's departure, though Alex doubted it and didn't pick up on anything. In no apparent rush, Alex and Nora walked to their car and drove off, guided by Duncan's notifications.

Though he didn't want to give in to it, deep down inside, Alex could feel an old sensation slowly returning. It was a shot of adrenaline not present for quite some time.

Much to his disappointment, it was beginning to feel good.

CHAPTER 17

This part of his past Alex remembered all too well. Despite some technological advancement, not much had changed either. Sitting on a target, conducting surveillance, got boring pretty quickly.

For three days now, they had monitored Tobias Baum's every move, with nothing to show for it. Nora gazed through the viewfinder of the digital SLR camera for the hundredth time. It was equipped with a powerful telephoto lens that was fixed on the Baum estate. She could clearly see arrivals at the security gate. Making identifications wasn't terribly difficult, because all guests, once inside, had to pass through a large, extended glass hallway. Ordinarily, one would think a man like Baum would have just a tad of paranoia, but Alex guessed that the glass was probably bulletproof, and if privacy was needed, shades were available for concealment. A vast majority of the estate was strategically shielded from onlookers by tall trees. The back of the property was virtually impenetrable as it backed up to thick trees that were part of the 180-acre Woluwe Park.

The villa Alex, Nora, and Duncan occupied, courtesy of Neville Schofield, was nearly fifteen minutes outside the city center, nestled among numerous impressive flats and detached terraced houses in the Woluwe-Saint-Lambert municipality. It was apparent the British had had their own reasons for monitoring Baum on occasion, and rather than totally close up shop each time he left town, the villa remained operational should it become necessary to spy on him again. Much to Duncan's delight, a sizeable amount of surveillance equipment was on hand as well. The living room window provided the best vantage on Baum's estate. At night, the room stayed dark in case there were binoculars scanning the area for people like them. For three days, it was mundane, normal activity. When Baum's car went rolling down the long driveway, Alex and Duncan were quick to follow. His destinations had been to his office in the city center, an antique store, an art gallery, and a couple of upscale bars one night. End of story. With that in mind, Alex hardly got excited when Nora announced, "Car approaching the gate." Duncan, on the other hand, put down the novel he was reading and donned a pair of headphones, keeping his left ear exposed. On a predawn jog during the first day, Duncan had inconspicuously attached a tiny listening device next to the intercom at the entrance gate. It allowed him to hear the words being uttered from the occupant inside the car as it came to a stop outside the metal gate.

Looking at the meters move on his instrument panel, Duncan relayed what he heard. "A man named Davis to see Mr. Baum," he stated. "They're buzzing him in."

Nora adjusted the binoculars' magnification, following the car as it rolled toward the house. A single occupant exited, but he was cast in shadow as he made his way to the front entrance, which was opening upon his approach. A few steps inside and Nora would hopefully have at least a glimpse of "Davis." He was patted down by a bodyguard as Baum approached from within the house. Nora could see a smile forming on Baum's face as he extended a welcoming hand. After exchanging pleasantries, Baum motioned for his visitor to proceed down the hallway.

"Come on. Come on," Nora whispered. "Give me a look."

The visitor answered Nora's plea when he turned his head toward the windows, admiring the overall craftsmanship and nerve of it all. Nora quickly adjusted the focus to get a clear, tight picture.

A firm press of her index finger snapped a series of pictures in rapid succession. She then released her finger and sat up firmly in her chair, the move made with such urgency it caught the attention of both Alex and Duncan. It was as if she'd seen a ghost.

"Motherfucker," Nora said behind clenched teeth. Alex and

Duncan looked at each other with puzzlement. Alex had to pretty much pry the camera from her hands in order to get a look. He only saw the backs of the two men as they disappeared from view. He looked to Nora for an explanation.

"What the hell was that about?"

She stayed silent in the darkness, the anger obvious from her demeanor. Alex set the camera to playback mode to see what she had captured. When Nora spoke, she shook her head toward the estate. "Lipton. Davis fucking Lipton. The asshole responsible for screwing Erica."

Alex knew the story. Erica Janway had been chief of station in Moscow. Davis Lipton was reportedly a totally talentless prick placed on a fast track thanks entirely to family influence. He was someone Janway definitely had her doubts about. He wasn't qualified enough to be under her supervision in such a vital and dangerous section of the world. But she was told he was there to stay. She understood why, but protested anyway. Stuck between a rock and a hard place, she did what she thought was the next best and most responsible thing. She made sure he didn't get in harm's way. That would ensure he wouldn't get his stupid ass killed or, worse, get others who knew what they were doing killed.

Janway was eventually blindsided by allegations of harassment brought forth by him. Her drinking, although she was on the road to recovery, suddenly became a major area of concern. Men had been allowed to do it for decades, but for her, the game was not being played on the same field, and Lipton had benefactors. So, pending an investigation, she was called home from Moscow for desk duty at Langley. She felt her career was being flushed down the toilet by some little pissant who didn't like being schooled, especially by a woman. Janway concluded the only recourse was to beat them to the plunger, so she filed a discrimination lawsuit. She had known she could kiss her career good-bye for sure at that point, but she wanted vindication before she walked out the front door.

Not wanting to risk the camera being tossed across the room, Alex placed it on the windowsill instead of handing it back to Nora. He placed a hand at the back of his neck. "And the hits just keep on coming," he said, a slight strain in his voice. "Bryce Lipton's son."

Duncan removed the headphones. "Senator Lipton? The chairman of the Senate Select Committee on Intelligence? That Lipton?"

Nora stared into the distance. "Yes. Fucking yes."

The room fell silent as the latest revelation was digested.

Alex finally spoke. "Nora, can you get your hands on ten grand by tomorrow afternoon?"

She stared at him, wondering what the hell he was thinking. She also noted there was a calmness about him which slightly put her at ease.

"Time to get some answers," he said. "Can you get the money?"

"Yes, I can."

CHAPTER **18**

Day was politely giving way to night. The sunset was worth a thousand snapshots, and yet, as breathtaking as it was, it couldn't come close to the beauty of the little girl in a floral dress. Her eyes were bright ovals of hazel, full of innocence and playfulness. Her golden hair was neatly combed, and her spotless yellow shoes were prized possessions, along with the freckled doll she snuggled. She had hardly touched her meal, but much to the large party's delight, she was proving to be a perfect angel. Besides, she had other interests. She playfully peeked around her mother's shoulder with those big eyes, only to disappear quickly, reemerging slowly once again. She had the stranger hooked. At first, he pretended not to notice, but that would be like avoiding an exploding star streaking across the night sky.

There was much to take in at the Palazzo Ouzeri restaurant along the Old Venetian port in Chania, Crete. The noise level was pleasant, the distant tone of people enjoying a respite from the rigors of everyday life. The food, relatively inexpensive, was nonetheless tasty, especially when accompanied by several glasses of Cretan wine. The smartly dressed man fit right in with the throng of people who were trying to relax. For most of the day he had hidden behind sunglasses: partly because the sun was bright, but mostly so he could observe without being exposed—and, most assuredly, so that he could be left alone.

The little girl totally disregarded any expectation of privacy he might have had. He guessed she was around four or five years old. After putting his sunglasses on the table, and feeling yet another wide-eyed inspection, he unexpectedly made a funny face that caught her by surprise. It produced an irresistible giggle as she was eclipsed behind mom again. Her mother recognized something had captivated her daughter's attention and turned around to see what all the fuss was about. She smiled in response to the man's seemingly innocent expression, and was quick to say "Thank you" when he noted she was "precious." The girl sat at a table of eleven, mostly adults, so the mother felt secure in not being overly protective. There wasn't anyone quite the girl's age to play with among the group, so she busied herself with her new friend, making outrageous faces in return. The mother admonished the girl by telling her to stop, but Nathan Yadin assured her it was okay.

"I'm just as guilty," he playfully admitted. The little girl's innocence was just what he needed at the moment. It was reassuring that he could still be touched in such a way.

This unscheduled getaway for him was meant to be therapeutic. If he worked in a more structured environment, the likely recommendation would have been to see a psychiatrist, and posttraumatic stress would have been the probable diagnosis. Yadin had never grown fond of killing, but he took pride in ridding the world of its ill citizens. Still, on this day, instead of totally enjoying the warmth and atmosphere of this gorgeous place in Crete, he was slightly troubled.

It was the woman.

He had nothing against killing women. They had, over the years, proven just as capable of devious acts as men. No, killing women was not a concern. Killing *that* woman, however, stuck with him. Other than her name, he only knew what Ezra had told him: that she had to die if the overall operation was to succeed. There was something about her, though, and hearing her speak, however briefly, stayed with him. Presented with the inevitable, she was not afraid. Others, when confronted with her situation, often begged for their lives or promised anything. He didn't want to question Ezra about it—at least, not at the moment. There was too much at stake, and jeopardizing it on something he couldn't get out of his mind seemed altogether silly. Yadin tried to put the matter to bed by promising when all this was done, he would learn more about Erica Janway. This was a first for him, caring about the dead.

For now, he fully intended to give in to what his body and mind were aching for. They needed rest. The first part of achieving that had him getting out of Paris shortly after his meeting with Ezra had concluded. He didn't want to take the chance of Mossad or anyone else figuring out that Paris was where he officially resided. He didn't bother to tell Ezra he was heading to Crete and couldn't be contacted for the next several days. Yadin knew Ezra's timetable. If there truly was a problem, an e-mail would alert Yadin, and that was the only thing he checked anyway. He was not the kind of person one easily got in touch with to begin with, so being totally out of contact was not unusual. Anyone looking for him had better have a damn good reason for doing so.

Yadin took a deep, cleansing breath as he soaked in the surroundings. This was what life was supposed to be about. People from different backgrounds experiencing the same things while enjoying and respecting each other's existence. He winked at his little friend. Families spending time together. He liked to think he was doing his part in making people feel safe. Tonight, at least, he would go to sleep with that belief. That would be after he answered another of his mental and physical needs. He would find a woman tonight to lie down with. He wanted his strong hands to gently caress the body of someone soft. A woman whose scent made the air around her more breathable. He wanted it to happen naturally, which would require him to be engaging, at the very least. He could be charming. Just ask his little friend in the floral dress. He smiled at her a last time as he rose from his chair. The night was young, and he felt like being part of the action. He liked the sound of it. Before he left the restaurant, he stopped to pay his bill and in doing so, requested that an assortment of flowers be given to the little girl. He also instructed that her table's tab be charged to his credit card. With that, he exited into the awaiting night in search of pleasure. So far, it was a good vacation.

CHAPTER 19

Technically, he was considered a senior citizen. However, at sixty-five, Senator Bryce Lipton hardly felt old. Perhaps that was because life kept throwing challenges at him, forcing him to stay active. Part of his unyielding drive was due to the fact he hadn't yet achieved all the things he deemed possible in the political arena. He had clout and prestige, but for him, as for the wealthy person who craves yet more money, there was never such a thing as too much.

Growing up, he had known wealth, but as the limousine pulled into the grounds of the stately manor, he noted that this was altogether something else. The house itself had to be at least fifteen thousand square feet, well secured behind landscaping that easily was over a million dollars. The drive from his Capitol Hill office was uneventful, no serious traffic tie-ups. It really was a manageable drive, should he ever have to get here in a hurry. He prayed that such a day would never come. These meetings were usually held at an address in the District. This was his first visit to the "castle."

The limo pulled up alongside a host of other chauffeur-driven stretch vehicles. There was a person dressed in a dark suit to greet him, or rather to open the door for him, as no words were spoken. Trying not to be overly impressed, Senator Lipton took his time exiting, his eyes taking in the enormity of it all. From the looks of everything, it was as if the property had a weekly salon appointment. Not a thing was out of place. The house sat on three acres of land that backed up to the Potomac River.

Property like this rarely came on the market—at least, not for regular people. For many motorists traveling along Chain Bridge Road, the smattering of homes and their super-sized opulence could only slightly be seen during the winter months when some of the foliage fell away. This avenue of prosperity, just across the Potomac River on the Virginia side, dwarfed what one imagined as being well-off.

As if he had stepped on an automatic opener, the double doors to the mansion gave way as he approached. Upon entering, he noticed but paid little attention to the two servants who held each heavy door open. A butler, or he could he be the concierge, officially greeted him in the expansive foyer.

"Good evening, sir," he said with a slight bow of the head. "Please follow me. Mr. Daniels and the others are assembled."

Lipton glanced at his watch as he followed the hired help down the hallway. He wasn't late, but he got the impression he was the last to arrive. How many cars did he see out front? He tried to count, but the house had diverted his attention. The walls of the hallway were lined with works of art, many of which he had seen before—only in pictures or a PBS special. He recognized a Renoir for sure, and because of his love of the sea, he slowed down upon encountering a piece of Winslow Homer's work.

They stopped at a huge wooden door, which, judging by the butler's knock, was thick enough to stop large-caliber gunfire. Laboriously the door swung open, and immediately the heavy aroma of cigar smoke greeted Lipton. There were six men in the room. Some puffed on cigars, and nearly all had some sort of beverage in hand. In unison, they all took notice of Lipton's presence.

"Ah, Bryce, damn good to see you." The greeting came with a smile and extended hand. "What can I get you to drink?"

"Scotch and soda will do."

"Coming up."

Lipton followed the estate's owner to the bar. According to *Forbes* and other business journals, Roger Daniels was sixty-four years old. If you believed what you read, Daniels worked out religiously every day. He also found the time to manage his nearly 22-billion-dollar financial empire that spanned the globe. Looking around, Lipton noted that if a bomb were to hit this room, the stock market would take a nosedive of historic proportion. Except for himself, this was a billionaires' club. A single billion wouldn't even get you on the grounds. Aside from Daniels, only one other individual was somewhat known by face in financial circles. The rest operated in relative obscurity. Yet, over the past three years, Lipton had come to know them all. There was no mistaking, though, who garnered top billing. This whole assortment was the brainchild of Daniels. At first these men would gather to exchange ideas and talk about future business opportunities and markets in the world. Then, Daniels realized their scope and influence could achieve so much more. To prove it to the others, he single-handedly engineered a coup d'état in a small corner of the world that wouldn't draw much attention. Thus was born the Global Watch Institute. With its unheralded financial arm, the institute did plenty of charitable work and was recognized worldwide for bringing food and medicine to the hungry and sick. It also had the kind of clout that was capable of influencing political elections, both do-mestic and abroad.

With a swig of his Scotch and soda, Lipton found himself con-versing and listening to the musings of men who could shape global economies just by picking up a phone and having a short conversation. Lipton admired that kind of power, but he knew he'd never achieve it the way these men had. He wasn't even close to being a blip on that radar. But there were other ways. He knew that, and so did Daniels, which was why the two had found each other.

"Gentlemen," Daniels said, immediately silencing the room, "let us proceed with the business at hand." He led the delegation to a long mahogany table crafted several centuries ago, restored to perfection. Everyone took a seat, looking to Daniels, naturally at the head of the table.

His face was thin, giving way to well-defined cheekbones. The grey sown between his remaining black hairs gave him an air of sophistication. He spoke four languages fluently, and his many travels around the world had produced an uncanny awareness that certainly served him well in monetary matters.

Daniels acknowledged each man before continuing. "My friends." Daniels extended the palms of his hands as he spoke. "We are on the brink of our greatest achievement. A daring and bold act for sure"—he raised an accusatory finger—"but, one that truly will reduce some of the madness that exists today and no doubt prevent, or at least halt for a considerable time, tragedies that surely will occur if nothing is done."

One of the billionaires, whose fortune was obtained by managing money for others, interrupted. "Playing devil's advocate here," he began, looking at his fellow members, "isn't the president heading in the right direction? Like some investments, the return takes time."

Daniels took up the argument. "Years and counting in Afghanistan. Way too long in Iraq. Thousands of US troops dead and a public that's fed up. Conflicts that have now spanned three presidents. We have a country that's losing its stronghold and its way." There were a number of nods of agreement. "*Time* is what we are running out of. Unthinkable before, other nations now test our resolve, knowing that a strong response from the US only weakens our global position. We had a terrorist madman responsible for attacks on US soil—the success of which spawned followers that grow in number by the day, thinking we are soft. Things must change. Things will change. We are here for the long haul. We have the means and opportunity to change the course of history. We can make this once formidable country great again. It's time for the weak and uninitiated to get out of the way. The question is, are we ready to proceed? Senator?"

Bryce Lipton enjoyed being on stage. He was the go-to guy for the various network and cable television outlets, a frequent contributor to the Sunday morning network political talk shows. He gave good, concise sound bites that fit within the framework of a story, and he did so in ways that endeared him to the camera. He could be engaging and sarcastic or a wolverine when on attack. For years, the one thing Republicans had lacked was charisma. They offset the deficiency in the past by promoting themselves as the serious party. Lipton understood none of that mattered right now. It was time to deliver. You couldn't dazzle these men with bullshit. Their vast empires were built upon one simple principle: results. They were poised, waiting to hear if the plan was worth their investment of money, time, and ideas. Lipton also understood if he failed here, his political future would be nothing more than a footnote.

"I think it's important at the moment to make sure all of us are still in agreement," said Lipton, taking command of the room. "Walk away now if you have second thoughts."

There were no defectors, not even from the one billionaire Lipton thought to be the weakest of the group. He came from a good East Coast family, attended the right schools, married the right girl and generally sided with the do-gooders of the world. It was a positive sign that he remained seated.

"Very well then," Lipton acknowledged. "A lot of hard work, as you know, has gone into this undertaking. To answer your question, Roger, everything is on schedule and moving forward."

"So Baum has procured the materials?" Daniels asked.

"Shipment is waiting for when we want it. He'll handle the transaction and then make a considerable profit on top of what he already has, thanks to you gentlemen. He'll then authorize the transport to Iran, and that will happen once the materials are inspected."

"And the Israeli contingent?" Daniels followed up.

"In the shadows, omnipresent, ready to move when we give them the green light."

"Are you absolutely sure we can trust them?" the billionaire whose profit was garnered from computer software chimed in. Ian Novak was a familiar face, having been the subject of several technology-related articles and interviews. It was a fair but bold question, considering one of the members of the group was Jewish.

"Frankly, this wouldn't be possible without their expertise and willingness to see this through." Lipton glanced at the lone Jew for a moment to see if there was any reaction. He kept quiet on the surface, but he had to at least suspect that others in the room, at some point, had wondered the same thing.

The most private of the men in the room, Dominick Rourke, spoke next. Lipton had developed a great deal of respect for him.

Rourke didn't scare easily, was Princeton educated, and carried himself with a quiet calm. He was also the youngest of the group and not married, which made it even more of a challenge to remain totally off the radar. Lipton anticipated a well-thought observation.

"Senator, my only hesitation at this point lies in the potential of this not being as secret as we'd hoped," Rourke said. "And certainly, once it's done, there'll be several loose ends that have to be tidied up. The potential for exposure is already there with the messy situation concerning the woman from the CIA. Compounding that is her protégé's being still unaccounted for, with knowledge of God knows what. To make this more troublesome, there is the fact that your son has history here. How long or difficult is it before someone starts connecting the dots?"

Lipton remained composed, despite the mention of his son. If he weren't sitting here and weren't a part of this, Lipton envisioned they would have done something already to remove what they perceived as a potential problem. As always, though, Rourke's thoughts were on point. Lipton could foresee the day when the young man from Arizona would be the head of this group if it lasted that long.

"Dominick." Lipton addressed him as if he were the only other person in the room. The technique worked well to appease the pompous egos of network news people. "My son is well insulated in this matter. Necessary steps, as you recall, were taken a while ago to put us in a position to proceed, and yet, the woman from the CIA persisted in being a threat to our success. Her removal unfortunately was unavoidable. It's true, her protégé is in the wind, but if she had anything of substance, I wager we would have felt the fallout by now. Still, the search for her is widespread and ongoing."

Lipton didn't feel the need to reveal that Nora Mossa had found someone to assist her. He was privy to the exhibition at Dupont Circle. Surely, though, she was fishing, and in this case, the body of water was huge.

"As far as loose ends, rest assured that measures are already in place to do what needs to be done."

Daniels formed a devious smile. He looked at the faces around the room and realized he was on the brink of completing a monumental achievement. There for the taking was a chance to change an entire culture. Huge profits would eventually follow, and they'd be in place to take those as well. And the best part was, no one would ever know. Daniels raised his glass in a toast. "If there is nothing else, I take it we are all in agreement in saying, the time has come." Hands went up around the table. There were no disbelievers. Daniels looked at the man who wanted to be president of the United States. "Senator, you have the green light."

Lipton nodded and instinctively checked his watch. In another part of the world it was way too early and risky for him to make a phone call or send a direct, unsecured e-mail, no matter how vague its wording. Besides, a procedure had been established, and even though it would take another day, he had to resist the momentum of the room. For the moment, as the last of his Scotch and soda slid down his throat, Lipton could rejoice in knowing that "Sandstorm" was now fully operational.

CHAPTER 20

Alex found that getting the ten thousand dollars he'd requested was a lot easier than calming Nora down. Her main purpose in life now centered on killing Davis Lipton. She was convinced of his involvement in her friend Erica's death. Alex needed more proof to be sure. That's where he hoped the money would come in handy.

Under the name of Nathalie Tauziat, Nora arranged for two separate five-thousand-dollar transfers to two different banks. Both ING and Deutsche banks were within walking distance of each other along Avenue Marnix. The first transfer came from a bank in the Cayman Islands, the second from an account in Cyprus. It was all done quickly and without incident. Alex had sent Nora into the banks on her own. She wore a wide-brimmed hat to circumvent surveillance cameras, making facial recognition that much harder. Anything that kept her mind off Lipton was worth doing.

The withdrawn funds were basically seed money from the CIA. An agent with Nora's status needed funds readily available in case of an emergency. She had been entrusted with a total of thirty thousand dollars. It was enough to offer a bribe or secure an escape route if needed in a hurry. She had split the money into several smaller fractions, depositing it in various banks around the world, under various names. There was a total of twelve thousand dollars under the name Nathalie Tauziat, an identity she had never used before or reported to her superiors. The remaining funds were under names the CIA knew, and they would stay there, because surely those accounts were being closely monitored by now.

A block away from the Deutsche Bank, she hopped in the car driven by Duncan. Nora then put all ten thousand dollars into two large brown envelopes. The packages bulged slightly despite the denominations being large bills. She made a call to Alex's cell, and he instructed that the money be delivered to him as fast as they could catch up. Sensing they were running out of time, Alex hoped his instincts would prove correct. He maintained a leisurely pace through the congestion at Louise Square, a nexus of people, cars, tramway and metro station. As he pressed on, the fashionable section of Avenue Louise lived up to its nickname of *le goulet Louise*— the Louise bottleneck. Two tramway lines and an endless flow of vehicular traffic marched through the narrow street. Taking an interest in all the distractions, Alex snapped pictures occasionally with a palm-sized digital camera. While Brussels passed by on a different pace, he was a man in no particular rush. He got another call from Nora, and turning around, he located the car making its way down the street. He maneuvered himself between two parked cars, giving off the appearance of wanting to cross the street as he waited for Duncan to pull up. Duncan slowed down as if looking for a parking space while Alex moved against traffic in the narrow space along parked cars. In an instant he took the two packages from Nora like a running back receiving a handoff from the quarterback. They disappeared inside his jacket just as fast. The car darted off, and Alex returned to the sidewalk. When he focused on the people, he didn't see what he was looking for, which he took as a good sign. He wanted to make it as easy as he possibly could. He continued on his previous path. A shopper's delight of designer stores, coffeehouses, and chocolate offerings lined the street. Alex made a point to stop and look through the windows of establishments as he passed. He paused in front of one shoe store to take a picture, studying the reflection off the curved glass front as he snapped away. A smile creased his lips as he saw what he hoped would be there. As he resumed walking, his pace quickened, and a couple of blocks later, he turned down a quieter street. With camera in hand, Alex gave the appearance of intently focusing to get a shot of the street's architecture. He never took the picture because the unmistakable shape of a gun barrel was pressed against his side. There was a considerable amount of mass behind it, semi-pinning him to the wall of the building, the free hand placed on his shoulder for added leverage. To an onlooker, it would seem like two acquaintances, sharing a private talk.

"You're either terribly horrible at surveillance or you want to get my attention," the voice breathed hotly into Alex's ear. He then shoved the barrel into his kidney for added emphasis. "Which, by the way, you have."

Alex tolerated the mild discomfort from one of Tobias Baum's bodyguards. "I admit, I'm a bit rusty, but I wasn't born yesterday. Can we go somewhere to talk?"

"Why?"

"Look, if I didn't want you to see me, we wouldn't be having this Hallmark moment."

Alex's solid build and casual demeanor made an impression. Even though he was holding the gun, the bodyguard had a sense this could go either easy or hard. It was still early in the day, and easy sounded good.

"I'm hungry, but then you should know that, since you've been on my ass for a while. There's a place to eat a couple of blocks back. This better be damn good," the bodyguard said as he withdrew the gun from Alex's side. He motioned for Alex to lead, staying a couple of steps behind, the gun now resting in a side pocket of his light windbreaker, his hand still firmly attached.

So far so good, Alex thought.

CHAPTER **21**

The two strangers sat across from each other in the quaint restaurant, separated only by a small square table. Neither had had to suggest their strategic seating arrangement next to the large window. Each could watch the other's back as they looked out upon the intersection of Rue de Florence and Rue Veydt. The restaurant was understated, the kind of place that had word of mouth to thank for its survival. For those who discovered it, the payoff far exceeded the expectations. If it weren't for the architecture beyond the glass, this could have easily been a culinary establishment located in New York's SoHo district. Having already placed their order, they took a nonverbal moment to determine who would take the next step.

The bodyguard unzipped his jacket but kept it on, resting a hand on his lap. A clear message that he was still armed. He didn't take his eyes off Alex as he took a drink of grapefruit juice. "It's your meeting," he said, nearly draining the glass.

"My name's Alex."

The bodyguard thought about it for a moment and then acquiesced. "Michael."

"Ex-military? Afghanistan? Iraq?" Alex probed. He then decided to provide the answer he knew wasn't forthcoming voluntarily. "Had to be Afghanistan. No one in his right mind would choose Iraq. Bad intel, poorly equipped, too many hostiles to identify. You could get blown up just getting a cup of coffee because some sectarian wants to martyr himself and impress a sheikh you've never even heard of. In the early stages, Afghanistan was where you could make some money. Your tour is eventually over, and instead of re-upping, you sign on with a private contractor and get assigned to security. The same government that had been paying you shit is now forking over thousands to protect its assets."

Nodding his head, Michael offered, "I'm impressed. Somewhere along the way, you took a political science course."

Alex chuckled. "Better to live it."

"So, Mr. Obvious, how long have you been following me today?"

"Since you left your apartment." That revelation got the bodyguard's attention. "You caught wind of me for the first time when you left the health club late this morning, after your workout. But then, that's when I wanted you to see me. Not this morning for your coffee and bagel stop. Not at the ATM or on the metro to get to the gym. With your morning being so free, I can only assume it's going to be a late night for Tobias Baum."

The bodyguard locked his gaze on Alex. He didn't look away as the waiter laid out their order. Alex said "Thank you" for the both of them.

"More impressed now?"

"I don't take kindly to being threatened," Michael said, his nostrils widening.

"Ease up," Alex consoled, getting ready to take a bite of his sandwich. "It's not about you."

"Who are you?"

Alex held up a finger, waiting to swallow. "We've established that already. I'm Alex, remember?" Before Michael could utter a protest, Alex reached inside his jacket and lobbed one of the packages onto the table.

Michael let it stay there briefly before carefully peeling back a portion of the package, revealing an indication of its contents. "I get compensated for my services pretty well already." He slid the package back over to Alex.

"I'm sure you do. That's to cover lunch." Alex slid it back.

"I don't plan on eating that much."

Alex took a sip of his iced tea. "Like I said, this isn't really about you. This concerns Baum and a certain business associate of his."

"How long have you been on me?" Michael questioned, and then another thought appeared. "No, make that 'us.' "

The cat was out of the bag, so Alex felt he needed to give a little. "For a few days now. Don't get all freaky about it. If I'm doing what I should, you're not supposed to notice I'm there. I'm interested specifically in the man who visited the estate last night."

The bodyguard contemplated his response. "Interesting. Since you probably already know more about him than I do, I'll just say he feels like an OGA employee. Perhaps you two have that in common. He reeks of it, though. You, not so much."

Alex continued eating, somewhat amused at being reminded of the military's euphemism for a CIA employee, OGA being Other Government Agency. If his tablemate was starting to talk, he wasn't going to interrupt. "You said earlier, 'Better to live it.' " Michael leaned in and lowered his voice. "Ex-CIA? Or perhaps Special Ops? No, I'll stick with CIA. Considering you guessed—correctly, by the way—that I did a tour in Afghanistan, I'll wager you spent some time there as well. When my military obligation was over, I wised up and saw the opportunity to make nice money working for an independent contractor. Guarding guys like Hamid Karzai was a hell of a lot less dangerous than chasing the Taliban or freedom fighters in the Hindu Kush Mountains."

Alex nodded in agreement. "Now, I'm impressed. And you're right about the Hindu Kush Mountains. Nasty place to get caught with your ass in the wind."

The bodyguard stopped toying with his meal and took a long hard look at Alex. Several seconds later he raised an index finger as he searched his mind for a thought. "There was a story once about an incident in Jalalabad," he began. "Turned out to be a real shitkicker of a dogfight. The kind that has you praying to Momma, God, anybody who could get you out of that hell alive. A so-called reliable informant led a small group of Rangers right into an ambush. They fought hard and hunkered down, but then two of 'em got snatched during the firefight. There was enemy fire all over the place, so no way in hell was a CH-47 going to risk flying in for a rescue mission. About two hours later, they're almost out of ammo when they hear a chopper a few clicks away. Next thing you know they have a clear path to the south and were told to hightail the fuck out of there. Our guys take off in that chopper, but word is a small unit, ten or twelve guys led by a ghost, stays on the ground to search for those two missing Rangers. Now, back at HQ, nobody's getting any sleep that night, and just before dawn, we hear a Chinook coming in. Damn if getting off that chopper in the early morning dust aren't the two missing Rangers, a bit bloody and banged up, but safe. That chopper also unloads a team of Special Forces guys, except for one individual who remained on board as it took off. Later in the day it's confirmed the mystery man was CIA. In and out. The rescued Rangers also say he found that 'reliable' source and put a bullet through his head. If memory serves me right, that ghost's name was Alex too."

"It's a common name. And one thing I've also learned, it's a pretty small world."

A hand was extended across the table. "I'm Michael Craftson."

Alex shook his hand. "Pleasure to know you."

Craftson took a moment to consume some of his food. He washed a good portion down with a gulp of water. "Now, you mentioned my current employer, and you're right, tonight is probably going to be a rather late one. Every now and then Baum likes to go clubbing," Craftson offered. "He has a meeting as well tonight, though. Look, I'm not really sure how much I can help you. He's a very careful guy. He just likes to get out every now and then, flash some cash, and feed on the excitement."

"Do you know how Baum makes most of his money?"

"I was briefed by my company before taking the job. Everything I'm privy to seems aboveboard. He trusts me to a certain extent. He has to, when you consider I'm looking out for his well-being, but when he has serious business to do, and I assume those are matters off the books, that's usually done in total privacy. On those occasions, I don't ask and he doesn't tell."

"When did you come on board? Were you around when his partner went missing?"

"I was hired shortly after the Ostermann thing. Before you

ask, he doesn't talk about it. He touched upon it briefly at the beginning, explaining that in his line of work, shit happens."

"So it didn't seem as if the Ostermann thing spooked him all that much?"

"It could have at one point, but by the time I arrived, he seemed cool. Maybe it's his business savvy, but he doesn't strike me as the kind who loses much sleep."

"Who's the other guy I see with you guarding Baum?"

"His name is Reynolds. Comes from a different service. Baum likes to mix things up like that, but I'm the one he likes to keep close. I suppose I got a glowing report from working in trouble zones around the world, with no slipups to my credit. But Reynolds is capable. There are three other guys that take over when we're off shift. That's when Baum definitely has down time—usually doesn't leave the house too much then, or certainly reduces his range of motion. The big stuff—extended time in public, serious business meetings—that's me and Reynolds watching his back."

"What do you know about the guy who visited Baum last night?" Alex cautioned Craftson with a shift of his eyes. A few seconds later, the waiter appeared and asked whether they needed anything. Craftson said they were fine. He didn't begin talking again until Alex said it was okay to do so.

"He calls himself Davis. I've never heard a last name," Craftson said, looking out at the comings and goings on the street. "But that's how Baum likes it. He doesn't want us to know everything."

"His last name is Lipton," Alex said.

Craftson raised an eyebrow.

Alex nodded. "Yep. His son."

A disturbed look engulfed Craftson's face. "So is there an operation in place to take Baum down?"

"I wouldn't know for certain, but I don't think that's what's happening here."

Craftson leaned back in his chair, none too happy. "Son of a bitch. This is damn good money."

"You mentioned this is going to be a late night for Baum. Why?"

Craftson seemed lost in thought. "Michael," Alex said sternly.

"Michael, I need you to focus here. Like I said, this might not be what it looks like on the surface."

"Then why else would a guy from the CIA, whose father happens to be a Washington bigwig, be fucking around with a dangerous person like Baum?"

"How do you *know* Davis is CIA?"

"Like I said, he smells like government. But unlike most, he doesn't do a good job of concealing it. He might as well be wearing CIA cologne."

"Which means Baum knows he's CIA too."

"I don't see how he couldn't. He's not stupid."

"So, there's your answer right there."

Craftson looked at Alex, seeking more clarification.

"If Baum knows Davis is CIA, he wouldn't do business with him, unless he was sure this wasn't a sting operation. No, the business is real. What it is and the motivation behind it is what I'm trying to figure out."

Craftson's nerves eased considerably. Alex's observation made sense. "Well, their business will probably conclude tonight. Baum likes to celebrate the closing of huge deals. We're supposed to be at the You Night Club around midnight. Davis and Baum are supposed to meet at twelve forty-five. Baum more than likely will bring his laptop along."

"Sounds like a transfer of funds," Alex spoke the words tossing around in his brain. "A couple of keypad strokes and millions are floating in the air from one account to another, all in a matter of seconds."

"Please tell me you don't intend to crash the party."

Alex was already attempting to visualize a club he'd never seen but more importantly, trying to work out how he wanted the night to unfold. He chose his words carefully, trying to ease the concerns of his tablemate.

"No, I won't interfere with Baum's business. But afterwards, I will have to get some answers from Davis, and something tells me he won't want to cooperate. At least, not at first."

Craftson exhaled. "You do remember who his father is?"

A knowing smile formed on Alex face. "Oh, hell. That's an added bonus."

Small talk ensued as the two men finished their lunch. Shortly after, Alex paid the bill and remained seated while Craftson exited into the afternoon sunshine. A few minutes later, Alex was on the phone with Duncan, requesting to be picked up at the restaurant. Alex was waiting outside when the rental car pulled up. He got in the backseat. As Duncan drove on, Nora turned in the passenger seat to engage Alex. Her whole demeanor was a question waiting for an answer.

Alex studied her near flawless face, trying to suppress memories. "You need to go shopping," he told her. "You have to find one hell of a sexy dress."

Nora smiled in remembrance of what was originally a stupid decision in Rome. "I don't have to go shopping. I'm sure I have something that'll work."

"Resourceful, that's always good."

Duncan peeked at Alex in the rearview mirror. "So, I take it things went well?"

Alex sat up, reaching inside his jacket pocket. "Yeah, that reminds me." He produced the two envelopes filled with money and handed them over to Nora.

Duncan casually took in the exchange. "So, you think you can trust him?

Alex's eyes shifted to the passing scenery. "I believe so. As it turns out, the world is a pretty small place."

CHAPTER 22

After dinner, like clockwork, Yosef Ezra retired to his study. He gently closed the French doors behind him and sat at his glistening mahogany desk. Waiting in a pile, as always, was the day's mail. His devoted wife never opened his envelopes nor even paid much attention to the return addresses. Her routine was to stack it neatly in his study before going about maintaining the rest of the household, which included making a delectable meal each night they didn't go out for dinner. And Ezra didn't really like going out too often, because his wife was an outstanding cook. He gave in only to please her, because every now and then she enjoyed dressing up and letting someone else prepare the food. Part of the deal was also that after investing long hours at work, he wouldn't spend too much time in his study to conduct more business. She preferred he stay at work if that was going to be the case. He went about clearing his desk efficiently, quickly shredding the junk mail, putting bills in another pile and scanning other correspondence as if he were the Emperor of Rome deciding a gladiator's fate, issuing a hasty thumbs up or thumbs down. His pace slowed considerably when he encountered the small sealed box. He carefully picked it up and shook it. There was something loose inside. He inspected the package's label. There was no return address. He grabbed his letter opener and sliced through the translucent tape that held the package closed. The inside was sealed with plastic wrap. He sat upright in his chair when he realized what was inside. His throat felt slightly dry. In the quietness of the room, he could hear his heart beating faster.

As if it were a precious gem, Ezra's aging fingers gently angled the box so that its contents would slide out. He watched as a small pile of sand came to rest on his desk. A note, the size you'd find in a fortune cookie, contained the word "Go." Ezra woke up his computer and composed two short e-mail messages that were virtually untraceable thanks to security software that utilized a network of IP addresses. The messages simply read: *Sandstorm. Green light.*

He hit the send button on both e-mails and logged off. Ezra sat back in his big leather chair, eagerly looking forward to spending the rest of the evening cuddled up with his wife. There was no turning back now. Years of planning, concealing, and manipulating were about to pay off. Certainly all of it was against the law, but no one would ever know. If all went according to plan, the consequences would force the world to focus on the end result and not the hidden steps that led up to it. For certain, Israel would be a much safer place, its aggressors less tempted to take measures that could have catastrophic results.

He knew history would prove him right.

CHAPTER 23

Dmitri Nevsky was not the most patient of men, and spending idle time in Gomel, of all places, did nothing to improve his disposition. This was one job he wanted to be done with, despite its nice payday. To him, even when the sun shined brightly, this part of the world seemed sorely lacking. The landscape was boring, the housing repetitive, the cities predictable, and the people, though hardworking, lacked perspective on the rest of the world. He felt qualified to form such an opinion because he grew up in such a place. He watched his father grow old fast because he worked too hard to provide for his family, and the return on his sweat equity was never a fair exchange. Their apartment was certainly too small for a family of five. After a while, playing with his two younger sisters no longer distracted him from focusing on the family's meager belongings. The inner workings of the street, however, were appealing to him. There he found what he was looking for. Nevsky discovered he was good at using his fists and that even bigger, older kids could be intimidated once his reputation grew around the neighborhood. That reputation eventually got the attention of the authorities, and a relationship was born.

Nevsky's first taste of a jail cell came at age fifteen. He was a frequent visitor until he turned eighteen. That was when a new association ensued, and it came with a uniform: the military beckoned. A hungry, strapping, feared young man like him was just the type the military needed to prevent its ranks from getting soft. He eventually attained responsibility and authority, which empowered him in ways he never thought possible. It would have been easy for him to become a career soldier, but influential men saw that as a waste. No, a man like Nevsky had a higher calling. He was handpicked to receive the education he'd turned his back on during his youth, and his penchant for violence was channeled into a craft—a much easier sell, since the military had taught him a sense of discipline. Nevsky had become a prized possession of the FSB. Though it wasn't like being a doctor, an educator, or a businessman, working for the government's enforcement and intelligence arm was a career. And it was one that made him proud. Plus, working in foreign countries widened his scope of the world and what it had to offer. Like his father, though, he eventually felt trapped in a system that failed to compensate him sufficiently for his efforts. After taking care of an assignment in Iraq, he'd decided he was done. Besides, it was getting more and more difficult to stay true to the cause. Determining how certain actions benefited his homeland was starting to require too much thought. On occasion, it was as if he was on loan to the Iraqis, or Saudis, or some other Middle East entity. Was it about oil? Maintaining relationships? Control? In the end, for him, it was about working with or for people he didn't like being around.

There were protests and veiled threats, but he was allowed to leave the government's service without looking over his shoulder because he'd been smart enough to document and hide vital information that could destroy careers. To the Russian hierarchy, Nevsky was certainly more dangerous dead than alive.

Over the last couple of days in Gomel, his mealtimes consisted of trying to consume anything packaged, preferably imported. He had trust issues, having read somewhere that a number of Belarusians still consumed contaminated food, a leftover gift from Chernobyl. It was probably a lie, but it succeeded in making him cautious. All he wanted to do was wash Gomel off his hands and wave good-bye. When the call from his employer came, he was more than overjoyed to hear it was time to move the cargo one last time. The conversation was not lengthy, the instructions clear. He listened intently, jotting down notes along the way.

After the call, Nevsky consulted a map of the region and began calculating the safest and quickest route. He didn't anticipate having any more problems, but in the world of black market goods, anything was possible.

CHAPTER 24

Nathan Yadin's eyes focused long enough to confirm it was late morning. Certainly an oddity, since he was usually an early riser. His body felt sluggish, but in a good way. To that end, he slowly turned to see the face that belonged with the feminine arm draped around his midsection. He moved ever so slowly, so as to not wake her. This little respite had rejuvenated him much more than he'd thought it would. In the precious few days he'd known her, the sex was delightfully good, but the mental stroking was what made it complete. They talked not about the ills of the world but instead about wine, art, and music. The weather even managed to be a topic of discussion—beautiful sunsets, gentle breezes, how good the sun felt upon their bodies, the stars dancing across the sky's canvas at night. In his other life, the weather would only come up in terms of how it might alter the variables of an operation's success.

Her name was Lauren, and he was attracted to her partly because there was nothing artificial about her. She was naturally attractive. The late-morning light that filled the room illuminated her makeupless face. If a woman could pass this test, she was indeed a find. Still, like most women, she felt her early morning look was not presentable to the masses. Yet, for the past couple of mornings, he took delight in seeing that face before she woke. Last night was another late one, topped off by lovemaking. If he was quiet, she would sleep some more. He, on the other hand, already felt a trace of guilt for sleeping so late. He carefully slid out of bed and dressed in athletic garb. He ventured out into the Chania sunshine, determined to jog at least several miles at a brisk pace. He marveled at the scenery, considering just how idyllic a life like this could be. He certainly had the funds to do it. There were no family responsibilities holding him back. And yet, it was not as easy as flipping a switch. The one thing really holding him back was his anger and hatred. The world was filled with evil, stupid people. He wasn't delusional enough to believe he could eradicate them all, but he had and could still make a small difference. One fewer sect of suicide bombers undoubtedly saved countless lives. One fewer terrorist might cause the next to question whether it was the right career path. Walking away now was just not a viable option, but the mere fact that he was starting to have the mental conversation indicated the possibility that such a time would arrive. Until then, moments like this would have to suffice.

At the end of his run, his lungs burned slightly from being put to the test, but they recovered quickly. Along with the rest of his body, they were used to the drill. A little discomfort up front went a long way toward preventing a lot of punishment on the back end. He stopped for coffee, juice, fruit, and any other breakfast items suitable for carrying. Entering the hotel suite, he expected her to be awake by now, so he didn't try to mask his entrance. He smiled when no signs of life greeted him. He glanced through the bedroom's French doors and could tell his return was beginning to wake her. He thought about setting the table inside and then decided it was a perfect morning to enjoy breakfast on the balcony instead. From outside, he could hear her call his name.

"Lauren, I've got breakfast," he responded. He stepped back inside through the wind-whipped drapes and immediately smiled upon seeing her. "Of course, you're going to have to put on some clothes."

She stood at the entrance to the bedroom, totally naked, part of her long blond hair covering a breast. The breeze from the balcony managed to blow strands of her hair aside so that both breasts were now exposed. She had a sheepish look on her still awaking face as he admired her nude form.

"I hope you like what I got," he offered, motioning back toward the balcony.

With pursed lips she said, "I've enjoyed everything you've done so far."

The invitation to flirt was answered as Yadin crossed the room to join her. They embraced and kissed. In the brief time he'd known her, he discovered she was a lot like him—minus the killing, of course, but she was lethal in her own right. Looking for a place to relax and unwind, Lauren had been drawn to Chania as well. She really didn't intend to meet a man during her self-prescribed R and R. Why ruin a perfect retreat with drama? Besides, she dealt with enough men in her high-pressure world of corporate takeovers and acquisitions. When she set her sights on a company, she was known for being a ball breaker. But when she'd first seen Yadin a couple of nights ago, there'd been something about him, a sort of kinship that sent signals across the room. There were other, more attractive men in the bar, but none possessed his sense of comfort. He was a man who seemed totally content to be by himself. He didn't look at every short skirt or tight-fitting pair of jeans in the bar. Instead, his taste seemed more refined. He was interesting enough for her to send a drink his way. Rather than take advantage of the compliment, he merely acknowledged her and raised his glass to say thanks. Men didn't ignore her, but the casual gesture intrigued her. She found his slight rejection appealing. Here was a man who was smart enough to accept a good thing, but not careless enough to commit to something he didn't know fully. It was enough to get her to follow up with a trek to his table. And now, here they were, no longer strangers physically, and surprisingly to both of them, growing closer emotionally.

There had to be a sense of reality here, though. Chania would come to an end sooner rather than later, and there were no plans made or thought of beyond what they were experiencing in the present. The morning after they met, they both agreed to do something unthinkable for them in the real world. It was proof of how much they both needed a break. The pact was to leave their cell phones off and no checking e-mail. It was crazy, but so was this.

She could taste the salt on his skin produced by his run. She was impressed by his dedication to staying in shape. He did some sort of lengthy workout every day, fatigued or not. She also appreciated his thoughtful side, something she hadn't expected. Stopping to get breakfast was an example of that, and she didn't want to waste his effort. She pushed back to look into his eyes.

"I'll put on a robe so we can eat breakfast on this beautiful day on the balcony," she whispered. "And then, judging by how you taste and how much I know I sweated last night, we can take a shower together." She planted a kiss on his lips and then nodded for him to go get started on breakfast while she headed to the closet to get a robe. First, though, she'd make a stop in the bathroom to at least run a brush through her hair and throw some water on her face.

On the way to the balcony, Yadin out of habit grabbed his dormant cell phone and placed it on the table next to him. He poured himself a cup of coffee and then felt compelled to break the pact. It had been a couple of days, and much was at stake. He turned on his cell phone and retrieved his e-mail from a nondescript account. He wasn't the type to get a lot of correspondence through the World Wide Web. There were three messages, all from Yosef Ezra. They didn't bear the man's name, but he was quite familiar with the moniker Ezra used for this mission. The first message had been sent a couple of days ago. There was no copy within the message; the subject line said it all. *Sandstorm. Green Light.* That same message was repeated in one sent twenty-four hours later. The third message still contained no copy, but the subject line conveyed a sense of nervousness and urgency. "Where Are You?" it read in bold letters. Yadin smiled, knowing the old man was probably on the verge of a coronary because he hadn't responded yet. Yadin could see him panicking. Agonizing that all his hard work and detailed planning would be wasted if something had happened to his most valuable commodity. There was no one capable of taking his place. Yadin decided to have some fun. He replied to the third message with the subject line, "I'm Fine. On Vacation." He went on to write that he'd received the two previous messages and that this was his last day of rest. Just as he sent the message, Lauren came walking through the drapes to join him. She immediately noticed the cell phone and then looked away with a smile as she sat down.

She reached for a Danish pastry and poured herself a cup of coffee, adding a side plate of fruit. "Thank you for breakfast," she uttered before feasting on a slice of melon.

He gazed upon her sun-bronzed skin, enjoying a sip of coffee as he did so. They sat in silence, letting the scenery and sound effects of the day fill in the gaps.

Finally, she spoke. "So, when are you leaving?"

He knew she realized he had broken the pact and what doing so meant. The outside world had finally come between them. "Tomorrow morning," he simply stated. There was no need for explanation. That, too, had been part of the deal. They were both strong-minded adults who understood that you take what life gives you and run with it for as long as the opportunity presents itself. For them, the past few days had been total bliss, and neither regretted their happiness, no matter the dose.

Lauren toyed with a large strawberry in her mouth, her full lips helping to squeeze it in half. "Well, in that case," she murmured, placing a leg in his lap, her toes beginning to explore his inner thigh. "I have the perfect way to spend most of the day."

CHAPTER 25

The faces Alex encountered as he looked around the noisy, crowded room reminded him of his early adulthood. That time frame where he thought he knew enough about life to be taken seriously. The You Night Club reeked of such playful entitlement. Young people with money in their pockets and the illusion of invulnerability.

He leaned his athletic frame against the railing overlooking the expansive dance floor below. Duncan was making the rounds, getting a feel for the layout, and like Alex, he was making a mental note of faces, eliminating those that seemingly posed no threat. Their task was taxing, because there were a lot of bodies squeezed throughout, and the techno music blasting from various speakers was numbing Alex's eardrums and getting on his nerves. He felt that being forced to listen to techno music and its repetitive beat was a lot like being brainwashed. He could deal with hip-hop, house music, rap, and of course his favorite, jazz, but techno made him want to bang his head against the wall.

Tobias Baum and his entourage had yet to appear, but Alex surmised a roped-off section was being reserved for his arrival. He hoped it would be sooner rather than later. The crowd was getting thicker by the minute, and faces were getting lost in the mix. The object was to stay close enough to observe without being exposed for taking too much of an interest. In this crowd, it didn't take much effort to locate Duncan. He stood above the rest, and his physical frame demanded and created space. The only other people in the club even close to his stature were the various bouncers, and upon Duncan's arrival, they gave each other a "If I need you, come running in a hurry" acknowledgment. Duncan and Alex had arrived together, bypassing the long line that had formed at the entrance. One perk of being a current or former professional athlete was that all you usually had to do was produce your league-issued player's identification card and clubs around the globe honored your presence by not making you wait in line. They arrived shortly after twelve thirty. The club had been open for an hour and wouldn't shut down until around six in the morning. Alex had to give Brussels one thing. People here knew how to party.

Based on information from Baum's bodyguard, the black market dealer was expected to make his entrance between one and one thirty. The meeting with Davis Lipton was scheduled to take place shortly thereafter.

"Anything?" Alex was forced to scream as Duncan sidled up beside him, handing Alex a rum and Coke in the process.

"Nope. Not unless the cloak-and-dagger set is hiring juniors and seniors in high school. Are we getting old or what?"

Alex smiled. "Speak for yourself."

"Ah, if memory serves me right, didn't you graduate two years before me?"

"I did, which only goes to prove the disappointment and resentment you must feel because I still have such a youthful appearance."

"I'll give you a run for your money any day."

"Let's save that run for another day," Alex said, directing Duncan's attention with a nod toward a slight commotion below.

The time was 1:14. Even for a criminal, there was something to be said for being punctual. Two bouncers from the club led the way, making passage for Baum and his bodyguards. Craftson was positioned in front of Baum, while the other bodyguard, Reynolds, protected his rear. The young crowd being shoved aside was slightly annoyed but wisely didn't protest. Alex had guessed right. Baum, who carried a laptop bag, was led to the area marked "private" on the second level. Craftson handed one of the bouncers a sizeable tip. As he left, the bouncer got the attention of a waitress.

He delivered instructions in her ear, turning his head in Baum's direction as he did so. Alex and Duncan took all this in, just about twenty feet away from where Baum was stationed. The section provided security in that it was set back from the ebb and flow, and his bodyguards could see in every direction. It also offered the appearance of innocence, suggesting nothing outwardly sinister could happen in such a public place. It was a sure bet that Craftson and his partner were carrying sidearms. If the bouncers had protested, citing club policy, Craftson would have insisted. The tip went a long way toward relaxing the rules. The waitress who'd been stopped by the bouncer made her way to Baum's section, armed now with a chilled bottle of champagne and several glasses on a serving tray. She popped the cork and poured Baum a glass, not bothering to offer the same to his protection. A numbing five more minutes expired with nothing out of the ordinary taking place. It was a waiting game more than ever now. The young bodies on display were full of vigor and noise. There were no arthritic knees, calcium deposits, contusions, or concussions gyrating in this crowd, though Alex noted some danced like they might be suffering from some sort of ailment. He peeked at his watch, annoyed that it read 1:34. Through the thickening of people, he could still see Baum was waiting, a pleasant smile on his face as two young ladies in extremely short skirts tried to pique his interest.

"Daaaa-uummm."

Alex was forced to turn away by what came out of Duncan's mouth. "What is it?" he asked, searching. It was not the excited, pissed off usage of the word. It was more like admiration.

Alex focused on where Duncan's gaze was fixated and then he, too, saw what demanded attention.

CHAPTER **26**

To be fair, there were a number of beautiful women in the club. But as Duncan had pointed out, most of them still had much to learn about life and probably finals to study for. There were a few more women further along the age scale scattered about, but none were truly breathtakingly beautiful until Nora Mossa walked in.

Space seemed to open for her as men turned around to take a long look. The blond wig looked very natural, falling just below her shoulders. Part of it draped her high cheekbones. The black, low-cut crisscross dress she wore accented just about every aspect of her athletic body. Her feminine but defined arms hung freely. Her firm breasts were snugly wrapped and accented. From martial arts training and jogging, her legs were strong, a fact well displayed by the mid-knee-length hem. Black, strappy high-heeled sandals completed the look. Nora made her way to the packed bar where a young man tapped his friend in the back of the head. When he spun around in dumbfounded disgust, his friend shifted his eyes toward Nora, and his look quickly turned into a sheepish grin. He backed out of the way, allowing her access to the bar. In return, she threw him a huge smile. It didn't take long for a bartender to fulfill her apple martini order. Nora again smiled at the two hypnotized young men as she moved on. "You still got it, woman," Nora warmly thought to herself.

Despite the collection of eyes upon her, no one noticed how skillfully Nora surveyed the room. She located Alex and Duncan, and though she couldn't read lips, she could tell Duncan was playfully giving Alex a hard time about something. Nora declined a couple of dance offers, raising her drink as an excuse as she went about heading for the second level.

"What?" Alex finally exhaled, lifting his head from his forward lean as he did so.

"Nothing," Duncan responded, shaking his head. "Nothing at all." Alex returned to canvassing the dance floor.

"I'm just saying," Duncan chimed with a faraway look. "I mean, most people, uh, most would have never . . . Damn, man! You used to hit that!" Duncan's eyes were wide in disbelief.

Alex took a sip from his drink. "Are you done now? Got it out of your system?"

Duncan raised his hands in defense. "I'm cool."

"Good, because it's time to get to work. The main attraction just arrived."

"You ask me, the main attraction is already here."

"Yeah, well, fortunately, nobody's asking."

One of the bouncers that had escorted Baum was on the move, providing the same lead blocking for Davis Lipton. Duncan had already left Alex's side to seek another vantage point. No matter what spot he chose, his height would be an advantage. Alex made his way toward the spot where the bouncer would emerge. As he came into view, Alex briefly cast his attention upon Lipton, who was inspecting the room, sizing up the female population. Lipton's wandering eyes narrowed noticeably when they got a glimpse of Nora standing nearby, her body swaying to the beat of the music. He was thoroughly distracted when he nearly lost his footing after bumping into something solid and seemingly unmovable. Lipton appeared annoyed when he realized it wasn't a structure he'd collided with but instead, a person.

Alex, who had purposefully aided in the collision by stepping just enough into Lipton's path, was also quick and strong enough to catch him before he totally fell on his butt. The gesture was not done out of kindness. It afforded Alex the opportunity to discover that Lipton was carrying a small-caliber weapon clipped to his waist at the small of his back.

Upon pulling him up and noticing Lipton's perturbed look, Alex couldn't resist.

"You okay, little fella?"

Lipton brushed himself off, knowing he had to have come across like a clumsy idiot. He mumbled something under his breath and shook totally free of Alex's grasp. The bouncer was about to step in, but Lipton motioned for him to continue, wanting to get the scene over with as quickly as possible.

Alex was amused as Lipton went on his way. He also shot a look toward Nora, careful not to fixate on her for long, because even though she wasn't looking directly back at him, he guessed her peripheral vision might catch him watching. He had to admit, she was wearing the hell out of that black dress. He then spotted a table filled with youthful, enthusiastic women. They'd been discussing him for some time. He surmised their location was a perfect place to keep a watchful eye on Baum's business meeting.

"Ladies, good evening," Alex said, giving all four eye contact as he sidled up next to them. "Everybody enjoying the night so far? My name is Alex. Can I buy you lovely ladies a drink?" The women welcomed the intrusion with inviting eyes and an expansive show of teeth. Alex heard the names, but they really didn't register long-term. He only needed their camaraderie for a short time.

Baum didn't stand to greet Lipton, preferring to remain seated as he shook his hand, offering him the space next to him. Alex noticed Craftson ever so slightly position himself just behind Lipton's right shoulder, all the while keeping his head and eyes moving back and forth on all the bodies that strolled by.

Alex could also see that Duncan had ensnared the interest of a few females. Everyone was blending in nicely, just faces in a packed house. Alex did his best to feign interest in what the young women at the table were talking about. Each of them seemed fascinated by his presence, asking him how he stayed in shape. He was far removed from the boys they were used to being around. "Former pro athlete," he informed them. "Football. Not the European kind. American." Two of the women were familiar with the game, having attended college in the states. The other two were heading into their senior years of higher learning. Alex sensed several other questions were forthcoming, so he reduced the probability by grabbing the hand of the nearest girl, asking her to dance. She jumped at the invitation, overjoyed to be the chosen one. With the music blasting so loudly and bodies bumping into each other, there would be little, if any, verbal communication, just a few flirtatious grins and some innocent physical contact. Of course, Alex forgot about youthful enthusiasm. His dance partner soon laid her back against his chest, one arm waving in the air, the other draped around the back of his leg, pressing firmly. He had no choice but to place his right arm around her midsection so that he could stay in rhythm and not topple over. A few beats later, she gently broke free of his embrace and, bending at the waist, rubbed her butt up and down his crotch. Fortunately, there was a change of songs, and he escorted her back to the table in time to see Lipton carefully and deliberately typing on the laptop. Leaning back with his legs crossed, Baum kept a watchful eye on his methodical dexterity. Alex assumed a transfer of money was taking place as Lipton slid the laptop over to Baum, and after a few more keystrokes, it was over. One of the other women asked Alex if he wanted to dance. He had to almost shout in her ear that he was thirsty. He told her he'd be right back and headed for a bar station that still afforded him a glimpse of Baum's area. Lipton and Baum were both drinking a glass of champagne now.

Without knowing any details, Alex had a feeling the world had just gotten a little more complicated and dangerous.

CHAPTER 27

Roughly twenty minutes after their champagne toast, Tobias Baum was on his feet, shaking Davis Lipton's hand, their business concluded. Baum's bodyguards assumed their positions, effectively forming a sandwich of protection. Craftson brought up the rear this time, and Alex needed to get in his line of sight. He made his way through the crowd as politely as possible, but it still was necessary to use his size to help persuade bodies to give way. Baum was approaching from about fifteen feet and slightly to his left. Throughout the evening, Craftson had managed to keep up with Alex's general whereabouts. Locating him now was simple, especially since he wanted to be seen. Neither at this point knew the intention of the other, but Alex was hoping Craftson would give him some kind of sign, and Craftson was gambling Alex would maneuver close enough so that he could communicate without breaking stride or having to talk. It was no accident that Craftson brought up the rear. Doing so allowed him to deftly reach into his pants pocket to pull out a ten-dollar bill. Alex was now about to pass the group, heading in the opposite direction. Craftson brushed Alex's hand, who in turn swiped the currency away, swiftly putting it in his pants pocket.

With Baum out of the club, Alex made his way back up to where Duncan was waiting. He gave him a thumbs-up sign and then followed Duncan's head nod toward Lipton.

It was a wonderful feeling to see a fish swallow the bait so completely. Lipton was already feeling extremely impressed with himself after completing his dealings with Baum. Now, this incredible woman was occupying his airspace. For her part, Nora wondered how long she'd have to keep up this charade. She wanted to jump right into foreplay, let him know that she was horny and ready to get the hell out of here. But that might spook him into thinking something was amiss. A woman like her just didn't fall from the sky and into your lap.

Nora had put herself in compromising positions before to take down a target or ensure an operation's success. In none of those situations, though, could she recall wanting to inflict as much pain as she wanted Lipton to feel. It made her nauseated to think they were supposedly on the same team.

You poor little bitch. Soon you'll be mine, Nora thought as she smiled at the smug son of a bitch's feeble attempts to be charming. In order to avoid hearing his voice, she took him to the dance floor, despite his mild protests about not being a good dancer. She kept him on the floor for a long time, working up quite a sweat. The heat radiating from her body made him want her even more, and every so often, she would coyly rub her breasts or pelvis against him while gyrating to the beat. He wanted to protest the awkwardness of being on the dance floor so long, but he didn't dare do anything to blow the possibility of sleeping with her. Nora started counting in her head when she saw Alex and Duncan exit the club. She wanted to give them ample time to get in place, and besides, the dancing was actually liberating. It allowed her to relieve a sliver of stress and forget momentarily the predicament her life was currently in. She still had to deal with this bastard who actually thought he had a chance to get her in bed. She pulled Lipton close so she could talk in his ear, purposely letting him feel the sweat drip from her body.

"Do you have a car?"

He enthusiastically told her he was parked a couple of blocks down.

"Great. So am I. Let's get out of here. You can follow me to my place where we can sweat some more," Nora offered with a nibble of his ear, pressing her body hard against his for further effect. She then led him toward the exit.

Once outside, the night air hit their heated bodies and the

cooling effect was refreshing. They began walking down the street, Nora positioning her body close to his as they did so. She engaged him in small talk, trying to take his mind off the surroundings, forcing him to concentrate only on her and the location of his car.

"This is me," Lipton pronounced, coming to a halt in front of an Opel Vectra rental.

"I'm just in the next block." Nora then drew him close and kissed him hard on the lips. That caught him by surprise, and he and Nora stumbled backward against the car, her back bracing them. He realized she was stronger than she appeared as her hands held him up until he could find firm footing again. He placed one hand firmly on the roof of the rental while the other found Nora's left breast. She could tell he was totally aroused as they kissed again. Thankfully, it was all about to end.

Nora shifted her glance toward Alex's hovering figure. Duncan was to his side, his frame effectively blocking the view of anyone back along the street toward the club. Nora withdrew her lips and quickly angled her head away from Lipton. He thought she was being coy and made an attempt to kiss her neck, but his intention was derailed by the fierce blow that came crashing down on the back of his neck. Lipton's body immediately went totally limp. Once again, Nora held him up, but this time Alex also grabbed hold, allowing her to escape from underneath. She searched his pockets and found the car keys, unlocking the doors. Alex threw Lipton's body in the back seat, unconcerned how it landed. Duncan came around and slid in alongside the unconscious man. Alex shut the door, and seconds later, with Nora behind the wheel, the Opel was out of its parking space and moving down the road.

Alex continued up the street to their rental car and took off in the same direction as Nora. As he drove, he knew there was no turning back now.

CHAPTER **28**

"You!"

Davis Lipton was barely coherent, his mind slowly surfacing from the fog. His eyes were watery and narrowed, but he recognized the man who'd bumped into him at the nightclub. Sensing a sizeable amount of discomfort that ran from the back of his neck and down his spine, Lipton made an attempt to raise a hand. It was then he discovered that duct tape secured him to an uncomfortable chair.

Alex straddled a chair across from him, his arms resting comfortably atop the back.

The pain made it difficult for Lipton to keep his head raised for any measurable length of time. It felt much better to let it hang at an angle. He had no idea where they were. The room seemed large, but it could have been just a matter of perspective, since there was very little furniture, save for a few chairs and cabinet. There were no windows, so the only light source was a pair of low-wattage bulbs. The space felt stale, like a little-used basement. He took note that there was only one legitimate way out, and that was through a door toward the back. From the small space under the door seal he could tell it was lighter on the other side.

With clarity slowly returning, Lipton nervously began piecing together his predicament. Now was as good a time as any to end whatever this was. "If this is about money, you've grabbed the wrong guy. I don't have any."

Alex cocked his head. "I guess not. Especially since you recently handed over ten million dollars."

The reaction was quick and faint, but the acknowledgment was there with a shift of the eyes.

"See," said Alex, pointing at Lipton's face in a circular motion. "That's confirmation. So, Davis, show me that you're a smart guy by making this easy. Why are you paying Tobias Baum ten million dollars?"

"This is a big fucking mistake. Do you know who I am?"

"Yeah, and for what it's worth, I dislike your old man a whole lot more."

Alex reached down for a cup of coffee on the floor. He took a taste before continuing. "Let's try this again. What was the money for?"

"I don't know what you're talking about."

"Look, I'm a patient guy. I can sit here all day. However . . ." Alex turned to reference Nora, who was leaning against the back wall, her arms folded, waiting for her chance to step forward. "She is a different story. Your dance partner really, and I mean really, doesn't care for you at all. So, what's it going to be? Are you going to answer my question?"

"Again, I don't know what you're talking about."

Alex addressed his coffee once more. "Don't say I didn't warn you." He rose off the chair, taking it with him to give Nora plenty of room.

Lipton fought through the discomfort to raise his head. Her hair was now shorter, brunette, and pinned back. The revealing attire had been replaced with sweat pants and a sleeveless work-out T-shirt. It was unmistakably the same woman from the club. He watched with interest as she stood a few feet away, in no apparent hurry as she went about sliding her hands into a pair of thinly padded gloves.

Her next move was rapid and, for Lipton, painful. Nora took a big step forward and with her weight behind her, delivered a solid right-handed punch to the side of Lipton's face. His head snapped back as if on a coiled spring.

Nora tried to hold back her anger. Not hitting him as hard as she could was a nice gesture, but her patience was running thin. "The man asked you why you gave Baum ten million dollars."

Lipton shook off the grogginess. "Again, you're mistaken."

Nora followed his lie with a series of left-hand jabs, placing them just below his right cheekbone. When his head stopped bobbing, Lipton spat out some blood. He searched the room for the man who'd sat in front of him.

"Hey, you!" he shouted. "Come get a grip on this cunt!"

Off to the side, near the back of the room, Alex and Duncan, who had been quietly observing everything, exchanged surprised, uncomfortable glances. They knew what response that remark would bring and felt no need to intervene. After all, he did just call her the C word.

Nora didn't react right away; instead, she inched her face closer to Lipton's, careful not to get so close that he could head-butt her.

"Davis, we all know you aren't cut out for this. You're just a little pussy, and sooner, rather than later, you're going to tell us what we want to know. Trust me when I tell you that I have no qualms about hurting you. Somebody is going to pay for my friend's death, and I don't mind starting with you."

"Death. What death? What the hell are you talking about now?"

His retort brought forth a combination of strikes that would have made Sugar Ray Leonard raise an approving eyebrow. Lipton's face was starting to bruise, and soon swelling would accentuate the damage. He fought against the throbbing but knew he couldn't withstand much more. He wanted to believe the woman wouldn't dare go so far as to kill him, but she had been right about one thing. He wasn't cut out for this.

Through moist eyes, Lipton managed to speak with confidence. "It's pretty easy for you to beat on a defenseless man tied to a chair."

Nora shook her head in disbelief. "Well, fuck me. Where are my manners?" She approached Lipton while reaching around her waist, producing a medium-sized, razor-sharp knife. She cut Lipton's hands and legs free of the chair. She then smiled and in the blink of an eye, slammed the knife down hard between his legs, sticking it into the wooden chair's seat. Nora stepped away a few feet.

"Pick it up and use it. If you get by me," she said, looking over her shoulder, "they won't bother you. They'll gladly let you go free." She could almost sense Lipton's mind contemplating his options and the validity of her remarks.

"Pick it up. It's the only way you're getting out of here without telling me what I want to know."

Lipton slowly rose from the chair, rubbing his wrists, trying to get some circulation back. He'd had some training in self-defense, and despite her beauty, he'd gladly slice her up if it meant he got to leave. After all, she was asking for it. He put his hand around the knife and dislodged it from the chair.

"Yes, that's it, Davis. Pick it up."

He accepted the dare and moved the knife around in his hand until it felt comfortable. Nora watched his every move. Lipton went into a slight crouch as he crept toward her. She still had a slight smile on her face, which angered him even more. Two more steps and he'd be within range to strike. He tried to get her off balance by faking a thrust to her midsection. She held her ground, reached out, and slapped his hand away, which gave her an opening. In a move far too quick for him to counter, Nora moved inward and followed with a fierce kick to Lipton's chest, the force of which knocked him back a couple of feet. He let out a pained sigh as he reached for his chest. He was certain a rib or two were either cracked or broken, and it became harder to breathe as several more blows caved in his stomach, delivered by Nora's gloved hands. She retreated immediately after striking, conscious that Lipton might try to unleash a wild knife attack. Instead, he struggled just to stay on his feet.

"You know her name very well," Nora said, her fist clenched, ready to go again. "First you lied and ruined her career. Now she's dead, and I'm sure it has something to do with all of this."

"Who's dead?" asked Lipton, assessing his injuries.

"Erica Janway, you son of a bitch!" Nora accented her anger with a hard, roundhouse kick to Lipton's jaw that airlifted him for a second before he crashed with a thud to the floor. As Nora approached, she gathered the knife that had flown out of his hand and put it back in its sheath at the small of her back.

She stood over his crumpled body, her feet ready to strike once more. Lipton understood what was coming next. Other than feebly raise a hand, he was physically powerless to stop it.

"What do you mean Janway is dead?" he cried, hoping communication would end the assault. He literally couldn't take any more of a beating. Hours ago, the woman had promised him pleasure, not pain. "If she is, I had nothing to do with that."

"You better start making me believe you."

Lipton nodded his head, and Alex and Duncan came forward to help him get back into the chair. "I tried to tell you," said Alex in his ear. "Now, be a good little boy and answer all her questions truthfully."

Nora brought Lipton a glass of water, immediately regretting that she'd done so. He didn't deserve an ounce of kindness. Punishing him some more was what she really wanted to do. But since he was now willing to talk, inflicting more pain might have an adverse effect, making him think there was no reward for being honest.

Nora grabbed the same chair Alex had occupied and sat in front of Lipton. "Lie to me one time and I'll hurt you so bad you'll beg me to kill you."

Lipton slowly filtered a few sips of water down his throat, each swallow uncomfortable and mixed with blood. "I think you cracked my ribs," he said holding his chest.

"I'd be disappointed if I didn't."

Alex and Duncan once again made themselves comfortable in the background. Alex took out a small notepad and pen, wearily checking his watch in the process. If there was anything to Nora's suspicions, a major blank could be filled in here, providing, at the very least, a framework for moving forward. One didn't fork over ten million dollars to one of the most notorious black market dealers in the world without getting some bang for the buck.

"Now," Nora began, "let's try this again. From the beginning. Why did you tell those lies about Janway when she was station chief in Moscow?"

Lipton hesitated for a moment but realized he had no other option. "They needed her out of the Russian sector. They were hesitant about proceeding with her in place because they felt she might get wind of what was going on."

"And what *was* going on?"

"A covert operation."

"She was CIA and chief of station. Why run an op around her? Rather than ruin her career, why not brief her as to what was going on?"

Lipton let go an agonized sigh. "Sure you know Janway? She didn't do anything without proper protocol being followed. She would have wanted confirmation from the highest level. Raising that flag and running it through channels would have put the op in jeopardy. Plus, the Israelis were insistent their involvement be known only to a select few."

"Israelis? What the hell are you talking about?"

"They were a part of it. A joint operation."

Nora was stunned for a moment. "The Mossad trusted you?" Nora chuckled. "I warned you about lying." She was about to rise from the chair when he cut her off.

"They didn't talk to me! I was told that was their position."

"Who told you? Who did you trust to the point that you'd risk your career by bypassing protocol?"

Nora looked at the pathetic figure as he tried to avoid eye contact. "Oh, my god," she said, not needing to hear the answer. "Your dad is involved. Your own father has been running you. What the hell has he done?"

"He's a good man. He serves his country."

"Your father had Janway killed!"

"I refuse to believe that. And like I said, I don't know what you're talking about. The last I heard, she was on desk duty at Langley, waiting for that damned lawsuit of hers to move forward."

"And you would have lied again."

"I would've done what was necessary to ensure the success of this operation."

"Good for you, Davis. You read the manual. But I'm going to go out on a limb here and guess it's an operation that you know hardly anything about."

"It's on a need-to-know basis, yes, but I've played my part."

"Well, let's see how much you do know. What was the ten million for?"

Lipton wiped his sweaty forehead. "I'm not totally sure."

"Davis, do we have to dance again?"

"No! No! What I'm saying is, that was Baum's final payment. There were more before this one. He was paid for purchasing materials that couldn't be bought officially. He also arranged for transport."

"There've been other payments? For how long?"

"This has been going on for two, maybe three years."

"This last payment was for what, exactly?"

"Centrifuges."

The mention of the word got Duncan to sit up. He interrupted before Nora could get another question out. "How many centrifuges are we talking about and who are they for?" By Duncan's tone, Alex could tell the man was on to something.

"This shipment, roughly three, four hundred, I believe. I'm under the impression it's for Iran."

"Iran?" said Duncan. It was more of a reaction than question. "And you're sure there have been other shipments?"

Lipton nodded yes.

Duncan started mentally calculating. "This doesn't make sense," he mumbled to Alex.

Alex opened his hands, wanting his friend to elaborate.

Duncan spoke to Lipton again. "You said earlier the Israelis wanted Janway out of the sector. You sure your father was being truthful with you?"

"He wouldn't lie to me. I don't know the scope of the whole operation, but I trust that part is true."

Duncan motioned for Nora to continue, and then he gave Alex a concerned look. "It doesn't make sense," he repeated. "Why in the world would Israel supply one of its biggest enemies with materials to facilitate their nuclear program? But, if what he's saying is legit, there's some crazy shit going on, and its way, way above our heads."

Nora let them contemplate the possibilities as she addressed

Lipton again. "You said something about Baum arranging transport. So, what happens next?"

Sensing this was his only chance to escape this predicament or even perhaps this room alive, Lipton played the only card he had left. "If I'm not out of here and at the delivery point within three days, a bunch of alarms go off and everything gets shut down. The entire operation. So you need me. You see, I have to give the go-ahead to one more intermediary who then takes care of the final arrangements."

That statement brought Nora to a critical point. Why not shut the whole thing down? Whatever the intent, it was an unsanctioned deadly operation already. She could bring Davis and his father to justice. Murdering a CIA analyst on American soil was a serious crime. But then, Nora realized the power and influence of the people involved and besides, she didn't really have any concrete proof. Bringing charges at this point would only give all the co-conspirators time to cover their tracks and hide like roaches when the lights came on. She was convinced a thorough beating of Lipton would determine the absolute truth of his words. At the same time, gathering information in such a manner wouldn't necessarily be easy. Lipton would eventually black out from the pain, and they'd have to wait for him to come around—and there was the added risk he might discover some hidden courage and try to hold out until his aforementioned deadline. Plus, she believed her original assumption was true. There had to be only so much Lipton knew. He was too much of a liability to be totally informed.

Alex could sense Nora's frustration. "Let's talk," he said, motioning for her to join him in the hallway, not the slightest bit worried that Lipton would try something stupid with Duncan in the room watching over him.

Once the door shut behind them, Nora ran her fingers through her hair. She was truly at wit's end, her mind churning, looking for an avenue to take that would lead to somewhere promising. Alex grabbed her gently by the arm to calm her nerves, the first real overt act of concern or kindness on his part since they'd been reunited. This was difficult for him too, but he didn't want to give in to his emotions. He had purposely kept a safe emotional distance, knowing that tension and despair could weaken one's resolve, making it possible for old feelings to rush back in.

"I think Duncan's raised a pretty good point," said Alex, making sure they made eye contact. "On the surface, the Israelis helping Iran build anything nuclear—and doing so on an accelerated basis—doesn't have an ounce of plausibility."

"But, if it's true?"

"If it's true, there's a whole lot more than meets the eye. To protect an operation of this magnitude, whatever its endgame, people would go to any lengths." He noticed her pupils dilating. "Yes, even frame and murder a former chief of station and the agent she mentored. An agent who might screw this whole thing up."

"What now? It seems like this thing is too big for us to stop."

"Well, I'm no stranger to screwing things up."

She nervously snickered. "Shit. We're like pawns on a big-ass chessboard."

"You're on the right track, though. We need help."

"Alex, if I thought there was someone else," her eyes diverted to a faraway place for a moment, "I wouldn't have reentered your life. I'm sorry."

He had no doubt her words were sincere. "We're not beat yet. I think there's someone I can trust."

CHAPTER 29

Growing up in Southern California, Sara Garland had the opportunity to run and frolic outdoors on pretty much any day she wanted. That lifestyle started early. Her father had been the inspiration, often dragging Sara along on his many Pacific Coast Highway quests for big waves to surf. By her mid-teens, no longer afraid of the unknown, she was on par with her father's expertise. When the waves in California got mundane, she upped the ante by tackling skydiving.

During college, she could drink any man under the table, so if there was any taking advantage to be done, she always had the upper hand. It was obvious that with her drive, life was going to be whatever Sara Garland wanted it to be. As a college senior, there were countless well-paying corporate positions thrown her way, but on a cloudy-day whim, she sat down for an interview with the Central Intelligence Agency. During a campus recruiting push, the spy agency advertised that it was looking for the best and the brightest, which caused Sara to snicker. Since she wasn't taking this too seriously, she remarked to her interviewer, "It's about time, because you certainly don't have them in ample supply at the moment." Instead of taking offense, the recruiter agreed, admitting that mistakes had been made in the past and that America was getting shoved a shitpile of disservice in every walk of government life. Two months after graduation, Sara was an agent in training.

For the past couple of days, the monotony had set in to the point where she found it difficult to sleep at night. To take some of the edge off, she'd gotten into the habit of exiting her Georgetown hotel around midnight for a brisk jog. Her travels would either take her down the Rock Creek Parkway and back or across the Key Bridge into Arlington. Any sane woman would have known better than to be out that late, alone, tempting fate, but she was actually hoping some misguided soul would see her as easy pickings. Either attempted rape or robbery would suffice, allowing her the opportunity to use the small handgun tucked away in a waist pouch. Ridding the world of one more worthless piece of trash would ensure a good night's sleep. Disappointed every time, Sara was back at Langley shortly after sunrise each day to begin anew.

On this morning, she was frustrated because she had nothing. She made herself a nuisance, albeit a pleasant one, to the group of geeks in surveillance. Adrian Jennings didn't like to disappoint, but with no lead on a place to begin video surveillance, he reluctantly told Sara that locating Nora Mossa was like finding a needle in a haystack. It could take days, even weeks for a normal person to pop up on a video source, even given a limited radius. Take a person of Mossa's expertise, with the world as a hiding place, and it could take months. She would know how to disguise her appearance and be savvy enough to avoid eavesdropping devices when possible, making use of crowds to shield her presence.

Jason Bonderman also had no good news to pass along. The last time Mossa had surfaced using her own identification markers was at the Starbucks in Dupont Circle. Since then, there'd been nothing on her financials. Bonderman was sure she was moving under a false name with access to funds. Mossa obviously wasn't stupid or desperate enough to use identification and accounts set up for her by the agency. The scenario that had unfolded at Dupont Circle proved Mossa had assistance. That realization and the importance of knowing everything about the woman had Sara scrutinizing Mossa's file, double-checking repeatedly in case she had overlooked some minuscule clue. Mossa's father was deceased, and her mother's phone and house in Oregon were being monitored. Her relationships of note were being checked and dismissed at every turn. Fortunately, it wasn't a long list. Still, a woman could have her secrets.

On her way to George Champion's office for a status update,

she forcefully blew a few bangs off her forehead. She didn't want to come across as inefficient, but there was virtually nothing to ascertain. As the elevator let her out on Champion's floor, she continued to comb through Mossa's dossier. One aspect of it proved especially maddening. How was she supposed to adequately do background checks when certain sections were blacked out, beyond her clearance grade? On several of her reexaminations, she'd caught the mention of a name that appeared only once among a number of pages. It could've been blacked out in subsequent references, but she had no way of knowing. Attempts to do further research on the name within agency records were met with a sharp roadblock. She casually dropped the name to Jennings and Bonderman to see if it triggered anything. Again, all she'd gotten were frustrated shakes of heads. It was probably nothing, but she wanted to totally eliminate the reference rather than to have it be a loose end.

Mrs. Prescot was cordial as always, offering Sara something to drink before showing her into Champion's office. Looking fresh for a man working on little sleep, Champion rose but didn't glance away from his computer screen as he offered Sara a seat across from him.

She wasn't sure if he was talking to her or reasoning with himself when he spoke, settling back in his chair. "Dredging through the morning briefs. North Koreans are having some inventory problems that are troubling at the moment."

Champion finally looked up and noticed Sara hadn't come into his office empty-handed. "I see you still have Mossa's file. You've been carrying that thing around like a newborn. I hope it's burped up something worthwhile."

Sara fidgeted in her chair. Her clothing seemed uncomfortably attached to her skin. "Sir, I've checked in with Bonderman and Jennings to the point where I think they're playing darts with my picture. Ever since Dupont Circle, there's been absolutely no trace of her." She patted the file in her lap. "Granted, she's talented, but she's getting help. She definitely has documents and funds outside the ones issued by us. The money will only last so long, but if she really wants to maintain deep cover, with the proper paper she could immerse herself in the landscape, establish a credible cover, get a job, and make new acquaintances. If that happens, finding her could take . . ." Sara cleared her throat, ". . . could take some considerable time." The speculation received a less than pleased look, but Champion knew what she was saying was true.

"However," Sara continued, wanting that look to dissipate, "I believe Mossa has an agenda that makes her susceptible to taking some risks. I think she's operating under some assumptions connected to Janway. Maybe they had a way of communicating that we don't know about."

"So you think she has an agenda? What the hell does she think can be accomplished out there virtually naked?"

"At this point, without us precisely knowing what Janway was working on, Mossa's probably the only person who might be able to shed light on who's responsible for her death. Others might come to that conclusion as well."

Champion locked his hands together and glanced at his computer screen again. "I reached out to the various agencies that also showed up at Dupont Circle," he said, seemingly referencing material. "Without giving up much detail, the Department of Defense admitted they're on some sort of watch at the moment because a number of sensitive materials around the world have gone missing or are currently unaccounted for by various governments like North Korea. So they're in a slight state of paranoia. And these days, when the DOD sneezes, Homeland Security grabs a tissue."

Champion toyed with his coffee cup, which Sara took as a subtle hint that her time was nearly over. While she was here, she might as well ask. Sara riffled through Mossa's file to a section she had marked with a red sticky note. "Sir, in going over Mossa's file repeatedly, I came across a name that appears only once, at least in the parts that weren't redacted. Therefore I have no idea if it appears again because I'm not cleared to read the entire file. It's probably nothing, but I'm just trying to be thorough. I even went so far as to Google the name."

"So you're asking for security clearance to read the remainder of her file?"

"I think it would be helpful."

"What's the name? At the very least, I might be able to grant you access to sections if the name appears anywhere else in her file." Champion smiled for a moment. "You Googled the name? What did you find out?"

"Well, the most hits pointed to an ex—" Sara was cut off because Mrs. Prescot beeped in over the phone's intercom.

"Mr. Champion?"

"Yes, Mrs. Prescot?"

"There's a call for you on line two. It's a bit unusual because it's not coming through normal channels, but the caller insists you know him and will take the call. I can get a number and give it to you later."

"Humor me, Mrs. Prescot. Who's on the line?"

"The gentleman says his name is Alex Koves."

Champion's eyes grew wide as he stood up. "Son of a bitch," he mumbled.

Sara had slowly risen from her chair as well once she'd heard the name over the speaker. Seeing Champion's reaction, she said, "That's the name, sir. Alex Koves. He's an ex—"

"Pro football player."

"Yes."

Champion gathered himself. "Well, he's much more than that. Thank you, Mrs. Prescot. I'll take the call."

Champion pressed the corresponding line, dispatching it from hold status. He took it off speaker phone and held the handset to his ear.

"Alex?"

"George," Alex playfully said on the other end. "How the hell are you?"

"It's been a long time. Alex, do you have something that belongs to us?"

"Well, you have to be more specific."

"You know damn well what I'm talking about."

"Yeah, but which *one* are you talking about?"

Agitated, Champion nearly bit his lip. "What the hell do you mean, 'Which one?'"

"George, we have to talk."

CHAPTER 30

The noise from the twin engines of the C-37A turbofan filled the spacious cabin with a gentle hum. If there'd been any ongoing conversation between its three passengers, the engines probably wouldn't have been noticed at all. It was a smooth ride with just a few hiccups of turbulence, which was expected as they traveled over the Atlantic.

Except for taking and making several calls on the plane's secure line, George Champion sat in relative silence. The plane was approaching the United Kingdom, but it wouldn't be landing. Instead, its flight plan called for flying over the country on its way to Brussels National Airport. Champion didn't need to look up to know that Sara Garland was monitoring his demeanor. The cabin's other passenger sat a few seats back, catching up on some sleep since there was no telling how long the next leg of the journey might be and while in the air, his assignment was certainly secure and safe.

Sara knew not to press for answers. Though she still didn't know much of anything about him, she was, at least, on her way to meet Alex Koves. It was obvious he and Champion had a prior relationship, which led Sara to believe Alex had been an agency employee in some capacity at one time.

He could have been a NOC (non-official cover) agent. But how a former professional football player might have any significance as an asset was beyond her scope of understanding at the moment.

When he wasn't making phone calls, Champion kept his head

buried in a file. Sara noted he didn't study the contents as if he were seeing them for the first time. Instead, he thumbed through it much like one reconnects with a favorite novel or crams for an exam. He appeared to know the material; he just wanted to be doubly sure. When he finally clasped the file closed, he shut his eyes and rubbed the narrow landing between them, trying to gently massage some stress away. All of a sudden, he rose and headed for the galley. When he returned, he had two glasses of Scotch. He handed one to Sara.

"You strike me as the kind of person who can knock back a few. I hope Scotch is okay."

With no hesitation, she swallowed a generous amount. "I've had my moments."

Champion reached for the file he'd been perusing. He held it out for Sara to take. She had an unsure look until Champion waved it in his hand, urging her to take it.

"It's the watered-down version," he said as she grabbed the folder. He concentrated on his Scotch while she glanced over it. After a few pages, Sara looked up, puzzled.

"I first met Alex when he was a junior in college," Champion said as he began to provide background on what was either buried in the pages in Sara's hands or omitted because they were in a much thicker, more secure document. He relayed how impressed he'd been to learn that Alex spoke fluent Arabic, thanks to instruction from his Lebanese girlfriend at the time. He then took it one step further by developing a passable understanding of Farsi. Champion pointed out that he had accomplished that while being a high-profile athlete destined for a lucrative career in the professional ranks, managing to also maintain an A average in business administration.

Sara returned her attention to the folder. Champion was with the agency then, and Alex had represented mission impossible in terms of recruitment. While Champion had ascended the ladder at the CIA, he kept up with Alex's pro career. During his fourth year in the league, in a playoff game against the Steelers, disaster had happened. Alex had emerged from a pile after making a crucial, bone-crushing tackle. His teammates were patting him on the back and smacking his helmet until it was noticed his balance was noticeably off. The third concussion of his career was deemed serious enough that it ended his season and ultimately, his career. Rather than shrink into self-pity, Alex accepted his fate and transitioned into a new career of money management, creating his own company.

A year after Alex had left the spotlight of the NFL, Champion paid him a visit in St. Thomas, where he'd worked in a modest office building. It took several days of convincing, but Champion had bagged his prize recruit. Alex missed the rush football had provided, and he was on board with the war against terror. Extreme training ensued, accelerated by Alex's proficiency in martial arts. He'd gotten a black belt during his junior year in college after realizing how much the discipline improved his overall quickness and strength on the football field. Since his money management career was a success, its legitimacy provided a perfect cover for his CIA employment.

Sara was so engaged, she didn't realize she'd emptied her glass or that Champion had refilled it. The folder's brief detail told her that Alex's early assignments sent him to Europe, where his command of languages again accelerated his development. From what she could decipher, he had helped identify and apprehend terror suspects and was part of operations that thwarted planned attacks against US interests and that of its allies, but Alex's biggest value played out in hotbed theaters like Afghanistan and Iraq.

Champion took a moment to point out that, for security purposes, the exact nature of Alex's assignments had to remain above her clearance level, but why he was no longer employed by the agency was an important detail.

"Following the invasion of Iraq, things, as you already know, were one chaotic mess after another, year after year," Champion said, pausing only to listen to the pilot announce they were about thirty minutes from landing. "It was a public relations nightmare for the White House. There was intense pressure to produce results. Alex was eventually put in place to cultivate and recruit assets in the region. He was a rising star. His expertise in the region put him in position to run point on a number of ops. He was given a big leash. And then one day, some officials in Washington felt that leash was too big."

"May I ask why?"

"Alex was adamant that a source our government was paying very well and held in high regard was working both sides, mostly against us. It ruffled a lot of feathers."

"Did he have proof?"

"Nothing that would convince a group of people who really didn't want to listen. What set Alex off was that a number of his assets were being targeted and executed. Their families included. Others just disappeared, presumably killed. Doors that were previously open to him all of sudden got slammed in his face. It got to the point where his life was very much in danger as well. We suspected the Russians, who were trying to salvage as much authority as possible during the collapse by assuring warring factions that they still had a measure of influence and would be rewarded in the aftermath for valuable intel. Still, the higher-ups didn't believe the person Alex pointed a finger at would betray them.

"Alex and Mossa were also dating at the time. I didn't know how serious it was, but apparently, they were very much an item. Their relationship, though, hit a wall when even she questioned him, begging him to drop the issue. But as I said, people Alex had befriended were dying around him. So he pressed. And pressed hard. Almost cost me my career as well."

Champion addressed the confused look on Sara's face.

"That's because . . . I did believe him."

"So you got a lot of heat because he was under your guidance and wouldn't back off."

"It got really dicey when part of the matter got resolved."

"How?" Sara fidgeted. "That is, if I'm allowed to know."

"Alex resigned."

"That had to be convenient for a lot of people."

"Yes. But he resigned right after he killed the man he had been accusing. In doing so, he also got the evidence he needed to prove the man's guilt."

"So he was exonerated."

"His actions pissed off a lot of suits who sit around and make policy decisions. The man's death caused a few political and strategic ramifications that had to be dealt with very delicately. A few lies had to be created as to how the man died. Alex, though, walked away from the agency and from Nora. Never looked back. Wouldn't take my phone calls or agree to meet. So now you're up to speed."

"I apologize if I'm asking for too much information, but who did he kill?"

Champion drained the contents of his glass.

"The former Iraqi foreign minister. He'd been on the payroll for quite some time. Alex is someone you really don't want to cross."

CHAPTER **31**

The European drew little attention to himself. Brief with his words, he was polite and courteous while going through the process of checking into the hotel. He appeared tired. His thin-framed glasses were a window to weary eyes. For good measure, he let loose a drawn-out yawn. He was apologetic, but the female front desk clerk understood. Had she looked, his passport would've indicated he was Swiss and had been in and out of several other European countries during the past week, hence his lethargy.

After handing over his credit card, the man ran a hand through his slightly unkempt graying hair, aware that he needed some basic maintenance, like a shower. It wouldn't hurt either to trim his equally graying mustache. Thankfully, the registration process didn't take long, something he had counted on after planning to arrive at such a late hour.

He'd arrived in Kuwait City only a few hours ago, spending an extra thirty minutes at the airport before hailing a taxi. He used the time to make sure there were no eyes taking a particular interest in his arrival. Once satisfied, he was on his way to the hotel. There were the traditional telltale signs that one was in the Middle East, but there was no escaping some influences of the West. There'd been a McDonald's and Starbucks in the airport. The hotels bore the names of very recognizable franchises as well. Yet, there still seemed to be enough of Kuwait's culture in place to distinguish it as a place in tune with its past.

The Swiss traveler uttered his thanks and took a couple of

steps before turning back to address the front desk. "I'm sorry," he said. "By any chance, did a package arrive for me?"

The clerk searched her area, sifted through a few unseen items, and produced a padded express mail envelope.

"Here you go, sir."

He didn't bother with a bellboy since he had only a single piece of wheeled luggage and now his express package. A few minutes later he was walking down a quiet hallway to his room. Once inside, he deposited his suitcase and envelope on the bed, removing only his toiletry bag as he headed for the bathroom. He took off all his clothes after adjusting the shower temperature. Before the bathroom mirror began to fog, he started probing sections of his thick hair. He went about removing several small, plastic pins, and moments later, the gray highlighted wig was off his head. He placed it on the countertop next to the pair of glasses that were prescription in appearance only. Next he applied a small amount of specialized gel to his mustache before pulling it free from his face. His thick eyebrows received the same treatment. When he was done, Nathan Yadin let out a sigh of relief and stepped into the shower. He took his time washing the day away. Periodically, he increased the level of hot water. Feeling totally cleansed, he dried off and wrapped a towel around his waist.

He made his way back into the outer room and stretched out on the bed, reaching for the express mail envelope. Yadin dumped out its contents. He casually rummaged through the items, briefly glancing at the face and name on a passport. The packet also included credit cards and a driver's license, along with nearly eight hundred euros. Satisfied, he put it all back into the envelope and slid it into the bedside table drawer. He unpacked only one set of clothes, laying them neatly on top of the dresser. After that, he returned to bed, tossing aside the spread. He allowed his mind to reflect on what lay ahead for only a few minutes before turning out the bedside light. As he drifted off to sleep, he thought of Lauren and the good time he had while briefly in Crete. He missed her touch and smell, wishing the respite could have lasted longer.

It didn't take long for him to fall soundly asleep.

CHAPTER **32**

The penetrating stare totally betrayed the words that were forth-coming, and in so doing, reduced their effectiveness. The cat was out of the bag, and it had left a huge mark.

Still, George Champion couldn't contain himself. The words had to be said. "Is this some kind of joke?" He shot up a protest-ing hand immediately. "No, you don't have to answer that, be-cause it's obvious you've been misled. The Israelis running point on a major operation for years against Iran, involving a high ranking member of Congress and utilizing a black market arms dealer whose life they've threatened. Just making sure I've got all of this straight. And you put this whole thing together in a matter of days?"

"Trust me; I'd rather not be here. I called in a few favors, did some legwork, and it sort of fell in our lap."

"The whole damn idea is preposterous."

"Now, where have I heard that before?" Alex said with a smirk as he leaned back.

"Oh, don't start that shit now. You still had a career. You chose to walk away. You weren't forced out," Champion coun-tered, realizing his voice might be getting too loud.

"What would my future have been? Reassigned like Janway?"

"Nice. So you're partially up to speed on some internal mat-ters, and now you're drawing conclusions."

Neither would admit it, but when they'd first cast eyes upon each other, there'd been a shared feeling of admiration, as well as regret that their paths hadn't crossed for such a long time. After exchanging a smileless handshake, Alex had led Champion to a corner booth in the dimly lit coffee shop. Sara Garland was on Champion's heels while his bodyguard located a seat that afforded him a view of his boss's booth.

Once seated, Champion made introductions. "Sara Garland, meet Alexander Koves."

Alex gave her a polite nod of the head. "Nice to meet you. I'm sure you're a wonderful asset to the agency, but good-bye, Sara Garland."

Champion came to her defense. "She's with me."

"I don't know her," Alex responded. "So, please go take a seat with Fred Flintstone over there."

Sara kept her frustration below the surface, mostly because she was somewhat amused by Alex's brashness. Champion was no longer his superior, and this whole venture across the pond was conducted because the former employee had something he wanted. It was all about leverage.

Champion caved and motioned for Sara to join their associate.

"His name is Roger, by the way," Champion said as Sara exited without fanfare.

Alex made note of the name, hoping he wouldn't have reason to actually remember it. "Thanks for coming," Alex said, casually noticing Sara's physique as she walked away.

"Didn't think I had much of a choice, but you could've saved the taxpayers a nice hunk of change if you had requested this meeting in Washington, since you were there recently."

"Yeah, well, at the time, it was important to assess the threat level. And since you didn't get a call . . ." Alex let the sentence linger.

"You honestly think I'd have a reason to harm one of my own?"

"Not knowingly."

Champion leaned in closer. "What the hell is that supposed to mean? These aren't the Kim Philby days," he huskily said, referencing a bygone era of betrayal within the CIA and British intelligence. "The names have changed dramatically, and so has the playing field."

"Come on. Not even you can believe that crap. The names behind the names are still the same. Outsourcing is the new deniability."

"We can debate this all day, but I happen to have a jet in a hanger with a crew that's accruing overtime at a rate that's increasing the national debt."

Alex was halfway through his cup of coffee when the waitress made an appearance. She refreshed his cup and asked what she could bring the booth's newest occupant. Champion inspected the place for a moment and then passed on ordering anything.

"Hold on a minute," Alex told the waitress. "George, I know you love coffee, and this may not be a shrine to Juan Valdez, but the coffee is exceptional."

Champion needed something to erase the taste of Scotch, so he yielded and ordered a cup per Alex's recommendation. They didn't want to interrupt any sensitive conversation, so the meat of their exchange would wait until after Champion received his coffee.

"I see your business is doing very well," Champion offered, trying to make small talk on at least an interesting topic.

"You pulled my financials," Alex retorted with a smile, appreciating the thoroughness. "You know, I can even make that government stipend of yours work for you. It's not too late."

The waitress returned with Champion's coffee, and after a couple of sugars, he took a hesitant sip. "Hmmm," he whispered, raising an appreciative eyebrow.

"See, there are times I know what I'm talking about."

"To that end . . ." Champion took another taste and then placed the cup down. "What *are* you doing? You're not in the game anymore. What's so important that I had to come all the way over here? And where is Nora Mossa?"

Alex began to tell his former mentor everything he'd been able to ascertain over the past several days. He watched intently as Champion soaked it all in, his eyes adjusting with each shocking revelation. Not wanting to write anything down, Champion was putting all the pieces together in his mind. Though he didn't interrupt Alex, it was beginning to sound like a fairy tale, a classic case of disinformation. There was a time he wouldn't have questioned

Alex's observations, but there was plenty of rust sitting across from him.

Alex, when he wrapped up, purposely left out any reference to Davis Lipton, sensing he would need it later.

Champion bumped his head slightly against the wall of the booth as he pushed back. "I'll say it again. This has to be some kind of joke," he said. "Somebody has put this tale in the wind to see how it would stick."

"I don't think you can wave a magic wand and bring Janway back. Seems like a big risk to take just to see how something might stick."

"It's time to end this charade. Where is Nora Mossa?"

Alex had been waiting for this moment, and without Champion noticing, he grabbed his cell phone and sent a prewritten text message.

"You want to see Nora?"

"If she still considers herself an employee of the CIA, I damn well demand it."

Alex's ability to see the front door of the establishment was aided by a high mounted mirror Champion couldn't see because his back was to it. Alex didn't really need the mirror, though. From across the room, Sara's reaction told him Nora had entered. Sara stiffened just enough, and then she gave Fred Flintstone a subtle nod. Sara was rising to position herself on Nora's flank when she totally disappeared from Alex's view. Standing high above her and the man from Bedrock was Duncan's imposing figure. He had stepped forward from the seat behind them.

"What do you say we let them have some quiet time?" Duncan said, with a suggestive hand in the side pocket of his jacket. "Everybody is going to be just fine. If you need anything"—he motioned to the chair behind Sara—"I'll just be right here." Duncan then sat down and motioned for them to do the same.

Champion sensed that Alex's sudden silence wasn't because he'd run out of things to say. Instead, he felt the presence of someone just outside his peripheral vision.

Before he could turn his head, Nora took a seat next to Alex.

"One field agent, as promised," Alex announced.

Champion had only met Nora a couple of times. Once was during a joint operation he'd conducted with Janway. She'd boasted about her young agent, and he, in turn, had bragged about his protégé, Alex. As a refresher, he had gone over her file, and seeing her now, he was surprised how subtle changes like shorter hair, of a different color, had changed her appearance.

"Miss Mossa, are you all right?"

"Yes, sir."

"You've generated a lot of man hours. You didn't feel that you could bring this . . ." Champion rested his eyes upon Alex for a moment, "this . . . concern to your superiors?"

"With all due respect, sir, not after Erica was murdered. Her assumptions are what got her killed, and she passed those along to me. I didn't think it was wise to sit around and wait for the cavalry to arrive."

"Not even if it was your own people?"

"Especially my own people."

An exasperated Champion raised his hands to shoulder height. "Okay, I've sat here and listened to the far-fetched story our friend here is pitching. Do you have anything of significance to add?"

Nora shot Alex a look, seeking reassurance. "I know it sounds completely ridiculous," she said. "Why would the Israelis aid a country whose leadership has, time and again, called for their extinction? A country that has even funded terrorist organizations in attacks against them. The answer has to be that the Israelis are running some kind of operation. Something spectacular. Exactly what that is, we have no idea."

"Even if it has legs on some level, you've implicated a high-ranking member of Congress. You've also suggested he's complicit in the murder of a CIA agent. Damn it, we're talking about Senator Bryce Lipton here. You know how much juice he has? He can call and get a tee-time with the president. Hell, he can darn near initiate a war on his own."

"You've essentially confirmed that he's in a position to pull something like this off," Alex chimed in.

"We have some proof, sir," Nora offered, cutting off Champion's anticipated fire-breathing.

"Proof. Now there's a word I haven't heard. What kind of proof?"

Again, Nora glanced at Alex, unsure if she should continue. This time he led the conversation. "George, when I called yesterday, remember I asked you, which asset?"

"I'm damn sure I don't like where this is going. What have you two done?"

Feeling the best way to get it over with was to get it out, Nora blurted, "We got the confirmation from Davis Lipton."

"Holy shit," Champion exhaled. "You got it how? Where is he now?"

"Sedated. Sleeping it off," Nora answered.

"Sleeping what off?"

"His injuries," said Alex.

If this had been his office at Langley, Mrs. Prescot would have heard his agitated voice, despite the thick door being firmly shut. As this was a public place, it took every ounce of restraint Champion could muster to contain himself.

With Champion's laser beam pupils burning through him, Alex said, "Don't look at me. I'm just along for the ride."

Champion diverted his wrath to Nora. "Injuries! Do you have any idea how many rules you've broken? This is your career, or what used to be one. What happens when Davis files a report? You think his father isn't going to get to the bottom of this? He heads up the Senate Select Committee on Intelligence, for God's sake! You interrogated a fellow government agent."

"Sir, the end justifies the means here. Davis is going to be fine. He only has a couple of cracked ribs and a slight concussion at worst—he'll be just fine. He's damn fortunate that's all he's got."

"Don't get cute. All this for what? Risk your career for what?"

"Sir, he admitted to setting Janway up."

"Setting her up how?"

"The accusations that got her removed from Moscow were all fabricated. He said his father ordered him to do it because they needed her out of the sector. They were afraid she'd get wind of their operation and wouldn't go along. As best we can tell, thousands of centrifuges have been moved out of Russia and into the hands of the Iranians for their nuclear program. Davis left no doubt that his father and the Israelis are involved. We were there when he transferred ten million dollars to a black market dealer. That kind of money had to come from somewhere."

"What about Janway's death?"

"I pressed him on that, and he seemed surprised. Claims his father wouldn't go that far. Frankly, I'm not so sure. You can see him if you'd like. Take him back with you and let the specialists at the Farm take a crack at him.

"Oh, no." Champion exhaled. "I have no intention of getting near him. All I can do at this point is make quiet, polite inquiries. Any exit strategy here? Since you're rolling the dice as you go along, what do you plan to do with him at this point?"

"We have one more card to play. He claims there's a final shipment that's supposed to be heading for Iran. But it has to be inspected and approved by a go-between before the order can proceed. Davis says he has to be the one who gives this person his marching orders."

Champion sat bewildered for a second, amazed he was giving this even the slightest consideration. "What makes you think Davis doesn't know you're CIA?"

"I don't think he's quite put that together yet," Nora confirmed. "He's scared and confused. I'm sure he doesn't believe that someone from the agency, knowing who he is, would dare interrogate him."

"I have a hard time believing it myself. When and where does he have to meet with this person?"

"He says there was a three-day window. If he doesn't make contact by the allotted time, all sorts of red flags go up, and the operation gets scrubbed. His contact and the merchandise will be in Tbilisi. If Davis is pulling our chain, this person won't exist, and there won't be several truckloads of centrifuges ready for transport. But my gut tells me he's not lying."

Champion was speechless as his mind raced. He was not happy with Mossa's conduct for sure, but he was even more pissed at the possibility that an operation was being run under his nose, utilizing assets from his department. If Senator Lipton was truly involved, how many other government agencies were being used as well?

"One more thing," Nora said, breaking the silence, "I don't see a connection, but Janway also made reference to North Korea several times in her notes."

Champion tried not to let on, but too many coincidences in this business generally formed the framework of a puzzle. There *was* that damning thing with the North Koreans. Despite assurances that they would be found, several IRBMs—intermediate range ballistic missiles—were mysteriously unaccounted for. Such was the state of cooperative politics with the North. Champion had a sickening feeling when he thought of where those IRBMs might be now. For the moment, though, he decided he'd keep that thought off the table.

"I'll look into it," he assured Nora.

Her eyes opened wide. "So, you believe us?"

"I'm not quite sure what the hell to believe, but as I mentioned, I'll look into some things. In the meantime, you take very good care of Davis Lipton—and you've only got a couple of days to let this play out. If Tbilisi turns out to be bullshit, you release him immediately. But understand, Miss Mossa, your actions in this whole thing will be severely scrutinized. I must be out of my mind for not putting an end to this right now."

Alex formed the hint of a grin. "Sometimes, George, you just have to let a hunch play out."

"Screw you," he shot back. "And don't think I'm not considering bringing your private-citizen ass up on charges for assaulting a government employee. Fortunately, the guy you roughed up in Washington is going to be okay."

Alex winced. "You know, I almost forgot about that. I'm truly sorry about it, too. But, if I may, he does need some field training."

"The situation was slightly outside his expertise, but I'll pass along your sentiments."

"How do you want us to keep in touch?" Alex asked.

For the first time since he'd sat down, Champion was able to foster a sinister smile. "Simple enough. From this point on, Miss Garland will be by your side."

Nora hunched her shoulders as she turned to Alex with a puzzled look.

Alex rolled his eyes as he glanced over to where his added baggage was sitting.

"I'll explain it to you in a minute."

CHAPTER 33

The rain began to pelt the pavement with more regularity, forcing the expansion of umbrellas. Champion didn't mind the rain, especially since he was moving faster than the flow of pedestrian traffic as he made his way up Fifteenth Street NW. It was just past one thirty in the afternoon when he reached his destination, and the lunch crowd was still packed inside the popular restaurant. On his own, he would have had to wait for a table or take a chance that a seat was available at one of the bars scattered throughout the establishment. However, once Champion informed the receptionist whom he was joining, he was whisked away promptly. Passing table after occupied table, he recognized a smattering of inside-the-Beltway political faces holding court. Thank goodness his own face was an obscure one. The noise level was deafening in pockets, producing a near-stadiumlike chorus. After a few more paces, his lunch companion saw him coming and rose to greet him.

"George." The middle-aged brunette affectionately gave him a hug.

"Amanda, so good to see you," Champion said, upon separating. "You look no worse for the wear. Power agrees with you."

"My, my, dishing out the compliments early," she responded, inviting him to sit down in the booth, which he did across from her.

"Thanks for seeing me on such short notice."

"Hey, I was in the neighborhood," she playfully pointed out.

Amanda Jergens did, in fact, work just a few steps away, at the most prestigious address in the world: 1600 Pennsylvania Avenue. Though her face, like Champion's, was less recognizable than some in the restaurant, there wasn't a place in the District with any political savvy that wouldn't seat her right away. Amanda trumped all of the restaurant patrons as White House deputy chief of staff.

"So, how goes life in the fast lane?" Champion asked, while perusing the menu.

Amanda sighed. "Potholes everywhere and too much time spent on fixing all the flat tires left behind by the previous administration. How are things in the dark corners of the world?"

"Hard to see the light some days, which is partly why I called you yesterday."

"Of course, I'm curious to know why you asked for what you did, but for now, I'll settle for your assurance that my man has nothing to be concerned about."

"I'll definitely tell you if and when there's something to lose sleep over. But I'm seriously trying to rule out your man."

"I realize that cloak-and-dagger is your modus operandi, but still, calling me on my personal cell and insisting we not use e-mail or print out copies . . . ," Amanda said with a raised eyebrow.

"Harmless as I hope it is, I don't want anything sticking to you. Asking to see the visitor's log for the past six months shouldn't raise any flags."

"Yes, there are literally thousands of names to sort through, unless you're looking for specific ones, which you are."

Seeing Champion and Jergens together at lunch or even in each other's personal space at a function didn't give anyone reason to question such encounters. Those in the know were aware of their deep-rooted friendship, formed in college and continued long afterward, when Champion introduced Jergens to her future husband. She'd been building a prosperous life in the private sector, one of those driven, no-time-for-serious-personal-life types, when Champion and his wife invited her down from New York City for a few days of sailing on the Chesapeake. She'd had no clue about there being a fourth person involved. That fourth turned out to be the US ambassador to Spain, and a few hours after setting sail, she found herself no longer upset with her good friends but instead very infatuated with the man that would become the love of her life. In college, Jergens and Champion were drinking and party buddies. They never took the relationship further, as both realized they enjoyed something special that was nonsexual in nature. Their careers took different paths, but their friendship had remained intact. She used to poke fun at his devotion to anything spy-related: books, movies, and real-life world events. She herself had a mind for business and making money. It was no surprise to Champion that after landing a lucrative job post-college, she quickly climbed the corporate ladder, eventually being hired as CFO of a major Fortune 500 company. Her success coupled with her husband's political connections led to a chance encounter with the man who would become president of the United States. He was so impressed with her credentials that he offered her a post in his administration. Jergens didn't hesitate to put her private-sector career on hold for what she felt was a higher calling.

"Let me put some of your fears to rest," Amanda said. "Only one person with direct ties to Israel has visited more than once in the last six months. An aide attached to the Israeli embassy, named Daniel Wassermann. He didn't meet with the president, and I'm sure the president doesn't even know Wassermann."

"I assume he didn't visit for the food, so who did he see and for how long?"

"The first time, five months ago, Wassermann spent forty-five minutes with Matt Mendelson, a special assistant to the president for economic policy. There happen to be seven people with that job description, by the way. The second time, Mendelson again, only this one was for roughly a half hour, three weeks ago."

Champion took a moment to absorb the names and circumstances. "Do you know Wassermann's title at the embassy?"

"Deputy minister for economic affairs. I had to research that one, because they don't always sign with name, rank, and serial number."

Champion developed a concerned look on his face. "And just how did you . . ."

"Get that information?"

"I told you I wanted to keep you sterile on this."

"You think you're the only one who's good at this cloak-and-dagger stuff? Apparently, young Mr. Wasserman has caught the eye of a few female interns. We had a small, girls-only evening snack yesterday, and I casually asked who he was and what he did."

"Did the interns have a clue as to what Wasserman and Mendelson have been meeting about?"

"Not a one. Look, could be just two young Jewish boys talking about bedding some interns."

"Surely that's frowned upon over there, even now."

Amanda laughed. "Common sense and human nature often clash. Now, as for Senator Lipton, he's been there three times, but given his title, that's to be expected. On each visit he met with the president. Twice he was accompanied by others, and the third, he had a good fifteen minutes of one-on-one time."

Champion again slipped into a minor trance. On the surface, everything seemed harmless, just normal business being conducted at the White House. The place was like a conglomerate unto itself: daily tours, press conferences, photo ops, lobbyists, food service. Uncovering a needle in the haystack would require constant monitoring, and that kind of access was impossible to obtain for an outsider.

"You seem disappointed," Amanda pointed out.

"Believe me when I say I'm relieved more than anything. Now, what do you say we actually have lunch?"

He didn't want her to agonize any further over what could turn out to be absolutely nothing. Her job was difficult enough. He also didn't feel the need to tell her Daniel Wassermann's life was about to go under a microscope.

CHAPTER 34

It was nearly unanimous that he be left behind. The only dissenting vote came from Davis Lipton. He realized that staying behind meant he had no more bargaining chips.

He couldn't believe he had been both careless and stupid enough to be in this jam. Who were these people? At first it crossed his mind they were part of a rogue organization out to make a profit on the knowledge they'd gained. But he later concluded they were much more. The beating he took from the woman was severe but skilled. She knew precisely where to place her blows to inflict damage. That took training. The way he was set up even indicated a certain degree of operational ability. They'd also taken him to the brink of believing that killing him was not out of the realm of possibility if he didn't cooperate. How did they know about Erica Janway? They were aware of who his father was, and that didn't scare them at all. His CIA cover was blown, too. Had Tobias Baum sold him out? After all, the black market dealer had been paid, so what did he care about Lipton? Perhaps doing so led to another nice payday. No, Baum wouldn't dare. Doing that would risk his personal well-being. The Israelis would exact revenge— unless that had been their plan all along. There were hundreds of scenarios running through his mind, but figuring out what had brought him here was not the most important thing. What mattered most was survival.

His captors persuaded him to tell them everything about the contact in Tbilisi. They told him they'd get the information they wanted even if he didn't cooperate. He was assured that route would be painful.

Self-preservation won out. He gave them what they needed to know. Including the truth that he'd never met the contact in Tbilisi face-to-face and real names were never exchanged. A few hours later, a doctor was allowed in to treat his wounds. It was only then that he no longer feared for his life. They wouldn't bother patching him up after getting what they wanted if they were just going to kill him anyway.

Davis slowly succumbed to the pain medication and drifted off. The first time he came out of the haze, he encountered a pair of new faces. The trio he had come to know and loathe was nowhere in sight.

CHAPTER 35

Even under an assumed name, traveling with Nora still presented a tremendous risk. Champion hadn't lifted the all-points bulletin for her, because doing so might raise suspicion, and at least for now, he was willing to see if this wild story had any merit.

With no direct flight from Brussels, the trip to Tbilisi took over eight hours. It seemed even longer as Sara Garland tried her best to get Alex to open up. He had no one to blame but himself. It was his idea to separate and travel as two pairs. Duncan sat with Nora, and he was saddled with Sara. He would have gladly paired her with Nora, but in the interest of harmony, it was best for now to keep them apart as much as possible.

Though he tried to ignore her, Sara was persistent in her attempts to extract information. He gave her the cold shoulder by putting in his earbuds and listening to jazz on his iPod. Searching for a way in, Sara even tried to test his jazz knowledge. She asked if he was more of a bebop-era fan, leaning toward the likes of Charlie Parker and Thelonious Monk, or if he preferred the modern-day flavor of smooth jazz like Boney James, Jeff Lorber, or Marion Meadows. Alex almost took the bait but instead murmured, "Nice try, but I'd be willing to bet you've never even heard a song by John Coltrane—or Pat Metheny, for that matter." The look on her face told him everything. Before she responded with "Got me," the earbuds were back in place for the rest of the flight.

Carry-on luggage in tow, they quickly made their way through the airport. On the remote chance that anyone had taken an interest in them, they took separate taxis five minutes apart to their hotel overlooking the winding Mtkvari River.

Not knowing what the next few hours would bring, they utilized forty-five minutes to refresh, change clothes, and equip themselves with all the items they felt necessary. Sara, shortly after their arrival, received a couple of express packages. The courier didn't bother obtaining a signature. He'd memorized her face from a photograph supplied by Langley, and his orders were to hand over the two boxes without question. She'd been given no notice before being assigned to monitor this situation, and making certain arrangements now required a number of people to be on top of their game in a hurry.

She laid the two boxes on a table while she finished getting dressed. She was sure Alex would be prompt and wouldn't wait, no matter how much she might have suggested otherwise. She swept her wet hair into a ponytail, securing it with an elastic band. Her black running pants matched her athletic shoes and lightweight jacket. She proceeded to open one of the boxes, pulling out a 9 mm handgun, making sure it was operational. Satisfied, she holstered it in her jacket, specifically designed for such an accessory. Two extra clips went into a hidden back pocket. There was a set of car keys in the box, along with a note detailing the location and make of the car waiting for use. Sara glanced around the room. If need be, she could leave everything behind. She took a moment to send a text message to Alex, Nora, and Duncan, telling them she was heading down to get the car. On her way out, she scooped up her passport, a tiny credit card wallet, and the remaining box, cradling it between her forearm and hip.

Informing the concierge that she was going to retrieve a car, she handed him the box for safekeeping, promising to pick it up in a few minutes. Once outside the hotel doors, she jogged off at a brisk pace. Two blocks later she made a right turn, and after a left on the next block, she located the vehicle and then climbed behind the wheel. She double-parked in front of the hotel just long enough to pop in and get her package. Three blocks later, she pulled over to allow Nora and Duncan to get into the car. Nora got into the backseat behind Sara to give Duncan plenty of legroom up front. Sara anxiously looked around before putting the car in gear.

"Where is he?"

Nora wasn't the least bit apologetic with her answer. "He left ten minutes ago in a taxi."

"Shit," exploded Sara, smacking the steering wheel as she cut off a car to reenter traffic. She hated that she had absolutely no control over Alex. He wasn't on the government payroll, and there was nothing they could hold over his head for coercion. He lived on an island, and for all intents and purposes, he seemed to conduct himself as an island. She had to dismiss the brash behavior for now, but she hoped it wouldn't become a major source of irritation later. She informed Nora that the contents of the box were for her, Duncan, and Alex, but since he wasn't here, getting it to him was more than likely out of the question. Nora was impressed with what was inside.

"Nice to have friends in high places," she said, locking a magazine into place in the Walther P99 Compact. She knew it wasn't coincidence that she was holding her weapon of choice. She inspected and loaded Duncan's gun before handing it to him.

With a frown on his face, Duncan said, "Hopefully, this meeting will get done peacefully."

Nora also extracted a pouch that contained a syringe and two vials filled with a sedative strong enough to bring down a horse in seconds. Going into an unsecured environment, it was best to have a fighting chance at an exit strategy if the need arose. Nora turned her attention to other items in the box that might prove useful. As care packages went, this one was pretty well equipped.

CHAPTER **36**

The cathedral stood as a testament not only to faith but also to the resiliency of the human spirit. Built originally in the sixth or seventh century, the place of worship had undergone numerous restorations. Most of those repairs were born of necessity, the cathedral having been destroyed by foreign invaders. Each time, Georgians had banded together to start anew once the turmoil had subsided. The current design dated back to the nineteenth century. It had taken two centuries to restore after the Persians tried to make a claim for territorial domination.

There were some traditionalists that still worshipped at the church, but the vast majority of new souls found solace in the more contemporary cathedrals.

The church, located in the old part of Tbilisi, had long served as the place of worship for the Georgian Orthodox faith. With its ancient architecture, which included a bell tower from the 1400s, it was also historical enough for sightseers to explore. An ardent observer would recognize it as one of the oldest remnants of Russian neoclassical architecture in the region.

It all made for a nice postcard, but the tall, muscular figure making his way up the hill wasn't interested in capturing memories or in the tales behind the architectural wonders of the region. His focus was the church, but by no stretch of the imagination would he be mistaken for a religious man. A mere glance showed he just didn't fit the part. True, people were capable of surprise, but it was difficult to fool a trained eye. And there was a set of such eyes watching the man as he approached the church. For the moment, the man was on the opposite side of the street. The eyes that were following him felt certain he would eventually cross. Even while walking up the hill, the man, the eyes noticed, kept a measured pace, and his breathing appeared to be under control and not labored. The average person would be forced to intake and exhale a lot more air.

There was about an hour and a half of daylight left, certainly enough sun to justify the large-rimmed sunglasses that hid the eyes. They belonged to a middle-aged man resting comfortably on a bench near the church, a hardcover novel in his hands. He looked content to just let time pass by, his legs crossed as he sat at an angle. His appearance was completed with a long, outdated, wide-brimmed hat that added shadows to his face, further aiding his deception. He'd done very little reading of the book—mindful, though, to at least turn the pages every couple of minutes. The slumped figure smiled, presumably reacting to a passage he'd just read, but in reality, it was in response to being right.

The tall, muscular man was crossing the street.

Alex was cautious, mindful of not drawing too much attention. Though the window was rapidly closing, he was expected. Cutting it so close would undoubtedly make his contact a little nervous. It was no different, really, than waiting on a friend, business associate, or even the cable guy to show up. There was a prearranged time agreed upon, and when that window grew smaller, the frustration and anxiety level increased with each passing minute.

Alex had decided to leave earlier than the others, fully aware his actions would get under Sara's skin, but to some degree, that was intentional. He wanted to send the message that it wasn't her place to dictate how things should go. The fact that Champion made her stay spoke to her qualifications. However, after so many years on his own, Alex wasn't in the mood to have a boss. Besides, he needed his senses free to scope the landscape on his own first. He had the taxi drop him off four blocks away, more than enough distance to spot a tail if one existed.

As he crossed the street, angling toward the old cathedral, he was convinced he'd registered everything of possible interest. Since dusk was on the horizon, the flow of actual tourists was ebbing, making the streets a little less crowded. A select few continued to marvel at the church, pointing things out as if they possessed a measure of understanding others lacked. Alex overheard a couple referencing the cupola and southern chapel added during one of the structure's many restorations. He was about to make his way up the short flight of steps when he froze, seemingly taken aback by the magnificence for the first time. He backed away, reaching inside his pocket. A second later, he had his cell phone, and he went through the motions of taking a picture. To an onlooker, it might appear as if he were sending a photo to someone who would appreciate the gesture. In actuality, all he sent was a short text message. He next dialed a number, pressing the handset firmly to his ear when someone answered.

"This is Alex. I need you to do something for me."

The voice on the other end waited for instruction.

"Are you in the room with him?" After a short pause, the person answered in the affirmative.

"Tell him you're talking to me and that I'm standing outside the church." Alex waited to hear his directions carried out. He also paused to let a woman pass him on the pavement before he continued.

"Ask him if he's certain the procedure he gave me is correct."

Alex heard Davis Lipton's response in the background. His willingness to cooperate so freely gave Alex reason for concern. He checked his perimeter to make sure he wasn't in earshot of anyone.

"Okay, do you have a silencer?"

The voice on the other end acknowledged that he did.

"Attach it to your gun and put it against his temple."

Alex could hear Davis protesting as he reacted to what was happening.

"Now, ask the son of a bitch if he gave me the right instructions. Tell him if something goes down in this church because he decided to get cute, you'll put a bullet in his head. Inform him that I'm about to go in."

Alex kept the phone to his ear as he slowly climbed the steps.

"Hold it!" The raised tone forced Alex to pull the phone away a little. "He says go to the first pew, grab a bible, make the sign of the cross, and then take a seat in the fourth row of pews on the right. Then wait. If asked, the name is McBride, not Thompson."

Alex shook his head. Davis was lucky *he* wasn't there with him. Before Alex opened the huge doors to the church, he spoke into the phone one last time.

"You still have your weapon out?"

"Yes."

"Is the doc still there?"

"Yes."

"There'll be something extra for the inconvenience, but shoot that asshole in the foot. Your choice. Let him experience the pain, and then get him patched up."

Before he ended the call, Alex could hear a faint, agonized scream.

His mood immediately got better.

CHAPTER **37**

Less than twenty-four hours ago, Karl Peters and every resource at his disposal had begun peeling away the layers of Daniel Wassermann's life. Officially, Wassermann had come to Washington two years ago, thanks to a promotion from his administrative duties for the Knesset in Israel. There were no blemishes to uncover, and Wassermann possessed a healthy appetite for young females. Being under thirty and single, that was totally understandable in the nation's capital. His personal phone records, Internet searches, and e-mail were bland. His movements during the past several hours bordered on predictability. He left home for work early in the morning, grabbed lunch outside the Israeli embassy, and returned to the job for several more hours before calling it a day. Trading a few body checks with commuters on the Metro, Wassermann was now back where his day began, inside his Adams Morgan–district apartment.

It all made for a very simple, routine life. Just the kind of cleanliness that got one bumped up the ladder. It was all just a tad too neat for Peters's taste. Through discreet channels, very little information was available about the young man, who somehow managed to remain relatively obscure even while having a high-profile social life and access to the White House.

Karl Peters though, was a patient man.

CHAPTER 38

Alex gazed at the large figure of Jesus Christ mounted high on the cathedral wall. With bible in hand, having made the sign of the cross, he exited the first row of pews and casually walked back to the fourth row, taking a seat after a few steps inward. There was a smattering of tourists milling about in addition to what appeared to be a few locals hoping that God was keeping business hours. An official of the church was on hand to answer questions but also to keep an eye out for the church's precious artifacts. Alex didn't see what he'd expected to see, which probably meant he was being carefully watched himself. Trying not to make any moves that might alarm or scare his contact away, Alex slowly retrieved his cell phone from a pants pocket, having just gotten a vibrating text message. It was from Nora, acknowledging his earlier message sent from the cathedral's steps. In short fashion, she informed him they would be in position soon.

Alex was distracted momentarily by an elderly woman seated a couple of pews ahead to his left. She was mumbling inaudibly; her emotion seemed genuine. He wondered briefly what difficulty life had dealt her that warranted a visit during the week. Surely her devotion had to count for something.

While the elderly woman continued her private conversation with the Almighty, Alex sensed the man easing next to him long before he took a seat.

"We were expecting you much earlier," the man said, picking up a bible.

"My benefactors work in mysterious ways," Alex responded.

The remark brought a slight smile to man's face. "Well, your prayers have been answered. Your shipment is waiting. I'm sure you, as much as I, would like to get this over with as quickly as possible. All the necessary arrangements have been made. I shall be in position to inspect everything at twelve thirty this morning. By daylight at the latest, your cargo should arrive at its destination, and I trust my final payment will be sent shortly after. In the meantime, enjoy a nice meal at one of the fine restaurants Tbilisi has to offer." The man began to rise but was forced to sit back down as Alex grabbed hold of his sport coat. Based on what Baum was paid, Alex assumed this mysterious partner was due a nice sum as well. Addressing one's greed was worth a gamble.

"No offense, but I'm not about to sign off on your final payment without being there to ensure everything goes off smoothly. There's too much at stake."

"I'm not comfortable with that."

"We can get someone else," Alex said matter-of-factly.

The man sat as if in prayer, contemplating his options. Half of his fee had already been paid, and it was a comfortable amount, but he was counting on full payment to cover his overhead. Protection, for instance, was not a cheap commodity in today's dangerous marketplace.

"Fine, suit yourself. But only you. If you're not alone, you'll have to get someone else. However, at this late date, I'm sure that will cost you more than just money."

Alex could tell he had ruffled the man's comfort zone with his demand. The swift acceptance indicated the man wanted his final payment badly.

"So, where shall I meet you?"

The man thought about it for a moment. "Outside the Tbilisi Opera and Ballet Theatre. You should have no trouble finding your way."

"That works for me. I'll see you there."

"Eleven o'clock." The man began to rise again, only this time, pausing and sitting back down was his idea.

"I almost forgot. Please wait ten minutes before you exit the church. If you try to leave earlier, that poor old woman will certainly be repentant after putting a bullet in you."

Alex glanced at the heartbroken woman a few pews ahead. She raised her hand above the pew so that Alex could see part of the automatic weapon otherwise concealed by her clothing.

"She's so sweet. Now, I'll also take your cell phone. I'll be sure to return it when I see you later."

Before Alex did as requested, he addressed the old woman, keeping silent as he mouthed, "You're going to hell." She responded by giving him the finger.

Alex slowly reached inside his jacket pocket and produced a cell phone, reluctantly handing it over. Little did the man know the phone wasn't his and that it was password protected. Alex's phone still rested in his pants pocket. The man left just as quietly as he had come. Alex watched his exit, taking in as much as he could before the cathedral doors glided shut. When he turned back around, the grieving woman was maintaining her cover while focusing on Alex. He lifted his arm to check his watch, which forced her attention to shift momentarily. He slid his other hand in his pants pocket and went about slowly texting Nora.

Outside the cathedral, the interracial couple flagged down a woman who'd been jogging. They politely asked her to take a picture of them with the sun setting in the background. It would make for a romantic memory. The jogger didn't seem overly pleased at having her exercise interrupted, but she obliged. As she angled the couple's cell phone to take the picture, Sara read the text message Nora had just received.

Man leaving church. Short thin blond hair. Dark rumpled jacket. Don't lose him.

A small flash filled the short space as Duncan and Nora embraced with affectionate smiles. Sara picked up her target easily enough as he strode away from the church. His pace exceeded others on the street, and Sara was relieved to see there was no vehicle in sight to pick him up. She was sure, though, that there'd be some form of transportation at the bottom of the hill, not far from where Nora and Duncan had left the car. Sara had handed them the keys about a half mile from the cathedral, opting to jog the remainder of the distance, needing to work up a sweat to give her credibility. She nodded after being bestowed with a "Thank you so much," adding an inconvenienced smile as she handed the cell phone back, stealthily retrieving the car key in return. She then took off jogging again, this time in the direction of the man she'd been told not to lose. For Nora and Duncan, there was one more thing to do before they made their exit. They held each other close as they continued their lovers' stroll. They were nearly upon the seated figure Alex had texted them about before he entered the church. Approaching quietly from behind, they could tell by the angle of his head that he was more interested in what was happening in front of him. He was making sure the man who'd exited the church went on his way unimpeded and had no one on his tail. The vantage point also afforded him a bird's-eye view of the cathedral's entrance. If need be, putting a bullet in the tall, muscular man should he emerge from the church too early would be simple target practice. With everything he was concerned about in plain view, his flank was of little concern. He was so startled by Nora appearing at his side, that he nearly dropped his book. He fumbled to secure it, wrestling with whether to keep his attention on the cathedral's entrance or the attractive woman suddenly next to him. He'd seen her before. In fact, one question was answered. She was as stunning up close as she was from a distance.

"Oh, I'm sorry if I've startled you," Nora said sheepishly, holding out a map in her hands. "First, I hope you speak English, and second, I hope you can tell me how far I am from something."

The man shrugged his shoulders, hoping the woman didn't notice he was buttoning his jacket to conceal the weapon tucked in at the waist. "I understand a little English." The dark sunglasses allowed him a good glimpse of her cleavage. It was enough of a look to satisfy, and then he brought himself back into the moment, remembering he was working. "What are you trying to find?"

It then dawned on him. Where was the big brown-skinned man she was with? They had been a couple, arm in arm, kisses on the cheek. The cheek! Lovers caught up in moments of endearment didn't settle for the cheek. The man began a quick shift in his seat to check behind him, unbuttoning his jacket as he did so. Duncan reached him before his torso was in position. The syringe was thrust quickly into his neck, the potent tranquilizer pushed through as Nora restrained his gun hand. He desperately tried to dislodge her hands with his free one, but the strength to resist rapidly drained from his body. A few seconds later, he slumped into unconsciousness. Duncan withdrew the needle and held him up as Nora situated the book back in his hands and adjusted his hat to cover more of his forehead. They let him gently slope into the corner of the bench, the side armrest holding him in place. Duncan then came around to grab Nora's waiting hand, and the loving couple continued on their way, passing the cathedral as its doors swung open.

Alex emerged looking slightly annoyed. He took note of the man sitting on the bench but didn't fixate and only casually registered the interracial couple passing before him.

The doors behind him slowly opened as the elderly woman was on his heels. She looked to her left with admiration. That Oleg was such a damn professional! She considered herself capable, but not yet in his class. He played the part so well. Look at him over there, looking so comfortable, so laid back. A book occupying his hands, his hat pulled down low, sunglasses covering eyes that she knew were watching everything.

She then looked up at the tall stranger next to her, a sardonic smirk drawn on her face.

"May God bless you," she spat out in barely audible English, making the sign of the cross. Alex looked down at her with a raised eyebrow and watched as she gingerly took each step before proceeding on her way.

Some people you never wanted to see again in your lifetime.

CHAPTER **39**

The rain continued its assault on the Beltway. Morning rush hour traffic didn't need any assistance to be a pain in the ass. Mother Nature could close schools and virtually shut down the government when snowfall reached an inch. Rain on the Beltway had the potential to push people over the edge. George Champion didn't need any more stress in his life. He avoided adding to it by being an early riser who found a measure of peace in avoiding the bumper-to-bumper congestion of people seemingly in a hurry to get to jobs they generally didn't enjoy in the first place.

Considering the pay scale, the consensus was that the majority of employees at the Central Intelligence Agency actually wanted to be here. They believed their overall reward was in helping to ensure that not only themselves, but also others could go home at night to a sensible and safe world. That ideology was tested on a daily basis, because there were days when it seemed the world was coming apart at the seams. There were no quick fixes anymore either. Not with rampant governmental oversight and more intelligence-gathering agencies on the federal dime than it seemed there were liquor stores in the District. Solving problems now had to get done one stitch at a time.

A slight buzz was permeating throughout the building. For a place that took pride in keeping secrets, the comings and goings of high-ranking visitors to Langley rarely went unnoticed. Earlier, while peering out his upper-floor window, Champion had noticed the two black sedans rolling down the driveway. They screamed "Washington bureaucrat," but to his knowledge, there were no official meetings on the docket today. Not that certain people on the Hill ever felt compelled to follow protocol anyway with their "We appropriate the checks that keep your butts afloat" attitude. One such politician had been in the building now for thirty-five minutes, meeting with the director of central intelligence. Champion hoped it was something his superior would handle, but then the call he dreaded appeared on his private line. The director wanted Champion to join him and Senator Bryce Lipton. That had been five minutes ago, and as he made his way to the DCI's office, a line from a sitcom ricocheted through his mind: "Lucy, you have some 'splaining to do."

How could Lipton know? Had Alex or Nora screwed up? Had they been apprehended? As he entered the director's office, Champion figured he was about to find out if the firing squad had ammunition.

Advancing in age, Adam Doyle was surprisingly spry. He was up and rounding his desk to greet Champion before the door closed behind him. Despite being twenty-two years younger, Champion doubted he could best Doyle in a marathon race. The man was downright religious when it came to running and staying fit. If memory served him correctly, Doyle routinely got in six miles a day before work. For a brief instant, Champion cast a glance toward Lipton, who remained seated, his posture locked down, facing forward. With a hand resting on Champion's back, Doyle guided Champion to a chair next to Lipton. Only then did the senator rise from his seat.

"You two have met, haven't you?"

They sized each other up. "Yes, briefly our paths have crossed," the senator said, his tone suggesting their prior interactions weren't anything special.

"Senator, good to see you again." The handshake was firm but didn't last long. "A couple of State dinners, I believe, maybe a function at the White House." Lipton nodded in agreement as he sat back down, tugging at a crease in his pants.

"Hell, everybody at least knows somebody who knows somebody in this town," Doyle said, returning to sit behind his manicured desk. Doyle spoke before the senator seized the opportunity. This was not going to be a place where Lipton could huff and puff.

"George, as you know, the senator has a personal interest in the agency, since his son is one of ours."

Champion acknowledged the fact with a nod. Doyle continued, sensing the senator's need to move things along, which was just fine with him as well.

"Is Davis Lipton working on anything vital at the moment?"

Champion could feel the elder Lipton's eyes on him like lasers. He knew he had to sell it, so he took a second to gather his thoughts. "Nothing of consequence has crossed my radar screen." Champion cleared his throat. Why not make this interesting? "And . . . it was my understanding"—he shot Lipton a cautionary glance—"from the AG's office that he wasn't to be assigned to any heavy lifting until the Erica Janway legal matter was concluded. Am I missing something here?"

The senator's face was emotionless, but Lipton couldn't help himself. "Not wanting to seem unsympathetic, but isn't the Janway issue a nonissue now?"

"Senator, her death is very much under investigation, so I'm afraid not," Doyle pointed out. "And besides, there were a number of depositions taken, and her legal team is very thorough. Her husband is steadfast on seeing this through." Like Champion, Doyle had known and respected Janway. "I'm sure you can appreciate that the AG wants to make sure we're on solid ground." The nononsense response was effective in establishing the boundaries. The CIA had taken its fair share of criticism over the past several years, but there were limits on how far an outsider could push.

Champion alternated his attention between the two men. "I'm still not sure what we're discussing here."

"Well, let me tell you," the senator said, seizing an opening. "I haven't heard from my son in a couple of days. He hasn't answered his cell or responded to e-mail."

"I take it that's unusual? You two converse that often?" Champion queried.

The muscles in Lipton's face twitched for a second. "Not really. It's just that a relative is ill and he asked to be kept informed in case a trip home was warranted."

"My apologies, Senator, but it's really impossible for me to know the status of all our field agents unless they're part of a large-scale undertaking, which, as I mentioned before, your son isn't." Champion addressed Doyle for reassurance. "I'll follow up with his station chief. Any chance he's just taken a few days off? A romantic getaway, perhaps?" Champion decided to measure the senator's ability to handle himself under fire. "Where was he when you two last touched base?"

Lipton took longer than he should have to answer, coming up with, "I believe it was Zurich."

"And you say that was a couple of days ago?"

"Yes."

A nightclub in Brussels for a meeting with a black market dealer is quite a distance from Zurich, Champion wanted to blurt out, but this wasn't the place or time for a showdown. Not yet.

"I'd hate to worry his mother," Lipton said, a sly smile forming. "None of us would get any sleep then." The Washington heavyweight then pushed off his chair and offered his hand. "Gentlemen, I've taken up enough of your time this morning, and I really have to get back to those whining children on the Hill."

Doyle answered for Champion as he led the senator to the door. "Senator, we'll certainly make some calls and get back to you. I'm sure there's nothing to worry about."

Walking toward the elevator, Senator Lipton wondered if he had just been handled. He could hardly press the point, but his son should have been in contact by now. Tobias Baum had been paid, so everything was relatively on schedule. The merchandise waiting to be inspected and shipped was the only holdup. His Israeli connection certainly wouldn't be pleased at even the hint of a problem after so much meticulous planning. Lipton was most worried, though, about the man financing the major portion of the endeavor. Roger Daniels had never been too keen on Lipton's son being part of the operation in the first place. Would he dare harm his son? There were degrees of power, and although that bastard had a ton of influence and money to burn, there were certain lines you didn't cross. If need be, Lipton could arrange for Rogers to never be heard from again. A black ops unit from the Department of Defense could take care of that, no questions asked.

As soon as Champion was sure Lipton had vacated the director's inner sanctum, he let it be known he wasn't done talking. Champion and Doyle had tremendous respect for one another, and after years of service, Doyle was set to step down shortly. He had gone out of his way to make the case to both political parties that without question his successor should be Champion. The two knew and trusted each other very well at this point.

"Adam, I have to get you up to speed on a pressing matter."

"I got the feeling you had something on your mind."

"You better sit down. I may not be your first choice to succeed you after this."

CHAPTER 40

Sara examined the landscape before her, and she saw several items scattered about that caused her concern. She prayed the man from the church hadn't come by bike. She wouldn't be able to keep up on foot if he had, and using a car to maintain surveillance on a bike would be a dead giveaway.

Establishing a rapid pace on the other side of the street, she eclipsed him without much interest. She was able to reach the car as he continued to walk past a smattering of locked bikes. She had the car headed back toward the cathedral, her cell phone already in use. Nora and Duncan should have taken care of the sentry by now, and Sara had a feeling she might need them. Out of the side mirror she was relieved to see that the man was fumbling for keys in his pocket as he stood next to the driver's side of a compact car. Nora answered her phone as she and Duncan came into view, making their way down from the top of the incline. Sara told them to pick up the pace as she readied the car by turning it around in the direction the man was now traveling. His compact was diminishing by the second.

Nora and Duncan weren't fully inside when Sara hit the gas pedal. Duncan grabbed hold of the car door handle as his back slammed against the seat. He shot Sara a less-than-pleased look as she worked the pedals. She offered no apology. They stayed a safe distance behind, allowing the target to maintain at least a block lead. Having six eyes on his car made the tail a lot easier. Checking constantly, they were convinced he had no protective escort. The traffic thickened as they entered Tbilisi proper. Several blocks later, motoring along the main drag of tree-lined Rustaveli Avenue, they suddenly were gaining ground on him. Duncan looked at the fast-approaching structures on either side of the street. From here he could see Freedom Square ahead, its multidirectional options a potential challenge. He then saw the car's turn signal engage.

"I think we got something here," Duncan said as the lead vehicle slowed in order to turn into a parking garage.

"I'm getting out," Nora said quickly, and Sara barely had stopped before Duncan leaned forward to let her out of the backseat. The uniformed doorman observed the strange scene but nonetheless tipped his hat to welcome Nora as she entered through the double doors of the Marriott Hotel. Sara made a beeline for the parking garage, trying to keep up. She let her hair down as she did so, taking no chances that the man, should he get a glimpse, be able to recognize her as the woman who was jogging near the cathedral. His car wasn't immediately visible when they pulled into the garage. Seeing no empty spots, she continued on to the next level. It was then she saw the car up ahead, just before it turned onto the next level. As they rounded that same corner, the compact turned into a vacant space. Duncan didn't bother telling Sara, but she got the message once his door flew open. She tapped the brakes, and he exited in a flash. Sara continued on, looking for the next available parking space. Duncan located the nearest exit, and by the time he heard the man's car door shut, he was already ahead of him, pushing open the door of a vestibule that housed a bank of elevators and a stairwell. Taking a calculated risk, Duncan punched the down button just as the man came through the door. The man noticed the stairwell, but seeing the elevator button was pushed, he elected to wait. Duncan turned to acknowledge him and produced a courtesy smile before returning his focus to the elevators.

Thankfully, the wait wasn't long. Duncan allowed the man to enter first, letting him punch the button for the lobby. Duncan got out his cell phone and sent a short message to Nora, telling her they were heading her way and to be in position. He had no way of knowing for sure, but Duncan assumed the man would be going to his room once he reached the lobby, since there was no way to do so from the parking structure.

Looking like she belonged, Nora had already done a quick assessment of the Marriott's lobby. She kept moving, utilizing her peripheral vision. The elevators to the guest rooms were fronted by high decorative pillars, and there were two restaurants on the level. Judging from the noise, one was probably more of a bar than a sit-down restaurant. There was one thing she couldn't account for, so she did the only logical thing when one needed information in a hurry: ask someone who would know. She sauntered over to the front desk and explained she was expecting a friend who was going to park in the garage and, not having a car herself, wondered if there was access to the hotel from there. The female clerk was most helpful and pointed to where the bank of elevators let out from the parking structure. Just as the clerk was asking if there was anything else, Nora's cell phone chimed with a text message

"Excuse me, this is probably her." Nora backed away and read the message from Duncan. She took a moment to text him back and then calculated her next step. Beating the man to the guest elevators presented a problem because most likely, he'd allow her to enter first. At that point, she would either have to punch a floor button or wait for him to ask "Which floor?" She settled for a riskier option that would require precise timing.

She hung back upon first noticing Duncan's imposing figure exiting the parking garage elevator. His size blocked her view of the target that followed a few steps behind him. Nora slowly moved toward the guest elevators, and when Duncan peeled away toward the lobby area, there was the man from the cathedral. He increased his step to get an elevator that was there, waiting. Once inside, he quickly pushed his floor button. Nora hoped she had timed correctly the rate of closure for the elevators. She accelerated her pace as the door began inching to a close. Six inches of opening was all that remained when she stuck a hand in the elevator door, forcing it to reopen.

"Whew, that was close," she exclaimed, appearing a bit out of breath. The man was slightly startled at first, but upon inspecting

Nora, he relaxed his posture. He was still standing close to the buttons.

"If I may, what floor?"

"Fourth . . ." Nora began, before realizing the number was already punched. "Looks like we're on the same floor. Thank you." Her accent revealed a Russian influence.

When the doors opened again, the man waited for her to depart first. Either he had manners or was being cautious. Getting her bearings straight, Nora turned left, and she could feel him do so as well. *Any minute,* she said to herself, her purse already slightly open in anticipation. Hopefully, his room wouldn't be at the end of the hall. She was relieved when her phone rang. As per her text instruction, it was Duncan calling exactly a minute and a half after she entered the elevator.

She answered and made sure her side of the conversation was heard. She slowed down, stepping aside to give the man room to pass. She protested into her cell that she really didn't feel like joining the person on the other end for a drink in the hotel bar. She instead wanted to freshen up before dinner, but she finally relented and agreed to come back down. She did so, though, only after taking note of which room the man entered.

CHAPTER **41**

They'd been traveling for nearly thirty minutes, the lights of Tbilisi proper fading from view. From briefly studying a map, Alex surmised the treacherous foothills of the Trialeti Range were to the right. To his left, he was able to follow the Mtkvari River before it snaked away from the city.

There was little conversation between the two men, except for the occasional directions given by the passenger to Alex, who was behind the wheel of the compact car. As instructed, Alex had been waiting outside of the Opera and Ballet Theatre, which was just letting out after a performance. The location was within walking distance from the Marriott, and Alex had taken the opportunity to clear his head as he'd walked along Rustaveli Avenue. He had arrived early on purpose and found a bench across from the Rustaveli National Theatre. The majestically lighted building was right next door to the Opera and Ballet Theatre meeting place. He had been in place when his appointment pulled up to the curb in the compact. The driver's side door was swung open, and Alex was told to drive.

When Alex asked what name the man should be called, he received a terse response. "You can call me Mr. Green."

Alex guessed it was meant to be a coy reference to his expected payday. "Mr. Green" was definitely packing a sidearm in his right jacket pocket. Once settled in the passenger seat, he sat at a slight angle that would allow him to use the weapon, should it become necessary.

Alex's attempt to learn where they were heading had been rebuffed with a simple, "Just follow my directions." Alex hoped that by this time, Nora, Sara, and Duncan were well into the process of retrieving information about Mr. Green.

Getting access to the man's room without a key or name presented a problem, but they'd brainstormed and felt confident there was a way.

Duncan purchased an envelope from the gift shop, filling it with a few sheets of blank paper to add bulk. He then proceeded to the front desk, explained to the clerk that his friend and wife weren't in their room as expected, and asked if he could check one last time. If they were still out, he'd appreciate it if the envelope were left in their mailbox. Since he also provided the room number, the clerk called to make sure, but got no answer. Aside from confirming what he already knew, the clerk gave Duncan a valuable piece of information upon accepting the envelope.

"Mr. Janko isn't picking up, but I'll certainly put this in his mailbox."

Duncan expressed his gratitude and made his way to the hotel bar. That was twenty-five minutes after Nora had walked up to the hotel desk, inquiring whether a room was available since her company had failed to make a reservation due to a last minute scheduling change. She had also expressed her preference for something on the fourth floor, away from the elevator, and she didn't care about a view. The clerk checked and was able to accommodate her request.

While Duncan was dropping off his envelope, Sara was stepping out of the shower in Nora's room. Instead of drying off, she slipped her wet body and dripping hair into a hotel robe, grabbed the room's ice bucket, and exited.

The desk clerk that had assisted Duncan was just as puzzled as some of the people in the lobby area upon seeing a woman clad only in her hotel robe approaching in a hurry, depositing water droplets in her wake. There were a couple of people ahead of her in line, but Sara apologized as she walked past them, her face reeking of embarrassment as she propped the ice bucket on the counter. Not wanting this to become more of a spectacle than it already was, the clerk rushed over to be of assistance.

"Something I can help you with, miss?"

Sara looked around, aware a number of people were taking interest. "Yes, thank you. I'm so embarrassed," she said in a rush, nearly out of breath. "I'm Mrs. Janko in room 412. I just got out of the shower and was on my way to get a bucket of ice when I realized I'd left my key in the room. Stupid me, it's on the dresser and I forgot to grab it on my way out. My husband is away at the moment, so I have no way to get in the room. Could you please give me another key or have someone let me in the room?"

Conscious others were watching and waiting, the clerk decided the best course of action was to get this resolved as soon as possible. "Certainly, let me code you a key. Janko, 412, you said?"

"Yes and oh my, thank you so much."

"Not a problem." The clerk finished activating the card and handed it over. Sara started to walk away. "Mrs. Janko," he called out. Sara froze.

"Yes?"

"A gentleman dropped off an envelope for you and your husband a short while ago. You must have been in the shower when he called."

She took the envelope and waved it by her head. "Again, thank you." Opening the door to Janko's suite, she cautiously waited for a second, listening for any indication she might not be alone. None came, so she went about searching the room for any information on Mr. Janko.

————————

Alex had followed a long stretch of road out of town, the area growing more remote with each passing mile. Faint nighttime lights were now separated by huge gaps of land. He exited the road and turned down a path that took them over a bridge crossing the Mtkvari River. He was now driving along a bumpy road sandwiched by heavy foliage and a succession of tall trees. He guessed his passenger had to have knowledge of this area, because roaming through it in the dark, without any guidance, was just asking to be lost. The headlights of the compact were the only source of light. After a few more jolting revolutions of the tires,

Alex saw what had to be their destination. In the foreground, about half a mile away, he could make out what appeared to be a transport plane, one side bathed by light as if it were a museum piece. Mr. Green told Alex to bring the vehicle to a complete stop and flash his lights on and off twice. His actions were met with a similar response just ahead of them.

"Proceed," Mr. Green advised. "Slowly."

Two men armed with semiautomatic weapons emerged from the shadows, taking a relaxed but ready position in front of their vehicle. Alex stopped when one of the men raised his hand. The man then came to the driver's side, his index finger positioned near his weapon's trigger, the other holding a flashlight. He motioned for Alex to roll down the window and then took a closer look inside. He didn't seem to take much interest in Alex, addressing Mr. Green instead.

"You were told to come alone," the man admonished.

"He's my business associate. It couldn't be helped," Mr. Green pleaded.

Looking none too pleased, the man backed away. His action led the other armed sentry to assume a more ready position.

"Damn it," Mr. Green said, just loud enough for Alex to hear. "I knew bringing you was a mistake."

"Easy," Alex whispered. "Easy."

The guard to his side was now on a cell phone, conversing in Russian. The call was short, and when he hung up, he instructed his associate to lower his weapon and move aside. Alex was then waved through as the vehicle in front of them pulled aside to give them access to the road. They followed the path as it curved before straightening out along the fence line, revealing an airfield. The foliage was less dense here, and Alex could clearly make out the plane now. A good-sized transport, its side-loading doors were open and waiting alongside several trucks. The whole space was strategically flooded with lights. There was another set of armed guards at the airstrip's gates, and they waved the car through. Alex proceeded to where the trucks and a couple of vehicles were parked.

"Now, I'll do the talking. Remember, you are my associate,"

Mr. Green said, much more comfortable now that the situation seemed manageable. "If I ask for your opinion, just agree with me. Understood?"

"You're the expert."

Mr. Green then realized he was without a valuable piece of information. "What should I call you?"

"Fine time to think about asking me that, huh? McBride should be easy enough to remember."

"And now is not the time to get cute, Mr. McBride."

Alex stretched to get rid of the unpleasantness of being inside the cramped space. There were several more men milling about, most of them visibly armed. Clearly their arrival had sparked interest, as the attention shifted to him and Mr. Green. As they walked around to the lead truck, Alex got the impression the airstrip wasn't used often and probably wasn't on too many maps.

Alex was forced to squint as the huge lights brought about near-daylight conditions. He glanced at the plane's wide-open side doors, which revealed a cavernous interior waiting to be filled. There were even more men, and for the first time, Alex noticed some of them were not of European or Eastern Bloc heritage. They were Middle Eastern and mostly in the background near the plane. The first voice he heard greeting Mr. Green was unmistakably Russian. A few feet behind, Alex saw only a portion of the man's face because of the lights.

"And who have you brought with you?" the Russian asked, his attention shifting to Alex.

Mr. Green sounded convincing. "He's my associate, Mr. McBride." Alex barely heard the words as his stomach lurched to his throat. He could see the Russian clearly now.

He searched the Russian's face for any sudden change. It had been years, but he was certain beyond a doubt that he was standing in front of a vicious killer.

He knew the name even before Dmitri Nevsky introduced himself.

CHAPTER 42

The names and the faces associated with them had stopped creeping into his consciousness on a frequent basis. It was as if the dead had finally moved on, releasing him from his personal purgatory. But when Nora had reentered his life, so did the departed. Alex had exacted a measure of revenge by killing the man who'd engineered their demise. That act of retribution had also cemented his exit from the CIA. The government's decision to utilize the double agent instead of bringing him to justice was too much to swallow. Men, women, and families had trusted Alex. He had sold them on democracy and the promise of a better, safer existence. All of that had systematically been stripped away by the man standing in front of him.

The Russian with heavy eyebrows and dark, lifeless eyes had been the executioner of Alex's assets in the Middle East after the former Iraqi foreign minister—the man the US government had trusted with sensitive information— betrayed them. He had passed that information along to Nevsky and the Russians, and to anyone else willing to pay to learn the identities of home-born spies.

Nevsky had been a butcher who took delight in driving home the message that helping or siding with the West carried dire consequences.

With relatives cursing his existence in a language he wished he didn't understand, Alex saw firsthand Nevsky's brutality. Ammar Handi's torso was found along the banks of the Tigris River, his identification stuffed in a shirt pocket. Once Alex had learned of his death, he'd tried desperately to warn and protect his family. He had been too late. As he'd entered their modest dwelling, Alex could only imagine the terror they'd experienced in their last moments. On top of a table was Ammar's severed head. On the floor beneath, in a puddle of blood, lay the body of his wife, a bullet wound ventilating her skull. In the corner of the room, slumped against the wall, was his daughter, the oldest, the wall streaked with blood from the point of impact. In another bedroom was Ammar's six-year-old son, his youth cut short by a bullet to the heart.

It was that night that Alex had decided to do what his government was reluctant to carry out, dismissing their argument to look at the bigger picture. His approach was much simpler. The asshole responsible for this atrocity and for the deaths of other trusted assets was going to pay with *his* life. So, despite a firm hands-off order from high-ranking officials in Washington, Alex got up close and personal with the man who so casually decided the fate of others. He died in a lot of pain, slowly.

Alex had been immediately jettisoned back to Langley to face a barrage of angry politicians who were hell-bent on teaching him a lesson about following orders and understanding what was at stake in the war on terror. Knowing he was right, Alex felt the only sane decision was to stop working for people who saw the world with blinders on.

He had one regret. His quick exit meant Dmitri Nevsky would live. For years, he'd tried to content himself with believing the perils of the business would eventually catch up to Nevsky. In time, he had learned to let it go.

"So you are the puny one's partner?" Nevsky said, those dark eyes probing. "You're in very good shape to be in your profession. You look more like muscle to me, and Mr. Green should know he has no need for such precautions."

Alex had fully expected to be dead by now. Maybe Nevsky, so heavily surrounded with protection, was toying with him. But his interest seemed to be that of a stranger's at the moment. It dawned on Alex that they had actually seen each other only twice before, and each occurrence was under less than favorable light in Tehran. Alex had obtained surveillance photos of Nevsky, and once at a restaurant, he heard him speaking loudly, celebrating. Because of the savagery, Alex had promised he'd never forget the face or voice. He'd given up hope, though, of ever seeing him again.

Alex didn't want to appear too comfortable, which was no act.

"I like to work out," he responded. "Helps alleviate some of the boredom."

Nevsky seemed warily satisfied. He returned his focus to Mr. Green. "Let's get this concluded. The Iranians are not happy about having to wait. You've nearly taken this down to the deadline."

"Blame that on Mr. McBride," was the reply as they followed Nevsky to the back of the lead truck. Nevsky nodded to a couple of his men. They moved like a pit crew servicing a racecar. The doors were swung to their sides and a wide ramp deployed to ease access. The truck was packed with crates, leaving just enough room for the contents to be extracted. A pair of men raced up the ramp and grabbed one of the crates. They carefully carried it off the truck, placing it to the side. They went back in and repeated the maneuver, this time grabbing a crate from a different section. While they did this, another set of men opened the first crate that had been brought out. Mr. Green made a move to take a closer look but Nevsky held him back with a firm arm across his chest.

"Mr. McBride. If you will, indulge me," Nevsky said with a wry smile, his head motioning to the open crate.

"But I'm supposed to inspect the merchandise," Mr. Green protested. "They're paying me directly."

"Yes, that's true. But you said he is your associate, so I assume he has some expertise in the area. And besides, Mr. Green, you were instructed to come alone." Nevsky addressed a Middle Eastern man who was standing nearby, quietly observing the proceedings. "Is this okay with you? It's for your protection." The Iranian remained silent, giving his approval with the wave of a hand.

Mr. Green could feel the sweat forming at the top of his receding hairline. He cast a wide-eyed look at the man he only knew as Mr. McBride. It did his nerves no good to get a smile in return.

Alex leaned closer to Mr. Green and could feel his accelerated breathing. "We're going to have to talk about a pay raise," Alex muttered, reassuringly patting him on the shoulder.

He walked past Nevsky, who had a satisfied look on his face, as if he had figured out the magician's tricks. "He worries a lot," Alex quipped. "He thinks I don't pay enough attention to details."

Alex was at the point of praying himself. He'd been all ears for hours as Duncan had given him an education on centrifuges. With unlimited Internet searches and access to a CIA database at his disposal, Duncan had given Alex a crash course on the latest advancements in the field and how the devices were put together. He had also worked the phone, calling every expert he knew. After their cramming session, Alex had felt secure enough that he could at least talk a good game, provided there were no major design surprises. Having studied and analyzed thousands of complex football formations and game films for years, Alex had developed an uncanny ability to retain large sums of information for a brief period of time. Eventually stuff got purged, but for now, he was counting on every ounce of retention.

Alex knelt down and scanned the cylindrical object. It was around five feet long, and as he ran his hand along the ringed exterior, he could tell it was well crafted.

"I need to see one open or disassembled," Alex said over his shoulder.

Without hesitation, Nevsky snapped his fingers. His men immediately brought around another open crate, this time from a different truck. A hole, virtually the length of the cylinder, had been cut out, so that the guts of the centrifuge were visible and easy to explore. Alex worked from top to bottom with his hands. Mr. Green stood close to Nevsky, observing intently his associate's inspection, straining to get a better view. Alex nodded his head approvingly. Duncan was quickly becoming his hero.

"Carbon fiber, excellent," he said, talking to no one in particular, but just loud enough for those close to hear. "This is very nice craftsmanship. All in working order," Alex said, still going over the merchandise. "But now, if you will . . . indulge me, Mr. Nevsky. I'd like to see one unassembled. Just the inside pieces, please. Specifically, the bottom bearing, the upper and lower scoop, and the rotor."

Nevsky stood in silence for a moment, summing up the situation. "So far you are satisfied with the IR-2?"

Alex rose to his feet, not bothering to look at him. "I'm satisfied with the IR-3, which we both know these are."

Nevsky exhaled, "Excellent," in Russian. "I'm satisfied on two fronts." Nevsky talked to one of his men, speaking strictly in Russian. He put his arm around Mr. Green. "They will bring you the individual parts to inspect. While you're doing that, I will have Mr. McBride look over the inventory. We need to get the merchandise loaded onto the transport as fast as possible. I don't want to continue being a torch in the wilderness much longer."

Nevsky led Alex to the back of each truck in succession, all of which were now open. They were also filled to near capacity with boxes containing centrifuges of the same type he'd just handled.

Taking in the magnitude of everything that had led to his standing in this isolated airfield, Alex was at least convinced of one thing. Someone had put some serious shit into motion.

At around one fifteen, Nevsky's phone rang. He walked a few steps away to gain some privacy. At times during the conversation, his tone was agitated. The candid discussion was in Russian, but Alex twice heard Mr. Green's name mentioned. When he ended the call, Nevsky gathered his thoughts before calling two of his men over. They listened, nodding all the while before being dismissed.

Alex bristled as Nevsky came back his way, reaching inside his jacket, his gaze solely fixed. The Russian was quite skilled at killing. If this had to be the place, so be it, but Nevsky would die first. With no weapon, Alex just needed him to come closer. Nevsky would feel totally safe with all his men about.

He was now fifteen feet away. *Keep coming,* Alex calculated. He looked around. Only one of Nevsky's men was casually interested, his focus shifting between his benefactor and the men now starting to load the plane. His automatic weapon was in a relaxed position.

Ten feet and closing, Nevsky's hand was still in his jacket, moving slowly.

Alex had made up his mind. He'd first render a blow that would make it easy for him to overpower Nevsky, despite the man's bulk. He'd use the leverage to shield himself against the closet guard, who would hesitate to take a shot with his boss in the way. Alex knew his time would be measured in milliseconds. The guard, unable to get a clear shot, would sound the alarm. Though wounded, Nevsky's survival instincts would likely kick in as well. If he was to have any chance of escaping, Alex would have to act quickly. That meant that with Nevsky in a headlock, the lethal thing to do was snap his neck. Alex would then hold Nevsky's slumping body up just long enough to retrieve the weapon from inside his jacket. After that, he'd shoot the nearest guard. Luck would play a major part in his next move. Hopefully, the guards would come running and expose themselves. He'd be able to surprise a couple and take them down, causing the others to exercise caution. In that opening, he'd sprint for the darkness and take his chances outrunning his pursuers. If he didn't make it, at least he'd die knowing Nevsky had left this world first and at his hands.

The Russian was now five feet away. . . . Alex needed just another foot.

Alex's adrenaline rush suddenly dropped, as if a ton of ice had fallen from the sky. When Nevsky's hand came out of his jacket, it held a pack of cigarettes. He shook a single one to the top and grabbed it with his mouth. His other hand produced a lighter. He took a long drag before matching it with an equally long billow of smoke.

"Damn things, I'm trying to quit."

The smell hinted at the tobacco's potency. Alex knew that in time, cancer would get the job done. "Those things can get you killed, you know."

Nevsky's eyes followed a smoke trail. "You sound like my wife now." He let the cigarette dangle from his mouth as he signaled with a hand. "Mr. Green," he yelled. "Get over here."

Nevsky took a couple more drags before flicking the cigarette to the ground, extinguishing it with a twist of his foot. "Just a few puffs. As I said, I'm trying to quit."

Mr. Green was now by his side. Nevsky stepped forward to watch the operation of crates being unloaded from the trucks and onto the plane. "Everyone is satisfied. The people on my end can now have a good night's sleep. The Iranians are probably praying to their God. And now it's time for you to go. Your money is in the back seat. Mr. McBride, good-bye as well."

Mr. Green wasn't going to wait around for Nevsky to change his mind. He motioned for McBride to get moving.

Nevsky didn't say anything as he unconsciously reached for another cigarette, but Mr. McBride bothered him somewhat. He passed the test, but still, the man seemed out of place. Nevsky didn't press it, but felt as if he'd seen him somewhere before, and in his line of work, gut feelings weren't dismissed so easily. But he was never going to run into him again, so it really didn't matter.

The dead were the dead.

CHAPTER 43

The stretch limo kept up with the flow of traffic as it glided down Rock Creek Parkway, easing through the remnants of the evening's rush hour.

Dressed in formal attire, Roger Daniels occupied the seat behind his driver. He didn't let on that he was slightly perturbed at having to interrupt his soothing massage of classical music. It was how he preferred to pass the time while being driven. Daniels could sense the worrisome crease on his own brow. He knew from years of self-observation that it was not a good look for him. Early on, like a poker player tipping his hand, it had betrayed him in some financial dealings. He was a quick learner, though. If he couldn't fully correct the problem, he'd learn to use it to his advantage. As his portfolio had expanded, Daniels had discovered the forehead crunch could be intimidating, conveying volumes in the absence of a spoken word. As one of the world's richest men, Daniels subscribed to the adage of keeping your friends close and your enemies closer. He had no illusions about Bryce Lipton, who sat next to him. He was a friend born of convenience.

Granted, Lipton possessed a number of personality traits that served him well. He was hard-working and bright enough to understand the big picture. A career politician, Lipton had the kind of power and influence on Capitol Hill that not even huge quantities of wealth could procure. Money could get you access and favors, but stability, whether in the form of respect or intimidation, could satisfy far more valuable wants and desires within the system. Thanks to years of getting his hands dirty, Lipton unquestionably operated in the inner corridors of power. Daniels had benefited from that access on a global scale. And yet, he felt there was more to conquer, and Lipton was a key to that.

For years, the senator had been satisfied with just being a major power player on the Hill, but associating himself with Daniels offered a new possibility, one difficult for a huge ego to pass up. Daniels had convinced Lipton that with his help, being president of the United States was attainable. Like himself, Lipton was a hard man to gain influence with, but Daniels had gambled and succeeded in offering the ultimate prize. The thought of having a president in his pocket was like mental Viagra for Daniels. It would be a luxury for four years, not four hours. He was even getting better at tolerating some of the man's shortcomings. For now, he'd live with it.

"Bryce, you know I would never—"

The senator cut him off. "Yes, but what about Ezra?"

Daniels exposed the crease, as if giving the thought some consideration. Truth was, the subject had come up in conversation with the Mossad spymaster more than once.

"Not even Ezra would exercise that option."

"For his sake, I hope not. This is my son we're talking about."

"Bryce, now is not the time to panic. We're so close to finally seeing this come to light."

Daniels stared out the window, aware of his destination looming on the horizon just opposite the Potomac. He flicked at some lint on his trousers.

"In fact, I talked with Ezra within the past hour, and the merchandise is being loaded as we speak. Now, in order for that to happen, your son would have had to make contact. That's how it was structured. The way *you* wanted it to be done."

"Yes, but I still haven't heard from him. Maybe we should talk with the man in Tbilisi."

Daniels's limo fell in line behind similar vehicles inching forward to allow their occupants to depart. The waiting attendants were hustling to assist and keep the line moving. Exiting from each car were Washington's elite: impeccably dressed, the women accessorized with sparkling jewelry. Like other monuments in the nation's capital, the Kennedy Center for the Performing Arts was a treasure. It had hosted its share of dignitaries, presidents, and some of the finest entertainment the world had to offer. Tonight, it would see hundreds of thousands of dollars pass through its doors for a fundraiser.

Before Daniels signaled his driver to unlock the door, he turned to Lipton.

"From what I gather, because they are in transfer mode, no one is reachable by phone. Too dangerous at this point. Someone could be listening. And besides, it's only a matter of hours before Ezra's cleanup program begins." He rested a hand on Lipton's arm. "Seriously, Bryce, you have nothing to worry about when it comes to your son. He came through. You should be proud. Think of the future."

Daniels motioned to his driver, and the doors were unlocked. An attendant swung the door open, and Daniels rose to exit. He peeked his head back inside. "Richard will drop you wherever you need to go."

The door closed, and the partition separating driver from passenger was lowered.

"Where to, sir?"

Lipton sat back. He didn't have an answer readily available. He sighed.

"Just drive for now."

CHAPTER 44

Sara Garland's field experience wasn't extensive, but she understood limitations. She knew that not even a so-called superpower's clandestine services could adequately staff every region of the world. There was no James Bond in Luanda, Angola; in Harbin, China; or in Barbados of the Lesser Antilles.

The Republic of Georgia presented a unique set of circumstances. Its location represented a golden opportunity to have an ally within arm's reach of countries worth monitoring. When the door had opened to possibly making friends with Georgia, the United States couldn't get a foot in fast enough. The move had angered Russia and had given Iran something to lose sleep over.

The association also allowed the CIA to justify placing a small staff in place full-time. Sara had put those scarce resources on alert upon departing Brussels. They'd already proven useful by delivering the packages containing weapons, money, and pharmaceutical supplies. More support would be available if Sara and Nora needed it, but there were limits. Removing a body or two was manageable. A killing spree, on the other hand, would be impossible to contain. More weapons and ammunition were obtainable, and a couple of doctors were on call to treat a knife or bullet wound if necessary. Money was there for emergencies and so was the ability to secure new passports. Some things they were better off accomplishing on their own. They were, after all, operating in foreign territory and had no knowledge of the personnel. The least amount of information they provided, the better.

Five minutes after entering Janko's suite, Sara let Duncan in.

Nora was in the hotel lobby, catching up on her reading while keeping an eye out for anything suspicious, like Mr. Janko suddenly reappearing. It took Sara and Duncan roughly fifteen minutes of searching before they discovered Janko's hiding place. His stash was taped to the back of a curtain, above the hem inside the lining. The contents of the oversized manila envelope were laid out on a table. There were several passports and driver's licenses: British, Czech, and Danish. Each contained the name Victor Janko, so that much was probably true. Sara took pictures of the documents with her camera phone and e-mailed them directly to Langley. There was also three thousand dollars in euros. Duncan took interest in a memo pad.

"Janko must have a sketchy memory."

"What do you have?"

Duncan tapped the memo pad with a finger. "Maybe he only remembers the passwords but I'm sure these are routing and bank account numbers." He handed them to Sara, who once again sent copies to Langley. They put the contents back in the envelope and returned it exactly the way they'd found it in the curtain. They double-checked the suite to make sure everything was in its proper place. Satisfied, they quietly left.

CHAPTER **45**

He didn't bother to silence the vibrating hum emanating from his phone as it danced on the night table. It would stop soon enough. Yadin remained motionless in bed, his eyes staring into the darkness.

He tossed the sheet aside and sat up on the edge of the bed. He checked the text message, which confirmed what he'd suspected. He sent a short text of his own and set the phone back on the nightstand. Thirty minutes later, he was refreshed from a shower, shaved and dressed in slacks, a polo shirt, and comfortable shoes. He grabbed an already packed suitcase and vacated the room. The hotel lobby was quiet this early in the a.m. A weary doorman was surprised to see a guest checking out at this hour. He was about to ask if the man needed a taxi when one pulled up in a hurry. All that was left for the doorman to do was open the door. His gesture was met with a tired, "Danke."

Yadin handed the driver his desired destination written on a piece of paper in Arabic and English. The Kuwaiti taxi driver, who was getting paid good money to be here at this hour, took a peek in the rearview mirror for confirmation and shrugged his shoulders. He had been cautioned the trip might be unusual, but if that was where the man wanted to go at this hour, that was where he'd take him. A couple of years ago, the taxi driver would never have made the trip, but the coalition forces and subsequent handover to trained Iraqi soldiers made the trip less of a life gamble. Still, one made the journey with caution. Providing the necessary paperwork, they passed through the border crossing with no problem.

In the distance, even in the darkness of night, Yadin could make out the Rumaila oil fields as they stretched for miles. Acts of sabotage on the various pipelines and wells were a rare occurrence now. The message had been ruthlessly sent: you don't halt the pursuit of serious money. Oil was a major income producer.

Yadin was thankful for the night air blowing through the open windows. It certainly helped to drown out the heavy cigarette smell and whatever other foul ways of life the driver preferred. Yadin passed the time going over what he'd already committed to memory. It was not unlike being an actor, prepping for a part, waiting for the cameras to start rolling. When a mistake could mean your life, going over the details again and again was not a problem. They rode in silence for most of the way, the driver recognizing his passenger was not the talkative kind. Yadin rebuffed the feeble attempts at conversation by pretending his English was not very good and Arabic was a lost cause. "Businessman" was all he gave the driver in shaky English. The driver formed a disapproving, sour look out of view. He considered his backseat occupant just another foreigner trying to rob the poor in a region rich with opportunity. But as long as his pockets were lucratively getting filled for trips such as this, the taxi driver gladly put up with such behavior. He had to put food on the table for his family. Still, there was something about his passenger that made him feel uneasy.

Relieved, the driver rolled the taxi to a stop. Looking around at the eerie isolation, he shook his head slightly before speaking slowly in English. "We are here." A handsome amount of money was handed over. The sound of the door shutting was akin to a drum banging in a cavernous, empty concert hall. Yadin watched as the taxi spun around and hurried away. He took a deep breath and walked toward the large, locked iron gate, the centerpiece of a fence line that ran for miles. On the other side, two men watched with interest. One was leaning against a Mercedes sedan, having a smoke. The other, behind the wheel, had awakened after the smoker tapped the hood a couple of times. The smoker barked orders for the uniformed guards on duty to open the gate. The second man shook off the last remnants of sleep and got out to join his partner. Both looked at each other as the stranger casually strode through the gate. His arrival was certainly low profile for one who was to be treated so royally. If he was that important, why not fly into Tehran and receive a dignitary's welcome instead of sneaking into the country under the cover of darkness just outside of Basra? The answer to that, of course, was beyond their need to know, and they dared not ask. Their orders had come from their superior, who'd received them from his boss, and ultimately, it was rumored, the directive came from none other than the secretary general of the Supreme National Security Council himself. They were directed to speak only when spoken to and to treat the visitor with the utmost respect. If there was anything he wanted, they were to get it for him.

The smoker flicked his cigarette away and stiffened as he closed the distance hesitantly.

"Dr. Mueller?"

In perfect Farsi, Yadin said, "You expecting someone else?" He flashed a wry smile and pushed past the pair. Not waiting to be invited, he opened the rear door on the driver's side of the luxury vehicle and threw his bag inside. His escorts didn't move.

Yadin was leaning against the open door.

"Again, unless you're waiting for someone else . . ."

CHAPTER 46

The engine of the compact reminded Alex it wasn't built for speed, but he pressed anyway, his mind on autopilot.

The names and faces of past associations once again nightmarishly ran through his mind. He knew why they were there, pointing a finger at him, their blank stares accusing him. The man who'd ordered their deaths had long ago been dealt with, but the executioner, with all his brutality, was unjustly still among the living. Dmitri Nevsky deserved to die, and Alex could have ended his life. He was that close. With his martial arts training and the element of surprise on his side, it could have been done in a matter of seconds. Clearly, though, he would have also been committing suicide. Nevsky had plenty of firepower around him. Survival wouldn't have been an option, and despite his guilt-ridden feelings, Alex had no plans to die on this day. He wanted to be back at his ocean-side house on St. Thomas, rum and Coke in hand, trade winds soothing his spirit, and music from Bob James or Coltrane playing in the background. That symbolized a relaxing day, and it was the kind of day he'd been having until Nora came back into his life. Now the departed were back as well.

"Hey, damn it, are you listening to me?" Mr. Green questioned impatiently. Alex snapped out of his daze.

"What the hell is it?"

Mr. Green displayed and aimed the small-caliber handgun Alex suspected was there all along. "Don't forget who's in control here."

Alex thought about violently veering off the road for a second, taking the gun from Mr. Green and then rewardingly smacking the barrel over his head. He let the thought pass. Besides, he couldn't afford to stop, because he was sure they were being followed. It had to be Nevsky's people, and they were good, keeping their distance. Alex wondered if a tracking device had been attached to the car, and then he remembered the briefcase in the backseat. Both the car and briefcase had been out of their sight, so either could easily have been tagged. The headlights appeared sporadically, but they were back there. Alex didn't want to let Mr. Green know what he suspected just yet.

"Yeah, you're in control. You're the guy with the gun."

Mr. Green was awfully glad he had the gun, because the big man was intimidating. "Now that my end of the deal is complete, you need to pay me the balance of what you owe me."

"Well, I can't very well do that right at this moment."

"You can wire transfer the money, yes?"

"I'll have to make a call, but yes."

"Good, I have a computer where I'm staying. We can conclude our business there."

"Speaking of making a call, I'd like my phone back."

Mr. Green reached inside his pocket and placed the phone on the dashboard. Alex put it away.

"Clever of you to lock the phone with a password. I should tell you someone has been texting you for quite a while. Perhaps you're in trouble."

Alex let the observation pass without comment, but he fully intended to see who'd been texting Davis Lipton's phone. His attention shifted to a more pressing problem. Alex noticed that the headlights were more prominent now, beginning to close the distance. He wondered about one thing in particular. Their business had concluded and they were allowed to leave, so why the tracking?

It was obvious Nevsky hadn't been pleased to see Mr. Green with a partner. Or had Nevsky's memory finally connected the dots?

CHAPTER 47

"What the hell are you doing?"

Alex didn't bother responding. Instead, he floored the accelerator and gripped the steering wheel tighter. In the rearview mirror he could see headlights gaining ground fast. They were less than two miles away.

"Slow down, damn it! Are you trying to get us killed?" Mr. Green once again brought his gun out for show. "I said, slow it down."

Alex gave him a no-nonsense look before returning his attention to the road. "I sure hope you know how to use that thing."

"I do. Why?"

"We've been followed since we left the airfield. I would suspect they're Nevsky's men. At first, it was a loose tail, but I don't think they're catching up to say we forgot something."

Mr. Green nearly pulled a muscle turning to glance out the back window.

"Why didn't you say something?"

Alex looked at him sarcastically. "Oh, Mr. I'm-in-charge, what would you have us do? Get out of the car, flag them down, and threaten them with your gun?"

"Shit!" Mr. Green screamed, staring at his prized briefcase in the backseat. "I knew it was a mistake to bring you along."

Alex understood that this car wasn't going to outperform the superior engineering behind them, so he had to come up with a plan of action now.

"If you value what's in that briefcase, I suggest you grab it now."

Mr. Green didn't quite understand the urgency, but he did as suggested. His hand was barely around the handle when instinct forced him to use his right hand to brace himself as the car veered off the road and screeched to a stop. The seatbelt did its job of holding him in place, and when his head snapped back hard against the headrest, he saw that McBride was already exiting the vehicle. He also heard him shout, "You don't have time to think! Get out of the car and start running into the woods!"

He wanted to protest this crazy maneuver, but as the trailing car's headlights began to illuminate his position, Mr. Green pushed himself free. Twenty seconds later, the sound of tires screeching and doors slamming shut echoed in the night. Agitated voices barking in Russian followed. Alex looked over his shoulder as he ran. As best he could tell, there were three of them. His question of how heavily they were armed was answered almost immediately, as two of them sprayed the area with machine gun fire. Alex crouched behind a huge tree and told Mr. Green, who was behind him, to do the same. From the muzzle flashes, Alex could tell the two men were advancing as they fired. They weren't seeking targets as much as they were attempting to provide cover fire for the third man to move ahead much faster in an attempt to locate their position.

The rapid fire was now concentrating to their right, so Alex instructed Mr. Green to move fast. Even over the crescendo of gunfire, Alex could hear the man's accelerated breathing. It was a clear sign Mr. Green wasn't cut out for this, but the adrenaline would serve him well, force him to keep moving. They continued to run at a good clip when Alex suddenly stopped and held out his arm to halt Mr. Green's movement. The gunfire had ceased. When Mr. Green was about to ask a question, Alex placed an index finger to his lips—the man's breathing was already making enough noise. At this juncture in the woods, all they could hear was nature. Leaves and tree branches rattled in the wind, and the native calls of insects surrounded them. Alex figured the Russians had stopped, attempting to get a fix on them by listening for footfalls.

Alex slowly dropped down and searched for a rock. The lead Russian was close. Mr. Green's hand was trembling badly as it snugly held onto the handgun he assumed gave him so much authority. Alex just hoped he wouldn't give their position away or stupidly dislodge a round.

It took a couple of stealthy passes, but Alex found a baseball-sized rock. He scanned as best he could the land and obstacles to his left. There was an opening suitable for his intentions, but in order to not alert the man canvassing from his right, he resigned himself to achieving a less-than-desired result. If he tried to throw the rock with too much force, he ran the risk of his clothing making too much noise or of exhaling air with a sound that would betray his position. A huge tree trunk gave him ample concealment. He slowly wound up his arm and let the rock fly high in the air. It landed about twenty-five yards away, and the aftereffects provided the symphony he'd hoped for. Once the rock disturbed a bit of brush, rolling a bit as well, to indicate movement, a flock of birds got spooked and noisily flew away. What followed was rapid automatic gunfire in the direction of the noise. The man to Alex's right took off in a sprint, firing into the darkness too. He passed Alex just a few feet away. The firing continued, and Alex took off in the man's wake, careful to establish a position on a line directly behind him. Alex quickly closed the distance, and he accelerated more once he saw his perfect opportunity. Alex was close enough now to hear the man's breathing, and at the same time, the man slowly began to realize someone was on his heels. Still running, he turned his head to see if his suspicion was correct. It was more than Alex could have hoped for. The man's direction gave Alex leverage. He reached out with his left hand and firmly grabbed the side of the Russian's face. The next move was more a credit to football than to his survival training. He kept driving with his legs for optimum force, and with all his weight, he slammed the man's head into the trunk of a tree. If not for the automatic fire, the sickening sound of a pumpkin being dropped from high up would have given him away.

Alex retrieved the man's weapon. The next part would be tricky. With darkness as his cover, he continued to run in the direction of the rock he had thrown, emulating the fallen man's hurried movements. Alex even fired a round. Once again he found refuge behind a thick tree, and he decided this would be the best place, because going any further exposed him to wide open spaces—an easy kill zone. In the midst of the excitement, the blood pumping, the thrill of the hunt, he decided to utilize a little trickery. He'd find out soon enough if it would work. Speaking rapidly and as if slightly out of breath, Alex bellowed in Russian, "Good shot. Good shot. We got them both."

He heard the other two men congratulate each other as they continued their approach. Alex hoped they'd relax their weapons.

"Where are you, Grigory?"

"Straight ahead," Alex responded, exposing part of his body just long enough for them to establish his position. They were close enough now that he could make out their faces. At that point, Alex stepped fully from behind the tree, the 9 mm ready. The two men were at ease, their weapons down by their sides. When their eyes adjusted and realized it wasn't Grigory, there was a panicked pause before they tried to react. Alex never gave them a chance to respond. Aiming at this proximity ensured each shot would be perfect. It only took two bullets, one for each forehead. The pair fell in unison, as if synchronized dying were a sporting event.

CHAPTER 48

"If I were you, I'd get that idea out of your head." Alex was dead serious as he addressed Mr. Green. They stood between the two vehicles on the side of the dark road, only a few feet apart. "You've got a suitcase full of money and you're alive to spend it. Cut your losses and move on."

Mr. Green was calculating his options. "But I have to return to my hotel."

"Are you just trying to get killed? Nevsky's men were sent to silence you and me and get the money back. He's going to be beyond upset when they don't return. Your hotel would be the first place I'd look."

"He doesn't know where I'm staying."

"So no one knows your hotel?"

Mr. Green had a distant look on his face as he thought about the question. "Only the Iranians," he confessed.

"The same people associated with the ones loading the plane back there?"

"I would assume so, yes."

"And you don't think—"

"No, they wouldn't set me up," Mr. Green was fast to respond. "They're supposed to pick me up later today and take me to Iran."

"What?" Alex said, shaking his head. "Why? I was under the impression your part of the deal ended back there."

"They want assurances the product is good. They've been valued customers, and I'd like to keep it that way. Besides, they say the president wants to meet me and offer his thanks."

Alex had to think fast. He didn't like the idea of being exposed on the road like this. There was the possibility Nevsky had already sent backup.

"So you've met with the Iranians before?"

"On occasion. But most of our transactions have gone through intermediaries. Besides," Mr. Green patted the suitcase, "they owe me money. A lot more than what is in here, I might add."

"Again, you and money. Look, I'm trying to talk some sense into you. Live to make a deal another day. In this world, I'm sure there'll be others."

"What are you suggesting? Are you trying to steal my profit?"

"There won't be a windfall if you're not around to spend it."

Mr. Green was about to slide inside his new Mercedes. "I suppose I should thank you. As a token of my appreciation, I'll waive the rest of the fee you owe me." He threw the suitcase onto the passenger seat and positioned himself behind the wheel, searching for the controls to adjust the seat.

"The Marriott," Alex called out.

"What?" Mr. Green leaned his head out the window to hear.

"The Marriott. That's where you're staying."

The pistol was back in Mr. Green's hand as he slowly emerged from the vehicle.

"If I know that, what makes you think Nevsky doesn't?"

Mr. Green pondered the situation. The performance he'd just witnessed in the woods wasn't lost on him. Besides, McBride was also holding a weapon.

"I have backup."

Alex checked the road and, thankfully, there were no headlights in either direction. "If you mean the man sitting on the bench outside the cathedral, I wouldn't count on it." There was a glimpse of disbelief on Mr. Green's face.

"He'll be fine. What I'm trying to get across to you is that you're in way over your head at this point. You need to step aside and get lost. Tonight, you got very lucky." Alex understood that included him as well.

Mr. Green put the pistol away with an affirmative nod. "Perhaps you are right. There will be other opportunities."

"Good. Now, tell me about the Iranians again. You said they're coming for you?"

"Yes, I'm supposed to be picked up sometime this afternoon."

"Do you have to take anything with you? Provide them with anything?"

"No. I suppose in case something goes wrong, they want me there for my expertise."

"Goes wrong?"

Mr. Green hunched his shoulders and raised his eyebrows. "Aside from being introduced to the president, I was told I would be part of something spectacular."

"And you have no idea what that something is?"

"Not a clue. I asked, but they didn't tell me anything more."

"All right," Alex said as he turned to get into the compact. "Remember. Don't go back to the hotel."

"But I have things there I need."

"Come back late tonight. It should be safe by then. I can't stress enough how important it is for you to disappear for a while. Your life may depend on it."

Alex started to ease into the compact but remembered one more thing. He walked back to Mr. Green's new set of wheels. "I almost forgot. Take all the money out and throw the suitcase away. There's a very good chance it has a tracking device in it."

Mr. Green stared at his bounty as if it were an unfaithful lover. When he looked back, Alex had the car back onto the road.

The rush of the past few hours had kept him going, but now Alex's body was telling him it needed to shut down. He tried not to listen, because there was much to be done. For the drive back into Tbilisi, he kept his mind sharp by concentrating on one thing.

How he was going to kill Dmitri Nevsky.

CHAPTER **49**

Alex stared at the hotel room clock, but the numbers didn't really matter. If he had to get people out of bed, too damn bad. The inconvenience came with the job.

From Sara he'd learned Mr. Green was in all likelihood Victor Janko, an engineer of Czech descent. Confirmation had come from Langley. She'd also gotten Alex up to speed on the other documents he possessed and his Swiss bank account numbers.

When Nora handed him a cup of coffee, he noticed how apprehensive she seemed. This whole ordeal had to be tearing her up inside. Someone she considered a dear friend and who'd been her mentor was dead. As a result, her life was in turmoil. Her seeking him out, after the way he'd so emphatically ended their relationship, was proof that she was truly at the end of her rope. And now, the pain she felt for involving others was hard to hide. On several occasions, he caught her looking at him with worried eyes.

Alex tried to shake away the cobwebs. He went to the bathroom to throw cold water on his face, running his wet hands through his hair. The reflection in the mirror confirmed what his body was telling him. He wasn't sure how much more he could accomplish. It seemed clear that whatever was underfoot was going to take place in Iran. With no cover story and no assets, he'd be walking into certain death if he made the journey. Even if he did go, he wouldn't know what to do next. As much as he'd been able to keep up from newspaper and Internet accounts over the years, he knew Iran had four potential nuclear facilities shrouded in secrecy. Refusing to allow the International Atomic Energy

Agency to inspect the sites was either an admission of progress or another defiant stance. It wasn't like he could just show up at the front gates and ask if the stockpile of centrifuges he'd seen a few hours ago was on the premises.

He had relayed all the night's proceedings to Sara, Nora, and Duncan, except for one thing. He omitted the presence of Dmitri Nevsky. The name would have no meaning to Sara and Duncan, but it would register in an instant with Nora. She knew how the name had haunted him, the one piece of unfinished business as he left the CIA. He'd tried to find Nevsky before, but shortly after his murderous spree in Iraq, he vanished into the wind. Nevsky would have known the territory was dangerous once his ally was taken out. For now, Nevsky's presence was something Nora didn't need to know about.

Peering out the window, down upon a relatively quiet Tbilisi, Alex came to the only conclusion his tired brain could hash out. "Sara, there may not be much time, because I don't know when the Iranians are due to arrive this afternoon looking for Janko or, possibly, Mr. Green. He seemed to at least be careful in that regard."

"So what are you thinking?"

"You need to call Champion."

She did the math in her head. It was a quarter to seven at night in Washington, and in all likelihood, the director of the National Clandestine Service was still at Langley. Alex started to suggest she use a secure line but thought better of it, knowing it would only insult her intelligence.

Champion had been in a meeting, but as soon as the call came through, he cleared his office. He took down everything Alex was saying and wished his once prized pupil were still under his command. When Alex finished his briefing, Champion was quick to follow up, wanting clarity in no uncertain terms, because he was sure his career would be on the line tonight.

"You say the Iranians are going to come looking for this Janko person in the afternoon? But you don't know exactly when?"

"That would be what I've been telling you." Champion could hear the sarcasm in Alex's voice but attributed part of it to fatigue.

"Hundreds of centrifuges . . ." Champion said, but it was more for his own clarity.

"What?"

"I'm just thinking out loud. You also said Janko was told something spectacular was going to occur?"

"You're totally caught up. Now you need to get someone here who's an engineer who can possibly go in his place."

"Yeah, Rocky, I'll pull a rabbit out of my hat. Like I have someone in the area with that skill set who can handle himself in a covert situation."

"Surely you've got some assets on the ground in Iran who can lend a hand."

"It's taken years for those individuals to establish a credible cover. Taking the risk of exposing them now could set us back years, and then we'd be making assessments with virtually no human intel. That's not a part of the world you want to go dark in right now."

"I'm sure you'll figure something out."

Champion was silent, and for a moment Alex wondered if he'd lost the connection. "You said you're pretty sure they don't know who Janko's associates might be?"

"That's right."

"But they did see you and him at the airfield?"

"We were pretty visible and there looked to be Iranians there."

"Well then, it's a no-brainer."

"What is?"

"What name do you want to go by?"

"Not a chance in hell," Alex responded when he understood what Champion was suggesting.

"I'm not the one who got involved here. You laid the foundation on this one when you went out of your way to help Nora."

"Let me remind you, I don't work for the government anymore."

"And let me remind you that you kidnapped one and assaulted two government agents. How much prison time do you want?"

"You don't have the balls to pull a public stunt like that."

"You're probably right. But how motivated will Senator Lipton be to making your life a living hell?"

Alex thought about what Champion didn't know at the moment regarding that matter. Once he got wind that Davis Lipton had been shot in the foot on his orders, the heat would intensify.

"You know this is bullshit. I'm not qualified for this anymore."

"From everything you've told me, you're the only option at this point. I'm going be honest with you . . ."

"No, please lie to me."

"I'll go the extra mile to keep you as safe as I can. But if it means exposing vital assets in Iran, that's not going to happen. Not unless you're stepping into Armageddon. You pull this off, and we'll probably learn some vital things we didn't know before."

Alex looked at Nora, who was trying to decipher the conversation by hearing only his half. He couldn't avoid the subject. "What about Janway?" he asked Champion. "That's what started this whole thing."

"Those responsible will be dealt with."

"Does that include the senator?"

"As soon as I get off the phone with you, I'll get to work on that. You're not the only one about to risk a lot. Now, so I can get them started on your cover story, give me a name. And since you've been away for some time, I suggest you make it one you can easily remember."

Alex wanted to protest some more, but exhaustion was washing away his resistance. He wanted to stay with the surname of McBride. It had served him well so far.

"Wayne McBride," he decided.

"Mr. McBride, get some sleep. You sound like shit."

Rather than offer a sarcastic response, Alex hung up. Nora immediately stepped forward with raised arms.

He tried to brush by her, pretending not to notice. "I need to get some sleep."

She halted his exit by grabbing an arm. "If I understand that conversation, I can't ask you to do this! It's foolish. Hell, it's suicidal!"

"There aren't a whole lot of options here."

"You've helped me do what I asked, which was to keep me safe. You've done that. You don't need to do anything more."

"What about Janway?"

"Now that I know which direction to head, I'll eventually take care of that."

"Hey, I hear Iran is beautiful this time of year."

"Damn it, Alex! No!"

He smiled. "I'm going to bed."

"Listen, I should have never involved you in this. Coming to St. Thomas was a mistake. Washington, Brussels, and even here are one thing, but trekking through Iran on a whim with little or no backup is sheer madness." Nora closed her eyes, hating herself at the moment. Once Alex made up his mind, there was no sense in trying to convince him otherwise. She pleadingly looked into his eyes. "Don't do it. Don't do it for me. I was wrong years ago, and I was wrong for seeking you out."

"You might be dead if you didn't, and on some level, if that had happened, I'd probably get involved anyway." If Sara wasn't in the room, Nora would have rushed into his arms and kissed him with all the passion they used to share. Instead, Alex turned for the bedroom, pausing at the door to reach into his pocket. He tossed Davis Lipton's cell phone to Sara. "Apparently someone's been burning up his phone with messages. Find out who it is, and if necessary, make an appropriate response. Don't want any more complications at this juncture. Wake me up if there's something important or if any Iranians come knocking at the door."

CHAPTER 50

Champion caught Amanda Jergens in transit. He could hear the intermittent blasts of police sirens in the background. That, coupled with her guarded tone upon answering her cell phone, led him to one conclusion. She was part of the presidential motorcade.

Upon seeing the caller ID, she almost didn't answer. Doing so meant apologizing and excusing herself from the ongoing conversation, interrupting the president in the process. The only reason she did answer was because of their lunch meeting from the other day.

She spoke just loudly enough to be heard, turning her head into the window and away from the rest of the occupants in the vehicle.

"This had better be good." Despite being a whisper, her tone came across loud and clear to Champion.

"I told you I'd call when there was something to lose sleep over."

She gave a reassuring smile to the commander in chief, who was mildly interested as he continued his discussion on economic matters.

"Does this concern any of the gentlemen we talked about the other day?"

"Yes, and as a result, there might be something in the works that needs drastic attention."

Amanda didn't like the sound of that. "Well, why don't you make sure it gets in the PDB?"

Champion laughed for a moment. "No way can this go in the President's Daily Brief. I need to see him tonight. One-on-one."

She closed her eyes and took a deep breath. *Why tonight? Why me?* It figured that, on what was supposed to be an uneventful agenda, things would get complicated under her watch. Her immediate boss, the White House chief of staff, felt the lax atmosphere was a good opportunity for her to spend time with the president. He reminded her that the most powerful man in the world had handpicked her all by himself. No small order on anybody's political menu. Being seen at his side only increased her prominence in Washington. These jobs weren't going to last forever. She also knew the chief of staff was relishing the opportunity to play Texas Hold 'em with certain congressmen from the Hill, all men who could bluff with the best of them.

Champion was in a similar situation. The spy stuff he could stomach. Dealing with flip-flopping, opportunistic, and partisan politicians was something he had yet to acquire a taste for. Nonetheless, after hanging up with Alex, he'd immediately gone to his boss's office. Director Doyle had greeted him warmly, as always. As a mentor, he'd always been even keel with his protégé, passing along knowledge of not only how the world operated, but on Washington's inner workings as well. It would've been easy for Doyle to pick up the phone and handle this matter, but he explained to Champion this was a perfect opportunity to impress the president. Champion mentioned that his only encounter with the White House's newest resident had come when he'd been the president elect, and on that social evening, there'd been hundreds of hands to shake and certainly more-important faces and résumés to remember.

"So you'll hit the ground running," Doyle pointed out with a sly grin. "Of course, if you're wrong and you screw this up . . . what was your major in college?"

Doyle was certain Champion would be the right person to succeed him. There'd be strong opposition for sure, and his confirmation hearing wouldn't be a walk in the park. Doyle knew the biggest objection, sadly, would come from his demographic: a bunch of old fart politicians who didn't relish the idea of giving such a high-profile job to a man in his forties. Never mind that Champion had done more to keep this country safe than they had ever accomplished on Capitol Hill while sitting on their butts.

Champion waited for Amanda to give him an answer. If she said no, he was prepared to go over her head. He prayed he didn't have to go that route.

Amanda assessed the request and the evening's itinerary. They were on their way to Woodrow Wilson Senior High School and, amazingly, on time for once. The president was to honor the school for its continued academic prowess and for the diversity of its student body. The school stood as a glowing example of the fact that when young people were determined and pointed in the right direction, a great deal could be accomplished. It was the perfect platform for the president to hit home his education agenda. Amanda felt she could make the meeting happen, but it all depended on how quickly Champion could get to the school. By her best judgment, making it from Langley would be pushing it at best, and no way in hell was she going to hold the president up. That went against everything the Secret Service had drilled into their heads. When in transit, follow procedure.

"George, how quickly can you get to—"

"Woodrow Wilson? I'm already here."

Amanda pursed her lips until they were like prunes.

"I'm beginning to not like you."

CHAPTER 51

After ending her phone conversation, Amanda tried to wait for an opening but was left with no choice except to interrupt the president. She spent several minutes explaining that an important member of the intelligence community needed to steal a few minutes with him at the school before he addressed the student body. When pressed what it was about, Amanda admitted she didn't feel comfortable mentioning any specifics in front of the press secretary and the secretary of education. She promised it wouldn't take much of his time, though that was a stretch, since she really had no idea what Champion was going to convey. In any event, she hoped her friend realized he was putting his career on the line. If this turned into a total waste of the president's time, she would be reprimanded but still a part of the inner circle.

Once the president agreed, Amanda called ahead to the Secret Service detail and conveyed what had to happen. Champion had already identified himself, and after her call, the agents whisked him inside the school while searching for a secure location.

Because it had no windows and each exit could be guarded, the Secret Service settled on the cafeteria's kitchen. After doing a quick sweep, they told Champion to stay put and left him in place, alone.

The kitchen was exceptionally sterile: white marble floors, white walls, and shiny stainless-steel appliances. Overhead fluorescent lights completed the environment. Outside the doors at each end of the kitchen, there was a Secret Service Agent posted. In the distant background, he could hear a muffled youthful assembly growing louder by the minute. He was isolated with his thoughts for roughly ten minutes, ample time to go over and over how he was going to present his case. It wasn't lost on him that this was also, as Director Doyle pointed out, a golden opportunity to impress the man who, with any luck, would see fit to promote him in the near future. That was an unnerving thought in its own right, but in all truthfulness, he didn't give a damn at the moment about becoming the next director of the Central Intelligence Agency. What concerned him was squashing those who were attempting to run their own unsanctioned endgame with US government assets.

He snapped to attention when the thunderous noise of the assembled masses came crashing through one of the kitchen doors when it swung open. A burly Secret Service agent came through first, shielding the people following directly behind him. He gave Champion an indifferent stare. If the need arose, he'd pull out his semiautomatic weapon and blast Champion into the next world while maintaining that same look. Satisfied, he stepped to the side.

Champion's attention immediately focused on the familiar face of Amanda, who was revealed when the Secret Service agent peeled away. The look on her face was not that of an old friend who was happy to see him. Her pace was quick as she headed his way, and flanking her was President Travis Hudson. He was taller and thinner than Champion remembered. He could imagine there were a few square meals left unfinished as a result of constantly being on the go. Hudson had been in office just past a year, but the stress of the job hadn't affected his fashion-model looks much. Pair that face with his eloquence and ability to rally people, and it was understandable why he was the man standing in the kitchen at this moment.

"Mr. President, this is George Champion." Amanda had informed the president of Champion's title while still in the sedan, where she had further explained the situation after the other occupants had departed upon arriving at the school. The president didn't quite understand the urgency of the situation or the unorthodox circumstances. He had asked Amanda why this meeting couldn't take place later at the White House. She had cursed her friend's existence for about the seventh time when she had to admit she wasn't clear why, only that Champion had stressed it was time sensitive.

"He *used to be* a friend of mine, sir," Amanda added. "George, President Hudson." They exchanged a firm handshake.

"Sir, thank you for seeing me," Champion said, feeling every bit out of place.

Hudson nodded with a courteous smile. "We've met before. At a function in the District shortly after I became president elect."

"That's correct, sir." Champion looked at Amanda for a second, wondering if she had fed him that tidbit or if his memory and powers of observation were that keen.

"Director Doyle and others speak highly of you. So, what's on your mind?"

What ensued was an awkward moment as Champion shifted his attention to Amanda.

"What?" she demanded.

Champion couldn't spare the time to be diplomatic. "If you don't mind, I need you to leave right now."

Amanda threw him another look, which told him he could add this move to the growing list of things there would be hell to pay for later.

"Fine!" Amanda said, making her way out. "I'll be right outside, sir."

Still not satisfied, Champion looked past the president at the lone Secret Service agent. Based solely on praise bestowed upon the man in front of him, President Hudson spoke over his shoulder. "Bob, give us a minute." The secret serviceman's demeanor didn't waver as he slid through the door, leaving the two men alone.

"The kitchen is yours," said the president. "What's on the menu?"

"Sir, I believe Senator Bryce Lipton is engaged in unsanctioned activities that are outside the scope of our foreign policy and could very well place our global standing in grave jeopardy. He may have also been responsible for the death of a CIA agent."

"Whew, you swing for the fences don't you?" an astonished Hudson remarked.

"I don't have the time to mince words, sir. In order to possibly prevent him and others from succeeding, I have to act now, but I need to know how far you're willing to let me take this, if at all."

The assembly crowd was getting impatient, and chants of "We want Hudson" echoed down the hallways. It would continue a while longer as the president gave Champion another five minutes before deciding they would discuss this at length at the White House later.

In the interim, the president gave Champion the green light to do what was necessary. As he headed for his awaiting fan club, President Hudson couldn't help but be impressed by the man from the CIA.

CHAPTER 52

The voices were faint, but the conversation was spirited and lively.

Alex sat up in bed, waiting for his body to finish its assessment. There were no aches, pains, or headaches. According to the bedside clock, he'd slept for four hours. He wondered how long they'd been going at it in the other room. There was at least coffee, its aroma motivating him to get moving.

He threw water on his face, put on a hotel robe, and headed for the coffee. His arrival halted all conversation. Looking back at him with blank stares were Nora and Duncan. They were seated around two tables pulled together. Papers and maps cluttered the surface. There was a box on one of the other chairs, and it too was full.

"I take it we had a delivery?" Alex asked while pouring a cup of coffee.

"Local office by way of Langley," Nora confirmed, a trace of friction in her voice. "Your new ID documents are here too."

"That was fast."

"Some things have changed during your absence. They're still building your background, though, filling in every gap that comes to mind."

Alex picked up on Duncan watching his every move. "What?" Alex demanded.

Duncan chuckled and spread his hands over the contents on the table. "Have you lost your *F*-in' mind? Houdini couldn't pull this off."

Alex rolled his eyes. "So, what do we have here?"

"He's right, you know," Nora chimed in. "There's way too much that can go wrong."

Alex took a seat at the table. "I'm excited, because according to Janko, we might be getting some sort of recognition. It would be rude to just blow it off."

Nora bit her lip, and Duncan shook his head. In the final analysis, if Alex concluded he couldn't pull this off, he'd say so and shut it down. He didn't owe anybody anything, least of all his government, and Nora had told him he'd already done everything she'd hoped for.

Though it had been years since they last spent any measurable time together, Nora knew Alex well enough to wonder what was motivating him to continue. He had always been a man of conviction and purpose. Rarely was doing anything stupid part of his agenda. There had to be something he was holding back.

Alex scanned the items on the table and tried to piece together as much as he could. "What am I looking at?" he asked.

Duncan cleared room on the table and positioned several items in front of Alex. He tapped a set of satellite images.

"The question is, where in Iran are those centrifuges you inspected going? The smart money is on a site known as Natanz," Duncan said, placing an index finger on the location. "It's one of several facilities the Iranians are working on. They've learned how to play the game of deception very well. In '81, an Israeli air strike destroyed a plant under construction. A preemptive attack today would be met by a number of antiaircraft defense systems."

"So why is the CIA sold on Natanz?"

"A ton of activity, for one. It's a uranium enrichment facility the Iranians claim will only be used to fuel nuclear power plants to provide energy. But with the right materials, it can be transformed into a weapons-grade program. It's about 160 miles south of Tehran, and the last estimate anyone could come up with was that Natanz is big enough to house sixty thousand centrifuges. That kind of inventory can produce enough uranium for twenty-five ten-kiloton nuclear bombs a year. The bomb dropped on Hiroshima was fifteen kilotons. Seventy thousand people . . . poof," Duncan said, extending his arms for emphasis. "The Iranians have been constantly upgrading the centrifuges at Natanz in search of a more efficient and powerful means of enriching uranium. As you can see, they started to build part of the facility aboveground. Then, they got secretive and creative." Duncan rifled through a pile, searching for another satellite image. Once he located it, he circled a section before handing it over to Alex. "That is a tunnel entrance—and it marks a blind spot, since satellites can't see underground. And with no International Atomic Energy Agency inspectors allowed inside . . ."

"No one really knows what the hell they have down there," Alex finished.

"That's the scary part. It's also heavily fortified. Watchtowers and guards all along the perimeter. Plus, the Russians officially deny they supplied them, but it's believed S-300 surface-to-air missile systems are on the premises as well. Those nasty little babies can track aircraft and fire at them from more than a hundred miles away."

Alex mulled that image over for a second.

"I know what you're thinking," Nora interjected. "If fighter jets were capable of making it past the defense systems, why not just drop crater or bunker-busting bombs? The answer is based on the amount of dirt and sand hauled away. The Iranians fortified the structure beneath the surface so it more than likely can withstand such an attack. They're hunkered down pretty deep below ground."

Duncan raised a cautionary finger. "Besides, if that reactor goes operational, you can't bomb it." He addressed Nora's quizzical look. "You wouldn't be able to because the fallout would make Chernobyl look like a two-alarm fire."

Alex exhaled as he examined more of the images, taking in the sequential building blocks of what appeared to be a humongous project. "There's still a way to take it down."

"Do tell, Yoda," Duncan said, waiting to be impressed.

"It has to be done from the inside."

"Yeah, and if I could wave a magic wand, I'd win the lottery."

Nora exhibited disbelief as well. "And just how do you propose to get all the stuff inside so you could take it down? The place is too well guarded. Everything and everybody going in and out is accounted for."

Alex nodded. "I understand that. But what if what you need is already down there?"

CHAPTER 53

He rode from the southern border of Iran in silence during the wee hours of the morning and was eventually deposited at the luxury hotel while most of Tehran still slept. The check-in process was conducted by his two transportation specialists, who departed his side only after he'd settled into the most expensive suite at the hotel, courtesy of the government.

Dr. Franz Mueller had proved to be vital in building the nuclear plant at Natanz. In return, the Iranians had made Mueller a rich man. The majority of the millions he received was handed over to the Israeli government. The rest, a sizeable amount, Yadin had pocketed for himself. It paved the way for certain luxuries like his prized piece of real estate in Paris, but more importantly, it was bringing a comfortable retirement into focus. That was, of course, if he survived this mission. His acceptance of the Iranians' offer to be present for their crowning achievement came as a shock to them. Throughout the building process, Dr. Mueller had only stepped foot on Iranian soil four times. His reason for staying away needed no further explanation than that being too visible risked exposure to the Israelis. The Iranians understood. He was much too valuable to have an accident or vanish into thin air.

Yadin turned on the television and channel-surfed, quickly losing interest in the late-morning talking heads that seemed to dominate the airwaves. He took a quick shower, got dressed in relaxed clothing, and kept a leisurely pace as he moved through the lobby, asking for a taxi once outside. One pulled up in no time, and before it whisked him away, he noticed that the Iranian couple that had been sitting in the lounge area was coming outside. As the taxi departed, Yadin saw the man signaling a car to come forward.

Let the games begin.

CHAPTER 54

"You son of a bitch!"

Sara was at Alex's side before the door closed behind her. Her flared nostrils were breathing fire, and unconsciously she clenched her fists.

"Who the hell do you think you are?" she demanded. Alex was still seated at the table with Duncan and Nora as she hovered over him. Out of the corner of his eye, Alex caught Nora beginning to rise. He slightly shook his head to get her to sit back down.

"What's your problem?" Alex calmly responded without looking up.

"You had him shot? Are you fucking kidding me? You had him shot!"

"Oh, that." Alex couldn't contain a slight smirk.

"Yes, that! You arrogant bastard! Do you realize how much trouble you've gotten me in? He's my responsibility."

Nora was confused. "Got who shot?"

"Your ex here had Davis Lipton shot."

Alex raised a hand. "What? The foot! I had them shoot him in the foot. That little shit gave me bad information prior to going into the church. I could've gotten killed. I just wanted to send the message I wasn't screwing around."

There was silence in the room as Sara maintained her prickly stance, debating whether to lash out further.

"I'm sorry if I've jammed you up a bit, but if there's nothing else . . ." Alex's change in inflection made it clear it was time for

Sara to back off. She ran a hand across her face and drifted to the empty chair around the table.

"Good. One big happy family again," Duncan said, without diverting his attention from the table.

Sara was about to mouth something but thought better of it. She threw Davis Lipton's cell phone on top of all the clutter. "All the messages left on his phone were from the esteemed senator himself. Seems as if he was very worried about his son."

"'*Was* very worried'?" Nora questioned.

"Yes, Langley eased his mind by responding with a couple of text messages. Should he get suspicious, the times and location stamp will indicate they were sent from Tbilisi. Essentially, they convey that Davis didn't feel it was safe to talk openly." Sara cast her gaze upon Alex again. "Davis gave us all the safeguard codes for contacting his father. He was very cooperative."

Alex couldn't resist. "Guess he didn't want to get shot again."

Champion relished the chill of the night air. The back of his shirt and underarms were soaked with sweat. It was the main reason he hadn't taken off his suit coat while inside. He began to grasp how, in moments like this, some people sought comfort from a cigarette. He'd prefer a shot of something alcoholic and had even been offered one, but considering the company, he steadfastly and politely declined. He wanted to take that decision back now.

The meeting was pushing past two and a half hours. Numerous phone calls had been made, reversing the nighttime ritual for an unlucky few caught getting ready to turn in for the night. They were told to prepare for a potentially long night. President Hudson decided for the moment that high-ranking members of Congress would not be brought on board. At this point, a leak was unthinkable, and there would be hell to pay if one occurred.

A stream of cool air rustled the crabapple trees and swayed the primrose bushes and grape hyacinths, filling Champion's nostrils with a soothing scent. He took a deep breath, taking it all in. Here he was, standing just outside the Oval Office, the gorgeous and historic Rose Garden in front of him. He leaned against the wall of the West Wing Colonnade, the connector to the private residence of the White House.

He maintained a calm exterior, but on the inside, there was an intense wrestling match going on, his heart and stomach a tag team of uneasiness. He hadn't seen his wife, Jill, since they'd gotten out of bed yesterday morning. They'd played phone tag for most of the day. His last message to her indicated that he'd spent time with the man they both voted for and that he felt good in thinking the right choice was made. They'd finally connected after he passed through security at the White House. He let her know he had no idea when he'd be home. Though he heard the disappointment in her voice, regrettably she was getting used to hearing that his time and attention was needed elsewhere. There was a very good possibility he would simply return to Langley, grab whatever shut-eye he could steal on his sofa, and start his day from the office. It wouldn't be the first time.

Inside the White House he was initially greeted by a still-perturbed Amanda, who'd said little other than, "Follow me," as she escorted him, her day also elongated. Midway down a corridor, she'd finally gotten it out of her system. "You really have stirred up the pot. If I'd known lunch was going to lead to this . . ." She cringed. "You shithead!" What Amanda didn't tell him was that she'd spent five minutes praising him when the president asked her specifically about his qualities.

She delivered Champion to Bill Stern, chief of staff and her immediate boss. After shaking hands, Stern offered Champion a seat.

"Do you know Senator Bob Langdon?" Stern was sure the name wouldn't come as a surprise. He sat down right next to the man from the CIA.

Champion didn't grasp the connection, but if this was a test of how well versed he was on Washington insiders, he'd play along. "From Wisconsin? Chairman of the Commerce Committee."

"Exactly. Way back when, he played football for the Badgers. Still fancies himself quite a competitor. Well, Mr. Champion, I had a full boat in my hands tonight. Kings over queens, and there was a sizeable pot on the table." Stern paused to let the picture sink in. "I had to fold that hand because I got an emergency call to be back here. I'm a bit competitive, too."

Stern spent the next several minutes mildly grilling the relatively unknown visitor who had managed to put several of the most powerful people in the US government on call. He didn't push too hard because President Hudson had already informed him he thought Champion had potential. Tonight would go a long way toward confirming that assumption.

When Champion finally walked into the Oval Office, National Security Advisor Warren Spencer and Secretary of State Ron Drake stood up along with President Hudson to greet him.

"Doyle feeling okay?" the secretary of state inquired with a firm handshake, a little disappointment evident on his face.

So much for the pleasantries, Champion thought. "He's fine, Mr. Secretary. Pillar of health, actually. I'll make sure he knows you asked about him."

Champion didn't really have time to take in the magnitude of his surroundings, commonplace for the men he was now seated around. The home court advantage was clearly theirs, but he wasn't about to be intimidated.

"You can be frank and open here," President Hudson assured. "Try and overlook Ron's cynicism. He generally doesn't like too many people, which, for being secretary of state, is a pretty bad character flaw. I may have to address his appointment before my term is over."

The remark drew smiles and eased some tension. The secretary of state had a reputation for lacking charm, but President Hudson was actually pleased to have a bulldog like him on the leash when dealing with certain foreign entities.

Champion could tell by their body language that both Spencer and Drake were anxious to get this moving. The president, on the other hand, looked as fresh as he had early this morning, when the various cable networks carried his remarks live as he visited a local homeless shelter, pushing the importance of volunteerism. His energy was intoxicating, and Champion couldn't help but wonder how long he could keep it up.

"Am I to understand this has come together in a matter of weeks, if not days?" The question came from Spencer, who was known for having one of the brightest minds on the Hill. He'd been Hudson's highest priority when the new president was collecting the people who would form his administration. It was a tough sell, too, since Spencer had been thoroughly enjoying the challenges of a very lucrative private sector career. He'd stayed as far away from Washington as he could, because the previous administration had soured his belief in politics. Eventually, President

Hudson wore him down. Spencer had come on board with the understanding that he would speak his mind, even if it meant offending those who had established careers doing what they claimed was in the best interest of the American people.

Champion hesitated before responding, knowing the answer would only increase skepticism, but sometimes you had to put all your cards on the table. "That would be correct, sir," Champion said, making a point of maintaining eye contact. "I totally understand the concern here. This is not something you can be wrong about."

"Damn right," Drake shot back. "This is Senator Bryce Lipton we're talking about."

As was the case so many times, it only became important when a prominent name was involved. What did that take? Five minutes? Already Champion wasn't the secretary of state's biggest fan. "It's also the murder of someone from my side of the fence and an illegally sanctioned operation involving a foreign government that could have us on the brink of another war or a jihad. A situation this administration would have to deal with for years."

That assessment was greeted with thoughtful looks from the three powerful men. It certainly wasn't the way President Hudson wanted to spend his years in the Oval Office. He had run his campaign on the strength of change and a different path for a country that had seemingly lost its way.

A decidedly more controlled secretary of state addressed Champion this time. "Just how certain are you of Senator Lipton's involvement?"

Champion began to lay it all out for them, underscoring that whatever was planned appeared to be imminent. He explained that even though the operation had just recently come across the CIA's radar, it had been in play for a couple of years, starting with Erica Janway's being set up in Moscow. Jaws literally dropped when Champion relayed the information that was confirmed by Lipton's son, who played a pivotal role himself. They didn't need to be reminded that Davis Lipton worked for the CIA as well.

"He gave up this information willingly? Ratted out his old man just like that?" Spencer asked, his forehead rows of skepticism. Champion realized he had to tread very carefully. "I'll merely say that he understood the nature of the question and its implications."

Drake chuckled as he shifted forward. "What did you do, kidnap the boy and torture him?"

"He was detained by individuals who do not work for the agency."

Drake wasn't chuckling anymore as the president followed up, seeking clarity. "So, you're assuring us the CIA did not commission or outsource Lipton's detainment?"

"To be clear, the CIA gave no such directive."

After Champion had given the latest developments, which included confirmation of Davis Lipton's statement that a large shipment of centrifuges was packaged and ready to be shipped to Iran, the president decided to take a break. But first, he asked Champion to excuse himself and give them a moment.

Outside, Champion could see that the trio was still talking. President Hudson got up to stretch and while doing so, picked up the phone on his desk. It was a short conversation. Champion caught himself staring, so he returned his attention to the Rose Garden. He assumed it wouldn't be a violation of protocol, so he began to walk down the West Wing Colonnade to get some circulation back into his legs. There was a Secret Service agent stationed nearby, and probably a couple more he didn't immediately see, so if he was violating a rule, he'd know about it in no time. His mind drifted again to wondering how many people who had shaped this country's destiny had made this very walk. It was impossible to ignore the significance. On his way back toward the Oval Office, he noticed a pair of legs extending from a bench. The woman's face and body were blocked by one of the pillars that lined the corridor. As he got closer, he was prepared to give a courtesy "Hello" and keep moving. He stopped in his tracks just short of the bench when he saw it was Amanda. He smiled when he noticed her hands were occupied with two bottles of beer, one extended for him. He graciously took it and flopped down next to her, loosening his tie as he drank.

"Thanks."

Amanda finished a long swallow of her own. "Don't mention it. Even shitheads deserve a break."

CHAPTER 56

With Alex taking a shower, Nora was alone in the outer room. She buried her face in her hands. The events of the past few days had happened at a whirlwind pace.

It was still hard to accept that her dear friend Erica was gone. Some of her anger had dissipated, giving way to grief. She'd never see her friend again or hear her reassuring voice that never stopped mentoring. Now, she felt the pain of having put her former lover in a situation that could cost him his life. There was no one to blame for that except herself. Despite her telling him that he'd done enough, Alex was determined to see this through, and Nora didn't understand what was motivating him.

Not knowing the Iranians' timetable, Sara and Duncan cleared out all the documents and took them to the room down the hall. Duncan continued to study everything as if he were cramming for the most important exam of his life. If Alex was going to go forward with this ludicrous plan, he wanted his friend to have as much information as possible.

Nora was deciding whether or not it was a good idea to join them: the Iranians were probably expecting Janko to be alone. Alex was already taking a risk in hoping they would accept him in Janko's absence. The possibility existed that they would try to kill him to protect the secrecy of their operation.

Nora wished she could convince Alex to stand down. She thought about going into the bathroom while he showered and shooting him up with the tranquilizers still at their disposal. Duncan would help her move him to the other room. He'd sleep it off until the Iranians came and left empty-handed.

She shook her head at what was a stupid idea. He would only get angry with her all over again. What she couldn't easily dismiss was a burning desire to reunite with Alex. Being around him again felt right. He was good for her nerves, and she felt safe with him. Alex, though, hadn't indicated in any way that he still had any lingering feelings for her. It didn't matter to her at the moment. Could he really resist if she slipped her naked body into the shower next to him, ready to give him the release they both desperately needed? He would certainly remember how good it felt when they made love. She made up her mind and began unbuttoning her blouse. Next she tugged at her skirt, pulling it down, not regretting her decision. She had her hand on the bathroom door handle, anticipating him accepting her.

Just then, there was a hard knock at the door.

CHAPTER 57

They clearly had no idea who they were really dealing with. To think two people would be enough was laughable. Especially two people with average skills. If he wanted, Yadin could easily kill them both without even drawing attention. Their demise, though, would only raise suspicion about Dr. Franz Mueller. Right now, they served a purpose. It wouldn't hurt for the Iranian agents to observe him in plain sight. What he had in store was akin to performing a magic act. They would see, but not comprehend the trick.

Yadin had no intention of losing them in the crowded, noisy Grand Bazaar. Because of its enormous size, he had memorized the path he needed to take, so there was no need for urgency. The historic bazaar consisted of numerous narrow, jammed alleyways, lined with colorful shops and hungry merchants eager to move their merchandise. Yadin stopped on several occasions, inspecting various items: clothes, jewelry, and rugs. He seemed particularly interested in watches, haggling over the price whenever one caught his eye. No amount of bargaining seemed to satisfy his price point, so he kept shopping.

The merchants who ran the bazaar were known as *bazaris*: conservative, politically very powerful, and growing more tired every day of a dwindling bottom line caused by their government's foreign policy. They were willing to ride the promises of their president a little longer, but patience was running thin. The prospect of losing businesses their families had run for generations didn't leave a palatable taste in their mouths.

One who held strong reservations about the government's direction was Reza Yasrebi. He never had a clue that his careless vocal opinions were the reason he was singled out. He was suspicious initially, but when a fellow Iranian approached him with the equivalent of five thousand dollars just to talk, he felt compelled to hear the man out. With the promise of fifty thousand more on the table, Yasrebi agreed to the man's terms. For the life of him, he couldn't come up with a reason not to accept the offer. There was nothing on the surface that seemed sinister about it, and he'd dissected the request from several angles during a couple of restless nights. In tough economic times, the decision was that much easier to make. All he had to do was keep a brand-new watch in its box, under lock and key, until someone came to claim it. That person would also pay him an additional four thousand dollars to make the transaction legitimate. It was that harmless.

As Yadin continued his browsing, he nearly got bumped by a fabric-filled wheelbarrow pushed along by an overzealous porter. He stopped at a storefront window, inspecting its offerings. Once he saw in the window's reflection that the male portion of his shadow was still with him, he moved on. The female was slightly ahead, pretending to shop. If they stuck to their pattern, each time he stopped, they'd exchange positions. The man would continue on ahead of him while the woman would assume the rear position. Yadin marched on, overshooting his destination on purpose before reversing direction. He had to suppress laughter because the woman was startled, caught unprepared by his movement. She stopped cold in the middle of the alleyway, and that resulted in two people bumping her from behind, nearly knocking her over. Yadin went inside the cramped store, in no hurry as he inspected items behind the display cases. One of the clerks let him browse before offering service. Exhibiting seasoned sales prowess, the man didn't speak Farsi at first.

"Looking for watch? You come to the right place. We have much to choose from."

Yadin nodded his head. Not bothering to look up he said, "I see that. Very nice collection."

"All price ranges too. And for you, a good deal. The best deal."

The clerk followed Yadin's footsteps like a tiger at the zoo locking onto potential prey, ready to pounce just in case the bars disappeared.

Dissatisfied, Yadin shook his head. "I'm looking for a watch with multiple time zones. I travel a lot, and it would come in handy. Something that's one-of-a-kind. I like unique things."

The clerk look puzzled as he scanned his display cases. He pulled out a tray for the man to see. "How about these? They are fine timepieces with dual time zones."

Yadin didn't even look. "No, I don't think so."

"But these are top quality. I give you great deal."

Yadin had performed the charade long enough. "Is the owner available?"

"Yes, but I can help you with—"

"The owner, if you please." Yadin's tone changed just enough to convey a degree of seriousness.

The clerk reluctantly disappeared behind beaded curtains that led to a back room. While he waited, Yadin noticed he was being watched from the outside by the male portion of his surveillance team. He paid him no mind. There was nothing he or the woman would learn from this shopping experience.

The curtains swung open and a slightly overweight, sun-drenched man emerged, his eyes curious and his mouth still working on a meal. The clerk on his heels whispered in his ear, and when he began to follow, the elder man waved him off. He walked cautiously closer, inspecting the foreigner.

"Hello. Welcome to my store, I'm Reza Yasrebi," he said with a toothy grin that was not reciprocated. "I'm told you seek a watch. As you can see, we have many."

Yadin closed the distance so his conversation would be more intimate. "As I mentioned to your clerk, I seek a particular watch. One with multiple time zones. Probably the only one you carry. I like unique things."

There was recognition on Yasrebi's face and the smell of his meal on his breath. "I might have such an item for someone of your refined taste. I keep it in back. Would you like to see it?"

"Nothing would make me happier."

Yasrebi excused himself as he went behind the curtain. He re-appeared holding a watch box. He placed it on the table and opened the box for his customer. Inside was a beautiful piece of craftsman-ship that took even Yasrebi by surprise. The potential owner of the watch had no reaction, but it was exactly as he described. The large face was cream-colored, and on its perimeter were several mini circles that contained their own watch faces, capable of being programmed for multiple time zones. The bezel and band were made of highly polished stainless steel. Yadin took off the watch he'd been wearing and replaced it with the new one. To Yasrebi, he merely appeared to be going through the motions of checking the watch out as he depressed three of the six side buttons. A few sec-onds later, unbeknownst to Yasrebi, the watch provided Yadin with feedback as it vibrated ever so slightly underneath.

"I'll take it."

"Ah, a satisfied customer. That is why people come to see Yas-rebi." He produced an animated, even larger grin. "And for you, the price is six thousand dollars."

Yadin paused to gather himself. Getting angry would only draw unwanted attention. Instead, he produced the look of a man who was not in the mood to negotiate. "What say we make it four thousand?"

"Four thousand for such a fine piece of craftsmanship!" Yas-rebi raised his voice slightly. "You are robbing me blind."

"If you think there's someone else who'll offer you more . . ." Yadin began to put away the wallet he had placed on the counter.

"No, no, no," Yasrebi protested, talking more with his hands as he calculated the promised additional payoff disappearing as well. "These are tough times. The watch is yours for four thousand."

After he paid and Yasrebi reboxed the watch, Yadin was out of the store and back among the horde of people. In the background waiting for him were Iran's version of Boris and Natasha.

CHAPTER 58

Alex squinted to see through the cascading warm water shelling him from the showerhead. He wiped the stream away from his face and stepped to the side in order to fully open his eyes. Standing in front of him was Nora, her blouse open and her skirt in hand. He made no attempt to cover up, and she wasn't concentrating in that direction anyway. It was the look on her face that got his attention.

"I think they're here. Someone's knocking at the door." Nora handed him one of the hotel robes as he stepped free of the shower. She followed him out of the bathroom to retrieve her gun and then returned, partially closing the door behind her.

Alex was still dripping wet as he peered through the peephole. There were two men. One was at least four inches taller than the other. Still, they were both shorter than he and would be in for quite a surprise when he opened the door, since they were no doubt expecting the shorter Janko, a.k.a. Mr. Green. He thought about Nora for a second. She wasn't supposed to still be here, but she could hold her own, and besides, she was armed.

"Can I help you?" Alex shouted, just as they knocked again.

"Mr. Green," the shorter of the two responded, "we are your transportation."

Alex unlocked the door and stood behind it as they stepped through. The shorter man, when he was forced to look up, realized it wasn't Mr. Green who opened the door, and he braced himself. The second man reacted by making a move inside his sport coat, but he paused when the shorter one held out a cautionary hand. He backpedaled as his focus shifted to the sound of running water coming from the bedroom area of the suite. The man turned back to look at Alex and noticed he was wet underneath his robe. The look of disgust was evident on his face.

"Clearly, you are not Mr. Green," the shorter man observed and then motioned with his head toward the bedroom. "Is he in there? Taking a shower?"

Alex understood what he was thinking. "No, he's not here."

"Not here?" The man looked at his watch, annoyed. "There must be some confusion. He knew to expect us."

"There's no confusion. Mr. Green had to leave suddenly. A family emergency. He instructed me to take his place."

"That was not our arrangement."

"As I said, it was an emergency."

The taller of two shifted slightly to establish better balance as he waited for instruction. Alex didn't want to startle them, but he used the moment of indecision to ease within arm's reach of a heavy lamp he had unplugged on his way to the door.

Before the Iranians could determine a course of action, their attention was once again drawn to the bedroom. This time the bigger of the two produced a sidearm. A woman was singing, and it was getting louder.

"Hey, hey," Alex protested upon seeing the weapon. "No need for that." The shorter one wasn't interested in his protest.

The playful singing was replaced by a gasp as Nora appeared at the entrance to the bedroom, her eyes focused on the gun now pointing at her. The man holding it slowly began lowering the weapon, not registering any danger from the woman wearing only a towel that covered her from the waist down. Even Alex focused on Nora's bare breasts, glistening from a fresh shower and heaving due to her rapid breathing. Selling her reaction, she took a second to regain her composure, and in doing so, she covered her breasts with her left arm. Her frightened look found its way to Alex, while her right hand never wavered from her side. In an instant she could reach behind her and grab the Walther P99

Compact held in place by the towel draped around her waist. If it became necessary, Alex would distract the gunman for the millisecond required for her to take him out.

Alex positioned himself even closer to the two men as they continued to gaze at Nora. They both were within reach now, and though they didn't realize it, they no longer had any advantage.

"Please put the gun away," Alex said, sounding sincere in his request. "You're making her very nervous."

The shorter one didn't take his eyes off Nora. "You are Mr. McBride, is that right?"

"Yes. How do you know that?"

"I was at the airfield last night. In fact, it was you and not Mr. Green who inspected the initial cargo."

"That's correct. I'm his associate."

"Here you are, but no Mr. Green. Much like the Russian, we don't like surprises."

Their presence answered one question for Alex. If they were here to transport Janko to Iran, they must not have been party to Nevsky's attempt to have them killed. Either that was his own call, or someone was tying up loose ends.

Alex decided to force the issue. They were sent for a purpose, and he doubted they wanted to be in a position to explain themselves to superiors.

"I totally understand if you're disappointed. As far as I'm concerned, my services were rendered last night and I'm done. My girlfriend and I can start our well-deserved vacation." Alex gave Nora a lover's smile. "Sweetheart, go and put some clothes on now. That is, if it's okay with our friends here."

The little one nodded his approval. "I'm afraid your vacation will have to wait a few days. You will come with us in place of Mr. Green. A guest of the Iranian government. We have a plane waiting for us."

"You're sure this is only for a couple of days? And why, exactly, am I coming?"

"Most assuredly a short stay. There are schedules to meet. As to why, Mr. Green has provided invaluable services on several occasions and therefore is very important to my government. His presence is required to insure quality control and to be available, should a question arise. Seeing as you are his associate and, based on last night, a qualified one, you can step in for him. So please, get dressed. "

"Sounds harmless enough. I've never been to Iran, so this will be a first. I'll tell my girlfriend I'll be back in a couple of days."

"That won't be necessary. She'll be coming with us."

CHAPTER 59

So far he wasn't dead, and that was a good thing. It was still early in the day, though.

The caravan of cars and SUVs totaled six, and they were moving at a good clip along the desert highway, heading southwest of Tehran. Civilization had vanished behind them. Alex noted that this stretch of road was devoid of pedestrian traffic. The vehicles passing in the opposite direction appeared to be of an official nature or military. He tried to put on a good front, but this was a bit discomforting. He had been away from this life for too long a stretch. His instincts weren't what they should have been, because if he'd been thinking clearly, he wouldn't be in the backseat of a Range Rover tearing through the Iranian desert to destination unknown. He'd committed the cardinal sin of allowing his emotions to guide him. Seeing Dmitri Nevsky alive had sent his world spinning off its axis, and there was only one way to get it back on track.

He couldn't stomach the image of Nora being hauled away and tortured. That would be her fate if his background didn't check out, and he was sure the Iranians were checking every facet of their backgrounds, as quickly as they could. With each passing mile, he felt better. His cover was holding. All he needed, though, was some overworked CIA employee forgetting to cross a *t* or dot an *i*. A deep inquiry by someone who knew what they were doing would eventually uncover inconsistencies. Thus it became a dangerous game of filling in holes faster than someone on the other end of a computer could dig.

Alex was weary, his brain and body feeling the effects of being tossed into what felt like a relentless storm. He and Nora were in the air on a private jet less than two hours after the Iranians had come knocking. As she'd put on clothes, Nora did her best to keep Sara informed, texting her about what was going on. Sara in turn had alerted Langley and made sure Duncan was ready to move. If Alex and Nora needed extraction, the options were scarce. With US forces out of Iraq, a border crossing there at this point was too risky. Sara decided the best and shortest option was to the north. Azerbaijan had no love for its neighbor to the south. Langley agreed with her assessment, and soon after, she and Duncan headed to the airport to catch a flight to Baku.

Nora hadn't liked it, but she had to leave the 9 mm behind. Not having it made her feel a little underdressed, but if they searched or x-rayed her bag, a gun would be hard to explain, and they already had enough credibility issues. During the short plane ride, the smaller Iranian had engaged Alex in small talk, a veiled attempt to acquire subtle facts that could be traced. In between chats, the Iranian would excuse himself to use the plane's phone, no doubt relaying tidbits about Mr. McBride while trying to explain why they were bringing a different man from the one they were supposed to pick up.

Upon touching down in Tehran, there had been no fanfare or lingering as they were transferred from the plane to a waiting car. They had been checked into the fashionable Espinas International Hotel on the outskirts of the city. Their king-sized suite afforded clear views of Milad Tower, which according to the bellhop was the tallest tower in Tehran and sixth tallest in the world. In the distance was Mount Damavand, its snow-capped peak the highest point in the Middle East. Mr. McBride had been instructed to be out front, ready for pickup at eight in the morning. The woman would have to stay behind.

The next morning, Alex had been prompt to meet his Iranian handler, whom he only knew as Farid. Another person, who appeared to be of African descent, was already in the backseat of the Range Rover. The man had merely nodded when he and Alex made eye contact.

They had been traveling for miles when finally something

besides the desert came into view. Initially, it looked like a series of giant candles. As the caravan got closer, Alex could see that several vehicles were already on the scene, haphazardly parked quite a distance from the candlelike devices. There was also a healthy allotment of Iran's elite Revolutionary Guard soldiers, heavily armed. The military presence was partly explained moments later, when they passed a series of vehicles adorned with the official flags of Iran. It was clearly the president's detail. Alex was looking out each side of the vehicle, taking in the magnitude of the situation. There were people lined up several yards off the road, and two steel bleachers, looking totally out of place, were filling up with bodies. The real shocker came as the SUV came to a stop. There was no mistaking the candlelike devices now.

Spaced about thirty yards apart were a series of ten missiles, standing at attention, ready to be launched.

CHAPTER **60**

The luxury yacht was impressive but not overly ostentatious—at least, not when compared to some of the other vessels anchored off the Turks and Caicos Islands. Besides, Roger Daniels's real showcase was docked in the Mediterranean. This wasn't the crowd he needed to impress, so the multimillion dollar yacht labeled *Cuda* was more about pleasure than business.

For all he'd done in his life, good or misunderstood, Daniels found it strange that he was struggling to sleep. He continued to nurse the three fingers of premium Scotch, hoping it would have a soothing effect. The water around him was quiet, and his yacht was far enough offshore that he only faintly heard the night cacophony of Nikki Beach activity as it drifted out to sea. There were plenty of lights still aglow at the resort and surrounding area, the young and wealthy extending the night. This was supposed to be the R and R he needed to wait out the world's reaction to what was going to soon dominate the headlines. After his Kennedy Center event, he'd boarded his private jet bound for Turks and Caicos. Shortly after touchdown, he had been transported to his yacht, every one of his creature comforts well stocked, one of which was the young, curvaceous woman on his payroll. For the pleasure she provided, the small expenditure was a bargain.

Upsetting the balance of another country wasn't what bothered Daniels. Nor was it the loss of life. That was sometimes the cost of doing business. Those who weren't in a position to alter the world's path didn't understand that. Having immense wealth and power was akin to being a god. Important decisions constantly had to be made, and as a result, for some, suffering was inevitable.

No, what kept Daniels awake as he sat on the main deck of his 185-foot yacht, whose abbreviated name was derived from a dangerous saltwater predator, was the potential weakness of the people he was forced to associate with on this venture. The risk of exposure was there, and if his involvement ever came to light, it would cost him billions and sabotage important business relationships. He'd lose leverage, and Roger Daniels had long forgotten what it was like to not have influence.

He had no worries about Ezra, despite the man's patriotic motivation. Ezra was a soldier in a winless war, but you couldn't convince him of that. What he ultimately wanted to accomplish, a civilized world wouldn't tolerate. Not again. Daniels was sure even Ezra understood that, so he'd settle for his enemy on its knees. Daniels admired his saber-wielding conviction.

Bryce Lipton, on the other hand, concerned him, and that feeling was deepening. So far he'd been controllable, but Daniels had seen men succumb to the trappings of power before. Lipton wasn't a stupid man by any measure, but he was also one who'd never been able to rise above the inside-the-Beltway ceiling, so his ultimate desire of becoming president had been an unobtainable dream, until Daniels stepped in and took interest. Now Lipton was thinking the impossible was within reach. Daniels had himself to blame for that. He'd been the puppeteer, giving Lipton a reason to believe. The truth was that if the American public continued to have faith in the current president, he'd occupy the office for two terms. But if by chance there was an opening and Lipton was put in position, Daniels could foresee the day when the dog turned on its master. The problem was, Daniels actually liked Lipton. Daniels was not, however, fond of Lipton's underachieving son, and that was the man's weakness. His son's work in Moscow should have ended his participation in their operation, but Lipton had insisted on the young man being involved further. The more the son participated, the more he knew, and Davis Lipton was a weak link. The elder Lipton at least had been adamant about insulating his son, keeping him out of the loop regarding the endgame and the major participants involved. It was a nice gesture, but Daniels wrestled with whether he could risk his empire on such paternal instincts.

He'd decided he couldn't. Daniels dialed a number on his satellite phone, and on the other end, Yosef Ezra answered.

"Hello, my friend," Daniels said, his heart no longer heavy now that his mind was made up.

"Hello. The hour is near. Our investment looks solid."

"That's good to hear. But I'm concerned about our family of shareholders. I think we need to buy them out."

There was silence for a moment. "This is a *related* matter?"

"Yes, and I know the timing is bad, but is it feasible?"

"One should be easy, but at this date, a buyout of the other could be difficult to dismiss as coincidence."

"I understand. Do what you can, but out of necessity, the larger shareholder must be taken care of first."

"I'll get my staff to work on it."

"Excellent."

The conversation concluded, Daniels drained the remaining Scotch. He didn't give much thought to what he'd just put into motion. It was something that had to be done. The country could afford to lose a senator.

A soft pair of arms reached around his neck, and then he felt the touch of firm nipples pressing into his back. Her perfume radiated in the night air as she kissed his cheek. Daniels only saw the woman a few times a year and had no illusions about her being solely devoted to him. But she knew that whenever he requested her presence, nothing else mattered. She was along for the ride, knowing all too well it would end abruptly one day. So far, though, the arrangement had gotten her a pricy condo, a large walk-in closet of designer clothes, and enough money so that she didn't have to punch a time clock. She just had to stay in shape and be at Daniel's beck and call.

"Roger," she whispered, one hand exploring the area below his waist. "Come to bed. Let me help ease what's troubling you."

He thanked the miracles of modern medicine. To think a little pill could aid him in pleasing a woman like this. He gently kissed a breast. Making love to her would be the perfect way to end the night, and afterward, he was sure he'd be able to fall asleep.

CHAPTER **61**

Looking out among the vast desert, Yadin saw nothing that impressed him. He appeared to be alone in his opinion. His lack of enthusiasm was easy enough to explain: he was supposed to be a dedicated German scientist. A man born with the serious gene stuck up his ass. Outward displays of emotion were not generally his forte. That, at least, he did have in common with Dr. Franz Mueller.

The nearly one hundred people around him were filled with anticipation, whether it was real or required behavior was difficult to separate. They appeared to hang onto every word President Akbar Shahroudi spat out, his speech full of passion, peppered with the right amount of venom. Even though he was a small man, his persona was on stilts. There was a hint of instability, which in this part of the world forced outsiders to tread lightly. Yadin had heard the rhetoric most of his life. "We cannot let the evil West trample our way of life, dictate their policies to us. They are afraid of the true path of Islam, because they have no souls themselves. We will wipe Israel off the face of the earth." It went on like that for roughly fifteen minutes before Shahroudi finally was ready to reveal what bolstered his confidence. He was truly a ringmaster performing before a circus crowd.

"Today, we send a message to the world that we will not be bullied. And this is only the beginning." The president left the podium and returned to his seat. Yadin wondered if half the audience expected the sky to turn dark with the snap of a finger. There were television cameras present to document the event that would certainly be played on the various American cable networks and subsequently around the world as soon as possible.

Everyone in attendance had been given a pamphlet explaining in detail what they were looking at. Yadin didn't bother to open his. He already knew that situated on individual platforms were six Shahab-3D medium-range missiles. They represented Iran's latest foray into striking targets outside its borders: they had an estimated range of thirteen hundred miles and were easily capable of reaching Israel. The guidance system, warhead, and missile body were all improved. A new reentry system allowed for better precision. Another advantage of the Shahab-3D was its short launch-to-impact time ratio, which enabled the guidance to remain relatively accurate over a long flight until impact. There was no question these missiles would be a test for Israel's Arrow 2 ABM defense system. The other four missiles were intermediate-range ballistic devices from North Korea. With an estimated range of three thousand miles, they were both costlier and deadlier. If his calculations were right, Yadin figured London was just over 2,700 miles from Tehran. The European Union would indeed lose a little sleep over that. Even though the attendees were a safe distance away, each was given a set of earplugs. They were instructed to use them now. A minute later, the show began, as one of the Shahab-3D missiles slowly lifted from its perch and jettisoned into the sky until it disappeared.

The president had a constant sardonic grin on his face, confident the world would take Iran seriously after seeing this exercise of bravado and power.

But, as Yadin knew, this was merely the tip of the iceberg.

CHAPTER 62

Alex and Nora watched the local television stations' reports of what took place in the desert. Because it was broadcast in English around the clock, they were drawn to state-run Press TV. The female anchor, dressed in traditional Muslim attire, was reporting what a glorious day it was for the country, another step forward in maintaining security, keeping the borders safe from aggressors.

There were no differing viewpoints from foreign representatives, so Alex could only imagine what the response must have been to today's aerial show. He was sure that in well-secured rooms across the globe, analysts with access to costly toys were dissecting every frame of today's launches. The pamphlets that had been handed out indicated a maximum range of three thousand miles. Governments would be working feverishly to determine how many missiles with that capability the Iranians likely possessed, and where the hell they'd gotten them. The Shahab-3D wouldn't be that much of a surprise, but the IRBMs were enough to make most of Europe restless.

Apparently, this wasn't the worst of it, either. During the ride back to the hotel, Farid told Alex to be ready tomorrow at exactly the same time and that his expertise might be called upon as well. Relative silence followed, until Alex broached a subject with Farid. He reminded Farid about the proceedings at the airfield and told him how impressed he'd been with the Russian named Nevsky. He asked Farid whether Nevsky would be in attendance. The answer had been no. Alex explained that it might be beneficial to him and his other clients to do business with the Russian and therefore, was there a way to contact him? Farid didn't offer much other than to say he worked for a large firm operating out of Moscow. It was enough of a starting point. More than likely, "large firm" meant organized crime syndicate. Alex stopped inquiring when Farid said that Mr. Green should know how to contact the Russian.

Nora was getting bored with the coverage, especially after being cooped up in the hotel for several hours. The highlight of her day was a stroll around Laleh Park in the center of the city. It afforded her the opportunity to tour the adjacent National Rug Gallery and the Tehran Museum of Contemporary Art. Of course, she'd been followed. The rest of her free time she spent getting a bite to eat and then working off a portion of her frustration at the hotel's gym. The diversions had momentarily served their purpose of taking her mind off Alex. The uncertainty of what he was experiencing nearly drove her crazy. When he returned, they talked about as much of his day as he felt comfortable relaying over dinner at the hotel's French cuisine restaurant. Now, back in the room, she could tell Alex was troubled.

"What's on your mind? If you're going to see this ordeal through, you have to be at your best, so what is it?"

Alex took a deep sigh. "It's Dmitri Nevsky. He was at the airfield the other night."

"Nevsky? Oh, my god!" Nora's eyes expanded with astonishment. She knew the savagery associated with the name.

Alex had a faraway look on his face. "Stood right in front of him. We even had a conversation. He didn't seem to remember me. Guess it was a long time ago. Otherwise, I would have been killed on the spot. I should give him a little credit, though."

"For what?"

"He did try to kill me later."

She now understood what was motivating him to go forward. Dmitri Nevsky represented a turning point in his life. Granted, everything that transpired was done under the guise of war, but Nevsky took pride in spreading fear among Iraqis who dared to dream that America cared enough to change their lives. It went beyond politics for Alex. She recalled from late night conversations how his frustration and anger had risen daily. Politicians on the Hill told him to stand down, that a greater good was being served. They didn't have to hear the pain in his voice and e-mails as the bodies of those who trusted him began to pile up. Regrettably, once she joined the list of doubters, he had become a lost soul and loose cannon. Of course, he'd been right about who was betraying their interests. To those on the front lines, his course of action was more than justified. What Alex never knew in ending their relationship was how hard in the aftermath she had been on herself. If it hadn't been for Erica's counsel, she might not have recovered sufficiently to have a career.

Nora looked at Alex with apprehension. If they left now, they could make it to the nearest boarder and cross without incident. He could return to his tranquil life in the islands, and she could face whatever punishment awaited her. Whatever the Israelis and Senator Lipton had cooked up would either succeed or fail. The world wouldn't spin off its axis, no matter the outcome. The rich would only find a way to get richer.

Alex's stoic demeanor told her everything she needed to know. There was no need to waste her breath on that idea.

She made a decision. The worst thing she could do was think about all the risks. She wasn't going to give her mind the opportunity to debate courses of action. Nora stood and sauntered over to Alex, who was resting with his legs extended in a chair. When she reached him, her blouse was totally unbuttoned, her bare breasts peeking through. She straddled his legs and, as if doing a push-up, rested her hands on the arms of the chair, inching her way down to kiss him. Alex had a perplexed, unsure look on his face, but he rose to meet her lips. He reached out to fondle a breast, her kiss bringing back memories. Nora sat on his lap, pleased to discover he was aroused. Alex intently watched as she took off her blouse. Nora pecked at his chest as she began sliding downward, a free hand massaging his groin. She playfully worked his zipper open and explored before undoing his belt and the snap on his pants. She then paused to look back up at him. With a wicked grin in place, Nora continued.

CHAPTER **63**

The cover hadn't yet been blown off of what would become one of the biggest stories inside the Beltway. In a town that prided itself on secrets, few really were. Members of Congress historically had a problem keeping their mouths shut. Some loved to read their secrets in print, attributed to "According to a source. . . ." A select few couldn't resist flaunting their connections by discussing sensitive topics during sexual rendezvous that, in their very nature, were supposed to be secret as well. And then there were the various news outlets. It wasn't just the Bob Woodwards and Carl Bernsteins anymore. Cable networks were staffed around the clock, and the Internet had opened a whole new can of worms. A carefully placed tidbit in an otherwise obscure blog could develop into an active volcano, spewing a mixture of truths and innuendos.

The president had gotten very little sleep during the past couple of days. He managed to join his wife in the residence to sleep for a few hours and had made a point of sharing breakfast with her, a precious twenty-five minutes. Then it was back to the Oval Office, where FBI Director John Layden and Attorney General Lewis Farber were waiting. Both men had been there for several hours the day before. The AG had assembled his best legal minds and put them to the test without mentioning Senator Bryce Lipton by name. He wanted to know precisely, given the facts they had, what charges could be brought forth that would hold the most weight. And he'd promised that if a single word got out of the building on this speculative case, a career would be ended. For Layden, preparation was a much simpler matter. Once he got an arrest warrant from Justice, he'd order his men to apprehend Senator Lipton. He didn't really like the cantankerous old bastard anyway.

The attorney general was in the midst of explaining to the president that he felt they had a good case. There was a litany of headline-grabbing charges they could throw at the senator. His high-priced lawyers would earn every penny looking for a way out. They'd also throw the book at his son, in an attempt to pressure the senior to cave in. It all sounded promising, and that was a blessing, because the president knew he couldn't be wrong about this one. He was about to give both men the go-ahead when the first call came in on the crisis line about Iran's missile exercise.

The White House was now bogged down with yet another issue, but there was growing speculation that one had something to do with the other. The secretary of defense had reported that his analysts were certain the IRBMs fired by the Iranians were of North Korean origin. That further backed up Champion's suspicion about North Korea's "misplaced" inventory. President Hudson spent the better part of the day on the phone with leaders from the EU. They'd all wanted to come together to form some kind of unified front. The British prime minister was prepared to move a fleet of warships in the Persian Gulf, just close enough in international waters to give the Iranians something to mull over. The president told none of his counterparts about what he was dealing with on the home front. Doing so might have given them the impression he was trivializing their concerns. A prominent senator's breaking the law did not seem to be on equal footing with the possibility of bombs dropping in Europe and Israel.

CHAPTER 64

The facility was immediately recognizable. The route was unmistakable. Salt Lake in Qom, southwest of Tehran, was the first landmark. They continued along Freeway 7, the Chocolate Mountains near Kashan an impressive focal point. The topography reminded Alex of the Sonoran Desert, except there were more agricultural fields than he'd anticipated. The various photos Duncan had laboriously gone over paled in comparison to what Alex was looking at now. Those photos had mostly been satellite imagery. The ground was level, partially guarded on two sides by mountains. Antiaircraft stations and guard towers protected the perimeter. No attack was going to take place without a sizeable resistance.

The SUV nearly circled the compound before being stopped at another security checkpoint. Heavily armed guards on either side peered inside and then waved the vehicle through. Farid sat in the front passenger seat, while Alex occupied the back with the African, who he'd learned was from Botswana. That was about all he got out of the man. Farid had made it clear the day before that no conversations about occupations were to take place. That was fine with Alex, especially for this trip. He needed to focus on every detail, and that wasn't easy, considering what had transpired between him and Nora. He hadn't been looking for it to happen, but he had certainly been a willing participant. Her body and its fluid movement were incredible, and the mental and physical release of making love was rejuvenating. He had no answer for what exactly the union meant, and for the moment, he couldn't afford to dwell on it.

The temperature in the desert was increasing slowly, the way the number on a scale might rise if a fat man were lowering himself gradually onto it, hoping for a different result to register. In an instant, an eclipse occurred, the sun disappearing as the SUV rolled ahead into near darkness. The automatic headlights flickered on, revealing part of the way. They were in a winding tunnel partially illuminated by lights mounted along the wall. The road gradually sloped downward, and about two football fields ahead was what appeared to be an opening. The tunnel's height was expansive as well, with ample room for trucks with large loads to pass through. The opening was meant to impress. Written in gold were the Farsi words, "Welcome to Natanz."

There were several elevator shafts, two of which had warehouselike doors, capable of accepting large loads. The other five elevators appeared to be for civilian transport. There was an area for parking a select number of vehicles, and the spaces were nearly filled. A group of around fifteen people waited by one set of elevators. Also present were a handful of Iran's elite Revolutionary Guard troops. There was another tunnel in addition to the one they'd just traveled down. Two soldiers with submachine guns dangling from shoulder straps stood watch. As an added measure of security, a heavy gate protected the tunnel. Farid instructed Alex and the man from Botswana to head for the elevators where the others were assembled.

It was difficult to determine the tunnel's depth, but they were well below the surface. Judging by the numbers inside the elevator as it descended, Alex determined that they passed one level and stopped on the second. The buttons indicated one level remained below. The doors opened, and the scene was perplexing. Before them was a long, wide corridor, and as best as Alex could tell, there was a reception line in place. The group ahead of them was making its way through, being greeted by a succession of what appeared to be high-ranking officials. Between moving bodies, Alex could see President Akbar Shahroudi. Alex had followed world events only sporadically over the past couple of years, so Shahroudi was the only one he knew by name.

As Alex's group approached, each member was detained momentarily. A person standing next to Shahroudi would sometimes consult a tablet and lean over to whisper in the president's ear before the group member walked down the line. When it came to Alex's turn, President Shahroudi exposed his perfectly aligned, white teeth. "Mr. McBride, it is a pleasure. We are so grateful for your contributions."

Alex wasn't sure what protocol demanded, but he didn't want to linger. He shook Shahroudi's hand firmly, but quickly. "Thank you, Mr. President, the pleasure is all mine."

Shahroudi nodded as if Alex had already said too much. The president turned to engage the next person. The exercise was repeated six more times as Alex made his way down the line, shaking hands and exchanging forced smiles. Once he was done, Farid was waiting for him. He pulled Alex aside and led him to a room off the corridor.

"Mr. McBride, we seem to have a problem," Farid began, the door locking shut behind them. The words got Alex's undivided attention. He watched Farid closely, but the man didn't have a weapon in his hand, nor did he appear anxious to produce one. Alex took in the medium-sized, soundproofed room. He didn't sense danger, since there were only two other men present, huddled behind computer screens. They barely glanced up, their attention focused on what was being produced from their finger tapping. Several large monitors hung across one wall. Some of them showcased the various worldwide news outlets, while a few others were set to financial channels.

Alex felt better about the situation. "What's the problem?"

"We've tried several times, but there appears to be an error with Mr. Green's bank account information. More to the point, the account is closed. We'd like to transfer the balance of what we owe. Since you are his associate, can you provide a valid number?"

Janko's closed account could mean one of two things. He'd heeded Alex's warning and was securing what he could in an attempt to lay low, or someone had already found him and was covering their tracks. Alex surmised that if the latter were true, he'd be having a different conversation at the moment. Farid was standing next to one of the men in front of a computer screen, waiting for an answer.

"Well, Mr. McBride?"

"You have to understand, it becomes necessary to change account numbers and sometimes banks. Have to be careful about who might be watching."

"A wise and necessary step, yes. Good to know you and your associate are so cautious."

Alex gave Farid one number and bank he knew by heart. His own. After a few keystrokes, Farid looked up, satisfied. "Done. As agreed, two million dollars has been deposited."

Alex didn't let the number faze him. "Wonderful. Nice doing business with you." As they exited, he wondered how in the hell he was going to explain that windfall on his taxes.

CHAPTER **65**

The bravado was bordering on the ridiculous. The idealists were expected to foolishly celebrate, but not him. Not yet. The Iranians overlooked his gruffness. He had, after all, gotten paid serious money to make sure this day would not only come, but that it would be a glorious and crowning achievement for Iran. If all went according to plan, it would certainly be a day to remember.

After clasping his last hand in the reception line, Dr. Franz Mueller was escorted to a motorized cart. They traveled along a couple of hallways before stopping a few feet away from a thick, steel-reenforced door. Entry was gained through the swipe of a security card. The room was full of control panels, instruments, and heavy equipment positioned throughout several stations. Activity was brisk as bodies scurried about with purpose. Dr. Mueller veered in the direction of three men in lab coats who were engaged in conversation. Upon seeing him, they stopped talking and greeted him with enthusiasm, handing over a lab coat in the process.

"How's everything looking?" Dr. Mueller inquired as he put on the white coat and a pair of blue shoe covers.

"Everything appears to be in working order, Dr. Mueller," one of the lab coats responded, offering a clipboard filled with charts and notes.

Dr. Mueller checked his watch and in doing so, casually adjusted one of the outer knobs. "Let's get going. The president will want to start soon, and"—he looked at each man—"we don't want to disappoint. Not on this day."

Given their orders, the lab coats all turned and disappeared behind another set of doors that required the use of a security card also. Attached to Dr. Mueller's lab coat was an identical card that afforded total access to any part of the facility. For the past couple of years, he'd gone over the blueprints for Natanz to the point where he could navigate the facility with his eyes closed. He knew where everything was because he'd helped to put it there.

In the beginning, it had been a joint venture between Israeli and US intelligence. The partnership had worked perfectly in slowing Iran's nuclear program. It required a tremendous amount of monitoring and was costly, but it had forced the Iranians to commit a massive amount of resources, turning up the political heat on its leadership in the process. The Iranians had no idea they were purchasing flawed equipment and parts covertly supplied by Israel and the US. The power supply had been a continuously troublesome area. It needed to be stable to ensure that centrifuges spun at the correct speed. Too often, the power supply failed, causing them to explode or malfunction. The supply of supposedly top-grade centrifuges had also contained flaws, causing more delays. Electrical parts suffered the same fate on occasion. And so it went, on and on, until the Iranians struck gold. They'd discovered a source that had widespread, reliable contacts and access to quality materials. The fact that this person also had extensive knowledge of the inner workings of nuclear materials was invaluable. The Iranians were desperate enough to go along with their new benefactor's insistence of secrecy. Their previous supplier, a Pakistani scientist, was virtually under house arrest in his native country after immense pressure from the West to shut him down. The landscape therefore was bleak, until Dr. Franz Mueller emerged. He had one stringent rule. Any attempts to investigate him or check into his background would result in the Iranians being cut off entirely. No exceptions. To prove his credentials and access to resources were legit, Dr. Mueller went through a trial period during which he delivered quality, reliable products without attracting suspicion from the West. Once the materials held up under use, the Iranians were convinced he was the real deal. Whatever Dr. Mueller wanted, he got.

The other lab coats in the room were quick to answer any

question Dr. Mueller threw at them as he went back and forth from the clipboard to gazing at his greatest prize, the two huge reactors in place on the floor below him. He was standing on an elevated crosswalk that provided a perfect vantage point for viewing the reactors' design. Dr. Mueller inspected or asked about everything that was relevant. They were pressurized water reactors that required a system containing a mixture of air and steam. Maintaining a desired level of pressure was paramount in such a design. The control rod drive mechanism, which was affixed atop the reactors, acted as sort of a gas pedal. When the mechanism was raised, more neutrons could crash into uranium atoms. If either of the two reactors approached dangerously high heat levels, the control rods would be lowered in order to cool it down. The reactor core on both looked to be in perfect shape. The coolant pump, steam generator, turbine condenser, condensate pump, and all the other vital parts passed inspection. Dr. Mueller looked over the charts that contained testing results from previous months and saw no evidence of any hiccups.

The years of planning appeared to be paying off. He took a strategic path to every vital area that needed his attention. When he passed two critical structural beams, one of the seven smaller faces on his watch turned a different color. In doing so, the watch also gave him feedback by slightly vibrating. Dr. Mueller and the team rode a cart to another section of the structure. Behind the wall nearest to him was the central electrical center. The majority of the essential electrical wiring originated from the large room. Two more of the faces on his watch changed and were accompanied by two short vibrations.

They were filing back into the cart when one of the scientists held back for a second, listening to the transmission coming in over his communication device.

"We're on our way," he responded, joining the others.

"Everything all right?" asked Dr. Mueller.

The lab technician put the cart in motion. "Yes, it's just that the president is nearly ready. He's in the centrifuge area."

"That's perfect. It's the last place I need to take a look at."

The technician floored the pedal, honking the horn to disperse those on foot.

"Is President Shahroudi waiting for me to brief him on the new centrifuges?"

"No, that's being taken care of as we speak. He's almost done."

Dr. Mueller had a quizzical look on his face. "By one of your inspectors?"

"I think it's one of the visitors. . . ." The technician focused on making a sharp turn. "The man who approved the latest shipment."

"The shipment from Tbilisi? The IR-3s?"

"Yes. That would be those."

Yadin wasn't pleased to hear that. Apparently there was a hiccup after all. The inspector from Tbilisi shouldn't be on the premises. In fact, the inspector from Tbilisi should be dead.

CHAPTER 66

They stood upright like shiny soldiers at attention, over a thousand of them, waiting for orders. The room itself was nearly the size of a football field. Row after mimicking row of centrifuges nearly filled the available space. There were lanes carved out for workers to navigate. It resembled a well-designed maze. Yadin's interest, however, was fixed on the group toward the other end of the room. Because of the room's size, all he could hear was garbled words, and even those drifted in and out due to the noise from the centrifuges that were online and the hum of massive air conditioners.

Yadin caught a glimpse of President Shahroudi. He was engaged in conversation, asking questions and listening to the responses. Among the assembled group, one man stood out. It would have been easy to assume he was a bodyguard. Even with a lab coat on and from a distance, the man, Yadin could tell, was in very good shape. As he got closer, Yadin noted the man was also the one responding to the president's queries most often. The conversation ended just as Yadin joined up with the group. The president displayed a look of content and then shook hands with the man Yadin didn't know. He had to be the inspector from Tbilisi. The entourage began making its way toward a rear exit when Yadin felt another vibration from his watch. He paused for a moment, realizing there was only one more to go. A lab technician ahead turned and noticed Dr. Mueller was behind them. He whispered to the president, who glanced around and then stopped in mid-stride. He produced a wide grin that wasn't returned by Dr. Mueller.

Shahroudi held out his arms. "Ah, Iran's good friend, Dr. Mueller." He was literally beaming now. "Your handiwork," he indicated with a wave.

"You are satisfied then?" said Dr. Mueller, stepping forward.

"In our wildest dreams, not even we could have expected all of this so soon."

"The centrifuges meet your approval? You paid a hefty price for them."

"Yes, Mr. McBride was just extolling the virtues of the IR-3s."

"Mr. McBride?" Dr. Mueller raised an eyebrow.

"But of course, you two don't know each other."

President Shahroudi motioned for his latest acquaintance to come closer. Alex tried to stay calm while his insides churned. He had just given the performance of a lifetime, thanks to Duncan's tutelage. He didn't know a damn thing about how anything else in this place worked, so the slightest probing from here on in would expose his lack of knowledge.

The president gently grabbed Dr. Mueller by the elbow. "Dr. Franz Mueller, this is Wayne McBride."

Alex could tell the good doctor was doing more than just shaking his hand.

"So, you are the man who inspected the IR-3s in Tbilisi?"

"Yes," Alex said, raising a hand to protest. "Well, there was my associate too, Mr. Green. I'm actually crashing the party. He was supposed to make this trip, but a family emergency called him away."

The explanation was plausible, Yadin thought. Perhaps Mr. Green had made a hasty, unexpected exit before he could be dealt with. An associate may have been kept out of the limelight, brought into play only as a last resort. In just a short while, it wouldn't matter anyway. The one thing that kept Yadin's interest, though, was Mr. McBride's physical makeup. His lab coat fit him snugly. From Yadin's various travels and interactions, men in Mr. McBride's line of work were rarely put together so well.

President Shahroudi once again aligned himself with Dr. Mueller. "If all is in working order, I think it is time, doctor, to let the world know we have arrived."

CHAPTER 67

True power in Washington is measured by the ability to get a table at one of the District's finer restaurants on a busy night with little or no wait.

A senator of Bryce Lipton's caliber had achieved centerpiece status, thus there was no such thing as a private meal unless he specifically requested the use of a VIP room. But where was the fun in that? The food always tasted that much better knowing others were in awe of his presence. Tony Engler, Lipton's chief of staff, sat next to his boss, calculating the chances of making an early exit to begin some semblance of a weekend. Across from them was an old ally from North Carolina, Senator Daniel Wakeman.

The trio occupied a table near the rear of The Prime Rib restaurant. The location offered indirect concealment, affording Lipton the luxury of knowing who was in the restaurant before they spotted him. He relished seeing the sheepish look that would engulf his fellow politicians when they realized he was present. Most came over to pay their respects, while others, those that were truly intimidated, settled for a wave or nod of the head. And then there were the civilians, the normal people. They were the ones who had to make reservations or wait over an hour for a table.

To the experienced men and women of the Hill, it was obvious that a number of up-and-coming politicians were being wined and dined by lobbyists. Lipton chuckled. He'd been there himself a long time ago. He continued to scan the room. There were voluptuous, beautiful women dotting the restaurant at every turn. Eye candy wasn't on the menu, but if you had something of substance to offer, you could certainly order it.

Lipton loved this place. It always generated the right kind of pulse, and the food was worth the expensive price tag. The menu decision was never easy. The crab cakes were a favorite, but he had a taste for meat this evening, so he settled on the house specialty of prime rib. His wife and doctor would not approve, which was why he had no intention of telling either, he thought to himself as he drained a glass of Scotch. He didn't have to get the waiter's attention for another round. It would be refilled soon enough. The service was naturally good, but for his table, it was impeccable.

Lipton began by attacking his prime rib. The portion was so huge it could feed a Third World family. The egregious thing was, not only was there no way he would finish it all, he would forgo a doggie bag, because taking it home was out of the question. He ran every aspect of his life except for one. Since he'd suffered a mild heart attack several years ago, his wife was now CEO of his health, and she ran a tight ship. If Elaine knew he was drowning in buttered mashed potatoes along with a Texas-sized piece of meat, she would lose her mind. She'd force him to walk several miles and impose a week of nothing but fruit and salads, sans the dressing. If she asked when he got home what he ate for dinner, he could stretch the truth by saying grilled asparagus, which at the moment lay untouched next to his prime rib. Without asking, he reached his fork over to stab a bite of salad from his staffer. Yes, he'd feel comfortable in telling Elaine he had artichokes and a salad for dinner.

The senator from North Carolina dined on the jumbo crab cakes while Lipton's aide tried to keep it simple, adding to his salad only a cup of lobster bisque. His intention was to finish as quickly as possible so he could join his girlfriend, who was waiting for him with friends at a Georgetown bar.

Between bites, the senators discussed innocuous political matters that on any other day might have been remotely interesting, but tonight Engler could barely stomach the banter. Finished with his meal, he could feel his phone buzzing inside his jacket pocket.

He assumed it was his girlfriend, agitated by now, wondering how much longer he was going to be. He was annoyed upon discovering the text message was from a fellow congressman's aide. He wasn't going to respond until the message indicated the aide was also at The Prime Rib. Engler looked up, searching. He found the beaming wannabe at the bar. From the text, he wasn't surprised to learn a favor was needed. There was a well-endowed, stunning blonde at the aide's side. She was definitely a step up from the regular stable of bimbos he managed to impress and bed. The text indicated the blonde was a big fan of Lipton's and could she meet him?

Engler was about to reply with a resounding "no way" when he had a moment of clarity. This might very well be the distraction that could spring him from captivity. He returned the text, saying it was okay to bring her over. After doing so, he leaned over to inform Lipton what was about to take place. The senator had a perplexed look on his face until he took in the physique heading his way. His pupils got large, and he smiled enthusiastically when he and the woman made eye contact.

Sensing he was missing out on something, Senator Wakeman turned around to see what the attraction was. Taking his cue from the others, Senator Wakeman rose to his feet. Only Engler addressed the man who emerged from behind the woman. He stuck out a hand for Engler to shake, and his expression said, "Thank you."

"Tony, good to see you," the aide offered, his eyes darting back and forth between the two senior members of Congress.

Engler then took the initiative. "Senator Lipton . . . Senator Wakeman, this is Don Emerson. He's Senator Dublin's chief of staff." Both men gave him an obligatory nod. They forgot his name pretty much as soon as they heard it. The woman displayed a degree of bashfulness to accompany the openness of her blouse. Two buttons left unfastened was all it took to reveal the trace of a black lace bra and a cleavage sculpted to perfection by skilled surgical hands. Close up, her face was average, framed by thick blonde hair. Thanks to high heels, she stood just as tall as Senator Lipton.

Trying to gain a little leverage, Emerson gently nudged the

woman to Lipton's side. "Senator, allow me to introduce Monica Freemont. You two have something in common."

Lipton was intrigued. "I can't imagine what that would be." The comment drew smiles from the small gathering.

The blonde flashed her teeth and arched her back just enough to brush against Lipton. "Senator, this is a pleasure. I'm so honored to meet you. I'm from Missouri as well."

"Ah, one of my constituents," Lipton replied. "Miss Freemont, what part of the state are you from?"

"Chesterfield. Born and raised. Oh, my God, my mom is never going to believe I've met you."

"Well, in that case," said Emerson, who desperately wanted to get into Miss Freemont's pants, "let's preserve the moment with a picture. That is, if you don't mind, Senator?" He produced an iPhone while he waited for an answer. Miss Freemont caressed Senator Lipton's arm.

"Senator, it would mean so much to me," she pleaded.

Lipton smiled, feeling youthful. He could remember the days when he chased down many a Miss Freemont. "Well, hell. Let's take a picture. My wife should know she'd better hold onto me."

Miss Freemont's left breast had nowhere to go but against the senator's side as they wrapped their arms around each other to get a tight shot. The aide was focusing the phone's camera when Miss Fremont protested. "Hold on." She separated herself to grab the drink from Lipton's hand. "Why don't you let me hold this? Don't want to give these Beltway Democrats any ammunition."

The senator laughed. "Thank you, my dear. We Missourians have to look out for each other."

Once again, Emerson raised the camera, and a couple of seconds later, the bright flash forced everyone to blink. That was all the time and misdirection Miss Freemont needed to drop a pill into the senator's Scotch. It dissolved quickly and went unnoticed.

Engler decided to go for his exit strategy. He reached for the iPhone and told Emerson to squeeze in so he could take a picture of him with the senators and the blonde he had no business being with. Engler took two pictures and then apologized for cutting the evening short. Senator Lipton was too engaged to be upset, so he bid his chief of staff goodnight. Engler got his counterpart's attention, cocking his head to let him know the ledger was now very much in his favor.

Miss Freemont continued to charm Senator Lipton, aware that her companion was breathing down her neck. She had two options to consider. One was to get the phone from Emerson while in public, delete the pictures and dump the loser. If that proved difficult, she'd probably have to go to his place and get him all worked up while finding the right moment to erase the pictures. She'd then make an excuse to leave before losing all her dignity. She took a long, hard look at him one more time.

It was definitely option one.

CHAPTER 68

His orders were to ensure President Shahroudi's safety. Yadin understood why, but it was difficult to accept. In all the confusion that would arise, it would be no problem at all to kill Shahroudi. But he had to see to it that the president escaped. He hoped the man was foolish enough to stay.

The control room was packed. Technicians stood or sat ready at their various positions of responsibility. There was a camera crew jockeying for room, their lens trained on the president, recording the moment for posterity. The day Iran changed its fate and standing in the world.

Yadin stood behind several people in the back of the room, close to the exit, avoiding the camera crew. Even though they had explicit orders not to capture Dr. Mueller on tape, he wasn't taking any chances. He glanced through the narrow window of the control room door, out into the hallway. He caught a glimpse of Mr. McBride. McBride's presence left him with an unpleasant feeling. He'd made it this far in a very dangerous line of work by listening to his gut. He learned long ago to leave nothing to chance. For the next five minutes, the room was silent as President Shahroudi gave another speech, this one carried all over the facility via its audio system. He thanked all those who helped bring about this day and promised their contributions would be remembered for generations.

Upon conclusion, his speech received thunderous applause, and he basked in the adulation. The president's eyes seemed to glaze over, as if he was imagining how history would portray him.

He gathered himself and strode over to a control panel. A technician rose to give the president access. Shahroudi stared at the two keys locked into place, absorbing their significance.

Yadin improved his position in order to see. Shahroudi reached out with his right hand and turned one of the keys clockwise. Before his hand was completely off the key, the facility began to take on new life, generating more noise. Shahroudi looked up in acknowledgment and then promptly turned the other key. Once again, the facility hummed. To the technicians, it was like a symphony. There was plenty of enthusiasm around the large window overlooking the reactors. With no one paying him the slightest attention, Yadin begin working the mechanisms on his watch. He didn't need to look down, having practiced these maneuvers hundreds of times on a replica watch. He was finished in less than thirty seconds.

While most spectators in the room were still nodding their heads and congratulating each other, Dr. Mueller grabbed a nearby clipboard and joined a group of technicians along one panel of instruments. He made notes of the readings, satisfied that everything was as it should be.

For seven minutes and counting, Iran had become part of an exclusive club. The country now had functional, weapons-grade nuclear reactors in operation. Dr. Mueller continued to make rounds, checking in at various stations. He kept a nonchalant eye on Shahroudi as he did so.

Fifteen minutes in, it happened.

All conversation in the control room came to a concerned halt. Everyone felt a nerve-rattling jolt as the cavernous structure reacted as if it had taken a blow to the midsection.

CHAPTER **69**

The bedside clock read 1:37 in the morning, and Bryce Lipton didn't know if it was guilt or heartburn that had awakened him. In either case, he knew his meal choice had been foolish. Washing down the prime rib and mashed potatoes with several glasses of Scotch had only added fuel to the fire.

He lay in bed, covered only by a sheet, and yet he was soaked in sweat. He slowly sat up, reacting to the pain he felt. The last thing he wanted to do was wake Elaine. She'd grill him with a hundred questions, and before you knew it, he'd be the embarrassment of the neighborhood because she'd overreact and call 911. He was damned if that was going to happen over prime rib.

Lipton tried to remain still and control his breathing, hoping his body would cool down. It wasn't working, so he slid out of bed as quietly as possible and headed for the bathroom, easing the door closed behind him. He turned on the cold-water faucet and repeatedly splashed his face, allowing the water to run down his body. He looked in the mirror and didn't like what stared back. His eyes were bloodshot, his coarse hair a mound of mess. He watched as he gasped for air, his breathing labored. Nearly stumbling, he steadied himself against the basin, trying to fight off an onslaught of pain and nausea. He opened the medicine cabinet and discovered what he needed, but the cap on his nitroglycerin pills bottle was difficult to negotiate with his trembling hands. Heavy droplets of sweat fell onto the marble flooring. He could hear his heart pounding and was frightened that he couldn't turn the volume down. Images were starting to blur.

"Elaine! Elaine!"

He tried to shout her name, but it wouldn't clear his throat. His heart felt as if there was a vise around it. The distance from the basin to the bed seemed endless, and he doubted if could make it that far. His muscles tightened as he tried to walk. He made it to the door and somehow forced it open. He leaned against the doorway and realized there wasn't enough strength left to reach the bed. With tears in his eyes, he stared at his wife, peacefully sound asleep. It wasn't supposed to happen like this. He didn't understand. There had been no warning signs, and except for tonight, he'd been good to his heart. Lipton saved everything he had for one last attempt.

"Elaine," he managed to say, the sound so guttural it didn't seem human. His legs could no longer offer support, and he fell to the floor like an abandoned puppet.

Elaine Lipton thought it had been a bad dream as she turned over in bed, reaching for her husband. Only when she came up empty and felt damp sheets did she open her eyes. She shot up to see her husband slumped on the floor at the bathroom door.

"Bryce . . . oh my God!" She first grabbed the nearby phone and dialed 911. She then raced to her husband's side and knew immediately he was in serious trouble. He was unresponsive and barely breathing. She climbed over him to enter the bathroom where she found his pill bottle in the basin. She dumped a pill into her hand and raced back to him. Forcing his mouth open, she shoved in the nitroglycerin pill. Repositioning him on the floor, she then began administering CPR.

Lipton's eyes were open, but he could neither speak nor move. He did feel the intermittent drops of Elaine's tears upon his face.

Damn it! He saw red lights rapidly flickering off the bedroom walls. He was going to be the embarrassment of the neighborhood after all.

CHAPTER 70

The news wouldn't make the early-morning edition of the papers. If word got out, there was a better chance of it appearing on the various news services' Web pages, but even that was unlikely. At 3:45 a.m. there would be a skeleton staff in place, and more than likely, not a very seasoned one.

National Security Advisor Warren Spencer didn't want the president riding in the backseat on this one, certainly not after the way the past forty-eight hours had developed. Spencer thought about waiting. The president generally started his day at five thirty with exercise. After two sips of freshly made coffee, Spencer alerted the Secret Service that he needed to wake the president.

Special Agent Jimenez was standing ready by the president's bedroom door when Spencer rounded the corner. Jimenez looked into Spencer's eyes as the two men stood inches apart, the agent waiting for the go-ahead. It came with a head nod. Jimenez proceeded to knock firmly several times on the door and then moved aside.

About a minute later, Spencer watched the door handle turn. He still wasn't completely used to the idea of following protocol when addressing his friend. On this occasion, however, he made sure he got it right when the most powerful man in the world opened the door.

"Mr. President, sorry to wake you."

"Spence . . ." President Hudson said, confused. This was the first time since taking office his sleep had been interrupted. "What is it?"

"Mr. President, I have to inform you that Senator Bryce Lipton has died."

CHAPTER 71

The massive jolt achieved the desired effect. Everyone in the underground complex was concerned. There were multiple safeguards in place, and much thought, time, and money had gone into the facility's creation, making it structurally sound. Those specifications made it capable of withstanding an aerial bombing.

Had the West, though, with all its wealth and technology, built a better bomb that could penetrate even deeper to deliver a destructive blow? Nothing short of a nuclear detonation was supposed to threaten it: the Iranians had built this place with extreme confidence, being proactive by digging even deeper than the original plan called for. And yet, something abnormal had just occurred.

Alex stared through the window of the control room, and what he saw reminded him of the daily routine on the floor of the Chicago Mercantile Exchange. Everyone was moving swiftly, checking instrument panels, barking feverishly, and dealing with their anxiety. Even President Shahroudi, surrounded by security guards, seemed on edge. The lone inconsistency was easy to spot. The only uncanny calmness belonged to Dr. Mueller.

Alex ducked out of the way as a couple of lab coats came bursting through the door, cursing in Farsi. Alex eased his way inside, knowing his entrance would go unnoticed amongst the mayhem. He was wrong in that assumption.

Yadin tried to gauge reaction as best as he could. The technicians were scrambling to determine what had caused the place to rumble. He was surprised that the issue of shutting down the reactors hadn't been raised yet. Perhaps they felt secure in knowing safeguards were in place to do just that in the event of a dire emergency. That belief would be tested once the fear escalated. Yadin registered all the moving parts and bodies as if he were painting a masterpiece of confusion. His canvas developed an imperfection when he spotted something that shouldn't be there: Mr. McBride. He wondered how long McBride might have been watching him. The thought prompted Yadin to join the madness, and he did so with a purpose, knowing the clock was quickly counting down to the next disruption. He corralled a group of technicians. After their conversation, two of them approached Alex, who was milling around at the back of the control room. They expressed urgency in insisting he come with them.

"Where are we going?" Alex asked.

"We need to make sure every vital apparatus is working properly," barked one of the techs, heading for the door. "We're heading to the centrifuge room. Your expertise may be needed, Mr. McBride."

"On whose authority, if I may ask?"

"That would be Dr. Mueller."

Alex followed the technicians but took one last look before he left the room. He wasn't at all surprised to see Dr. Mueller watching him exit.

CHAPTER 72

"What, exactly, did Dr. Mueller say we were supposed to be checking?" asked Alex, looking out at the sea of centrifuges running in unison.

"He said to monitor the situation here. Make sure everything is running smoothly while the source of what caused that disruption is located." The tech was doing his best to shield his nervousness. Alex had his own set of doubts. Why did Dr. Mueller specifically request he be brought here? The good doctor had taken too keen an interest in him, considering what he should have been preoccupied with.

"Who is Dr. Mueller?" Alex figured it might be of some comfort to the tech if he were able to ease his fears by talking. There was a good chance his defenses would be down.

"There is little to be known about Dr. Mueller. He fiercely guards his privacy. But most of this facility exists because of him."

"So you don't know where he came fr—" Alex couldn't finish the sentence because the explosion was ear-shattering, potent, and—worse—close. As the tech's body slammed into him, it knocked the air from his lungs. The force of the blast sent both of them hurtling backward in the air. Alex fell to the floor, rolling over several times before stopping just short of a wall. The tech wasn't as lucky. His body continued flying, its path abruptly interrupted by the same wall Alex had managed to avoid. His ears still ringing, Alex didn't hear the thud of the collision, but the tech's body gave way to gravity and fell to the floor. His neck was twisted in an unnatural position. Alex was sure the man had saved his life by absorbing the brunt of the explosion. His own head was a scrambled mess, but Alex concluded it wasn't in his best interest to stay put. He groggily rose to his feet, hugging the wall for balance as he inched toward the exit. All the techs he'd entered the room with were down and motionless, their lab coats tainted with crimson. The other workers in the room looked to have either suffered a similar fate or were crying out in agony. The centrifuges were heavily damaged, and those that were still operational made a noise that only heightened his desperation to vacate the area. As his eyes began to focus, he saw that, in addition to the explosion, it looked like a number of centrifuges had ripped apart on their own. What was it Duncan had said? If they ran at a higher, inappropriate speed, it was possible for them to do just that.

He could hear sirens now, the explosion impossible to mask. Any minute, he expected to be joined by teams of emergency responders. He staggered into the hall and encountered chaos as his head began to clear. No one seemed to have the slightest interest in what was going on in the centrifuge room, and between the blasting of the sirens, he learned why. The female voice filtering through the broadcasting system in Farsi was issuing a warning of her own.

"Danger of reactor failure. Initiate immediate shutdown procedures." The voice was eerily calm, but the message was scaring the hell out of people who had no intention of the underground facility's being their gravesite.

Alex saw a worker jumping behind the wheel of the cart he had ridden to get here. He raced to catch up, and with the worker's back exposed, it was easy to grab hold and throw him roughly to the floor. Alex hopped in the cart and began retracing his route. Alex was convinced the explosion was designed to cripple the centrifuge area and hopefully take him out in the process. His blood began to boil. This was the second time within a few days someone had tried to kill him. Dmitri Nevsky had failed. He couldn't do anything about that at the moment, but Dr. Mueller was accessible.

CHAPTER 73

By now the centrifuge section would be in shambles and "Mr. McBride" presumably a memory. Yadin ignored the high-pitched screams of technicians as they relayed what their monitoring stations were reporting. He had hoped President Shahroudi and his handlers were smart enough to evacuate, but they were dazed by everything happening around them. Yadin could wait no longer. He regrettably had to get the man out. He approached the entourage with urgency.

"Mr. President, you need to get out of here. Now!" The message was delivered loudly. No one dared to talk to the president like that, but clearly, this was no ordinary situation.

"What is going on?" an agitated Shahroudi shot back, not sure if going anywhere was safe.

"I don't know yet, but I don't want to take any chances with your safety." Yadin tried to sound sincere. If the president was unsure about departing before, the next words he heard persuaded him quickly.

Not unlike the voice of propaganda used by the Germans and Japanese during World War II, the voice from the loudspeakers was soothing while delivering news of dire consequence.

"Warning. Warning. Danger of reactor failure. Initiate immediate shutdown procedures."

Dr. Mueller was precise in giving Shahroudi's bodyguards a route back to the surface. He sent them on their way with a sense of urgency based on knowledge of future events.

Alex was out of the cart when he gave way to Shahroudi and

his men, who, besides their weapons, carried a serious look of purpose with each rapidly advancing step. Alex managed to grab the last guard to inquire about Dr. Mueller. The guard was in no mood to protest and hurriedly told Alex he'd find him in the control room. Alex stopped at the door before going in. The room was a lot less populated now, with just five technicians frantically moving. Watching it all stood a relaxed Dr. Mueller. Alex couldn't hear, but he saw all the techs stop what they were doing and give Mueller their full attention. They must have heard what amounted to a stay of execution because they all abandoned their stations and rushed for the exit. As they pushed through, Alex entered. The soft covering on his shoes helped mask his entrance as Mueller faced the huge window overlooking the reactor floor. Alex knelt, using console panels for cover as he moved forward. The back of his head felt wet, so he touched it; after inspection, he concluded the blood on his hand wasn't enough to warrant concern. He let go of the thought of what might have been if not for that technician taking the brunt of the blast.

He peered around a corner and caught Mueller checking his watch. Alex was about to advance when it became necessary to grab onto the console for support. The structure had begun to shake violently as a loud boom permeated the environment. The woman's voice over the loudspeakers was even more nightmarish now.

"Warning. Warning. Reactor failure imminent. Automatic shut-off protocols are offline."

Throughout it all, Dr. Mueller hadn't moved.

"You're either quite resourceful or very lucky, Mr. McBride. Considering you've gotten this far, I'd say it's the former." The words startled Alex, and he realized there was no point in remaining hidden. He stood up, keeping a watchful eye on Dr. Mueller. Knowing he was being studied, Mueller let his arms hang naturally, exposing his open hands, informing Mr. McBride he was not armed—at least, not in a conventional way.

"I take it this is your handiwork?" asked Alex, trying to gauge which side, right or left, Mueller felt more comfortable with.

"Impressed?"

"Ask me again when I get out of here."

"You assume that you will."

"Something tells me you have an exit strategy."

Mueller slowly turned around. "There are some things worth dying for."

Alex looked into his eyes. "You don't strike me as the martyr type."

Mueller smiled. "Isn't there something you'd die for?"

"Off the top of my head . . . nothing comes to mind."

"And yet, here you are, Mr. McBride."

"I never said I was smart. I'm just helping out a friend."

"Must be one hell of a friend."

"And what about you? Mossad wouldn't trust this scale of an operation to just anybody. It's all going to come crumbling down, and I don't just mean this place. Senator Bryce Lipton helping to run a rogue operation with a foreign government . . ." Alex whistled. "The Justice Department and the media are going to have a field day with this one."

"I seriously doubt it will get that far. Besides, how do you think the world will judge your country if it can be proven America is involved? And let me caution, what you think is an off-the-books operation could simply be above your pay grade."

Alex saw something flicker in the man's eye.

Mueller rotated his wrist to glance at his watch. "Time is what I don't have, but it is time to end this."

The move was so quick all Alex could do in response was angle his shoulders sideways. Mueller had produced a knife from the cuff of his shirt and thrown it with deadly force and accuracy. The only problem was that McBride had been a hair faster: the sharp blade sailed past, clanging against an instrument panel instead. With Alex slightly compromised, Mueller ducked behind him just enough to deliver a sideways kick just above the hip. Having braced for the blow, Alex recovered quickly and once again surprised Mueller, this time responding with a long step that maneuvered him in position to use his right hand. He sent Mueller a couple of steps back with a karate chop to the face. Alex readied himself for what he assumed was coming next. If Mueller was a Mossad-trained agent, odds were that he was proficient in the fighting style of Krav Maga—swift attacks aimed to inflict as much damage as possible to vulnerable body parts, the goal being to neutralize the opponent quickly. Alex was right. Mueller came back with a flurry of movement. Two kicks found Alex's thigh, and he failed to block a series of blows to his neck, one connecting on each side. He was fortunate enough to turn and lower his jaw just enough to avoid a direct blow to his Adam's apple. Sensing he had the upper hand, Mueller closed in, and Alex let him. The moment Mueller made his intention known, Alex dodged the lethal right hand. He shifted to his left, and carrying the majority of his weight with him, he rifled two sharp blows to Mueller's midsection. His stomach was flat and strong, but the doctor definitely felt the impact. Alex locked Mueller's right leg with his own and then rose to fire his left-hand palm hard into the doctor's jaw. Mueller stumbled backward and fell to the floor. That strike would have left most men nearly unconscious, but Mueller was back on his feet, showing no sign of giving up. He charged at Alex, aiming for his midsection. Alex crouched and extended his arms as Mueller came at him. Rotating his hips, Alex tossed Mueller aside. There was a loud sigh as he crashed into a metal console. Once again, Mueller rebounded immediately. He came at Alex using his hands and feet in a furious attack. Alex blocked what he could, but a right hand had a clear path to his left kidney, and a series of kicks connected just above his groin. Alex's knees buckled, and his back arched from a stinging sensation climbing upward. His reflexes deflected a blazing left fist to his nose. He managed to defend himself from a flurry of strikes, finally going on the offensive by thrusting his large frame into Mueller's chest, creating space. In the blink of an eye, Alex delivered a direct kick to Mueller's stomach, doubling him over. Alex was in the process of delivering a fluid roundhouse kick to the head when Mueller sprung to life, ducking to make the intended strike harmless. Mueller then lashed out, attacking the big thigh muscle of Alex's firmly planted left leg. Next he sent Alex hard to the floor by sweeping his leg from under him. Mueller was on him in seconds, attacking the left side of his back with a series of well-placed, powerful jabs. Vulnerable and in tear-evoking pain, Alex tried to crawl away, cursing the fact that his skills were rusty for this kind of encounter. Dr. Mueller certainly had the upper hand.

When no finishing onslaught ensued, Alex turned his head to see Mueller walking away. At first Alex thought Mueller had designs on retrieving the knife, which was nearby, but there was something else that had captured the doctor's attention instead. Mueller didn't even seem to acknowledge Alex's existence. Instead, he made a beeline to an instrument panel. He punched several buttons with purpose. For the first time since he'd been in Mueller's company, Alex thought he recognized concern. There was a lost look on his face.

Recovering, Alex gingerly got to his feet. "What is it? You finally appear worried."

"You aren't as stupid as you look," Mueller responded as he rushed to the large windows overlooking the reactor floor. He shook his head and ran to another control panel, frantically tapping more buttons. He moved to an adjacent computer screen, typing so hard on the keyboard that he nearly broke it.

"Anything I can do?" Alex asked, feeling totally helpless. He picked up and pocketed the knife in the process. He had no intention of leaving anything to chance.

"Not unless you have an advanced degree in nuclear engineering. The reactors were supposed to shut down. That they didn't is troubling on several fronts." Mueller considered his options. "I'm in a generous mood right now, so you need to get out of here."

"Not until you tell me what the hell is going on."

Mueller shook his head. "On second thought, maybe you are as stupid as you look. If those reactors aren't shut down, they'll make Chernobyl look like child's play."

"You're telling me that wasn't the purpose all along?"

"Not really," said Mueller, going from instrument panel to instrument panel. "Who is the female friend you mentioned?"

"I didn't say it was a woman."

"You CIA?"

"Past tense."

Mueller stopped what he was doing. "I need your help with something." Without hesitation, Alex followed him to a door that led to a staging area. There were a number of protective suits hanging from a wall. They resembled astronaut gear. Mueller explained he needed help putting on one of the suits, since shutting down the reactors could only be done manually at this point.

"What should I really call you, McBride?" Mueller asked as he assembled the various items he needed as quickly as possible.

"Alex."

"I'm Nathan." They didn't bother to shake hands. "I have to ask you something. There was a woman in Annapolis. Erica Janway. Was she a good person? Loyal to her country?"

It was a strange question but Alex was able to piece together its significance. "No question. She was a mentor and friend to the person I'm helping."

"So your friend became a target as well."

"Exactly."

Yadin began stepping into the suit. "This operation has been in the works for a number of years. In the beginning, your country and mine covertly supplied the Iranians with faulty parts and materials, hoping that setback after setback would cause them to abandon the idea of achieving nuclear status. It succeeded in delaying their goal, but they were persistent. Once your country backed off, feeling enough had been accomplished, a decision was then made to start giving them legitimate parts in order to gain their trust. These parts were just enough to whet their appetite. They went on to spend billions. In order to build their program, they had to go through the fictitious Dr. Mueller. The stipulation was they had to trust me beyond question or their program would be dead. They were idealistic and desperate enough to accept the terms. As a result, we pretty much had total control in building this facility. We controlled the blueprints, the parts, and managed the go-betweens they had to deal with. All orchestrated."

Alex checked the suit for any defects. "You built it to tear it down?"

"Precisely, and at a tremendous cost to the Iranians. What they had no way of knowing was that mixed in with legitimate materials were craftily altered items that would pass expert inspection. And since I normally ordered them, after a while, not even those got a second look. The materials were designed to work perfectly until they were triggered to malfunction." Yadin had one arm in the suit and was about to insert the other when he showed Alex his watch. "This is a very special piece of equipment. It emits certain high-frequency signals and can be set much like an alarm clock to go off at different intervals. Some of these walls are made of a C4 base mold. The electrical wire going through them gets a charge, and boom! The centrifuges you inspected in Tbilisi were designed to malfunction and spin at uncontrollable rates when set off."

"But now you've got a problem?"

"Yes, those reactors. The warning signals were supposed to just be a scare tactic. They were false notifications. There shouldn't be a real meltdown in progress."

"Well, you can see the irony. Faulty parts not responding?"

"There were numerous safeguards in place. The reactors were supposed to be shut down and buried in a deep grave. The potential disaster hopefully would have been enough of a deterrent to prevent further endeavors and give pause to other countries in the region."

Yadin was outfitted with the entire suit except for the protective helmet. "I suspect others wanted to make more of a statement, which means I was deceived. At this point, I can't trust anything that was arranged to ensure my safety. But you have to go. I've bought you a little time by delaying the next explosion. It's going to be huge. The escape route won't be open for long, so you've got to get to the surface. When you get out, pay attention to which direction the wind is blowing and go the opposite way. Even if I can't shut this down, you might get lucky."

Yadin explained the exact direction Alex needed to take. He doubted if anyone else knew the path existed. Alex walked Yadin to a nearby elevator that would take him down to the reactor floor. Yadin stepped in, fully insulated, a tool box in one hand. With the other he punched the appropriate button. Just as the doors were about to close, he held them in check.

He had to speak louder through the airtight helmet. "Tell your friend I'm sorry. They told me Janway was a threat, a cancer to the operation. Someone who had betrayed her country. You know about Senator Lipton, but the real puppet master is a billionaire named Roger Daniels. If your friend wants closure, don't try to get it in a court of law. He has too much influence."

Yadin released his grip, allowing the elevator door to slowly clamp shut. Alex took a deep breath before hauling ass as rapidly as he could.

CHAPTER **74**

Alex had no choice but to trust the Mossad agent who called himself Nathan. As he sprinted down corridors, knocking bodies out of the way, Alex was aware he was taking the word of a man who'd tried to kill him just minutes before. The same man who'd killed Erica Janway. And yet, as the structure around him was on the verge of buckling, there was no other option except to follow the man's instructions to the letter.

The door Alex was looking for was right where Nathan said it would be. It was down a narrow passage off a main hallway. The halls leading to it were obscured by shadows, so it was understandable that in a panic situation, no one would have thought an exit existed. He was about to punch in the last digit of the access code on the security panel when he heard the unmistakable sound of a pistol assembly slide being locked into place. He muttered an expletive under his breath and slowly turned to see the demure presence of Farid pointing a pistol at his head. What made Alex nervous was the assault weapon in the shaking hands of a Revolutionary Guard soldier flanking Farid.

"What are you doing, Mr. McBride, if that is indeed your real name?"

"Trying to get out like everyone else," Alex hurriedly said, realizing there was no time for this.

"You arrive here for the first time today, and you're familiar with a part of the building that is well hidden. And," Farid motioned toward the security panel, "you know access codes as well."

The Revolutionary Guard soldier seemed to be questioning the wisdom of being here. His eyes were darting from side to side, not liking this poorly lit area at all. Farid, however, was waiting on an answer.

"Dr. Mueller gave me the code and told me how to get here."

"And where is he now?"

"Trying to shut down the reactor so that this doesn't become our final resting place." While Farid was measuring the merits of the situation, Alex reached in his pocket and brought the knife to rest on his shielded side. Just then, what little light there was flickered off and on as the ground moved. Chewed up pieces of concrete dislodged from above, adding to the mayhem. The soldier's attention was diverted upward as he used his free hand to cover his head. Alex had the opening he needed. He grabbed Farid's gun hand and wrenched it nearly to the point of breaking. He also kicked Farid's left foot away to knock him off balance. Farid yelped with pain and had no choice but to let the gun fall from his hand. By the time the soldier realized what was happening, he couldn't react. Alex started his right hand from well behind his head with blinding momentum. He didn't stop until the weight of the guard stabilized. By then, though, his Adam's apple was shattered. Alex followed up by stabbing him in the heart, removing the blade as he turned to catch Farid trying to retrieve his gun. Alex kicked the weapon away and thrust the knife into the back of Farid's neck as he stepped over him to reach the security panel, where he once again entered the code.

Despite all that was going on around him, Alex was alone in a quiet, long corridor just wide enough for electric carts to travel in either direction. As promised, a cart was parked and waiting. Alex had it moving in seconds, his foot fully depressed on the pedal, willing it to go faster. Its speed was slowed by the upward climb, which resembled a paper clip in design. The hallway led to a dead end with one exit door. Alex entered the same pass code as before. The green light gave him access to a stairwell. It was difficult to judge how many flights there were, but the only way to go was up, and he didn't think about it. He started off taking two stairs at a time. Six levels had been cleared when he heard a deafening explosion below him. It rattled the stairwell, and parts of the wall cracked open. There definitely was no going back. His lungs burning for air, Alex was grateful to see there were no stairs after two more levels. Not knowing what was on the other side, he took a couple of gulps of air before flinging open the exit door in front of him. The bright sun was blinding, forcing him to stop dead in his tracks. He raised his right arm as a shield, helping his eyes adjust as he pressed forward. There were frantic people running everywhere. He narrowly dodged a jeep that zoomed past him. Not even the blaring sirens could drown out screams of "Get out! Get out! Save yourselves!"

Alex made a run for a sedan that was loading up but was too late. Its doors closed and the vehicle jetted off. Fifty yards away, he located another vehicle. From the corner of his eye he saw that others had designs on the SUV as well. Taking off in a full-blown sprint, Alex reached the vehicle before the other men, who'd had a shorter distance to travel. As he opened the driver's side door, an arm forcefully grabbed his shoulders, trying to drag him away. Alex squatted to dislodge the hand. Still low, he pivoted and began to rise. He struck the man in several key body parts with extreme force and speed. The final blow was an open hand thrust under the man's chin. He fell to the ground dazed and unable to respond. Seeing this, his friends backed away and ran off to find another means of escape. Thankful the keys were in the ignition, Alex put the car in gear and floored it. He was about four miles away from the compound when in the rearview mirror he saw a sea of dirt and sand rise high in the sky, as if a giant fan had been turned on.

Several miles later, he phoned Nora and instructed her to be waiting with all the necessary paperwork and credentials outside the hotel. Panic wouldn't have reached Tehran yet, so they would have a head start before the roads jammed. When he pulled up to the hotel, Nora jumped into the front seat. All she carried was her purse and a pillowcase filled with nothing but essential items. Alex drove like an ambulance driver to exit Tehran. Nora explained that they had to head north toward Azerbaijan. She studied her phone. Sara had e-mailed a detailed map with their route well marked. Once on the highway, it was all just about speed. Alex stayed on the Tehran-Karaj Freeway for several miles, veering onto Freeway 1 toward Rasht. From there, they hugged the coastline along Road 49 en route to the border crossing at Astara. Along the way, Nora made contact with Sara again. If everything went according to plan, they'd soon be safe.

Getting everything to go according to plan was no small and inexpensive feat. The CIA had to enlist the services of a highly respected career diplomat who was an expert on the region with well-placed friends. He decided to help despite his hurt feelings. Just a few months prior, his nomination to be ambassador to Azerbaijan had been unceremoniously derailed in Congress due to opposition from Armenian-American interest groups. An easier route would have been to ask Israel to intervene, since they had a working relationship with the country, but based on the current situation, President Hudson thought it was an unwise request to make. Not knowing who was a part of this sordid mess, he felt it best to keep the Israelis in the dark on what they already knew.

Arrangements and payments went down to the wire, but when Alex and Nora joined the line at the border crossing, a couple of Iranian policemen took particular interest in their vehicle. They approached and demanded to see identification. Satisfied with visual confirmation, the guards stepped back and ordered Alex and Nora to exit, instructing them to leave the keys in the ignition. Alex didn't know what to make of it, but he felt their luck had possibly run out. They were marched toward the border crossing.

Alex formed a big smile when he saw Duncan and Sara waiting on the other side. Sara gave the guard standing next to her a nod, and he in turn did the same to his counterpart on the Iranian side of Astara. A few minutes later, Alex and Nora crossed the border.

"You crazy, amazing son of a bitch," Duncan remarked as he gave Alex a huge bear hug.

CHAPTER 75

Al Jazeera news network was the first to report it. The news was met with some skepticism, but the entire Arab world took note, especially Iran's nearest neighbors. Shortly after, CNN got wind of the story, making it accessible to the world. Other cable news outlets followed suit. About three hours after video aired of President Shahroudi proudly proclaiming Iran had joined the ranks of countries with nuclear power came word of a major catastrophe. One announcer uttered the words that drew people closer to their televisions and radios: "Nuclear disaster."

The Iraqi government responded by taking air samples. So far everything was all clear, and the wind, thank Allah, was blowing away from its borders. Turkmenistan also monitored the situation with uneasiness, putting the country's health care system on alert. The prevailing winds were blowing in a southeasterly direction. That set off a panic in Afghanistan and Pakistan. Word of mouth was spreading among border colonies, and people and possessions were left behind as a mad exodus inland began. Government officials tried to inform the escaping masses that test results were yielding no cause for concern. Having endured years of being lied to by various governments, they marched on.

There was no official confirmation or denial from Iran, but the story was sensitive enough to warrant talk of an immediate meeting by the League of Arab States.

In the United States, various governmental agencies were up to speed on what happened long before any news report. Satellites that routinely monitored the comings and goings at the Natanz facility yielded pictures of a complex that was there one minute and virtually swallowed by a giant sinkhole the next. Since it was early morning in Washington, the right people were already up, prepping for the day when they got the call. Al Jazeera was reporting hundreds of casualties as the first shaky pieces of mobile phone video were broadcast. The images weren't specific but they did convey panic, showing mostly workers scrambling to escape the area.

There was much speculation in the Arab world that the West had masterminded the incident in response to Shahroudi's bravado, backing up their promise that Iran would not be allowed to become a nuclear state. But calmer, more rational analysts conveyed the fact that such a strike so quickly after Shahroudi's announcement was implausible. That there were no reports of military planes or missiles crossing the necessary borders to carry out such a response gave weight to their observations. The United States immediately offered assistance through the Iranian embassy and NATO after attempts to reach President Shahroudi directly were unsuccessful. Most of the European Union duplicated the gesture, only to be rebuffed.

Yosef Ezra watched the events unfold at work with colleagues. One would have been hard-pressed to find sadness in the room of Mossad employees. From their point of view, an unnerving threat was now off the books. Plus, there was no doubt Iran would now have less money to funnel to hostile groups like Hamas. The cost in human life was tragic, but the Iranians had brought this upon themselves.

As more details slowly filtered in through news reports and assets in the region, it was clear something had not gone according to plan. There was no evidence of a radiation leak of any kind. If those reactors had malfunctioned like they were supposed to have, there would be condemnation from all over the globe for Iran's miscalculated steps. Its surrounding neighbors would be at the brink of war if radiation encroached upon their borders. Afghani chieftains alone would be up in arms if their precious poppy fields were contaminated for years to come.

There was one other uncertainty that kept Ezra relatively

quiet. What was the status of Nathan Yadin? If the reactors' cores hadn't been breached, it was conceivable Yadin was responsible. Ezra had never encountered a more dangerous man. Yadin was more than a walking, thinking, killing machine. He had a high IQ to supplement his deadly skill. Judging from the images, it was entirely possible Natanz's collapse was now Yadin's tomb. Surely he wouldn't have had enough time to prevent the reactors from leaking and then escape. Ezra rubbed his weary eyes. Yadin was capable of the impossible. He'd seen that over the years. For that reason alone, he had built in an insurance plan on Yadin's planned escape route. All the ambush team had needed for success was the slightest indecision on Yadin's part. Ezra wouldn't be at ease until he knew for sure, but if Yadin was buried beneath tons of sand and metal, only time would ease his fears.

Several hours had passed since the first report, and the rest of the world showed its resiliency or lack of concern by adhering to daily routines as if nothing happened. The night pulse of Brussels was just beginning to thump. Restaurants and bars were jammed with patrons, their noise indicating life was meant to be enjoyed. The navy sedan with tinted windows cautiously moved along, just another clog in the chaotic driving conditions of Brussels. There were five occupants in the car, four of whom could see clearly: the driver, the man in the front passenger seat, and the two men sitting in the back, bookending Davis Lipton, who sat blindfolded in the middle. The man on his left made him extremely nervous as he bounced to the music blasting from the car's speakers, all the while pressing a silenced weapon against his stomach. They'd been traveling for nearly thirty minutes, mostly due to the traffic, but also because they were scouting for the right location. Without warning, the car came to an abrupt stop and the rear doors opened just as quickly. A firm hand pulled Lipton by the shirt while the man on his left supplied a push in the back as he was led out of the car. They turned him around and forced him to sit down on what felt like a bench. He was instructed not to move, which was fine with him since his bandaged foot still ached from being shot. He heard their footfalls as they hurried away, and then a car accelerating quickly, horns blasting in protest. Lipton sat there for a good five minutes, listening to the night noise of cars zooming by and people engaged in conversation. He also heard a few giggles as foot traffic crossed in front of him. Taking a chance, he removed his blindfold, grateful he was still alive, his captors nowhere in sight. He had to find a phone so he could call his father and warn him.

CHAPTER 76

Home was about seventeen hours away, and Alex was determined to make it there today. He desperately needed to feel the comfort and familiarity of sand beneath his feet and the sound of the ocean.

For the last couple of days he'd done little besides recuperating mentally and physically. Being close to death several times tended to zap one's energy.

He debated getting another cup of coffee. It would be at least another forty-five minutes before his flight began boarding. Airports were the worst. The only thing that made his wait tolerable was spending it in the British Airways First lounge, away from the jammed terminal traffic. This little perk and the first-class ticket home were courtesy of the CIA. Alex sat isolated, purposely situated away from any television set. The news of Iran's nuclear facility "mishap" still garnered plenty of media attention, but he had no interest. The Natanz facility had nearly become his final resting place. He loved sand, but not to that degree.

From Azerbaijan, Alex, Nora, Duncan, and Sara had been transported by private plane to RAF Croughton base outside of London. Alex spent nearly an entire day being debriefed by the CIA chief of station and other experts on what he'd seen and encountered.

Upon being excused, he'd made sure the CIA was covering the tab for a suite at one of London's finest hotels and for his first-class return trip home. George Champion had arranged for him to have carte blanche to make whatever travel and accommodation

arrangements he pleased. Alex took Duncan and Nora out for dinner, sparing no expense. Alex had extended his gratitude to Duncan for being such a good friend: he, too, got a first-class ticket
home. Sensing that Nora and Alex had unfinished business to address, Duncan had said his good-byes, receiving a heartfelt hug
and kiss from Nora.

Alex and Nora had grown quiet as they nursed another bottle
of wine. She had searched her heart and began to explain that
words were not enough, but Alex had cut her off, telling her it
wasn't necessary. He asked if she wanted closure. She didn't quite
understand: the whole operation was over, wasn't it?

"Not exactly," he had told her, wondering if she truly possessed the hunger to see it through to the end.

Her response had been firm. "Let me have it."

It was a detail he'd refrained from telling the CIA. "The man
you want is named Roger Daniels."

Nora had consumed the revelation as they'd finished the last
bottle of wine. The emotion fueled by a last dinner together led to
their spending the night and experiencing one another quite possibly for the last time. There had been no promises made the following morning as they went their separate ways.

When Alex heard his plane's boarding announcement, he made
his way to the specified gate. Situated in his first-class seat he
smiled, thinking of the one last good deed he'd performed. Because they'd both invested with his money managing company
before, Alex had Nora and Duncan's banking information. They
deserved to enjoy the $700,000 windfall deposited into each of
their accounts, courtesy of the Iranian government.

CHAPTER 77

A bullet in the head from a long-range rifle was too easy and impersonal. Nora had decided her target deserved to suffer, and it needed to be personal. Roger Daniels's unlimited access to luxury made things problematic. He didn't fly commercial or wait in line for a dinner table. Stores stayed open for him after closing to the general public. Nora had spent more than a month chasing him around the globe, observing his habits. She concluded his love of the sea and younger women would be his downfall.

Nora had discovered that during his Caribbean jaunts, Daniels would give the majority of his crew a night off, leaving just a skeleton staff of two people. He didn't do it out of kindness or appreciation. Instead, the situation allowed him to put on a show, often having sex at night, on the open deck of the *Cuda*, the young woman's forced moans of passion drifting out to sea as if the ocean would be impressed with her lover's prowess.

On this night, Daniels's yacht was positioned about a mile and a half offshore. Nora was anchored just under a mile away, watching in the darkness from the twenty-seven-foot cabin cruiser she'd rented. When the time came, she would have to be ready. The slightest hesitation could put her in jeopardy. To prepare, she'd slept as long as she could during the day, not wanting to chance being lulled into a nap by the rhythmic sway of the ocean or the calmness of the night. Once darkness fell, she slipped into a diving suit, checked the oxygen tank for a third time, and set it down next to her for easy access. She sat low in the boat, peering over its side from time to time with night-vision binoculars.

Then she waited.

The bulk of the crew left for shore presunset on several din-ghies. One crewmember returned a short time later, piloting the dinghy with a shapely blonde in a V-neck sundress on board, the wind tossing her hair. Daniels was waiting and helped her board. There were now only two crewmembers on board. Nora medi-tated as the couple had drinks and dinner. She maintained calm through extensive foreplay and tried to concentrate on the task ahead while the pair engaged in their unabashed sexual exploits. All was quiet for over an hour with no movement on the boat. It was just the moon, the waves, and anticipation. Nora's interest piqued when a faint light on the deck was eclipsed. She grabbed the binoculars and saw the woman standing alone, adjusting her dress. Shortly after, she was joined by the crewmember that had transported her. There was no sign of Daniels. When Nora saw the crewmember get into the dinghy, she knew her wait was over. She heard the engine engage as she put on the oxygen tank. She slipped on the goggles next and, not wanting to risk making noise, she climbed over the side backward. She reached back in the boat with both hands and grabbed the Submerge underwater scooter. It was heavy at fifty pounds, but once she lowered herself in the water and went under, the DPV—diver propulsion vehicle—required her to expend little physical effort as she stealthily headed toward Daniels's yacht. She rose to the surface just prior to reaching the craft. She checked toward shore and saw the dinghy still hadn't reached land. If her understanding of the routine was correct, the crewmember would make sure the woman made it home safely. There was also a good possibility he would join his mates for a nightcap before returning to the yacht, giving Nora less to worry about.

She tied the DPV to the yacht below the surface so it wouldn't clang against the side. She cautiously climbed aboard, listening for any sounds of movement. Nora unzipped the airtight pouch at-tached to her waist and withdrew the 9mm weapon. From the same pouch she extracted a silencer and screwed it into place. She took off her dive fins, stacking them in the darkness so they wouldn't be noticed should the lone crewmember decide to take a stroll. Having studied the yacht's schematics, she easily found the main sleeping quarters. The door leading to the master bedroom was ajar, and she could hear soft snoring. She eased the door open to find Daniels sound asleep on the bed, clad, thankfully, in his underwear. She closed the door behind her and crossed to his side of the bed. She laid the gun down on the nearby table and produced a small box from a separate pouch attached to her utility belt. She opened it and withdrew a small liquid bottle and syringe. She filled the syringe, tapped it with her fingers, and deposited the entire solution into Daniels's neck. He sat up as if being stung by a bee.

"What the hell!" he said, reaching for his bedside light. He squinted to see whose life he was about to ruin when he noticed the gun barrel pointed directly at his forehead.

"It's really for show," Nora assured him. "I have no intention of shooting you. But to get the thought out of your mind, you aren't capable of taking it away either."

Daniels rested his head against the backboard, rubbing at his neck. "What the hell did you do? Who are you? Some Greenpeace protester? Save the whales? Is one of my investments encroaching on sacred land somewhere?"

Nora shook her head as she packed up the syringe and bottle, placing them back in the pouch. She took a seat at the end of the bed, resting the gun on her right leg. "Tubocurarine."

"What?"

"You asked what I did to you. I gave you a shot of tubocurarine. It's a neuromuscular-blocking drug. A highly concentrated dose. And this is about Erica Janway."

She saw a trace of recognition in his eyes. Daniels then surprised her, revealing a sarcastic smile that nearly caused her to shoot him. "Ah, you must be Nora Mossa. You may not understand this, but your friend's death served a greater good."

"Well, thanks for not insulting my intelligence. All her death did was solidify your interests and further your efforts to shape the world."

"Please don't tell me you're so blind as to not realize that's exactly what our government has done for centuries. Men like me are suppliers, capable of intervening or lending assistance when the government either can't or won't advance a necessary agenda."

"What you're saying is, rules don't apply to you?"

Daniels swallowed, beginning to feel the weight of his head. "Even in your line of work, that often becomes a gray area."

"Erica Janway was a good person. A patriot."

"Good people die . . . die . . . every day," said Daniels, the words becoming difficult to get out. "Janway's death at least paved the way for a more . . . more . . . manageable Middle East. Chaos sometimes leads to stability."

"Fortunately, nature balances things out."

"Whaaat duh you meeeeean? Whaaat arrrrr youuuu duh . . . doooing too meeee?" He could barely keep himself propped up.

"Bad people die every day too." Nora got up and hovered over his pathetic existence. He was hardly powerful now. She leaned over and grabbed the oversized pillow next to him.

Breathing heavily, Daniel's realized what was about to happen. He couldn't raise his hands to defend himself. Couldn't scream. His wide bloodshot eyes were his only form of protest left. He wanted to yell, "This is madness! Do you realize all the good I do in this world? I can make you rich beyond your dreams!" As the pillow began to cut off his flow of oxygen, Daniels knew this was one deal he couldn't negotiate.

Ten minutes later, Nora was climbing back into her rented boat, not feeling the least bit remorseful about exacting revenge for her friend, or for the countless others, she was sure, whose deaths Roger Daniels was responsible for.

CHAPTER 78

The last month had been extremely tiresome and nerve-racking for Yosef Ezra. His first full night of sleep had come just last week. After searching and searching, Ezra had begun to finally believe Yadin was buried in the Iranian desert. All of Yadin's known financial accounts had been monitored around the clock with no activity. His perceived favorite haunts had yielded nothing. Ezra went so far as to have Yadin's mother under surveillance. The team put in place to provide him with an escape route out of Iran had waited for days, but he'd been a no-show. Ezra had debated that bit of news for weeks. Was it proof of Yadin's demise? Or was it a smokescreen? Yadin was the most ruthless, efficient, and intelligent operative he had ever cultivated. Over the years, no one had served the Mossad and its interests better. But Ezra had begun to see the signs. Yadin had started to question assignments more, his thirst for killing waning ever so slightly. He had also begun to think about the lure of a normal life, and for someone with his expertise, that was a bad thing. Ezra had wrestled with the decision, but in the end, he felt it had to be made. At least Yadin would go out in a blaze of glory, not that the masses would ever know about it.

Some within the ruling party had begun to whisper Ezra's name in association with the Natanz incident. When asked, the rehearsed line consistently came out that he was flattered that others thought he was capable of such a grand achievement. He had been told the inquiry was generated by the United States through a White House dignitary at a Washington cocktail party. That same official had strongly suggested Daniel Wassermann be called home from the Israeli Embassy. To maintain harmony, the "request" had been granted, but the Israelis let it be known they were not pleased with the implication.

Ezra's call for additional security shortly after Natanz had been granted without protest. All high-ranking officials had been encouraged to increase their level of safety in case of backlash over what had happened in Iran. The Israelis had gotten out in front of the situation by maintaining their innocence, warning that serious consequences would follow an unprovoked attack against its land or people. All Ezra could do was smile, knowing only a select few held the secret.

More than a month had passed since Iran's mishap. Middle Eastern countries considering nuclear power took a long, hard look at the costs, both financial and human. Hundreds had perished at Natanz, and billions of dollars had been wasted, a portion of that amount pocketed under several umbrella corporations of the Global Watch Institute. President Shahroudi was under extreme internal pressure, and the people were growing more restless with each passing day over the country's economic woes. Iran's neighboring states were still none too pleased with what might have been. In the end, Ezra had come to grips with there being no radioactive fallout. The destruction alone had yielded the desired outcome. He was feeling much better about his situation, and Israel was a safer place today than it had been in a long while. A part of him wished he could take credit for Natanz, but that would surely result in the Arab world knocking loudly at Israel's door.

A sure sign of his growing confidence was Ezra's comfort with being seen in public more. At some point, he had to move on with his life. He made the gesture of reducing his security detail to just one person at a time. Even then it was a rotation of three people he'd handpicked, their loyalty beyond question.

He was feeling especially euphoric this evening, sitting in the audience of the Tel Aviv Performing Arts Center with his two granddaughters, enjoying a rendition of *Cinderella*. He found himself laughing, not so much at the age-old tale, but because his granddaughters were having such a great time. It was cathartic to laugh, but his best intentions were interrupted by his cell phone buzzing for the third time. He didn't recognize the number on the display, but it was damn annoying. Only certain people knew how to get in touch with him on this phone. He turned to his girls, telling them he'd be right back. At the end of the row, he engaged his security guard, who did his best to remain in the shadows. Ezra raised his phone and told him he had to return a call, instructing the guard to watch over the girls. Ezra eased the guard's protesting stance, indicating he would be fine on his own for a few minutes.

Once in the hallway, Ezra decided the first order of business was to visit the bathroom, since a growing prostate was making these trips more and more frequent. One of the inconveniences of growing old, he told himself. He found himself about to panic at the sight of a uniformed janitor outside the men's room and a "Temporarily Closed" sign on a stand next to him. The janitor had his back to him and was mopping up the floor.

"Excuse me. Is the men's room open or closed?"

The janitor didn't break from work and didn't turn to look up. He tiredly said, "A toilet overflowed. Had to clean it up. I still need to mop a bit, but it's open."

Ezra thankfully pushed through the door. He saw a stall that had a sign plastered on it. "Out of Order."

At least the place didn't smell, and from his observation, it looked pretty much spotless. After he relieved himself, he heard the door open and registered the sounds of the janitor, his bucket rolling across the tiled floor, ready to pick up where he left off, no doubt. At the basin, Ezra decided to return the call of the person who was persistent enough to keep buzzing, but not considerate enough to leave a message. He heard the phone ring through his handset and after a couple of rings, lowered the phone from his ear, curious about the sound he was hearing. He saw the janitor's mop sweeping back and forth around a corner, so the source of the sound wasn't there. He was certain there'd been no one else in the restroom when he entered, and the janitor had only walked in a moment ago. Ezra ended his phone call and gingerly walked back to the bank of stalls. He hit the redial button and then, unmistakably this time, another phone began ringing inside the stall marked "Out of Order." Ezra withdrew a weapon and crouched low so he could see underneath the stall's doors. There were no feet touching the ground, and yet a phone continued to ring. He inched closer, cautious, his weapon pointed at the stall, ready to fire. Standing to the side, he swung the door open with his foot and took aim with his weapon. No one was there, but a phone sat on top of the toilet seat. He moved to it but didn't try to pick it up, conscious that doing so might trigger an explosive device. He could read the caller ID, and staring back at him was his cell number. What he heard next nearly gave him reason to soil himself.

"Why, Ezra?"

He closed his eyes. The Devil was at his door. Ezra bent down and laid his weapon on the toilet seat before he was asked to do so. He turned to face his nightmare.

Yadin steadied the large-caliber, suppressor-equipped gun in his hand, not exactly the tool of a janitor. "Did I not do everything you ever asked me to?"

Ezra looked lost. Slightly ashamed, even.

"You were friends with my father. You provided for my mother. Why, Ezra?"

There were no exit-strategy words. The truth was the only avenue available. "What was at stake was larger than you—or me, for that matter. I placed Israel first."

"And you thought I couldn't be trusted?"

"You're a killer, Nathan. A finely tuned machine, but you also have compassion. I've been in this business a long time. I recognized the signs that you were starting to question your contribution. What we ultimately had planned I knew you couldn't live with. You wouldn't have accepted it."

"Senselessly killing thousands of innocent people? No, I couldn't stomach that. There's no justification for that end. As you've seen, we did enough."

"But how long will the message last? We have been in a war for survival for decades."

"And how much money did men like Roger Daniels make?"

Ezra at first was surprised Yadin knew the name, but then he remembered who was standing before him. Very little was ever left to chance.

"Daniels was necessary to accomplish the mission."

"And what does it say, Ezra, that our own government didn't sanction the mission? The American woman from the CIA, I understand she deserved better."

"You don't see it now, but again, a necessary step. She was on the verge of ruining years of hard work and planning. An operation of that magnitude had to be allowed to run its course, no matter the sacrifice."

"I still didn't want to believe it, but then I staked out my so-called exit team. Even a blind man wouldn't have stepped into that trap."

"So it *was* you who shut down the reactors. You risked your life for those that have sworn to bury us?"

"I did what was right at the time. Besides, it was your call to let Shahroudi live. Fortunately, I was in charge of the blueprints, and I made some modifications, just in case. Still, I almost didn't make it, Ezra, and you nearly succeeded. Nearly got away with it all. But like the play your granddaughters are watching, the clock for you has struck midnight."

Yadin pounced with the quickness of a leopard, knocking Ezra backward and off balance. He tripped over the toilet seat, and only Yadin grabbing him by his suit coat lapel kept him from falling to the ground. Yadin positioned himself so that he had leverage. One arm pressed against the back of Ezra's neck, holding it firmly in place while the other squeezed from the front with an unbreakable hold. As Ezra was about to lose consciousness, he tried to pry Yadin's hand lose. The move forced Yadin to tighten the pressure with his other hand. It was as if an anaconda had taken hold. Ezra's watery eyes were bulging, and slowly his feet stopped kicking as he lost the strength to fight back. His arms fell, dangling at the sides of his limp body. Yadin sat Ezra upright on the toilet seat and then retrieved the mobile phone that had been knocked to the floor during the altercation.

The janitor unlocked the restroom door and dragged his bucket and mop along as he exited. He paused to relock the door. The "Temporarily Closed" sign was still in place. The janitor started whistling as he headed down the hallway and out of sight.

CHAPTER 79

The peace and tranquility was all the therapy Alex needed. The events that nearly cost him his life all seemed trivial at the moment, nightmares that eroded with each foray into the ocean.

He had his Cruzan rum and a steady supply of cola and ice to go with it. The sun, as always, was a constant companion. To make the setting perfect, Alex's collection of jazz music shuffled from bebop to smooth jazz as it played through strategically mounted speakers. He drifted in and out of sleep, his body eradicating the effects of jet lag.

When his mind did wander, it led him to Nora, Duncan, and the mysterious man named Nathan. If indeed that was his real name. Alex didn't see how he could have made it out of that Natanz grave alive, but there had been an aura of the survivalist about him. In the end, Nathan had saved his life, and for that Alex was grateful.

He had no concrete idea where his relationship with Nora stood. Part of him wanted her back in his life, reluctantly admitting it was good to be around her again. But he had brushed off her attempts at affection more than once, and the answer as to why wasn't immediately forthcoming.

As far as Duncan was concerned, an old friend was always a good friend, and being around the tech-savvy behemoth was a blast, whether they were drinking to excess or trying to save a piece of humanity. He really needed to see Duncan more often, so he made a note to invite him to the island for a short stint. He loved the big guy, but he'd kick his ass out after a couple of weeks.

Alex was slightly annoyed. Even with his eyes closed underneath sunglasses, he could feel the sun was taking a while to emerge from behind the clouds. He then realized the clouds were not at fault.

"So this is how you spend your days."

Alex opened his eyes, recognizing both the voice and silhouette. He sat up on his elbows and, shaking his head, said, "I have to get a guard dog."

"I've got a proposition for you."

"Not interested."

"Yeah, but you'll listen, 'cause deep down inside, you know you miss it."

George Champion carried his suit jacket over an arm as he admired Alex's slice of heaven. He looked around for a chair or something to sit on, but finding nothing, he lowered himself into the sand next to Alex.

"Freddie Hubbard," the man from the CIA guessed as he listened to the music. "'Red Clay.'"

Alex downed more of his rum and Coke. "I'm impressed."

"Well, you got me hooked on jazz." Champion pointed at Alex's drink. "Any more of those?"

For the next two hours they sat on the beach talking, listening to jazz, and knocking back rum and Cokes. Before Champion departed, Alex had promised he would seriously consider what was being offered.

Alex told him, though, that regardless of his decision, there was one thing he had to take care of first. Champion didn't bother to ask what it was, because no matter how hard he might have pressed, Alex wouldn't have told him.

There was one name Alex couldn't stop thinking about, but he was determined to find the person it belonged to.

There was a score to settle with Dmitri Nevsky.